FRIDAY NIGHT FEVER

THAT SEVENTIES SERIES - BOOK 1

ANDRENE LOW

Squabbling Sparrows Press

Squabbling Sparrows Press

*S*am squares her shoulders and rolls another liquorice allsort of white internal memo, coloured copy paper and dark blue carbon into her IBM golf ball typewriter. Yet more drivel from Peter Crisp, her boss.

Crispy Critter is thirty-five going on fifty and middle management right down to the comb-over and a body that looks as though it's been put together like custard. He's a cheap bastard who drives a Nissan Sunny with rust flakes so bad that anything over 60kph make it look positively autumnal.

As her platform shoe hits the foot control of the Dictaphone, Crispy's nasal voice fills her head. "To Barry Davison, R17 Forestry Project, Year Ending 31 March 1978. Barry, please call me at your earliest convenience to discuss."

This is followed by asthmatic breathing, but nothing else.

If that's all that's in your sodding memo, why don't you pick up the phone and ring him, ya lazy prick?

Sam hears these words as clearly as Crispy's and the golf ball spits them out onto the memo paper.

"Blast!"

Rolling the wad of paper out of her typewriter, she holds the lot in one corner and flaps it until the sheets of carbon drop limply onto her desk.

Mrs Darren Walters. Mrs Darren Walters. Mrs Darren Walters.

Sam's expecting Darren to make it official the following weekend when he's up from the base on one of his regular fortnightly visits.

Her hand once again strays to the handle of the top drawer of her dark, walnut veneer desk. She slides it open just enough that she can gaze at a picture of Darren in his army fatigues, sent with one of his many letters.

If there's one thing Sam loves, it's a guy in uniform. Not as much as a guy who's ditched the uniform altogether. But close.

Looking at her soon-to-be fiancé reminds Sam how important her well-paid, awful job is. Her goal of saving enough money for a wedding more over-the-top than her parents are willing to pay for is getting closer every day. It's only the thought of a five-tier cake, live band and bucket-loads of frangipani that have stopped her telling her boss to shove it.

Taking a ring off her right hand, she puts it onto the wedding finger of her left. Joy bubbles away when she holds her hand under the light spilling from the Anglepoise lamp on her desk. She admires the wedded look but, hearing the elevator *ding* its arrival, turns it from married to stretching before putting her hand under the desk and swapping the ring back. As the elevator doors open, she automatically smiles at the new arrivals, but rather than head in her direction they disappear down the corridor.

Retyped without additions, she takes the one-line wonder into Crispy's office for his signature and waits patiently while he goes through his usual wank of reading it, with fountain pen poised expectantly. Then, after enough time that he could have proofed the Magna Carta, he signs his chicken-scratch signature with the flourish of minor royalty.

Back at her desk, she finds Mrs Johnson from Personnel waiting for her. This is the woman who'd first interviewed her for the job. A second-hand car salesman couldn't have done a better sell on how great the job was.

One careful lady owner, my arse!

"How are you settling in? You're not finding it too challenging?"

"No. We typed more than this at secretarial school."

"Is that right?" Mrs Johnson unclasps the large tan diary that has been protecting her meagre bosom, swings it open and scribbles furiously before snapping it closed. It's back on boob patrol seconds later.

Before the woman can ask anything else, a bellowed, "Sam, in here, now!" erupts from her boss's office.

Mrs Johnson's mouth drops open at the tone, but she remains mute.

Sam picks up her pad and pen and heads into Crispy's office and sits, although it hardly seems worth it. The stuff she takes down in shorthand is as wordy as that on the micro cassettes he leaves in his heavily brass-detailed out-tray.

"Shut the door." His voice is controlled, with a hard edge.

She jumps to do his bidding. A confidential memo would make a nice change.

Her hand is still on the doorknob when he starts berating her.

"How dare you discuss my work with that woman." His voice is low, as though he suspects Mrs Johnson is still hovering.

"But she—" Sam turns toward him.

"What happens in this office is none of her business," he hisses.

Sam looks down at Berber carpet, the colour of camel dung, before stuttering, "But I ... only told the truth ..."

"Good god, the truth is the last thing that woman needs to hear. Now I'll have to stop her riffling through every damn piece of correspondence I've ever produced. Any more screw ups like that and I'll have to let you go."

"Yes, Mr Crisp," says Sam, in a small voice.

Mrs Darren Walters. Mrs Darren Walters. Mrs Darren—

"Of course, we could discuss it over a few drinks."

She groans inwardly; god, not again. "I'll have to ask my, ah, fiancé if it's all right."

"It could be our little secret. We wouldn't need to let anyone know."

Especially not your wife, you cretin.

At 4.59 pm she flips the switch on the side of her sage green typewriter before dropping a cracked, grey vinyl cover over the top. She smashes the off button on the top of her lamp, grabs her oversized shoulder bag and heads for the elevator.

Crispy had left earlier; up to the senior management offices for the usual Friday night drinks. He'd been bouncing like a puppy in anticipation of mixing with the upper echelons.

God knows what they think of him.

She slumps against the wood panelled back wall of the lift. She can hardly wait to report this latest Crispy instalment to Jennie. Sam and Jennie share everything and always have. Best friends from kindergarten, the confidences have gone from dolls and kittens to boys and clothes and everything in between.

There'd been a lull in their relationship last year, when Jennie had been dealing with her fiancé, Steve, and his battle with cancer. Steve and Jen had been planning a trip overseas until he was diagnosed and they'd had to postpone. Steve lost the fight, leaving Jennie adrift and while she'd talked about finishing her fine arts degree, her heart hadn't been in it and she'd ended up working for her parents.

Jennie's now decided to go on with the trip as some sort of tribute to Steve. Sam hopes Jennie will be okay on her own and knows she'll miss her friend more than she can imagine.

The lift stops spongily on the ground floor and the doors rattle open, and Sam's brought back to her surroundings. After peeling herself off the wall, she strides across the marble lobby and up to the automatic front doors. It takes a second for them to register her presence before they slide asthmatically open. Walking through them, she breathes in deeply. Even with undertones of diesel, the air tastes fresh after the air-conditioned staleness inside.

The closer she gets to her car, the springier her gait. A girls' night out with Jennie is just what she needs to wash away any lingering traces of Crispy. A nice, big glass of straight scotch might be in order, although antiseptic would be more appropriate.

Later that night Sam's room is a fug of hairspray and Magie Noire perfume as she goes through the rigmarole of getting ready to go to the pub. Half a can of Wella super strength 'black death' hairspray and a round brush has her blow-waved blonde hair flicking back away from her face on both sides. If she were any more Farrah Fawcett she'd be getting calls from Charlie.

With the dryer safely back on its hook on the side of the dressing table, Darren's dog, V8, pops her head out from underneath the bed. V8 loves being in the thick of things but has a pathological fear of the hairdryer. Sam thinks it must have been something that happened to her as a puppy, but because Darren had picked up the dog at the SPCA they had no way of knowing.

It was as much a mystery as her breed, which seems to be Wolfhound mixed with Staffy and a little Labrador thrown in for good measure. As far as Sam can tell, the main Labrador trait V8 had inherited was the biscuit one; the dog only had to hear the kettle being switched on to appear in the kitchen seconds later.

It hadn't taken long after the adoption for Darren to realise he couldn't keep V8 down on the base and he'd asked Sam's parents if they would look after her. For Sam's mum, it had been love at first lick.

"It's all right girl, all finished." She bends down and sweeps the bulky fringe of hair clear of V8's eyes. "Although

I think you could do with some hairspray to keep this mop of yours under control." Sam grabs the can of spray and some hair clips from her dresser but V8, suspicious, is already squirming her way through the nearly closed bedroom door.

Sam puts the hairspray and clips back before looking down at the neckline of her dress and frowning. Opening the top drawer of her dressing table, she rummages until she finds an old pair of school socks. Stuffing one into each cup of her bra, she then rearranges her boobs so they look natural. Picking up the red dress she'd finished making the night before, she steps into it, and sucks in her tummy so she can zip it up.

After a thorough search, she wanders out into the lounge looking for a favourite pair of earrings. Her parents are watching the news, although Sam's mother does a double take at the red dress.

"Do you think you should be going out dressed like that when Darren's down at the base?" Her mother absently strokes V8, who's inching her way up onto the couch one leg at a time.

"It's not that bad!" says Sam, looking down and getting an eyeful of cleavage. "And anyway, Darren trusts me."

"If you're sure," says her mother. Her dad hasn't taken his eyes off the telly.

"I am!" Sam lifts the lid of the crystal bowl on the mantelpiece. Empty, apart from a moth carcass and a couple of perished rubber bands. Closing her eyes, she thinks back to when she'd last worn the earrings, then goes out into the hallway leaving her parents to the doom and gloom on the telly.

Downstairs, she opens the door to the granny flat where Darren stays when he's in town. Picking up a T-shirt of his from the end of the bed, she holds it up to her face. Just breathing in his scent kicks her heart rate up a notch. She keeps breathing from the T-shirt, before dropping it in the laundry hamper behind the door in the tiny bathroom.

She finds her sterling silver earrings behind the lamp on the bedside table.

Back up in her room, she opens her wardrobe and looks critically at herself in the mirror on the inside of the door before sliding hangers until she finds a more modest black and silver dress. Sam still can't believe she's managed to snare Darren and isn't about to screw it up. He's cool; everyone looks up to him, even the guys, and he's definitely a trophy. She wishes she could be viewed the same way, but even though she has the blonde hair and long legs, she's a pair of knee-highs short of the minimum cup size.

Sam skips down the curving front steps soon after Jennie pulls up in her lime green Morrie Thou'. Jennie is anal about time and being even a little late makes her left eye twitch. 'Kermie', as the car is affectionately known, has finally shuddered to a standstill by the time Sam reaches the bottom of the wrought-iron-framed pebblecrete steps.

Before she can open the car door, Jennie is out and around into glare of the headlights where she stands with arms wide, eyebrows raised and head cocked to the side. The denim flares are flattering and make her athletic body look curvy. Her short hair is its usual explosion of curls, the colour a deep auburn that could almost be mistaken for black, until the sun hit it. This, coupled with large hazel eyes, would make her look like a pixie if it weren't for her measuring close to six foot.

"You look good. I love the embroidery on the jacket."

"You don't think it's too much? I did bring some other stuff just in case."

Eyeing the bulging carry bag on Kermie's back seat, Sam knows if she doesn't stop the wardrobe panic in its tracks they'll end up back in her room for another hour, while Jennie works through every possible combination of the clothes she's brought with her. Jennie'd never been like this when Steve was alive. Losing him seemed to have knocked her confidence. "You look perfect. Come on, let's get there before all the good seats are nabbed."

Peeling the 'Farrell's Plumbing Supplies' magnetic sign off the passenger door where it's been missed by Jennie, she puts this, along with her own carrier bag of gear, onto the back seat. Farrell's is owned by Jennie's parents and explains the assortment of pipe joints and general plumbing paraphernalia that litter the footwell on the passenger side. Sam slides her feet in amongst them until she makes contact with the car's floor before slamming the door shut.

She's spending the night at Jennie's as it's easier to stagger into the sleep-out behind Jen's parent's place than dodge every creaky floorboard in the hallway at home. She tends to keep sober when Darren is in town, not wanting him to see her all messy from too many drinks. But she's not averse to a few when he isn't around.

Jennie pulls out and they belt along on their way to the pub. Belting for Kermie is 45kph, his top speed without risking mechanical disintegration. Jennie can proudly boast to having no speeding tickets but only because it's a physical impossibility.

The girls talk loudly so they can hear each other over the assorted clatters and clunks that give Kermie his personality, although a lot of these are the result of the pipes and spare parts rattling around Sam's ankles. "I think next weekend might be the one," says Sam.

"One what?"

"The proposal." Sam hopes this news won't upset Jennie.

"What makes you think that?" says Jennie, evenly.

"He asked me to book a table for us at The Fontainbleu in his last letter."

"Wow, that's flash. What are you going to wear?"

"Not sure. I'll go through my wardrobe tomorrow."

Even at Kermie's sedate speed, it only takes ten minutes to get to the pub. The trip home, via back roads, will be more than double to avoid running into the booze bus. Even though

Jennie's a light drinker; it's safer to dodge the breathalyser altogether.

The bar has as much class as you can get with mock Tudor. It's supposed to be "oldey-worldey" but only manages "slightley-tackey". The pseudo-oak bench seats are upholstered in velvet with what looks like a subtle pattern but is an accumulation of stains so numerous, the original colour no longer shows.

The carpet's the same but with more adhesive qualities. Fortunately the drinks are cheap and there's usually a good covers band.

Despite their being early, the only table available is a beige plastic-topped, metal monstrosity and the result of the landlord's decision to "jazz the place up a bit". It's from the same school of design as the fake open fires. The matching plastic chairs have cracks vicious enough to leave your arse looking like that of a stripper's after a sales convention gig.

"Do I look okay?" Sam checks her dress with her hands.

"Yeah. Why?"

"Nothing. Must be my imagination."

"It's fine." Jennie spins her around so she can three-sixty the outfit.

"Then why are people staring at me? Damn, I knew I should have worn the red dress."

"Relax you look fine."

"God, you wouldn't believe the crap Crispy tried on today," says Sam, after they've settled themselves as comfortably as they're ever going to.

Jennie's so transfixed by the bright green drink that's put down on their table, she doesn't respond.

"It's a Grasshopper," says Tania, owner of the drink and a friend to both of them.

"Gizza sip." Sam grabs the glass and helps herself to a large gulp.

"Well?" say both of the others.

"Not bad. Why's the glass so clean?" Sam compares it to the state of her own.

"It was fresh out of the box ... I think it's their first cocktail. Ever," says Tania.

Standing, Sam waves at the barman, points at the glass and indicates three with her fingers. He grimaces before going out to the back, grabbing a ladder on his way.

They're onto their fourth round of Grasshoppers when Jim, Tania's fiancé, turns up. He's tall and thin with a mop of wildly curling blond hair and Sam thinks he looks a bit like Roger Daltrey from The Who. He bends over and kisses Tania's strawberry blonde curls before lowering himself into the saved seat next to her.

"Sorry I'm late, love." Jim squeezes Tania's shoulder. "Got held up by a bloke I'm doing an engine rebuild for." Jim has a tidy sideline in mechanical repairs and it's paid for more than one overseas trip for him and Tania. At 5'2" and seven stone dripping wet, Tania is a bundle of energy who keeps Jim firmly in line. Sam doubts there'd be much money being made at all if it wasn't for Tania's influence on the freewheeling Jim.

Round number five and Sam and Jennie are in need of the ladies. They make their way easily through the tables and chairs but things slow down when they get to the three-deep mob standing next to the bar that runs the length of the room.

At first, the crowd looks impenetrable but Jennie spots a break and goes for it. Sam follows in her wake. They don't push and shove but edge their way through, moving people to the side by placing their hands on any backs they encounter and applying pressure in the direction they want them to move. It's an art form.

They move through Brut 33, then a patch of Charlie onto some Aqua Manda and even the odd whiff of Opium. Jennie's squeezing her nose to hold back a sneeze by the time they're spat out into open space by the toilets. "I wish people wouldn't slap on so much stuff," she says nasally.

They push open the swing door into the ladies and are happy to find it's empty; they hadn't been bursting when they'd left the table. Sam heads into one of the two cubicles, locks the door and hastily pulls her knickers down before carefully lowering herself into a hover position over the toilet. There's no way she's sitting down, with the glistening shine on the toilet seat having nothing to do with elbow grease. Still, she wishes the publican would use something to reduce the gag factor of old pipes and unscrubbed lino.

She's started a controlled pee when a couple of girls pinball their way into the ladies. The new arrivals bounce off washbasins and walls in turn and Sam's glad the lock on her door is strong when one of them falls hard against it. The new arrivals push at the doors of both cubicles and get a shouted "Busy!" from Jennie and Sam.

God, they must be hammered if they can't read the bright red ENGAGED showing on the locks.

"I can't believe the silly cow doesn't know he's screwing around," slurs one.

Sam's ears prick up.

Great! Some juicy gossip to take back to the table.

"Guess he's pretty convincing," says the other.

Give us a name! We need a name.

Sam would rub her hands together but it would throw her off balance and she'd risk bum touching porcelain or head smacking into the door.

Come on, even just a first name.

"He's got a nerve staying at her parents' place when he's up here."

Sam's heart falters.

"They even look after his bloody dog."

Her chest is frozen; breathing shallow.

No name, please no name.

"He's got balls, all right," slurs one of the girls.

"And I guess he knows how to use 'em." Her friend laughs drunkenly.

Her legs give out and Sam sinks to the toilet seat. It's cold and wet.

"Come on, let's go to the other bogs before I piss my pants," says one of them.

They stumble their way out and the door hisses slowly

closed behind them blocking out the raucous sounds of the bar. The relative silence is broken by Jennie, who's now outside Sam's cubicle. "Sam? It could be anyone."

"He wouldn't do that to me!" says Sam, wiping, then standing up and grabbing more paper to dry the backs of her legs. After pulling up her knickers and arranging her dress, she yanks down on the chain by her head before turning and opening the door.

When the roar of the old cistern refilling dies down, she adds, "Darren wouldn't do that to me, would he?"

"No? ... No!" Jennie yanks on the circular towel searching for a dry patch, before drying her hands on her jeans.

"He wouldn't!"

Sam's conviction is kyboshed when Jennie says, "I know how we can find out for sure."

2

*B*ack at the table when the band stops for a break, Jennie says casually "Hey, Jim, we're hoping you can help with something."

"Yeah, shoot," he says, looking at Jennie.

"Just heard some girls talking about a bloke who's screwing around," says Sam, causing him to turn toward her.

"It sounds suspiciously like Darren," says Jennie. Jim's head snaps back.

"Can't help, sorry," is his choked response, as his gaze swivels between Sam and Jennie.

"Can't help, or won't help?" says Tania.

"Yeah. Spill or we'll tell Darren you told us anyway," says Sam, smelling blood.

"Well, ah, all right. But you didn't hear this from me." He looks over one shoulder then the other before leaning forward. "You know that Aussie barmaid at the Mirage Hotel down by the base, the chick they call Head Girl?"

"Cheryl? There's no way! Darren said she's a real dog." Sam's breath rushes out and her shoulders relax.

"Yeah, well. Apparently she's more lap dog than Doberman and Darren was the one who gave her the nickname Head Girl."

13

"I think I'm going to be sick," says Sam, bile popping up at the back of her throat. She swallows quickly.

"But it's not like you're ever gonna meet her," says Jim, earning him a sharp kick to the shin from Tania.

"I'm outta here." Sam stands abruptly and heads for the door. She gets more of the same looks as when they first arrived. Sam realises they have nothing to do with her outfit.

"Wait for me." Jennie hurries behind her, catching up with her around the side of the building where she's getting rid of all the cocktails. Jennie holds Sam's hair out of the way but there's not much more she can do until the final Grasshopper is released into the wild. Sam still feels nauseated but this has more to do with Darren than any alcohol still in her system. Straightening, she sways a little when she takes her hand away from the wall.

"You all right?"

"Yes. No. Not really."

"Do you truly think he's about to pop the question?"

"Why else would he get me to book The Fontainbleau? It's too flash just for dinner."

"You'll have to cancel the booking. You can't just pretend you don't know!"

"I can't do anything, can I? Not without dumping Jim in it. Although the fact I know and Darren doesn't know I know ..." Sam forces a smile and even rubs her hands together with what she hopes passes for glee.

Despite this show of bravery, she's hurting. What Darren doesn't know is Sam's choosy about sharing her toys. As a three-year-old, she'd smashed her entire tea set rather than let a girl she didn't like play with it. She'd got one hell of a hiding and it had put an end to her ability to entertain at home, but she still felt it had been worth it.

Next morning, Sam's head is threatening to shatter like a drop-kicked piggy bank, the result of crying quietly most of the night.

Even now, tears are stuck in her throat where she's jammed them in an effort not to wake Jennie, who's gently snoring in her bed on the other side of the sleep-out. Thank god she'd arranged to spend the night here; breakfast with her parents would have been impossible.

Looking at the dust swirling lazily above her where it glows in the sunlight that's slipped under the bottom of the too-short curtains, Sam takes a shuddering breath. It's loud enough to interrupt Jennie, who barks her throat clear before rolling over and focusing on Sam's face.

"You're a mess," she says, pushing back the covers and staggering over to Sam's bed. "Move over."

Sam scoots over as far as she can and Jennie crawls in and drags Sam into her arms. This is all it takes to have her sobbing loudly.

"You'll be all right," says Jennie, into Sam's ear while stroking the back of her head. "You'll get through this. You don't think you'll ever laugh again, but you will."

"Jennie, I'm so sorry. Listen to me going on about my problems. Are you doing okay?" Sam pulls back to look closely at Jennie.

"It's been thirteen months." As Sam continues to peer at her, Jennie adds a forcible, "I'm fine. Really!"

Sam's drops her head back into the crook of Jennie's arm.

"I was so sure he was the one. I've even been practicing signing my married name. What if he does propose next weekend? What will I say? I'll have to tell him The Fontainbleu was booked out. Why did he do it? What's wrong with ... me?"

Jennie's answer to this jumble of thoughts is to continue stroking the back of Sam's head.

Eventually Sam is out of tears, her chest hurts and her sinuses are chocker.

Jennie's still beside her but has fallen asleep again, her

snoring more than a match for anything Sam can come up with. Sam falls asleep too, exhausted. She's woken later by Jennie mumbling. "You could come travelling with me. I know it was what Steve and I were going to do but I'd love it if you came. You can always come back home if you're not having fun."

Sam stares at the ceiling. "You're flying out to Melbourne on the eleventh, right?"

"Yep, only thirteen more sleeps to go."

Sam isn't looking forward to facing everyone and their pity; it's not like her job is any great shakes and Crispy Critter wouldn't let it rest until she shagged him or he forced her to quit.

"You're on, I'll come with you! But by jeez, I'm going to stick it to Darren before I go."

"Ooh, it's going to be a blast," says Jennie, coming fully awake.

Sam can tell by Jen's expression that she's not talking about their trip.

<hr>

Sunday afternoon and Sam's sitting leadenly on her bed stewing over Darren and wondering about clothes for work in the morning. Something neck to knee in a heavy serge that'll keep Crispy's eyes at bay would be good. A sob jumps into Sam's throat and tears pattern her faded jeans. She's wiping her eyes when her mother comes in with some clean clothes.

"What on earth's wrong?"

"Nothing." Sam desperately scouts around for a reason for her tears.

"Nothing?" Her mother sits on the bed.

"Well, it's … ah …" Sam falters, clambering through her head opening files in hopes of finding a good excuse.

"Go on."

"My, ah, boss." Sam has no trouble filling her mother in on the situation at work, making Crispy out to be bad enough that she's in tears at the thought of going to work in the morning.

"But you can't let him get away with that." Sam's mother puts her arm around her shoulders.

"But I can't quit, it'll look bad on my work record and the money's good," says Sam, before blowing her nose.

"I wonder if that's why the last girl left. Do you know her name?"

"Sure, she Dymo-labelled it onto everything on the desk that wasn't screwed down."

"Good. Go get the phone book!"

"Morning, Sam," floats out of Crispy's office when she tiptoes past the next morning. "Come in, Sam. No need for pad and pen, just your lovely self."

"Be right there," she mutters to her boss's summons in a perfect, whiney imitation before going in to see him. Standing right up against the front of his desk, her hands stray to her knotted stomach muscles.

"When shall I book the restaurant?"

"I'd rather not."

"I was thinking of this nice little place in Parnell, it's out of the way and they have accommodation, too. For dessert, I like the idea of covering you in whipped cream and licking it off."

Sam's close to gagging at this suggestion but manages to say, "I'd rather poke my eye out with a stick."

"Good, I'll make a booking for ... what?"

"Forget it, Mr Crisp. I do not want to go out to dinner with you, and I certainly don't want to be your dessert." Sam's voice is strong and clear although she's shaking.

"You know how it works, Sam. No dessert and ah, well ... no job."

"I thought you might say that, so I phoned Gina, your old secretary." Thank god her mother had thought of that. It hadn't been hard to track down Sam's predecessor.

"You did *what?*" Crispy's face is mottled with rage and he looks ready to blow.

"We're going to have a chat with your wife. She's bound to believe three of us."

"Three?" he squeaks.

"Yeah, Gina got hold of Mary. You remember *Mary*, don't you?" In truth, Gina had been onto it like a lawyer seeking damages.

"Get out!" he yells, his hair flopping about like the lid of a grand piano caught in a cross wind.

"Not without a reference."

"I'll send it on," he says through gritted teeth. "Just get out of my sight."

"Na uh, not without a reference. And let's have them for the others, too. I'll even write them."

"You little bitch!" he screams and Sam's glad she's on the other side of the huge, spit-flecked I've-got-a-small-penis desk.

Sam types up three glowing references; even she thinks she might have pushed how fabulous they all are, then takes them into a seething Crispy for signature.

This isn't strictly necessary, given his signature is such a scribble she can fake it; it's simply the perverse pleasure of making him sign them. He doesn't even bother reading them. Probably a good thing as she feels that vein in his forehead would pop for sure.

Before walking out of the building for good, she stops at the personnel department where she takes her dad's hand-held recorder out of her pocket, ejects the micro cassette and pops it on Mrs Johnston's desk with a note.

It'll be time the last Crispy Critter pulls that sort of crap.

"How'd you get on?" says Sam's mother that evening. "We thought you'd be home before now. Surely you don't have to work out your notice?"

"I'm not leaving, Crispy backed down. I even got a pay rise." Sam spouts the lies she's been practicing quietly all afternoon in the library down the road from the office. She practiced so much that eventually one little old dear had asked if she was all right.

"Are you sure that's a good idea?" says her father.

"I've got him on tape – I can keep him in line." If she keeps up the pretence of going to work, she can tell her parents the trip to Aussie is only a holiday; that way they won't have to know about Darren's cheating until after she's gone. Better to slip away without all the fanfare.

Sam's awake before her alarm the following morning, irked that she has to get up and pretend to go in to the office. She could have been having a lie-in. But if she can keep up the pretence and get away cleanly, there's less chance of further humiliation in front of everyone. If such a thing is possible. She still can't work out what it is she's done wrong for Darren to cheat on her. She's not sure she wants to know.

Thinking about what he's done has a lump working its way up her throat before erupting in a hiccoughed sob. But she consciously swallows her tears. As it is, having hardly slept, her eyes feel like tinsel. She lies there working through plans while waiting for the alarm to ring.

"Morning, dear. There's bread in the toaster and tea in the pot," says her mother when Sam drifts into the kitchen.

"Thanks." Sam takes her usual spot at the table. "Um, one of the other … ah … things I negotiated with Crispy, is a holiday, so I'm going to go to Melbourne with Jennie." Sam's surprised at how easily this lie comes. She hasn't practiced this one at all.

"How long for?" says her mum.

"A month." She then digs her hole a little deeper by adding, "With pay."

"A month with pay! But what about Darren?" says her mother.

"I'll let him know next time he's up."

"But what about the airfares? You'll have to dip into your savings," says her mother, feeding a toast soldier to V8, who's in her usual spot under the table.

Sam gets the spade out again. "I, ah, got a bonus from Crispy."

"You *did* back him into a corner," says her dad.

Sam finishes breakfast and heads off to "work". She's going to spend the day a few suburbs away organising a passport, sorting out airline tickets and putting in a request for travellers' cheques. Working out what to pack so she doesn't exceed the maximum twenty kilos will be the real challenge.

While the first day is easy to fill, as the days progress, it gets harder and harder. She resorts to spending most of the day hiding in the sleep-out at Jennie's place, reading magazines and working through her packing list. She's careful to be away before Jennie's parents get home.

Her back hard up against the headboard and her legs stretched out before her, Sam runs her finger down the spines of the teetering stack of magazines on the bedside table. Grabbing a handful off the top, she dumps them in her lap. *Cleo, Cleo, Cleo, House & Garden, Cosmo.* Sam's nearly through the pile on her lap when she comes across a well-thumbed copy of a bridal magazine. Flicking through it she comes to a page with the corner turned over. Jennie would have looked incredible in that dress.

Stroking the page, before finally turning it over, her breath catches in her throat. The dress on the next page is gorgeous and Sam knows it would look amazing on her. The tears pool above her lower lashes and spill over; she drops the magazine and swipes at her eyes with the back of her hand. She gropes for the steno pad and pen next to her on the bed and adds another item to a rapidly growing list.

27 – itching powder in grots.

3

The following Friday sees Sam ready well before Darren arrives, as she's a lot less anxious about outfit selection than usual. A brand new and frighteningly sexy dress hangs in the darkest recesses of her wardrobe. She's not putting it on until just before they leave so it's a nice surprise for Darren, and she can get out of the house without her mother seeing it.

"Sam, Darren's here," announces her mother.

"Thanks!" Sam yells back, before putting the finishing touches to her makeup.

Before leaving the sanctuary of her room, she examines herself in the mirror and takes a few calming breaths. Heading down the hall, out the front door and onto the front porch, she looks down at the no-good-two-timing-spineless-slimy-son-of-a-bitch and calls out, "Hey, babe, you're here! Be right down." He meets her grin with one of his own, although she knows his isn't glued on with bright red lipstick.

Skipping down the stairs, Sam throws herself into his outstretched arms.

Darren picks her up and swings her around, all the time checking if her parents are around. Seeing no sign of them he drags her even closer and into a kiss. He lifts his head. "Missed you," he breathes into her ear.

"Oh, have you?" says Sam, dreamily.

"God, yes, it's so lonely down at the base."

"You're a bit later than usual." Sam pulls back, double crossing the front of her robe and tying the belt firmly.

"Yeah, the car's seriously in need of a tune up. I even had to stop for gas."

"I'm pretty much ready. I'll get dressed and we can head out."

"That's not like you. You get off work early?" Darren goes to the boot of his car to take out his bag.

"Yeah, super early today." She had spent the day reading books about Melbourne from Jennie's mountain of research materials. Back up to her room, she finishes getting dressed while Darren unpacks and when her black satin dress slithers into place, she trembles in anticipation. She's filling it out beautifully thanks to a pair of socks in each cup, not that she planned on him finding them later.

"You look hot, especially from this angle." Darren waits for her at the bottom of the stairs.

"It's not too short?"

"No! It's choice."

Sam makes it to the bottom of the stairs, progress being slow due to her new shoes, and stands next to Darren.

"Bloody hell! How high are those heels?" He looks down at her platforms then up at her face.

"Six inches. It doesn't bother you that I'm taller than you, does it?"

Jim is the first person they run into at the pub. "Hi, Dazzer. Was thinking you must be up this weekend." When Sam moves from behind Darren to stand next to him, Jim adds, "Jeez, mate, have you shrunk?"

"No! Sam's decided she needs to clean the ceiling with her damned hair."

"Yeah, that and checking out people's bald spots," says Sam, laughing.

Darren moves swiftly to face her and she mentally ticks off item #32 on the list. All going well, he'll have ground his teeth to stubs by the end of the night.

"Where's Tania?" she asks Jim.

"Had to work late, so Jennie's picking her up."

Seeing Darren isn't rushing to the bar, Sam announces, "I'm going to get a drink."

Darren, busy hitting Jim up for tips on how best to tune his car, asks her to get him one, although he doesn't offer to buy one for Jim who's swilling the dregs of his beer in hopes of being included in the round. Darren stuffs a twenty down Sam's cleavage.

Bloody cheek.

Last time he did that she thought it was cute; now it made her jaw hurt.

I'll get him a drink all right.

Fishing the $20 out of her bra and holding it up, she offers to get Jim a fresh beer.

Let my cheating dick of a boyfriend pay Jim for the info for a change.

Darren's eyebrows rise at her presumptuousness, but she's off before he can say a word.

Score another point! And one that wasn't even on the list.

"Hi, Paul," says Sam, to the barman.

"What can I get for you?"

"I'll have a DB, a Scotch and Dry and Darren is dying to try a Grasshopper."

"For gawd's sake, not those things again."

"Go on, he'll probably only want one."

"It's all he's going to get," mutters Paul, as he grabs a cocktail glass from under the bar. It must be one of those used by the girls the week before and looks none too clean. He grabs the blender and she can see it's been rinsed with the same care.

"Christ, what the hell is this?" says Darren, when she hands him the drink.

"It's a Grasshopper. We were drinking them last week,

even Jim had one. You liked it, didn't you?" says Sam, handing him his beer.

Short of accusing her of lying, Jim mumbles, "They're different, that's for sure."

Darren looks at Jim. "If you're sure, mate." He chugs the whole glass in one go. "Bloody hell, that's disgusting. It tastes like rotten milk. Even smells like it!" He shoves the empty glass under Sam's nose.

"Smells fine to me," Sam manages to gasp without breathing in. One whiff and she'd be back examining the bushes down the side of the building.

"If they're so good, why aren't you having one?" says Darren, suspiciously.

"Too many calories. Don't want to put on weight! You might start looking at other women," says Sam, causing Jim to choke on his beer and Darren's face to colour. "I'll get you a beer if you like? Have you had dinner? Can I get you a pie?"

"A pie! From here? Jeez, Sam, what are you trying to do, poison me?"

"No? Some crisps then?"

"That'd be good. We'll look for a table."

Darren slides another twenty into her cleavage and takes the opportunity to gently squeeze one of her boobs. When he frowns, Sam glances down surreptitiously. Knee highs don't have the same bounce back quality as flesh but everything looks the same as it did before, so it must just have felt weird to him.

"Here, hold my drink while I fight my way back to the bar." Sam shoves her full glass in his direction to take his mind off the uneven texture of her boobs.

"Sure, anything for you, love."

"Sure, anything for you, love," mutters Sam, as she shoves her way back to the bar. "How about you get the bloody drinks?"

It's dawning on her that while Darren might pay, she's been the one doing all the fetching and carrying. She absently rubs the muscle twitching just below her ear.

Tania and Jennie arrive while Sam is making her way over to the table Jim and Darren have nabbed. Her co-conspirators spot her, wave and head toward the bar for drinks. As she slips between the tightly packed tables she gets subtle thumbs ups from a few of the women she passes; apparently her plan for revenge isn't as secret as she'd like. Still, as long as no one lets on, she should be fine.

"Have you told Darren about our big trip yet?" says Jennie, soon after she sits.

"What trip?" Darren looks at Jim, who's spluttering into his beer causing some to slop over the edge.

"We're coming down to see you! A girls' road trip," says Sam.

Darren spits out the mouthful of beer he's just taken and snaps up his head to look at Sam. "You can't visit me at the base. There's nowhere to stay."

"We're all sorted. Jennie booked us into the Mirage." This stroke of brilliance had been Tania's idea.

"Look Sam, I'm on call all weekend so I wouldn't be able to see you." Darren pulls his beer-dampened T-shirt away from his body and flaps it aggressively.

"Never mind, we'll still come down, it'll be good to get out of town and we can amuse ourselves at the pub meeting all your mates."

Saturday morning and Darren's still making lame excuses for why she can't visit him down at the base.

"Darren, is there some reason you don't want me down there?"

"No. Course not. What time's the booking tonight at The Fontainbleu?"

"They were fully booked. So I've booked us in for the next weekend you're up."

It's with a sense of relief that she stands next to Darren's car on Sunday afternoon and watches him sling his weekend bag in the boot before slamming it shut. She's managed to keep him away from her parents all weekend, worried they'd say something about her forthcoming holiday to Aussie.

He gives her a perfunctory peck on the cheek rather than partake of the usual tonsil hockey, obviously still miffed that he hasn't been able to get his end away over the weekend. She'd put him off by faking a gloriously bloody period. Any time he'd become too frisky she'd added more detail until her descriptions were akin to the storyline of the Texas Chainsaw Massacre.

Following Darren's car as he backs it down the driveway, Sam waves at him through the reflection of clouds scudding across the windscreen. She's standing on the footpath when he pulls to a halt and his head juts out the window. "Nearly forgot, I've had a shift rotation, so I won't be up again for three weeks."

"And you've just remembered this now?"

"It slipped my mind." Darren's face is devoid of emotion.

"I'll need to change the booking then?"

"You're still coming down?"

"For The Fontainbleu." Sam's unable to stop her eyes from rolling.

It's with mixed emotions she waves him off. She's sad to know she won't be looking him in the eye as she metaphorically knees him the goolies.

Wednesday evening and Sam's sitting on the lambskin rug in the granny flat, surrounded by the entire contents of Darren's wardrobe. He doesn't keep much stuff down at the base as he's mostly in uniform, so there's a lot to get through. She's singing along tunelessly to a Bee Gees album at full volume. Her new headphones were an unexpected gift from her dad.

Sam grabs her seam ripper and cuts through every second

stitch in the crotch of Darren's best pants. She's dropped the hems with stitching so neat he won't be able to tell. Let the bastard think he is shrinking.

She puts the pair of pants, now sporting a ball-breezy crotch, with the clothes she's already worked on. She's particularly proud of a pair of jeans where she's sealed the inside of the legs, near the bottom, with invisible hemming tape. Next time Darren follows his usual, wanky dressing style of putting both feet in then leaping up and pulling the jeans on all in one go, he'll crash in a heap, hopefully smacking his head on the way down.

Sam jumps when someone taps her on the shoulder. Turning, she finds her mother holding the downstairs phone out to her. She takes the headphones off in time to hear "... for you." Followed with, "What on earth are you doing?"

"Just fixing a few things for Darren." Slowly she puts the shirt she's about to work on down behind her. Her mother isn't stupid; the less she sees the better.

"Hey, it's me," says Jennie. "I just tried to change the booking at the Mirage and Head Girl said they don't have room for us that weekend."

Both Jennie and Sam burst out laughing. They don't have any intention of visiting the base and trying to change the booking is just another way to tighten the screws.

"Wow, he doesn't want us down there, does he? Mind you, he probably needs a rest after what we put him through last weekend," says Sam, laughing.

"I can't believe he hasn't caught on."

"Did I tell you about flicking a can of sardines on the vinyl roof of his car before we went for a walk at the beach on Sunday?"

"What happened?"

"We got back to the car and it was like a seagull convention. The roof was covered in bird poo, took him hours to get it clean. He was spitting tacks but didn't twig it was me. As usual he'd walked on ahead leaving me to catch up."

It takes a while for them to stop giggling. When Jennie

stops, Sam starts, and vice versa. It's a while before they can carry on with their conversation.

"Only one thing left to do now." Sam squelches a final snigger.

"Sam, are you sure about that?"

"Yep, it's the only way I'll know for sure. I'll let you know how I get on."

"What if he wants to go through with it?"

"I'll jump off that bridge when I come to it."

Sam hangs up, pulls a crumpled piece of paper from the back pocket of her jeans and takes a deep breath before dialling the number scrawled on it.

"Mirage Hotel, Cheryl speaking," says a woman with a distinct Australian twang. Head Girl herself.

"Hi, wondering if Darren Walters is there at the mo?"

"No, but he's due in later today."

"Can you let him know Sam, his *girlfriend* from Auckland, called?"

"Any other message?" Cheryl's reaction to the girlfriend comment leaves her in no doubt that while she's been in the dark, Cheryl hasn't.

Bastard!

"Just let him know my parents won't be happy about an extra mouth to feed."

Less than ten minutes later the phone rings. "I'll get it," yells Sam, up the stairwell when she hears footsteps upstairs.

"Hello?"

"You stupid cow! How you can you be pregnant? You were bleeding like a stuck pig last time I was up there?" spits out Darren.

"Yeah, I might have lied about that ..." Sam's heart pulses nauseatingly in her mouth.

"You know you'll have to get rid of it. I can't deal with the responsibility of a sprog right now."

"Now hang on a bloody second ..."

"You can't get it done here. Cheryl's told me about a place you can go to in Sydney."

"I don't believe it. You want me to go to someone recommended by your whore!" says Sam, shakily.

"What do you mean, 'my whore'?"

"Give it up, Darren." Overcoming her hatred of confrontation, Sam adds, "Everyone knows about you and Head Girl. Even me."

"Who told you?" says Darren, suspiciously.

"I heard about it at the hairdressers." Sam's not about to dump Jim, or herself, in it.

"Jeez. Look, I'll send you a cheque for the trip to Sydney and we can talk things through next time I'm up."

Eventually the dial tone cuts through Sam's shock and she slowly hangs up the phone.

***

A couple of days later and Sam gets home from another day at the "office" to find a letter on her bed from Darren. Actually there isn't a letter, or even a note, just a thousand-dollar cheque on its own. She looks at it until she's crying so hard her nose is running. Her first impulse is to rip it into a million little pieces and jump up and down on it, but her practical side kicks in and she tucks it into her wallet.

The stupid bastard hadn't even crossed it, so she's going to cash it as soon as she can; especially as it's made out for five hundred dollars more than Tania thought she'd get. That'll be five hundred dollars more pain for Darren when Sam can safely let him know how completely he's been stitched up.

4

*S*am's lying in bed fighting nausea when the alarm worms its way inside her head, stopping only when she slams her hand down on the snooze button. Staring blearily at the digital display, it takes a while for the large red three-thirty to swim into focus. No wonder she still feels drunk, they'd only hit the sack a couple of hours ago.

"I think I'm going to be sick," says Jennie, from the bed on the other side of Sam's room.

Jennie's parents' business is open on Saturday so she's getting a ride to the airport with Sam. There'd been a tearful goodbye when Jennie's parents dropped her off at Sam's place the afternoon before. Eventually the girls had left both sets of parents to it and gone off to the pub so they could say goodbye to all their mates.

"I think I'm still drunk." Sam has difficulty getting these few words out. There's a slight slur to them.

Her mother bowls into the bedroom and flicks on the main light blinding both the girls. "Come on, you two. You have to be at the airport by five, I want you up, now!" Without stopping, she swings around and heads straight back to the kitchen.

Groaning, Sam pushes her duvet back, and then slowly swings her feet to the ground. Prising the rest of her body off the mattress proves harder. When she's upright, the spins are so bad she sits back down and puts her head between her knees. "Oh, god."

"I need coffee," groans Jennie.

As if in answer to Jennie's anguished plea, Sam's mother comes back carrying two mugs. "I thought you might need this." She steps over a lamp and puts the coffees on a small table between the two beds. Before leaving she picks up the lamp and puts it back in its proper spot, bending the shade back into shape.

The girls nurse their coffees, taking small sips at first to see how it will sit in their stomachs. Luckily, it mixes well with the alcohol still sloshing around in their systems, making them feel a little drunk again. Still, it is a hell of a lot better than feeling a little hung-over.

After quick showers and breakfasts of dry toast, Sam and Jennie pack their final bits and pieces.

"Thank the lord everything fits." Sam pulls the zip closed on the second of her two suitcases. She's had trouble with the final mix because she's had to sneak good clothes in amongst the holiday gear. If her mother saw any work clobber, the game would be up for sure.

There's been a lot of standing on the scales with her bags to make sure she didn't go over her allotted twenty kilos of checked-in luggage. She hopes Tania is right about the airlines not weighing carry-on bags because, despite its small size, hers weighs more than both her suitcases put together. Not knowing if she'll be able to buy her favourite lotions and potions in Australia, Sam is taking as many as possible. The trick will be to carry the bag as though it doesn't weigh close to thirty kilos.

"Yeah. Hard to believe this is it for the next couple of years." Jennie is sitting on the lid of her one massive case and leaning forward between her legs to snap the locks closed. Looking at the size of the case, Sam's glad she's opted for two much smaller bags and ones with wheels at that. By the time she'd packed the three pairs of platform corkies she's taking with her, one bag was close to being full. Her thought is punctuated by the thump of Jennie's case as it hits the ground after being dragged off the bed.

"Ready?" says Jennie.

"Ready! Just need to grab my jacket and handbag and I'm good to go."

Sam tries wheeling her bags out into the hallway but it doesn't take long for the small wheels to snarl in the shag pile, forcing her to pick them up and lug them to the front door one at a time. Jennie, unable to lift her shipping container, drags it across the carpet to the front door leaving a wide swathe of shagged carpet in her wake. They're parallel to the faint remnants of a matching swathe from when she'd dragged the case in the afternoon before. Sam's mother was in for some major carpet grooming.

Back in her room, Sam opens the wardrobe to get her favourite white denim jacket. Apart from this, the wardrobe is damned near empty; most of its contents packed in the pale blue, vinyl suitcases standing next to the front door. Sam's mother's wedding dress hangs forlornly at the far right.

Sam has been wearing the dress regularly since she was five, when her mother gave it to her for dress-up. Because she'd always been careful with the dress, it's still in beautiful condition. She touches the gorgeous fabric, looking longingly at the pattern of watered silk before it disappears behind a veil of tears. Her hand trails down the row of tiny covered buttons that run down the spine of the dress. There was no need to undo these when she was little. Now that it fitted, she'd need a husband to get out of it.

Her hand stops on the last button but one, it's loose and comes away easily when she pulls sharply on it. After popping it in the top pocket of her white denim jacket she snaps the dome closed.

Jennie comes up behind her. "You all right?"

Before she can answer, her parents are there. Her mother to hurry them along, and her father to work on a hernia by loading their bags into the back of the station wagon.

. . .

Sam and Jennie make it to the airport on time and check in their bags without being over the limit. Sam is holding it all together until it's time to go through to customs. She's trying hard not to cry knowing it'll freak out her parents given she's supposedly only going on holiday. This is made difficult by the golf-ball-sized lump lodged firmly in her throat.

Her mother swallows hard, too. "Sam, promise you'll ring as soon as you get there."

"'Course. I'll ring as soon as we get to Jen's cousin's place."

"Have a great time." Her dad gives her a tight hug.

"I will, Dad."

"Don't do anything silly, will you? If anyone asks you to carry a package for them, say no." Sam's mother is convinced the world is crawling with drug runners looking for mules.

"See you in a month," says her dad.

"Yeah," says Sam, weakly. The "'Bye, you two," comes out croaky when her voice catches. After giving her parents a final, quick hug, she shoots through the double doors and into customs before she falls apart. Given the abruptness of her departure, it takes a few seconds for Jennie to catch up.

They then go through security to make sure their paperwork is in order and they aren't taking anything dangerous onto the plane. The only dangerous thing Sam has is her carry-on bag. It shocks the security guy who takes it off the conveyor belt after it's been through the scanner. Sam has to hold back a snicker at his involuntary doubling over and muttered "Bloody hell."

They're making themselves comfortable in the departure lounge when their rows are called. "Wow, we must be near the front if we're being called this early." Jennie looks down at her boarding pass for the first time, as does Sam.

"Row 38! That doesn't sound near the front to me," says Sam.

They make their way down the airbridge and in through the front door of the plane. It's much bigger inside than they're expecting and a lot wider than anything they've flown on in New Zealand. They catch a glimpse of what must be first class through a curtain to their left.

An immaculately groomed hostess just inside the door looks at their boarding passes before peering at their faces. "Are you girls all right? You don't look well."

"Box of birdies," says Sam, with fake enthusiasm. She's all for admitting when she's feeling lousy with a cold but will never admit to a hangover to this superior creature.

"Hmm," responds the hostie.

By the way her nostrils flare and her smile falters, Sam thinks they might still smell of alcohol.

"Please go to the back of the plane and you're on the left hand side," says the hostess, her painted-on smile back in place. It's as perfect as the rest of the meticulously applied make-up and matches the vigilantly coifed hair that must owe as much to hairdressing skill as half a can of extra-hold hairspray making it more of a rock cake than a bun.

"Thanks," says Jennie.

"You're welcome."

"Thanks," says Sam.

"You're welcome. Have a pleasant flight," says the hostess. Sam doesn't think she's meant to hear the "Nowhere near me, thank goodness," the hostess adds under her breath.

Snotty bitch.

Sam can't believe at one time she'd wanted to be a hostess but as far as she could see, they were only waitresses with altitude.

Sam is already moving before she looks up to see the aisle disappearing into the distance with hostesses, and the occasional steward, dotted along it at regular intervals.

Bugger, I still have to lug my bag for miles.

They trudge down the aisle, being greeted by every hostie as they go.

"Morning."

"Morning." "Morning."

"Morning."

"Morning." "Morning."

"Morning."

"Morning." "Morning."

By the time they find their seats, Sam's ready to go into *mourning* she's so fed up with chipper hosties. Anyone would think it was a sensible hour.

Short of the toilets and a couple of jump seats, their row is the last on the plane. Jennie's been allocated the window seat but promises they can swap over halfway through the flight. Sam jams her bag under the seat in front of her to avoid risking serious personal injury by trying to put it in the overhead locker. She's also not keen on something that heavy sitting above her in a cupboard made out of plastic.

They rummage through the magazines and gizmos in the elastic netting pockets positioned depressingly close to their knees. Concentrating on reading all the small type on the safety sheet out of Jennie's pocket proves too much for their hangovers. Sam figures they'll have to panic like everyone else.

Once the plane is moving toward the runway, the hostesses do a final check on seat belts and overhead lockers before they retreat to their fold-down seats in readiness for take-off.

As they hurtle down the runway Sam's eyes fill and she quietly grieves the end of her life as she'd planned it. No going back now.

Jennie looks away from the window. "You'll find a new dream."

"I'm not sure if I want a new one."

"Give it time." Jennie gives Sam's hand a reassuring squeeze.

It doesn't take long for the excitement of the flight to wear off, there being nothing to see but clouds and ocean. Certainly it's more interesting flying within New Zealand where there's always something to see, even if it is just more green. They don their eye masks and settle down to catch up on lost sleep.

Even with the world blocked out, Sam finds it hard to sleep. Darren's no great loss but heading overseas wasn't what she'd planned for, either. Her hand comes to rest over the small satin-covered button, snug in the top pocket of her jacket. The inside of her mask is damp with tears before she manages to fall asleep.

As the smell of the cooked breakfast cuts through her consciousness, her stomach gives a nasty lurch. She comes around fully, when the hostess wheeling the food trolley down the aisle, slams it into her.

"Ow!" She pushes up the eye mask and rubs her elbow.

"Would you care for breakfast?" says the hostess, oblivious to the collision. Before she can respond, the hostie leans in for a closer look, and then her nose wrinkles. "Probably best if we don't." Releasing the foot brake, she puts her full body weight behind the trolley to get it moving toward the galley.

"Hell, I must look rough."

"Huh?" Jennie lifts one corner of her eye mask to peer at Sam.

"I was saying I must look rough 'cause the hostess decided I shouldn't have breakfast, simply by looking at me. I don't look that bad, do I?"

"Well," Jennie slides her mask up onto her forehead, "I know I'm looking through blood shot eyes but ..."

At this point, one of the few stewards on board wanders past and looking at them says, "Can I interest you girls in some coffee?"

"Yes, please!" they enthuse.

After coffee, Sam and Jennie pull their masks back down and fall into a sleep so deep they only wake up when the plane thumps its arrival at Melbourne. They never did swap seats but, leaning over Jennie, Sam's able to see their new home town for the first time. Heat shimmers off a runway edged with foliage burned an arid, sandy brown.

It takes them so long to get from their seats to the exit that by the time they go through the final cabin the cleaning crew is already on the plane. Sam's shoulder is in agony from the weight of her carry-on bag, and she hopes it won't be long before they can snag a trolley. Jennie will need one to get her bag out of the terminal.

Unfortunately, they have to wend their way through immigration before they even get near the trolleys. The weight of Sam's small bag proves too much and she resorts to shoving it along the ground in front of her, leaving scuff marks on the lino in the process. By the time they clear customs and find their check-through bags, they're dripping with sweat.

"You'd think the cheap bastards would turn on the air-conditioning," says Sam, as they fight to get their hire horse of a trolley to head in the direction of the exit.

"Yeah, weird a terminal this flash doesn't have air-con," says Jennie, as the automatic doors of the terminal open in front of them.

They both stagger as they're hit with a wall of heat so solid they have to fight their way through it.

Sam struggles out of her jacket. "We're going clothes shopping, pronto."

5

A few minutes of the heat outside and Sam's head feels as though it's going to explode. They're fighting off another wave of taxi drivers when Jennie's relatives pull up in front of the terminal. The girls are grateful that Jennie's cousin, Greg, is a mountain of a man who has no trouble heaving their bags into the back of his small truck. His wife, who hasn't bothered to even look in their direction, stays put in the cab.

"Where do we sit?" says Jennie.

"You'll need to go in the back, Nadene gets car sick and so doesn't like to be cramped."

Stepping on the tow bar, the girls climb up to join their bags in the back and are horrified to find that not only is it incredibly dusty, it's a good ten degrees warmer than outside. They're still standing there wondering where they should sit when the truck accelerates away from the kerb. Sam, still upright, grabs a side with one hand and her friend with the other, preventing Jennie from falling out of the back. The girls drop in a heap on top of their suitcases and don't dare move for the remainder of the trip.

Any hopes of it cooling down once the little truck is moving are soon suffocated by the waves of hot diesel fumes buffeting in through the wide-open back. The wind swirling around them is hot enough to dry flannelette sheets, although they'd smell like an engine bay when done.

Jennie's relatives run a caravan park in a suburb called Sunshine. The girls can stay indefinitely, so long as they're happy to pay the full going rate. The place is bloody miles from anywhere and has seen better days, unfortunately a good thirty-five years before their arrival.

Greg and his wife drop the girls outside the caravan that is to be their new home, then drive off leaving them to it. For all the interaction they've had with her, Nadene might just as well be a dummy.

The peeling aluminium hulk in front of them is so far out of warranty even a heritage museum wouldn't touch it. Any paint that remains has oxidised to a soft grey that matches the metal showing through. The rubber window surrounds are cracked and hard. They crumble at the slightest pressure, as Sam discovers when she pokes one experimentally. "Bloody Norah, is this for real?"

"Maybe the inside is nicer?"

By the time they've lugged their bags inside, they've used up all of the available floor space and are blinded by their own sweat.

"I can't believe how bloody hot it is in here." Sam crawls over built-in furniture and suitcases so she can open every window in the van. When finished, she's not sure it's made any difference. If anything, it seems even hotter.

Jennie pushes up on the skylight, only to have her hand smash straight through the fatigued plastic. It's as tired as everything else in the van. The whole inside has a 'baked' feel to it. "There's no way we can stay in here."

"On the bright side, at least we can be sure there aren't any creepy-crawlies in here," says Sam, looking at the assortment of desiccated insects in the bottom of the tiny sink.

Jennie peeks over the safety of Sam's shoulder. "I thought cockroaches could survive anything."

After peeling off their damp travel clothes and donning their thinnest outfits, they retreat to the communal kitchen hoping it will be cooler. It is, but the coolest spot is the tiled floor. They throw down a sarong to protect them from the fine film of grease and remains of many a sloppily eaten fry-up.

It's dark when they head back to the caravan but by midnight they're back on the kitchen floor where it's at least cool enough to get some sleep.

Three nights of sleeping on bacon bits and the scrag-ends of burnt sausages is as much Sunshine as they can bear. They move to a hostel for "young ladies" in South Melbourne. It's a little more expensive than the caravan park but at least they'll be able to sleep in their beds.

The landlady is a Rubinesque, slow-moving woman whose eyes work independently of each other, which has the girls constantly on the move trying to either keep, or avoid, eye contact. She's wearing a large kaftan-style outfit because Sam suspects that other than your average pup tent, nothing else would fit, although pup tents came in more flattering colours.

They sign their lives away and receive their keys along with a small lecture. "There will be no men, alcohol or drugs on the premises, you are expected to keep your room tidy and vacuumed and the front door is double-locked from midnight till six a.m."

"That all seems fair," says Jennie.

"You are expected to clean up after yourselves in the kitchen and laundry and under no circumstances are you to use hair dye in the bathrooms."

"Why's that?" says Sam, curiosity getting the better of her.

"Because last time it happened it took me three weeks to get the tiles clean, that's why." The landlady crosses her arms over breasts so large and unsupported they merge seamlessly with her stomach.

"Fair enough," says Sam.

"I'll be keeping an eye on you," she says, looking at Jennie and Sam simultaneously.

It isn't until they're safely in their new room that laughter gets the better of them.

"I can't believe we agreed to all that with a straight face," laughs Jennie, holding her stomach.

"Well, we could hardly say the reason we're moving is to get *closer* to the men, drugs and alcohol, could we?" Sam throws one of her suitcases onto her bed and proceeds to pull everything out.

Jennie looks at the mounting pile of clothes on Sam's bed. "Here's hoping she doesn't do snap inspections 'cause I think you're about to break the tidiness rule."

"Come on, the place needs some brightening up." Sam artfully drapes scarves and belts over the head of her bed.

The place has a faded elegance. Very bloody faded. The wallpaper in their room is so washed out it looks like mottled beige Kraft paper and the floral pattern on the carpet has mulched down to a point that Sam thinks you could grow cabbages in it. Her candlewick bedspread is barely pink and so moth-eaten she can see her sheets through it. On the plus side, it'll come in handy if she needs a mozzie net.

The communal showers prove much more colourful.

Unfortunately the colour is grey; the sort of grey she can feel with her eyes shut. Obviously their landlady hasn't touched the tiles since the famous hair dye incident.

***

Next morning sees the girls pounding the pavements in search of gainful employment. Sam hates registering for secretarial work with all the shorthand tests, typing tests, and character assessments to make sure she's not a homicidal maniac. She hopes her shorthand and typing speeds are good enough that they won't care if she fails the last test.

Because Sam is after temporary jobs, she's working the following day at a company that imports catering equipment. By the end of the week, Jennie – who prefers the security of a full time job – has snagged one with an insurance company.

The Friday night of their first week in the hostel and Sam and Jennie are lying on their beds and wondering about going into town, when Sally, from down the hall, puts her head around the corner. "Hey, are you guys keen on hitting a nightclub tonight?"

"Sounds good," they both reply.

"What time are you going?" says Jennie.

"Around ten."

"Is it worth it when we have to be back here by midnight?" says Sam.

"It is when your brother's a locksmith and you have a spare key," Sally says, her laughter following her down the hall.

"My god, it's already gone eight. We're going to have to race if we want to get ready in time." Jennie bounces off her bed to survey her half of the wardrobe. "What on earth am I going to wear?"

"I know exactly what I'm wearing." Collecting her stuff, Sam heads for the showers leaving Jennie desperately sliding hangers back and forth. She hasn't gone far when she remembers her flip flops. A pair of angler's waders would offer better protection against the tinea lurking in the shower tray but would make shaving her legs difficult.

Sam gets back to the room after her shower to find Madam Jennie the Wardrobe Psychic still peering intently into the cupboard as if it's a crystal ball.

"What about your blue outfit? That looks good."

"But I've worn it a million times."

"Yeah, but no one here's ever seen it, so it may as well be new. You can wear my denim jacket."

Jennie sorts her ensemble and the girls are at the front door by ten. There are seven of them in the group; Jennie and Sam have met all of them already over breakfasts in the shared kitchen. Sally and three others are from country towns in the surrounding areas and are in Melbourne for work and, more importantly, to find a husband who isn't related to them by more than marriage.

Brenda is different. She's from Brisbane, not looking for a

husband and isn't that keen on work either. With her waist-length black hair, creamy skin and gorgeous figure, Sam thinks Brenda could get work modelling. She had suggested this over breakfast one morning and was told, "Piss off! Me model? There are much easier sodding ways to make money than that."

Brenda's voice is the one thing about her that isn't stunning. She sounds like a trucker; but with a much wider vocabulary.

Sam and Jennie can't help but be impressed when they walk into the nightclub with the others. The ground floor is Jazz and Blues, the second floor Rock & Roll and the top floor, where they are, is all about Disco. A wide, mirrored staircase spirals its way up through the heart of the place, so massive it's a destination in its own right, with the beautiful people lurking there so they can be reflected in their own glory.

"This place is *cool*," yells Jennie, as they all squeeze into one of the thickly upholstered booths surrounding the dance floor.

Sam looks up and notices the whole ceiling is mirrored like the staircase. "Un-frigging-believable." This, coupled with the mirror balls scattered throughout, makes the whole place sparkle, although the effect is softened by a thick haze of cigarette smoke. She knows her clothes will reek in the morning, even if she hangs her dress out of the window overnight. "Check it out," she yells, over the diaphragm-thumping music and points up.

They're all admiring the ceiling when a waiter arrives and puts a glass of champagne down in front of Sam. "Compliments of the gentleman over there," he says, right into her ear so she'll hear him. The Bee Gees are belting out their latest hit at a level that will have her ears still ringing when she wakes the following morning. The DJ seems oblivious to the volume, no doubt dazzled by the fit-inducing effect of the strobe lights.

"What? Oh, thanks," mouths Sam, swivelling to see who he's talking about, as she'd been looking at the ceiling so she'd missed where he'd pointed.

No one acknowledges her when she sweeps the room so she turns back to the others.

"Hey, if he's not brave enough to show up himself, stuff him!" she shouts, before taking a sip of the bubbles.

She's not finished when another arrives. This time the waiter has been given better instructions about letting her know who it's from.

He's standing at the bar with some of his mates, his head not reaching the shoulder of any of them which is why Sam missed him earlier.

He's pock-marked and sleazy and she wishes she hadn't drunk the first glass now because she can hardly turn down the second. Picking it up, she smiles weakly then turns back to the others hoping her lack of response will give him the message.

"Hi there, hope you enjoy champagne?" is shouted at her a moment later.

"Yes, thanks very much!" she shouts back.

"I join you!"

"There isn't enough room!" yells Sam.

"Eees fine, I grab chair!" Which he does, plonking himself down at the end of table and suffocatingly close to her.

"I am Tony," he says, shouting inches from her ear and deafening her more than the music. This is followed by a questioning look.

She nods her reply. The music's pumping. Great if you're dancing.

"And your name eees?" he bellows at her.

"I'm Pamela." She then rattles off other *Dallas* cast names for the rest of the girls. Sam isn't sure Tony believes her, given the resulting laughter by the others, especially when she finishes by introducing Jennie as Miss Ellie.

"Eees my imagination – I detect accent, yes?" says Tony

into her ear, even closer than before, causing her to crawl inside her own skin seeking shelter.

She'd rather he yelled.

"No. I don't think so. English is my first language," yells Sam, maintaining her distance.

"Aaaah, you a Kiwi. Wheresaboutsyoufrom?"

"Auckland!" Sam says, in a slightly elevated voice. Thank god the DJ's having a break; her vocal chords are taking a hammering. The hold music isn't much quieter but at least she doesn't need to shout to be heard. She's glad the strobe lights have been given a rest, too; you never knew when latent epilepsy might rear its ugly head.

"How long you have been here?"

"This is our third, no wait our fourth week."

"Our? Who is 'our'?"

"Huh?" Sam is confused both by his thick accent and what he wants to know.

"Who you travel with?"

"I think he means me, love," says a deep voice from behind Sam. "Sorry I'm late, got held up at the base."

"The base?" Sam freezes.

But Darren can't have found me already. He wouldn't know where to look.

"Yeah, those manoeuvres took longer than expected."

"Manoeuvres?"

But it can't be. Look around, look around.

Sam's still frozen despite her internal pep talk. She looks at Jennie; her friend's face shows confusion.

Her brows knotted, Jennie mouths, "What?" to Sam.

She turns reluctantly. It's not Darren, thank goodness. She has no idea who he is but he's much, much better looking than the sleazy little man sitting next to her.

He's grinning broadly at the thoughts that must be flashing like a slide show across her face. "Well, aren't you going to say something?"

Sam looks at Tony, then back at the stranger. "John, sweetheart. I was wondering when you'd turn up."

"Your boyfriend?" Tony's voice is a study of disbelief.

"Sorry, he's going to need that seat. You don't mind do you?"

Tony can't do much given the size of his competition, the fact the guy's in uniform and there are four more similarly attired blokes backing him up. He stands, grumbling, throws the chair at his replacement and storms back to his mates at the bar who are all doubled over at his expense.

"John" sits, smiles at her and says. "Hi, I'm Chris," his voice a tad above normal volume.

"I'm Sam. You've got no idea how pleased I am to meet you. I wasn't sure how to get rid of him."

"Yeah, you're the third chick I've seen him hit on tonight but you seemed more polite than the others. It looked like you could use some help."

"You're not wrong. So I take it you're all off to a fancy dress party."

"What makes you think we're not in the Navy?"

"You mean apart from the whites not matching, the jackets being so tight your buttons are about to pop and your hair being way too long?"

"Are you in the Navy yourself? You seem pretty up with the play on things."

"Yeah, something like that," says Sam, noncommittally.

"You're right, though. We're on our way to a party. Thought it'd be a laugh to call in here. The bouncer even let us in for free."

"Wow, might have to get a uniform of my own. Could save a fortune."

"With a gym slip and knee socks?"

Sam laughs and shoves at his shoulder. "Not that sort, you weirdo."

She can't believe the connection she has with him. She's sure she saw sparks pass between them. Their bond is electric, her whole arm's tingling.

"Sorry, the uniforms are nylon."

"Right. So I know you're not navy, so what do you do?'

"Auto design," he says, looking up.

Realising he's checking out her cleavage in the mirrored ceiling she says, "Careful, you're starting to remind me of my sleazy little mate over there."

"Perish the thought. What are you doing in here anyway? It's a real pick-up joint and you don't look the sort." He's now yelling as the music's started up again, with the Village People letting everyone know how macho they are.

"If it's so bad, why are you here?" She leans closer rather than shout at him over the music.

He leans forward at the same time which has his breath gently tickling her cheek. She's damn sure the static effects of the nylon uniforms aren't that far-reaching, so she's at a loss to explain this sudden surge in her national grid.

"You, too?" he says, into her ear.

"Don't know what you mean." Sam pulls back.

"Hey, mate, you ready to go?" yells one of the other sailors, putting his hand on Chris's shoulder. This is followed closely by him spitting out, "Bloody hell," and rapidly flicking his hand. "The static in these sodding uniforms is lethal."

"Yeah, if our boys had been wearing these at Gallipoli we could have fried the Turks," yells Chris, over his shoulder, before turning back to Sam.

"We're heading off now. Perhaps we could catch up some time?" he shouts.

"Not worth it, we're heading onto London soon!" she yells back in automatic self-preservation. God, with all the shouting and the cigarette smoke she's going to sound like Marlene Dietrich in the morning. Still, it was always fun to wander around saying you "vanted to be alone".

"Might see you around before you go." He stands before heading with the others across the dance floor toward the exit.

"What the hell did you do that for? He's gorgeous." Jennie looks at Sam and shakes her head.

"Exactly! He's bloody gorgeous," Sam yells back just as the track finishes.

"You're pretty cute yourself."

Sam's head whips around to find Chris back beside her. "Forgot my hat."

"Right," is all she can choke out.

"Forgot this, too." Without warning, he kisses her full on the mouth, pulling away and dragging on her bottom lip with his teeth as he does so. "Just so you know what you're missing," he whispers into her ear.

6

Back in Auckland, Tania's waiting for Jim to arrive at the pub. He should have been here by now, but Tania knows how time can get away from him once he has his head buried in an engine. She's startled when Darren throws himself into the chair next to her.

"Sam back yet? If she's around I'll sit somewhere else."

"No, ah, not yet."

"Jim's in tonight though, isn't he?" Tania nods and he continues "Great, I've got a question I need to ask him about the tuning on the car."

"Excuse me, I'm off to the loo." If she stays with the cheap prick, she'll ear-bash him about taking advantage of Jim.

She's threading her way through the crowd on her way back to the table when she sees Jim has arrived and is making his way over to Darren. Perfect. Time to get the show started. Standing on tiptoes Tania gives a "thumbs up" to the barman, who gives her a conspiratorial wink before he goes out the back.

Tania stalls for time so she arrives just after the barman who stands next to Darren, a bottle of champagne and a glass in his hands. Darren looks up, sees the bottle and says, "Sorry mate, I don't drink that poofter's stuff, must be for her," jerking his thumb in Tania's direction.

"Nope, it's been ordered especially for you," says the barman.

"Who by?"

"Sam, before she left."

Darren's quiet for a few seconds before demanding, "What the hell for?"

"To celebrate your impending fatherhood," says Tania.

"Not my fault."

"I should hope not, it'd be sick. And illegal," says Tania.

"She wasn't *that* bad," says Darren.

"You didn't find the flea collar off-putting?" says Jim, unable to stop himself laughing. Jim hadn't uttered a word to Darren before now, on pain of abstinence from Tania.

"What?"

"It's okay, Darren. We know all about it." Tania grins before adding, "Can I have one of the puppies?"

"Are you talking about V8?"

"Yeah. Sam told us V8's expecting although it came as a shock as they thought you'd had her fixed. I know Sam called and left a message for you at the pub. She even wrote a card to go with your Champagne."

"Where is it?"

"Here." Tania pulls the small card from her bag.

Darren opens it and reads it to himself. "I don't believe it." Darren throws the card on the table where Jim grabs it and reads it aloud.

"Congratulations Darren, hope you don't mind that I didn't 'get rid of it'. Thanks for the money, it's come in handy." This is followed by bellows of laughter from the nearby tables who've overheard the whole exchange.

"How long's she away?" Darren says to Tania, with a healthy dose of spit.

His face darkens when she explains that Sam's gone with Jennie on her big OE and so won't be back for years. That Sam had decided to go after she'd learned Darren was screwing around on her with Head Girl.

"Sam isn't pregnant?" says Darren.

"Sam pregnant? What made you jump to that conclusion?" says Tania.

Unable to cope with the continued laughter, Darren jumps up, spilling the drinks on the table in the process, and makes his escape.

"She was lousy in the sack anyway," he yells, to the bar in general when heading out the door.

7

Sam and Jennie stall halfway up the path at the address Brenda has given them.

Stunning pink flowers wend their way up the trellis on the outside of the huge, two-storey brick house. The garden is a riot of colour, with bumblebees staggering from flower to flower in a nectar-induced high. The scent of the blooms is almost overwhelming, the air thick in her lungs. "This can't be the place." says Sam. "It's way too flash."

Because of the hostel rules concerning men, alcohol and drugs, Sam and Jennie spend a lot of time under the huge Jacaranda tree out in front of the hostel. There, they can indulge in these pastimes, along with the other girls, without fear of molestation by their pup-tent wearing landlady. It's here they get talking to Brenda who's also had a gutful of the strict regime. She knows of a furnished three-bedroom flat going for a crazy cheap rent that even includes power and phone. Sam and Jennie jump at the chance to move in with her.

Even though Brenda is what Sam's mum would call "a little rough around the edges", she does own a car, which will mean an end to those arm-lengthening trips home from the supermarket.

"Looks a bit too flash for the rent, doesn't it?" says Jennie.

They're walking back down the path to check the number on the letterbox when someone with an accent says, "Are you Brenda's friends?"

"Yes," they both reply, turning to find a tall man standing on the top step. He looks Italian or maybe Greek and must have been a complete babe when he was younger. Even though he's close to her dad's age, Sam thinks he's still hot; with greying temples and dark brown eyes that scream *come to bed* and not in a hot cocoa and jammies kind of way.

He's wearing tailored slacks, topped off with a fitted white t-shirt and the shiniest pair of shoes she's spotted since primary school. Even shinier is the wide, gold wedding band on his ring finger. He's carrying a man-bag; the first one she's seen outside a magazine. Sam swallows her whistle of admiration.

"Well, come in then. It's too hot out here. Brenda will be along soon." He opens the door and gestures for them to head inside. "Go ahead, look, I'll stay here." He pulls a cigar out of his bag followed by an engraved cigarette lighter and what looks to be a track guide. As they start into the interior of the flat he's settling himself on a bench in a shady part of the garden.

"Boy, he's cute. He reminds me of Steve," says Jennie, followed by a small sigh.

"We can look for somewhere else if you like," says Sam, softly.

"All I said is that he reminds me of Steve. That's all. Come on, let's check the place out. Who knows where Brenda is."

They're looking through one of the bedrooms when Brenda bursts in. "Sorry I'm late traffic was a complete bitch for a Saturday morning so what do you think of our new landlord?" she says, in one strident breath.

"Very cute and married by the looks of things. Mind you, we might be able to come to an arrangement on how we pay the rent," jokes Sam.

"Too late, why do you think the place is so sodding cheap!"

"What! You didn't?" says Sam.

"Multiple times," says Brenda.

"How can you do that?" says Jennie, aghast.

"I can give you a book, if you like," says Brenda.

"Not that! I know how to do it. But sex should be special. It should be with the right guy."

Brenda rolls her eyes. "Screw me, that's 'virgin' on the ridiculous."

"You mean verging," says Jennie, a little primly.

"Yeah, whatever." Brenda leaves them, wandering into the next room.

The house has been split into four flats, with the one they're looking at taking up nearly all of the ground floor. Because they don't have access to some rooms on their floor, it makes for a strange layout with doors permanently locked and a lounge that only has two tall, skinny windows. It steals the rest of its light from the rooms that branch off it. There are two double bedrooms and a single that all open off the lounge

The kitchen is what a real estate agent would call 'compact' while the bathroom is more 'compactor'. It's tiny, but it's nice and clean.

Sam's standing in the separate toilet squinting up at the ceiling fifteen feet above her, when Brenda comes in. "Whoa, it's gonna be like taking a leak in a grain silo."

"Yeah, we'll be screwed if the bulb ever blows," says Brenda. "Not that you'll hear me complaining. Stefano's hot."

They move that afternoon, much to the annoyance of the hostel's landlady. Because Brenda found the flat, she gets the main bedroom, Sam dibs the smallest because it's got the biggest wardrobe. Jennie's room, too, is "just right".

Following a sleep-in and a day at the beach, it's late afternoon on their first full day in the flat before Sam finishes arranging her clothes in the wardrobe that spans the entire end of her bedroom. The room itself might be tiny but the wardrobe is a thing of beauty with all her clothes fitting in with lots of room to spare. She closes the louvered double doors with a sigh of satisfaction.

"Phone's free," says Jennie, passing the doorway to Sam's room.

"Thanks." Sam goes out to the hallway where the phone sits. She's not looking forward to this conversation with her parents because, apart from giving them the phone number of the flat, she's going to have to break it to them that she's staying on indefinitely.

Perching herself on the seat part of the wrought-iron telephone table, she takes a deep breath, picks up the phone and dials. She tries to make herself comfortable while waiting for them to answer. The sun streaming in through the window by her has heated the plastic seat covering so that it's hot on the backs of her sunburned legs. The sun is also responsible for the foam padding having disintegrated to caramel coloured dust, puffing its way through the seams at the first sign of a bum coming to rest on it. The only thing between Sam's cheeks and the plywood base is white vinyl with a gold star pattern. It's bloody uncomfortable so hopefully the phone call won't be a long one.

It's half an hour before Sam wanders into the lounge rubbing the dented backs of her legs. Jennie is sitting on the couch, her feet up on the coffee table and a book on Melbourne open on her lap.

"How'd it go," says Jennie.

"Stupidly well."

"What did they say when you told them you were staying on?"

"I didn't have to." Sam's still shaking her head in disbelief. "Mum suggested it after she broke the news to me that Darren had moved out."

"No surprises there. When did he go?" Jennie's finger marks her spot in the book.

"He cleared everything out this morning while mum and dad were at church. Mum's fuming because he took all her good wooden hangers. I didn't dare tell her that it was because I'd superglued all his clothes to them," says Sam, laughing.

"What about V8? Your mum's going to miss her."

"The bastard left her behind. Didn't want to deal with the puppies. When I said he'd given me money to get rid of them, Mum went through the roof. She's going to use the money I left behind to get V8 spayed after the puppies are weaned. Plus it'll pay for dog food for a while."

"So it all worked out okay then."

"Yeah. When I heard he was gone I thought I'd better check in with Tania."

"And?" says Jennie.

"Went exactly as planned!" There's the briefest of lulls before they both crack up laughing.

Their first Saturday morning in the flat and Jennie and Sam are off to the local Laundromat to do their week's washing. Brenda hadn't made it home the night before and they'd got sick of waiting for her, and her car.

Like all laundromats it looks to be at least twenty years old with the machines all original. They look to be in reasonable condition but it's always a worry with old machines that your clothes will come out covered in rust spots. But, looking around, Sam can see others bunging whites into their machines with gay abandon, so they must be all right. She's onto her fourth machine before she finds one where the dials are readable enough that she'll know what cycle she's selecting.

The chairs, arranged in a row down the middle of the black and white tiled room, are unpadded, hard-backed and generally unforgiving. Every surface in the place is coated with a thick layer of dryer lint so they feel as though they've stumbled into a fuzzy felt picture.

Sam looks up from pouring soap powder into what she hopes is the correct drawer of her washing machine. Being brought up with top loaders she's still nervous the laundromat's front loaders will leak on her. "Hell, this is one posh neighbourhood."

"What do you mean?"

"Take a look at that." Sam points at the huge, plate-glass window at the front of the laundromat.

"The dog's blue."

"It's the same colour as her hair."

Jennie's eyebrows pop up another notch. "Their jackets match, too."

"The floral looks better on the dog."

"She's coming in here," says Jennie. "You'd think if you could afford a Merc and a blue dog you could spring for a washing machine."

Beneath the blue hair, the woman is five foot nothing, twig thin and has a general air of command.

Her eyes are a pale blue more commonly seen on Angora goats, while her lips are the colour of packet orange cordial. Sam suspects she's been wearing the same shade of lipstick for the past sixty years and considers it her signature colour. Unfortunately, with everything else about her being faded with age, it's as though her lips arrive before she does.

Looking at the immaculate pastel floral Jackie O suit, Sam is conscious of the cut-off jeans, singlet and flip flops that make up her own laundromat ensemble.

They sit bemused as the owner of the Mercedes proceeds to put on a load of washing, all of which seems to belong to the dog while chatting away to the mutt as though it's a two-way conversation. She then leaves to take her "darling Sapphire for a little walkie". The dog doesn't respond, not once.

"An outfit for every occasion." Jennie wanders over to look at the load of little spotted, striped and floral jackets sloshing around in the machine. "He seems to prefer pastels over bold patterns," she muses and then shouts, "Oh, my goodness there are *hats*, too," jabbing the front of the glass with her finger. "Look there's one, and there. Hah, they match the jackets."

"I don't suppose the dog picks the stuff himself. He'd be happier covered in mud." She strolls over to check out the machine.

They're both peering into the curved, front glass when the Blue Lady/dog combo returns to check on the load. "Can I help you girls with something?" Her tone indicates flared nostrils.

"We were admiring your dog's outfits. He's very fashion conscious," says Jennie, turning.

"He's a she, if you don't mind."

"Sorry, I guess I thought blue for boys," says Jennie.

"It's not blue. It's what my hairdresser calls Gentian Silver."

Jennie turns to Sam and mouths, "blue".

"So your hairdresser colours the dog?" Sam has to ask.

"Of course he doesn't! He gives me solution and the people at Sapphire's salon take care of it."

Rather than wait inside and risk sullying her expensive suit by sitting on the lint-coated laundromat chairs, she retires to her car to wait.

"One day I will be rich enough to have my dog match my hair," says Sam. Closing her eyes she can see herself in a magnificent wedding dress, but the face of the groom refuses to come into focus.

Chris stands with his back to the bar. A bottle of beer hangs limply from his right hand; his left elbow is propped on the dark mahogany behind him. He scans the room for any sign of his mate, Mark. If there are any cute chicks between the bar and the door then that could explain Mark's absence. Chris hooks his heel over the brass footrail and boosts himself up to put him a head above everyone else.

Nope, Mark's not there. At six foot four, he's hard to miss.

The place is filling up with an older crowd, here to listen to the regular Wednesday night jazz band. Given it's a converted 1920s villa, filling the place to overflowing isn't a problem. If the original inhabitants could see their front parlour now, packed like it is, they'd be horrified.

Chris absently chugs on his beer only to realise he's finished it. He turns and orders another. He's halfway through it before he checks his watch again. Damn, it's already gone seven and this should have been Mark's round.

"A bottle of VB thanks," says Mark, to the barman as he comes up next to Chris.

"Mate, your timing's spot on, as usual." Chris takes another pull on his Castlemaine.

"Don't sweat it, I'll get the next one for ya. Sorry I'm late, ran into an old friend."

"How old?"

Mark swigs gratefully on his beer before answering. "About twenty-two."

"Hey, there's that chick who was with Sam the night I met her." Chris angles his face toward the far end of the room.

"Sam?"

"Yeah, the blonde at Clique Disco the night we were off to the navy fancy dress."

"Why bother with the blonde?" says Mark, drooling over Sam's friend's Barbie doll figure, waist-length jet black hair and full, made-for-head lips.

"She's all yours, mate, after I get Sam's number." Chris pushes himself off the bar and heads in the direction of Barbie. "Hi, there," he says, when he stops next to her.

Chris feels like a slab of meat when she scans him from head to toe without saying a word. He also has the distinct impression she's found him wanting.

"You're Sam's friend, aren't you?" he says, stopping any putdown.

"Might be. Who's asking?"

"Chris. I met up with you guys at Clique's," At her lack of response he adds, "I was dressed as a sailor."

"Ah right, what's long and hard and full of seamen?" she says, before cracking up.

"So I was wondering if I could get Sam's number from you."

"Not bloody likely."

"Well, can you give her mine?"

"Sure. But it'll cost ya."

"You're joking."

"Twenty says I'm not."

Back at the bar, Chris takes a healthy pull on his beer before saying "I don't believe it, I had to pay her to give my number to Sam." He takes another swig to get rid of the nasty taste in his mouth. "Money-grubbing cow."

"I thought you must have been sorting out some fun when I saw cash changing hands," says Mark.

"Hell, no!"

"You don't mind if I …?"

"Knock yourself out."

Mark swaggers off in Mercenary Barbie's direction. Chris gives him five minutes; max. He's overestimated. Mark isn't even able to speak before Chris lip reads, "Sod off!" Mark spins on his heel and makes his way back to Chris.

"Too rich for you?"

"I think I'm too young." Mark looks at Barbie who is flirting with an older guy who's made his way over to her lair.

"You shoulda dropped a hint about the trust fund."

"Yeah, right! How long do you think it'd last after she arrived on the scene?" Mark scans the room for a replacement.

9

*F*riday night and Sam's hanging onto the strap above her head as the old-fashioned green and gold tram rattles its way up St Kilda Road. As it takes the corner into Domain Road and trundles along beside the Botanical Gardens, she has to brace herself.

Her stop is coming up so she starts to make her way along the tram in hopes of evading the conductor. Not paying had started as a sort of game between her and Jennie but continued when they worked out how much money they were saving. There are things they'd much rather spend their dosh on. Like shoes. Spotting Jennie through the swaying crowd, Sam manoeuvres herself into the space next to her.

"How was your day?" says Sam.

"Okay, I guess, although I live for the day when they trust me with something other than the filing."

"Hey, one of the girls at the place where I'm temping was telling me about a new disco that's opened on St Kilda Road. You up for it tonight?"

"Sounds good. What are you going to wear?"

"Don't know. Might start with my silver platforms and work my way up." Sam looks over her shoulder to check on the whereabouts of the conductor. He's getting closer. She nudges Jennie, prompting her to pull the cord to stop the tram.

"From what the girl at work was saying, we'll be up to our armpits in cute guys too," says Sam, as they step down from the tram.

"So long as there's good music, I'll be happy." Jennie loves to dance.

"Never mind the music, I'm going to sample the local talent."

"Are you over Darren enough for that?" Jennie looks sideways at her as they wander slowly up the hill toward home.

Sam stops completely. "I think so. It's about time I checked out some other guys."

"If you're sure? But remember, sometimes it just feels like you're over something. Then it all comes flooding back." Jennie's not focusing on Sam.

"I am over him. Really!" Sam's hand subconsciously flattens over the button hanging between her breasts on a thin silver chain.

"Be careful you don't lose yourself along with the memories."

They continue up the road talking about outfits before turning off the footpath to take the short cut home. They walk through the back gate and nearly trip over Brenda, who's sprawled on a rug working on her tan. Sam can't help but be envious of Brenda's figure, shown to advantage in an incredibly small red, spotty bikini.

She takes in the golden colour of Brenda's skin. "You must've got off work early?"

"Told them I wasn't feeling well and came home at lunch time." Brenda rolls over, motioning for them to get out of her sun.

"But haven't you told them that heaps of times before?" says Jennie, stepping to the side.

"The penny'll drop soon but I don't care. It's a crap job so I figure I may as well milk it for as long as I can. Plus I like looking nice and tanned when Stefano comes around."

"Is the rent due already?" says Jennie.

"It doesn't feel like two weeks since we last paid," says Sam.

"Yep, it's due, there's a note on the calendar." Brenda holds out her hand.

"Damn, there go those new shoes," says Sam, handing over some notes.

Jennie hands over her share too. "You're just lucky I got paid today."

"Don't whinge at me, it's on the calendar." Brenda stuffs the notes inside her bikini top where Stefano will, no doubt, retrieve them later.

"Hey, are you up for a trip to a new disco in St Kilda Road tonight?" says Sam.

"What time are ya thinking of going out?" says Brenda.

"Nine-ish."

"Yeah, why not? I'll wear my white jumpsuit. It'll glow under the black lights. My tan will look wicked."

Later that evening, Sam stands in the middle of the lounge waiting for the others to finish getting ready. She's watching telly with the picture just visible behind a cloud of swirling white static. The wood-veneered TV on its cream plastic pedestal came with the flat, so they can't complain about the crap picture quality. But it's bloody tedious that every programme looks like it's been filmed in Alaska. Sam wonders if Brenda can have a word with the landlord and work her magic on getting them a set with a picture quality closer to the equator.

Sam moves around the room, doing the occasional squat. She'll sit down when her cream canvas flares have stretched enough that she won't risk doing herself an injury.

"Jeez, that outfit's bitchin'," says Brenda, coming from her room where she's spent over an hour on hair and make-up. "How wide are the flares?"

"Twenty-eight inches! Tricky if they wrap around each other though. I've been arse over kite a couple of times now."

"What about the platforms? They okay for dancing?"

"Hell, I can run for a tram in these babies." She demonstrates by twirling around the room.

Jennie jumps into the lounge and assumes a Frida-style pose. "Abba, eat ya heart out."

"Aw, off a duck, I feel boring in white now." Brenda admires Jennie's bright-blue satin flares and matching waistcoat. "I love the sequins down the side of your pants."

"Thanks, Sam added those for me."

They're standing outside the disco when Sam sees Chris sitting in the back of a car stuck in traffic. He rolls down his window when he spots her and calls out, "My offer still stands."

She moves to the edge of the footpath. "What offer?"

"To go out sometime," Chris calls back.

"Don't think so," says Sam, although not loud enough for him to hear. He's opening his door when the traffic frees up and the car moves on, forcing him back inside. As the car picks up speed, he yells, "Call me!" back at her and holds his hand to his ear to mimic a phone.

Call him? Not likely.

There's no way Sam's setting herself up to be hurt again so soon after Darren.

And what the hell does he mean by "call me"? I don't even have his number.

"Wow! It's like Saturday Night Fever in here," says Sam, as they walk into the disco.

"Duh except, it's Friday," says Brenda, without missing a beat.

. . .

"Come on, you guys." Jennie drags the other two in her wake. "I love dancing when the strobe light's on."

It's crowding midnight and Sam's dancing herself into a trance when she looks up from their pile of handbags and spots your typical Latin Lover. He's even got a white satin shirt open to the waist.

He catches her eye and raises his eyebrows; Sam smiles in response, meeting up with him in the middle of the flashing Perspex dance floor.

Due to his appalling English, they don't talk much as they dance. She suspects he hasn't long been out from the homeland. Because of the Aussie Government's "come one, come all" immigration policy, there are more Greeks in Melbourne than Athens and the bars are crawling with Greek guys on the pull. The Greek girls are all safely tucked at home or only allowed out with a chaperone.

He's spunky like most Greek men, but looks like he's got a cat superglued to his chest. Sam can hardly make out the obligatory two kilos of gold chain hanging around his neck.

He pulls her hard up against him. Any closer and his genitals might as well be hers. She hopes her voice doesn't start to drop.

"We go back your place!" he says, after a while.

Sam suspects they can't go back to his place because his mama might still be up. On first arriving in Melbourne, she and Jennie had been shocked to discover that most of these strong, virile Greek men still lived at home with a woman who sported a better moustache than they did.

Before she can give her Nana Mouskouri impression a whirl, they're in a taxi heading back to the flat, leaving the others to dance the night away. Even allowing for her new, untried method of dating, she's duty-bound to sleep with him, given he'd gone to the expense of buying her a drink. At least that was how it seemed with most of the Greek guys, although if they were ugly, even they realised it would take a hell of a lot more than one.

It's a first for Sam, sharing her body with someone whose

name she can't remember, let alone pronounce. Because it's so impersonal, it's also liberating. Knowing it won't lead to wedded bliss takes away a lot of performance anxieties and if her heart's not involved, can she truly be hurt?

Physically, yes. The gold chains he refuses to remove get caught in her pubes.

By the time Sam's got the two of them apart, using her nail scissors, he's sporting a bald patch in the middle of his chest and she's looking like she's had a Brazilian rather than a Greek.

"Sam, you alone?" Jennie stage whispers through Sam's bedroom door the following morning.

"Yeah, come on in."

Jennie sits on the edge of Sam's bed. "Are you all right?"

"Well, I'll think of him whenever I have a bikini wax."

"What do you mean?" Jennie leans back on her hands but immediately jerks them back again, looks behind her and jumps up. "What on earth is that?"

"Mostly it's his chest hair."

"Mostly?"

"There's also some of my pubes."

"Like that makes it okay!" Jennie wipes her hands down the old T-shirt of Steve's that she's wearing as a nightie. "Apart from that, are you all right?"

"Yeah," says Sam, thinking. "It'd be almost like it hadn't happened if it wasn't for my pubes."

"Do you think that's a good thing? The not happening bit I mean!"

"Jennie, for god's sake stop your worrying, will you?"

"Details, we want details," calls out Brenda, on her way to the kitchen.

"White and one," calls out Sam.

"Black, two sugars," yells Jennie.

A muttered "crap," comes from the depths of the kitchen.

Brenda's soon back with three coffees. She hands one to Jennie, puts Sam's down on the bedside table and says "Right, give," as she sits on the end of Sam's bed.

"Where do I begin?" Sam picks up her coffee and takes a sip.

Brenda stands abruptly, sloshing coffee everywhere. "What the bloody hell did you get up to last night?" She stares down at Sam's bed. "It looks like an effing poodle exploded in here."

10

$\mathscr{L}$ ooking at the bulging duffle bag sitting in the middle of her bed like a plump two-year-old, Sam wonders again if she's packed the right gear for the weekend. Unable to come to a decision the night before, she'd ended up packing for every eventuality. She'd rather have too many outfits than not enough. As it is, she'll be able to change her underpants at four hourly intervals without having to resort to turning them inside out.

Her tummy gurgles, reminding her she hasn't had any breakfast. A large slab of white toast plastered with smooth peanut butter will fill her up; and smother the large flutter of Monarchs and Painted Ladies circling in her stomach.

Zipping the bag closed, Sam hopes Brenda's all right with her borrowing it, but isn't going to check now. Given the amount of banging and crashing from the direction of Brenda's room when she and Jennie came home last night, she reckons Brenda is going to be in a hell of a mood with a hangover to match. A PS at the end of the note she's leaving for them both should be okay.

With breakfast over, she manhandles her bag out into the hallway. She's brushing her teeth to rid them of fat and peanuts when she hears knocking at the front door. After a final swish, she spits, and then rinses the sink and her brush.

75

She's only got the one brush and so she's taking it with her. She's still holding it when she opens the front door.

Chris looks at the bright green brush. "You travel light for a girl."

"Hah, in your dreams." Sam steps to the side to reveal her bag. Bending down, she slides her toothbrush into one of the side pockets. "I'm ready, let's go." She hefts her bag up off the floor.

"Here, let me." Chris takes the bag from her and grunts in surprise.

Sam's dismayed to see the couple in the back seat have lips firmly locked, although they pull apart briefly when Chris opens the boot. He has difficult fitting her bag in with most of the space being taken up by an enormous suitcase. She looks at Chris with eyebrows raised.

"Don't look at me, it belongs to Sonja, Mark's, ah, Yugoslavian friend."

She expects the other two to part when they get in, but no. Chris tries a round of introductions but it's pointless. He starts the car and the radio roars to life, drowning out what sounds like cows walking through mud coming from the back seat.

"Can you swing by Mrs Farquhar's place so I can drop something off?" says Sam, loud enough to be heard over the radio and farm sounds.

"Yeah, sure, I know the place."

Chris doesn't hide his thoughts about the architecture of the house on the drive there. As Sam pulls the silver, sequinned jumpsuit from her shoulder bag on arrival, his bark of laughter has the other two pulling apart to see what's going on.

"What the hell is that?" says Mark.

"A jumpsuit for a poodle." Sam leans down and unlaces her boots before hobbling across the gravel and then more smoothly up the front steps. The marble feels lovely after the rough driveway and it's warm on her feet. She stands on the coir welcome mat and pushes the doorbell.

Moments later Mrs Farquhar and Sapphire are at the door.

"Oh, Sam, thank goodness you arrived before we went out. Have you got my little darling's jumpsuit ready for the christening this afternoon?"

"Yes, I finished it late last night."

"I'd invite you in but we are just about to leave." Sapphire is already out onto the porch and giving Sam's feet a good sniff.

"Not a problem, I've got people waiting for me anyway." Sam gestures to the car and tries to distance herself from Sapphire's inquisitive nose.

"Oh, right." Mrs Farquhar peers out at the car. "The boy driving looks familiar?"

"Chris?"

"What's his family name?"

"I'm not sure," says Sam, embarrassed.

"Really? How odd." Mrs Farquhar's eyebrows are knotted, her nose wrinkled. "How odd."

Sam's relieved when Mrs Farquhar's attention is diverted. "Let's have a look at my little darling's outfit then."

Sam puts the jumpsuit into Mrs Farquhar's outstretched hands and the woman breaks into a smile. She holds it up so she can look at it from all angles. "Oh, Sam, I think this is some of your best work yet."

"I think so, too. Here, let me put it on so I can double check it fits." She removes the peach satin coat Sapphire is wearing and hands it to Mrs Farquhar. She hopes the silver jumpsuit fits, because if it doesn't, she'll have to go back home and fix it.

Feeding one of Sapphire's front legs into the new outfit, Sam then works her way around the other three before snapping it closed along the poodle's backbone.

"It's perfect! Who's mummy's beautiful girl then?" Mrs Farquhar bends down to kiss the top of Sapphire's head, as the dog stretches up and balances her front paws on one of Mrs Farquhar's knees. With this little ritual over, Sam removes the new outfit and gets Sapphire back into the peach satin number. No sooner has the zipper tag been tucked out of sight, than Sapphire is back sniffing at Sam's feet.

Sam backs away from Sapphire. "Well, I'd better not keep the others waiting."

"I'll bank the money for you on Monday."

Sam hobbles back to the car and its three slack-jawed occupants.

While they're cruising down the driveway, Chris re-introduces her to the couple in the back before they have a chance to re-engage lips. Sam vaguely remembers Mark from the night she'd first met Chris.

"If I hadn't just seen that with my own eyes I wouldn't have believed it," says Chris.

"Completely bloody bonkers," says Mark.

"*Luda, luda, luda,*" says Sonja.

Sam leans around to look at her. "Luda?"

Rather than add anything, Sonja spins her finger next to her head.

Arriving at the campground, Sam's disappointed to see they're staying in an on-site caravan, although it's a far cry from the wreck Jen and she had stayed in at Sunshine. And it's a big one, so with luck she and Chris will get some privacy. He hadn't flirted on the trip up but that may have been due to the loudness of the music. They've unloaded the car before the other two emerge.

The caravan is owned by Mark's family, so he and Sonja get the double berth at one end while she and Chris have to make do with the table that folds down between the two bench seats at the other end. At least that's what she hopes will happen.

The caravan is a shrine to Formica. Every surface is covered in the stuff with fake mahogany the most common theme. Luckily the squabs, carpet and curtains are in bright orange geometric patterns.

"We'll catch you guys later." Mark drags a giggling Sonja toward a plastic concertina door down the narrow hallway.

"A woman of few words," says Sam.

"She doesn't speak much English."

"How do they communicate?"

Before Chris can answer the caravan starts rocking.

"Is he always like this?"

"Nah. Used to be different."

"What happened?"

"He had a bad bike smash about three years ago. His girlfriend got killed."

"Oh, that's awful. The poor guy."

"Yeah, it wasn't his fault but he took it hard. He only found out after that Stacey was pregnant."

Setting out for a walk around the lake, Sam and Chris are in a sombre mood. Back an hour later they find the caravan still rocking. Returning after another hour, they find the van still rocking; harder than ever. They're about to leave again when they hear Sonja scream Mark's name over and over. Their accommodation shudders to a standstill.

"I hope the caravan survives the weekend," says Sam.

"It might fare better than Mark."

11

A week on from The Night of the Poodle and Sam is again enjoying being on the pill and living in a different country from her parents.

Forcing her eyes open, Sam looks around the strange bedroom. She hadn't seen much of it the night before as the bulb had blown seconds after the man of the house switched it on. If it wasn't for a couple of surfboards propped in one corner, the beige walls, carpet and drapes would make her feel she was in the middle of the Sahara. The whole room is in soft focus because of the gunge in her eyes.

God, I had a skinful last night.

She rubs her eyes vigorously before looking at the head of straw-like bleached hair on the pillow next to hers. Thankfully, he's facing away from her and working on a light snore. The satin sheets make for a quick escape; although their cherry red colour is garish in the harsh morning light and does nothing for her headache. Her brief impression the night before was that they'd looked much sexier.

Sam pauses to get her balance and looks down at, ah, Len? Her mouth feels like it's been dried it out with a paper towel but she thinks this has more to do with him not having showered after a late-afternoon surf than a case of the dry horrors. Salt coats the hairs on his arm, lying on top of the bed covers. She vaguely remembers saltiness when she licked his chest.

Not keen on the idea of sex when she's sober, Sam's going to dress in the bathroom and sneak off. Well, she would if she could find her blasted knickers.

She looks high and low, because if her bra hanging from the lazily rotating ceiling fan is anything to go by, they could be anywhere. She's down on her hands and knees looking through the dunes under the bed when a flash of memory has her lifting the side of the sheet. Damn and sod it all: her lucky knickers look a hell of a lot better on her!

She tiptoes out of the bedroom and down the hall in search of the bathroom. She's buck naked with her arms full of her clothes, handbag and shoes, so hopes he hasn't got any flatmates. There's no way she could execute a quick cover up.

After pulling the bathroom door shut slowly, and quietly, behind her, she rinses her mouth. Lifting her head, she's reflected in all her glory in the bathroom mirror. Bloodshot eyes, hair a rat's nest and skin the grey only a full-on hangover can achieve.

Unable to look any longer, she grabs a towel hanging limply on the towel rail and uses it to dust her knees free of the sand collected during her sortie under the bed. Pulling on her jeans, she then carefully zips them up. No undies make this a tricky business; she sure as hell doesn't want to risk ripping out any more pubes, they're looking moth-eaten enough as it is.

She's easing the glass-panelled front door open when she hears scratching behind her and turns to see surfer boy standing in all his glory rearranging the family jewels. They're firmly squished into her bright green knickers. Well, most of the jewels because one ball hangs out the side of the crotch, and his erection's close to ripping the sheer fabric.

"Where are you off to in such a hurry? It'd be a shame to waste this woody."

"Hmm, romantic as your offer is, I'll have to pass."

His mouth drops open and while the big head and little

head are fighting for blood, Sam says, "See ya," and nips out the front door.

"But I want to make love to you again," he says, when she's halfway down the path. She can hear him clearly, he's right behind her.

"It's wasn't making love, it was sex." She turns to face him. "Nice, uncomplicated sex."

"You used me for sex?" He draws himself up to his full height which results in his now wilting penis popping over the top of her lucky knickers.

"Oops." Sam is unable to stop the gurgle of laughter that follows.

She's giggling her way to the front gate when his muttered "filthy slut" causes her laughter to die. She'd call him on it but her heart isn't in it and she's not all that sure she'd win the argument.

Luckily he lives on a main road and she's not at a tram stop for long before one heading toward the city rumbles up. It gets her close enough to home to be able to walk the rest of the way, although her platforms weren't designed for it.

The following Friday night the girls are checking out an RSL Club. Sam's as keen as any of them to keep changing watering holes. The bars are interchangeable as far as decor and general atmosphere goes but this way she reduces the risk of running into any of her earlier conquests. The term "fresh meat" pops up, but is firmly tamped down again.

Brenda scans the room. "I can't believe how young the guys are."

"They're not that young?" Jennie looks around.

"There's no-one here over fifty."

"Fifty!" say Sam and Jennie.

"Why would you be interested in someone that old?" says Jennie.

"You mean apart from being filthy rich and so grateful for

a feel they'll buy you anything you want?"

"Ooh, that's awful." Jennie's old-fashioned when it comes to sex. She'd only gone to bed with Steve after they were officially engaged. Steve had been patient that was for sure. But he'd loved Jennie so much, Sam was sure he would've waited a lot longer.

"What about the wrinkles?" Sam can't comprehend sleeping with a guy as old as her dad.

"God, you two are lame. Give me an old guy who's easy to manage any day."

"Wow, he looks like Burt Reynolds," says Sam later, peering at a guy who's been checking her out. "You know, like in *Smokey and the Bandit.*"

"You're right," says Jennie, although she has to squint and close one eye to come up with the match.

"You have got to be effing joking," says Brenda.

"I'll catch you guys later." Sam stands unsteadily and grabs her handbag.

"Sam," says Jennie, "don't you think you should give it a break?"

"Jeez, Jennie, give it up. You're not my mother!" Even with a large percentage of her bloodstream comprising alcohol, she can see she's hurt her best friend, although this doesn't stop her continuing. "Stop ruining my fun!"

"Yeah, you keep telling yourself you're enjoying it. You might end up believing it," says Brenda.

Sam scowls at both of them in turn before lurching in the direction of the Burt look-alike, bumping into tables on her way.

Sam prises open her eyes the next morning. God, she must have been hideously drunk last night if the body sprawled over her is anything to go by. That's one hairy back; surely she didn't have sex with it? It'd be like shagging the hallway floor back home, although she remembers him pouring enough alcohol down her throat when they'd arrived back at his place that she wouldn't have been able to tell what she was shagging. Her head is pounding, her vision sparkly and she wishes the nausea would bugger off.

The bedroom is depressing. The decor is all right but there's a faint smell of dirty socks and jocks; the sheets she's lying on feel clammy and shiny from lack of washing. The smell of stale perfume from some earlier inhabitant wafts up from her pillow.

She's trying to extricate herself when he wakes.

Damn and blast it all to hell.

He drags his body up until it's covering hers, holds her head firmly on either side, then leans forwards and kisses her. He shoves his tongue into her mouth filling it and she doesn't know if it's the overwhelming stench of garlic or the sheer amount of saliva that has her starting to heave, but it's enough to make him pull back.

She'd give anything to still be drunk.

"Sweetie, aren't you feeling so good? Never mind, this will take your mind off it." He hawks a big wad of spit onto his fingers and proceeds to move his hand down her body, leaving a snail trail of saliva as he goes.

Sam freezes; she can hardly say no as they've obviously been at it like rabbits all night, if the deep ache inside her is anything to go by.

Before she can clear her head of hangover enough to think of a way out, his slimy hand makes contact, causing shudders of revulsion to work their way up her body. He takes this as a response and concentrates on the task although he eventually realises she's rather quiet.

"Come on love, respond a little. God knows, I couldn't shut you up last night."

"I'm not in the mood." Sam hopes he'll give up if he doesn't have a willing partner.

What in god's name was I thinking of, going home with this creep?

His face is covered with a heavy layer of sweat; drops of it condense on his forehead, looking ready to give in to gravity at any time. While his hair might have looked slick last night, now it just looks greasy and maybe not as clean as it could be. He'd looked so much better after half a dozen whisky and cokes.

"Baby, you can't give up on me now … we need to take care of Mr Salami. I'll soon get you in the mood."

He goes to work on her like she's a science project and she can't help the small sob that escapes as she stares blindly at the ceiling. Her eyes overflow and the tears disappear down each side of her face and into her ears blocking out some of the grunting.

He doesn't notice. He's too busy looking after Mr Damn Salami. Thankfully, it's over quickly. It's the first time Sam's been sober for sex since she broke up with Darren. She feels violated and raw, although this is nothing compared with the bone-deep shame that not even a bucket of alcohol could wash away.

"Is this the place?" he says, later that morning.

"This is fine, thanks." She has the door of the late model black BMW open before the car's even stopped.

"Give me your number. I want another session. Last time I had such an enthusiastic blowjob, it was from a hooker in Bangkok."

Bile bubbles up into Sam's mouth. She swallows convulsively, and then breathes slowly through her mouth, willing her stomach to settle and save adding to her humiliation.

She isn't forthcoming with her number, so he prompts her by handing her pen and paper. Sam writes down the number of the local deli which she's memorized for cases like this. Let him eat some salami of his own.

"Great, I'll call you later on today and we can catch up

tonight. I've got some toys I want to try out on you."

"Oh, yeah, um great," says Sam, too hungover to inject fake enthusiasm into her reply.

"You should be grateful. There are girls lining up to go out with me."

Unable to get a positive response, he forcefully grabs her head and gives her a long kiss, which has her close to heaving again. His breath still stinks of garlic even though he's brushed his teeth and she can't stop herself from wiping the saliva off her chin as soon as she's out of the car.

He sits there waiting for her to go in and when she realises he won't leave until she does, she opens the gate, turning to shut it behind her. Leaning against the rough wood she looks up at the house hoping there's nobody home. She puts her ear up to the gap in the boards of the gate, but can still hear the gentle idling of the BMW.

Damn, what the hell's he waiting for? Surely he's not going to sit there until I go inside the house?

Sam looks up at the house again and is horrified to see a curtain twitch.

She just needs him to drive away.

The front door is easing open when she hears the faint sound of a car pulling away.

"Can I help you?" The lady of the house peers out of the partially open door.

"Does Jennie live here?" She stalls, hoping last night's partner will be well down the road.

"No, I think you must have the wrong house."

"OK, sorry to bother you." Sam re-opens the gate but stops up short when faced with the dark BMW still sitting at the curb. Damn it must have been another car she heard. Waving half-heartedly, she opens the letterbox, as though to clear the mail, then retraces her steps, much to the amazement of the homeowner.

Sam would much rather face the woman standing with arms folded at the top of the stairs than have Salami Boy knowing her real address.

12

*L*ying on the bed, looking up at her feet, Sam rotates them slowly first one way, then the other. Her legs are pointed at the ceiling in hopes of catching the slight breeze coming in through the open window next to her. It's stupid hot and even though she's just had a cold shower, and is only in her undies, she's already covered in a fine sheen of sweat.

"Sam, are you ready?" calls Jennie, from the lounge. Not getting a reply she pops into Sam's room. "Obviously not." Jennie's voice is tinged with annoyance.

"I'm going to give it a miss tonight, Jen." It has taken a lot of grovelling on Sam's part to get back into Jennie's good books after the "you're not my mother" outburst. Even so, their relationship is still slightly strained. "I don't want to risk running into that creep."

"He'll have found another little friend for Mr Pastrami by now," says Brenda, joining them.

"Salami," she automatically corrects Brenda

"Hey, it's all Italian lunch meat to me."

"Don't even joke about it. Every time I think of him I get the heebie-jeebies." Catching the lace curtain with one foot, she drags it to the side in hopes of increasing the air circulation.

"Suit yourself," says Jennie, leaving the room.

"See ya," Brenda follows.

Sam can hear the impatient honking of a taxi at the front and when this is followed by the sound of the gate shutting, she gets off her bed. Standing in front of the dressing table her hand strays to the wooden mug tree where she hangs her jewellery. Nestled in amongst the brightly coloured bangles and assorted junk jewellery is the silk-covered wedding-dress button on its fine chain. She lifts it free and looks at it hanging over her fingers.

With her free hand she opens her underwear drawer and lifts out a small silk bag full of lavender. After loosening the cord on the top, she drops the button and chain in before tightening the cord again. Plonking the bag back in amongst her knickers and bras, a few tears slide from under her closed lids.

Shaking her head to rid it of unwanted thoughts, she turns toward her open wardrobe. She stares into it for a few seconds before riffling her way toward the less accessible depths, grabbing a floral denim dress off its hanger.

After digging out her travel mending kit, she gets the kitchen scissors and settles in for a quiet evening of sewing. She isn't sure the Blue Lady will even want the new outfit she's going to make for "darling Sapphire". For all she cares. It's more a case of anything to blot out the images running through her head like a B-grade porno.

***

For a few weeks, she doesn't leave the house other than to go to temp assignments or to do her laundry. She's not keen on running into Salami Boy, as he's now known around the flat.

Jennie and Sam are sitting in the laundromat watching their machines with about as much enthusiasm as a party political broadcast when the familiar Merc pulls up outside.

"Blue Lady's here," says Jennie.

Sapphire, bowling into the laundromat ahead of her owner, looks especially sharp in a small floral denim coat.

"Ooh, I love Sapphire's outfit," says Jennie. "Very Mary Quant."

"You don't know anything about it, do you?" says the owner.

Sam, mesmerised by the bright orange lips moving as if of their own volition, finally stammers out, "Don't you like it?"

"On the contrary, it's fabulous and much better made than anything else in her wardrobe."

"In that case look at these." Sam drags three more outfits from the depths of her large shoulder bag.

"When have you been making these?" says Jennie.

"How much do you want for them?" has both girls' heads snapping up.

"I hadn't thought."

"What if I give you what I paid for Sapphire's last birthday outfit?"

"I guess." Sam wonders more about what a dog would wear on their birthday than what it would cost.

"Good, $25 each it is." The Blue Lady riffles in her Oroton handbag and pulls out two fifties. "There could be more where that came from if some of the other mothers like them too."

"Mothers?" says Sam. "Oh, right."

"I'm Cynthia Farquhar by the way. You can call me *Mrs* Farquhar."

Lugging a large bag of still-wet washing between them, the girls stagger home from the laundromat.

"How did you get the outfit to her?"

"Flicked it into a dryer-load of Sapphire's clobber."

The girls have an entire range designed by the time they heave the washing through the back gate. They nearly trip over Brenda, who's in her usual spot. She's topless.

"Crap – is the rent due already?" says Sam.

"Nah, the light bulb in the dunny blew and so Stefano is coming around to change it."

The following Friday night sees them out at the Piano Bar of the Old Melbourne Hotel. Given it's a haunt for out-of-town sales reps attending conferences, Sam feels sure she's not going to run into Salami Boy here. For one thing, the ratio of men to women is all wrong.

The hotel is fashioned along the lines of an old English coaching inn but unlike the oldey-worldey pub back home, the place is clean and the furniture not prone to attack. This is offset by the price of the drinks that appear to take into account the majority of the people in the bar are working their way through healthy per diems.

They inch into the packed lounge, then force their way through a pin-striped pathway toward a large marble-topped bar. The piano, after which the lounge gets its name, is audible but not visible, although Sam can see a gap in the starched collars that mark its position.

"Bleedin' hell, I haven't seen this many suits since I was last in court," says Brenda.

"There must be a church conference going on.' Jennie points out a group of priests in one corner.

"Catholics, if the amount of alcohol is anything to go by," says Brenda.

"My goodness," says Jennie, recognizing one of the priests. "Sam! Look, isn't that sailor boy?"

"Oh, no, not him!" Sam's about to do a runner when he sees her and makes a production out of crossing himself, before fighting his way across the bar.

"I thought you must have left for London when you didn't phone," says Chris.

"How can I phone when I don't have your number?"

"But I gave it to ..." Chris looks at Brenda. "I want my twenty bucks back!"

"Sure you do." Brenda looks at a spot behind Sam and Chris.

Seeing Brenda's eyes dilate, Sam turns and spots a 'fog' of grey hair near the piano. Seconds later Brenda's off like a jaguar after an ailing wildebeest. Jennie trails after her.

"So is this fancy dress?" She looks the priestly attire, "Or have you dedicated your life to God?"

"Party, although I've already got bookings for a couple of weddings. I can take confession if you like."

"No, thanks."

"Come on." Chris gently drags her toward the door.

"Where are we going?"

"My confessional." He leads her out of the bar, along a dimly lit hallway and straight into a cleaning cupboard. He pulls the door shut behind them cutting off any light and causing her to trip over something sitting on the floor. Her hand flies out to keep her balance and she plonks it straight into something slimy on a shelf.

"Ooh, gross." Sam straightens, wiping her hand on an unsullied piece of shelving.

"How can I help you, my child?" floats out of the dark in a soft, ecclesiastical voice, although his hands inching their way around her waist don't feel priestly at all.

"This is daft," says Sam, before sneezing. "And dusty."

Chris starts pulling her toward him, but she stops him in his tracks by blurting out about Darren, plus a few edited highlights.

If he wants a confession, then by god he's gonna get one.

By the time she's finished, there are tears dripping from her lashes and she's got a bad case of hiccoughs.

"Right, okay, well. That wasn't what I was expecting. C'mon." Chris opens the door and walks back along the hallway with Sam blindly following him until she realises they're leaving the hotel.

"Hang on, when you said let's get out of here I thought you meant the broom cupboard."

"I thought we could go back to my place."

"Weren't you listening ... to what I just ... said?" hiccoughs Sam.

"Yes, and that's why nothing's going to happen. I feel a bit guilty that it was me who set you off."

"What about ... your party?"

"We go to heaps and it's always the same old faces. We know it's a different party by what people are wearing."

"Oh, all right ... I'll go tell the others."

As she fights her way back into the bar to let Jennie know she's leaving, she wonders at the logic of going with Chris. Crazy as it sounds, she trusts him and she's made her decision whilst sober. It just feels right. Shoving one final suit to the side, Sam pops up next to Jennie and gets an idea of what her eye make-up must look like by Jennie's grimace of horror.

"Oh, no! Did you run into Salami Boy?"

"No, thank god. Just having a meltdown. I'm going to head off." Sam doesn't mention who she's leaving with, to avoid the inevitable argument.

"I'll come with you." Jennie lifts the long strap of her handbag over her head in readiness for pushing through the crowd.

"No, don't be crazy. I'll be fine."

It takes the taxi a good twenty minutes to get to Chris's place and when they pull up outside Sam is too shocked to hide her surprise. "You live here?"

She stares at the building. With its clean block work, minimal windows and flat roof it looks more like somewhere you'd spend a penny than spend the night.

"Sure do, but don't be put off by the outside. It's completely different inside."

"Okay," says Sam, unconvinced.

Seeing her scepticism, Chris adds, "It was built for a Japanese guy who was out here working at the Nissan plant."

He opens the large wooden double front doors and Sam feels like she's been transported to the downtown Tokyo of her imagination.

"When he buggered off back to Japan, he left a few pieces of furniture," says Chris.

"You sleep on the floor then?"

"I wasn't taking it that far, like my comfort too much."

Sam loves the place. At the centre is a courtyard full of tropical plants and raked gravel; there's a glassed-in corridor running around it that gives access to every room in the house.

"Make yourself comfortable." Chris points at the couch. With its dark green leather and clean lines, it looks like something out of *The Avengers*. The leather is buttoned all over at regular intervals with the whole thing supported on angled black metal legs. Thankfully, there are a few cushions dotted along its length to add comfort. Sam grabs a few of these when she settles herself into the corner at one end. While watching Chris turn on the mahogany clad stereo and lift its smoked glass cover, she arranges the cushions to her liking.

"Cat Stevens okay with you?"

"Yeah, great, I haven't listened to him in ages. I love his stuff."

Chris flips through a section of LPs housed in the unit below the stereo before selecting an album. *"Tea for the Tillerman* it is."

"Wow, how many do you have?" She eyes the vinyl-jammed alcoves.

"Not sure exactly, around a thousand." Chris slips the LP out of its cardboard sleeve. The acetate is removed next with the LP balanced between his thumb and index finger to avoid fingerprints. Holding the edges of the LP safely between the flat of both hands, Chris angles it toward the light checking for dust and scratches, before placing it onto the turntable.

As it spins, he brushes the surface before placing the needle on the first track. After a couple of clicks, "Where Do the Children Play" pours out of the metre-high speakers sitting on each side of the room. The emblems on the gold fabric that covers the speak fronts vibrate with the base notes.

The music rolls over her, releasing tension and the last of

the trembling although her hiccoughs have yet to stop. On his way back to the couch, Chris grabs a bottle of scotch and a couple of glasses. He sits close to her and pours the drinks.

"Have you got any ... coke?"

Chris winces at this suggestion "Try it, it's a single malt. You're meant to drink it neat."

She takes a tentative sip. "Phew! That hits the spot."

Sam's on her third drink when she falls asleep. She surfaces just a little when she feels Chris pick her up and carry her to bed.

He puts her down, pulls off her shoes, tucks a blanket around her and leaves her to her hiccoughing.

Sam's still getting her bearings the following morning when Chris comes in with a mug of coffee in each hand. "Hey, sleepy head. I guessed white and one, hope that's all right?"

Sam can't believe she hasn't got a hangover, although the sight of Chris dressed in low-slung jeans and no shirt makes her mouth go dry. The coffee's welcome.

"I fell asleep on you, sorry."

"That's okay." Chris sits on the edge of the bed.

"I was surprised you weren't next to me when I woke up."

Chris stands immediately and leans casually against the doorjamb. "I said nothing would happen."

She sips some coffee before asking, "Can I get a ride back into town? I've got some doggie coats and hats I need to sew and it's easier in the daylight."

Chris is visibly confused by the sudden change in subject. "You need to do ... *what?*"

Sam explains her new sideline in canine couture.

"It sounds like the sort of thing my grandmother's friends would do. They treat the bloody animals like children."

"Weird, but it pays well."

Chris goes over and slides open the door of the wardrobe. He retrieves a bright green-and-gold check jacket, loud enough that you couldn't have a conversation while wearing it. "Could you use this?"

"It's brilliant. I can already see it made up as a Sherlock Holmes outfit."

"You can see that? And you're sober!"

Sam walks into the flat and is pounced on by Jennie. "Where on earth have you been? I've been worried sick. I thought you must have run into Salami Boy after you left, or been attacked or something."

"Sorry, I ended up going home with Chris."

"I was about to ring the police! I was rehearsing the phone call to your parents!"

"Hell, sorry."

"I thought you were giving the casual sex a rest."

"But I didn't sleep with him!"

"Weren't ya drunk enough?" says Brenda, who's sprawled on the couch. "You're going to end up with crabs or a dose of the clap, if you haven't already!"

13

Saturday morning and Sam's up early, the heat making it impossible to sleep in. After making breakfast, she and Jennie eat out in the garden. Brenda is a no-show.

"I guess she's managed to pick up another old guy." Sam lies back on the grass and idly spins a daisy between her fingers.

"Yeah, although I've never even seen her show more than a passing fancy for anyone other than the landlord and I suspect his wife keeps him on a tight leash."

"Hey, I'm off to the Laundromat this morning to wait for Mrs Farquhar. You want to come?" says Sam, as they take their dirty dishes back into the house.

"Why not." Jennie rinses her plate before stacking it.

Ready to leave, Sam looks for Jennie only to find her rummaging through a pile of dirty clothes in the bottom of her wardrobe.

"Don't bother with that."

"Laundromat, laundry," says the ever-practical Jennie.

Their machine is shuddering to a stop after a particularly climactic spin when Sapphire and her mother come in, looking frazzled. Although Mrs Farquhar more so than Sapphire.

"Thank goodness you're here. We've been invited to a christening and Sapphire hasn't got a thing to wear."

"What were you thinking of?" Sam is at a loss to make any sensible suggestions.

"Sequins. Pale pink sequins, with a feather trim."

"Aren't you afraid she'll outshine the dog being christened?" says Jennie.

"It's not a dog being christened!" says Mrs Farquhar, with a face that could make ice. The "you stupid girl" hangs unsaid in the air.

"I could visit a fabric shop later today."

"There's no time. I'll drive you there now."

"Now? But what about our washing?"

"Surely your friend can take care of that?"

"I can't get this lot home by myself," says Jennie.

Mrs Farquhar starts for the door. "I'm willing to pay you $100."

"I guess that's okay, the fabric and bits and pieces should come to around $30."

"I'll buy the fabric. The $100 will be simply for making the outfit." She opens the door and stands next to it, exuding confidence.

The opportunity to make a quick hundred is too much for Sam. "I'll come back and get you," she says, over her shoulder to Jennie. Seeing the stony look on Jennie's face she turns her back fully to Mrs Farquhar and whispers "A hundred bucks, Jen! That's half a week's wages!"

"Fine, leave me then, don't worry about me."

"Lovely, we'll be off then." Mrs Farquhar drags Sam out of the door, a feat made difficult by Sapphire yapping and jumping around their feet.

Don't stand on the dog, don't stand on the dog.

"You'll have to sit in the back. Sapphire gets car sick."

Sam pours herself into the two-door Mercedes. The back seat is a glorified perch that forces her to sit with her legs sideways. Only one butt cheek is safely in place when Mrs

Farquhar floors it. The woman's driving is lethal and Sam's halfway through the Lord's Prayer for the third time when they screech to a halt outside a fabric store.

"Come on, stop dawdling. We haven't got all day."

"Sorry." Sam meekly follows Mrs Farquhar into the store.

The place is full of incredible fabrics. Sam's stroking a bold striped satin when Mrs Farquhar appears at her elbow causing her to jump.

"No, no, that won't do at all. It would clash with Sapphire's colouring."

Sam finds the perfect thing on a remnants table at the back of the store. It's pink, shiny and wouldn't look out of place in a strip club.

"Now for the feather trim," says Mrs Farquhar, zipping off to haberdashery with Sam tagging along.

"This'll be perfect." Mrs Farquhar holds up a length of pink feather boa.

They buy matching cotton and press studs for ease of entry and then leave the store with Sam dragging her steps as they head to the car.

"Step lively girl, we can go to my home, measure Sapphire and discuss styles."

Jennie will be peeved she missed this.

Sam grits her teeth as they dodgem their way to Mrs Farquhar's house. The place is huge and in the early pretentious style – Hollywood meets Regency England with highlights of Las Vegas Brothel. Sam is surprised that Mrs Farquhar lives just around the corner from them, although she's a million miles away socially.

"You'll have to take off your shoes." Mrs Farquhar indicates the white carpet. "We'll go to Sapphire's room and I can show you what I like of hers now."

Dutifully unlacing her leather boots, Sam puts them inside the front door. Her hand is just clear of them when Sapphire stuffs her head in one of them right up to her ears that flop over the top and hang down either side. The poodle must have no sense of smell whatsoever given how fast the fluffy ball at the end of her tail is wagging backwards and forwards.

"Who's a clever girl," says Mrs Farquhar, in the silly voice she reserves for the small blue dog. She pats the visible top of Sapphire's head before leading the way upstairs.

The staircase is wide enough to take three people abreast and sweeps up in a wide arc through the double-height foyer. It's also carpeted in white, although Sam can see the middle of each tread tends to a faint grey from constant traffic. The banister is black and so highly polished she can see a distorted image of herself in it. This is supported by turned wooden spindles. Sam is surprised these aren't gold; they would be far more in keeping with the rest of the house.

Sapphire has a room at least five times the size of Sam's. The bloody dog's even got a double bed complete with a pale blue satin cover and bone-shaped pillows. A basket, full of balls, leather chews and assorted bits of fluff, sits next to the bed. The dog has a newer model telly than the girls have at the flat.

Mrs Farquhar walks over to a huge, mirrored double wardrobe and slides open the doors with a flourish. Sam is confronted with a collection that would do Liz Taylor proud, although the average length of the garments means the bottom seven-eighths of the wardrobe is strangely empty. The outfits are hung in colour order apart from a couple of jewel encrusted capes that hang at one end. Their matching tiaras sit proudly on the shelf above.

"As you can see we've tended to go for pastels rather than anything bold as we feel they suit her skin tones better."

"We?" says Sam, weakly. The woman has to be bonkers if she discusses wardrobe selections with the bloody dog.

"Her stylist from Canine Capers and I."

Sam starts breathing again, albeit with less depth than usual.

"Right, I guess you should select some outfits you like and I can have a look at those." It's a couple of hours before they're both happy with the style. One thing Sam has noticed is her finishing is better than that of any of the other outfits. No wonder Mrs Farquhar is so keen on her working on Sapphire's ever-increasing wardrobe. If she has her way, Mrs Farquhar will need to fit another rail. At $100 a pop for special outfits, it won't take long to save for her – and Jen's – airfares to London.

"I'll need to start on this today if I'm to have it ready by next Saturday. The hand sewing is slow."

"I didn't realise you made them by hand. I've got an old machine you can use. George, my late departed husband, bought it for me as an anniversary present! I don't know *what* he was thinking."

They wend their way into the bowels of the mansion and Mrs Farquhar shows the machine to her. Sam's gobsmacked to see it's a top-of-the-line model and that it's crowning an even newer-looking automatic washing machine.

So, why the hell does she bother with the laundromat?

The washer, although connected, doesn't appear to have seen much action. There's a birthday card stuck to the front. It would seem George wasn't too clever on the present front and obviously failed miserably with the domestication of Mrs Farquhar.

Back at the front door, Sapphire is lying next to Sam's boots with a satisfied look on her face. Sam checks the boots for bite marks and missing laces but there's no outward damage. Sitting on the steps outside, she pulls them on. The first boot is warm to her foot, no doubt due to all that doggie breath. The second has a large amount of drool in the bottom; something she discovers when her foot slips into place.

She looks back at Sapphire, standing at the door with Mrs Farquhar.

Hasn't the bloody dog got enough toys without adding my boots to the mix?

"If you put everything in the back I'll drop you home."

"That's lovely, but I only live around the corner and it's a beautiful day, I'll walk." She shudders at the thought of more of Mrs Farquhar's driving.

"Walk? But what about the sewing machine?"

"It doesn't weigh much, I'll be fine."

Forty-five minutes later, Sam staggers into the flat loaded down with everything and dumps it on the floor in the lounge. Her arms feel longer, her back's killing her and she's sweating so much she can hardly see; but she's alive and doesn't feel nauseous.

Brenda is watching a movie. Her eyebrows move up her forehead when she sees the state of Sam along with the pink sequins and feathers. "You going on the game?"

"No, this is for Sapphire to wear to a christening next Saturday afternoon."

"You are joking?"

"A hundred bucks says I'm not. Where's Jennie?" Sam looks around. "I want to update her on the visit to Mrs Farquhar's place."

"Not here."

"Blast it." Sam runs out the door.

By the time she staggers into the laundromat, she's close to throwing up. She needs to exercise more. Jennie's sitting up straight, arms crossed tight. Two huge bags of dried and folded washing sit next to her feet.

"I'm so sorry I was so long," pants Sam.

"She took me to her place, straight from the fabric shop. She wouldn't take no for an answer. She insisted!" Sam is relieved to see Jennie's posture relaxing. Forgiveness should be imminent.

Brenda is still watching television when they get home, but now has the sequinned fabric draped across her chest and the feather boa wrapped around her head. "Woof."

"Good dog." Sam pats her head.

Brenda tosses the fabric back in the general direction of Sam's bag. "Chris called while you were out."

"Did he leave a number?" Sam picks up the fabric and feathers off the floor, noting the boa has already started to moult.

"Nope. Said he'd phone back."

14

It's Thursday night before Chris calls back. Four days in which Sam has jumped for the phone every time it has rung. She walks back into the lounge after hanging up and plonks herself on the couch next to Jennie, who's attempting to watch a documentary on TV. Given it's about Antarctica the picture looks fairly authentic. Sam's grinning broadly and the backs of her legs are sporting the obligatory phone seat dents.

"Chris?" Jennie keeps her eyes on the screen.

"We're going out for dinner on Saturday."

"Dinner on a Saturday night, that's serious." Jennie gives Sam her full attention.

"Don't think so. Says he wants to take things slowly."

"When guys talk about taking things slowly, it's serious. Does this mean I'll be travelling on my own after all?" says Jennie, archly.

"I wouldn't abandon you like that."

Jennie opens her mouth as if to reply, then stops.

"What?"

"Nothing. So Saturday night. Still a bit serious if you haven't slept with anyone twice since Darren."

"I don't count crashing on the couch after three scotches and sleeping in the spare room going the whole way."

"You were serious about that? Oh, wow, you know what that means?"

"What?"

"First date!"

"Oh, god, I haven't been on one of those in over a year." Sam's eyes widen. "Crap, even longer 'cause I didn't even go on one of those with Darren. We just hooked up at the pub. How the hell am I even supposed to behave?"

<hr>

Chris calls for her dead on 7.00 p.m. on Saturday night but rather than going to a restaurant for dinner as she expected, they drive away from the city. Chris stops for fish and chips, throwing Sam for a loop. Their final destination proves to be Brighton Beach where Chris parks before they scope out the sand for a good spot.

Sam isn't sure how to behave; it's not what she was expecting, at all. If nothing else, she'd been hoping for a glass of wine to calm her nerves.

"Right, you hang onto the greasies while I sort this out." Chris passes the newspaper-wrapped parcel to her to hold, while he takes a picnic blanket from the bag he's bought along, flicks it in the air and helps it float down smoothly to the sand. "Make yourself comfy." He drops to the blanket and Sam's relieved to see him pull a couple of glasses and a bottle of wine out of the bag.

They finish eating and Chris tops up Sam's glass. "Right then, let's hear all about you."

She downs her glass in a couple of gulps and gets a small hit from the rush of alcohol.

"Relax. I want to understand your problem with guys."

"I don't have a problem – I'm here with you aren't I?"

"But you don't need to be smashed. We can still have a good time without you being hammered." Chris looks pointedly at her empty glass.

"Oh. That seems to be what guys want these days." She

holds her empty glass in front of her like a shield.

"Not all of us. I'd rather you were with me in mind, not just body. Right, let's start with your first boyfriend."

"Oh, that's easy." Sam puts her wine glass down carefully on its side on the blanket. "That would be Nigel from next door. He used to beat up anyone who messed with me and I wrote him love letters."

"What happened?"

"He moved. Well, his parents moved and he had to go with them. He was seven."

"Understandable. Who was next after that?"

"Then when I was eighteen, I—"

"Hang on a second," says Chris, interrupting, "no more in between?"

"It took me a while to get over Nigel and I wasn't confident as a teenager. I was flat as a pancake and wore a padded bra. I didn't like to let them get too close."

Chris bursts out laughing.

"It wasn't funny!" She crosses her arms tightly over her breasts.

"Come on," he says, dragging her into an embrace. "Surely you can laugh about it now?"

"It gets worse. I realised at my first sports day at high school that without padding I'd still be ironing board flat in my swimsuit."

"You pulled out?"

"I wish! Mum sewed cups into my cossie."

"Go on," says Chris, when she stalls.

"When I dived in, the cups shot out the armholes of my swimsuit. I ended up looking like I was wearing water wings!" Sam finishes in a rush.

"We need to take your mind off that with a reward," says Chris, laughing before enfolding Sam and sharing the rest of his laughter with her.

As he lifts his head, Sam says, "Are you going to reward me for everything?"

"If it'll help," says Chris, smiling.

"Okay, when I was ten—"

"Hang on, I thought we were up to eighteen?"

"That was before the reward system kicked in."

"Right." Chris pushes her down and kisses her thoroughly. "We should be up to eighteen now," he says, looking down at her, his hands busy on the buttons down the front of her shirt.

"Seventeen," Sam whispers, and draws his head back down to lengthen the kiss, loosening a few buttons on his shirt in return.

They become aware of their surroundings when they hear someone telling them to get a room and look up to see an old man glaring down at them.

"Do you mean me and your dog?"

Sam's confused until she looks past Chris's shoulder and notices the small terrier busy humping the back of his thigh. The old man notices at the same time and yanks hard enough on the leash to have the little humper airborne.

The old man sees they aren't moving and storms off dragging the dog behind him. Not easy given its gaze remains firmly locked on Chris's leg.

"He might have a point. I was starting to forget where we were." Chris brushes Sam's hair back from her forehead. "Come on, let's go." He refastens buttons for both of them. "We can go back to my place and have a soak in the hot tub.'

"I'll have to pick up a swimsuit."

"No, you won't."

15

At his place, Sam follows Chris to the back of the house and into a bathroom much larger than the one she'd used the first time she'd been at his place. It's easily the size of the lounge back at the flat and, when she briefly takes her eyes off Chris, her impression is that it's fully lined with cedar including the ceiling. Like the rest of the house, it's in the Japanese style. "You could fit ten people in here."

"The Japanese guy who owned the place before me used to. When the company had visitors down from Japan he'd invite them around here for a bath followed by a meal. I've kept the tradition going because of the Brownie points it gets me with management."

Looking at the strange assortment of items in the room, a frown settles on her face. "What should I do?"

"Take your clothes off in there," says Chris, indicating a door. "There are towels in the cupboard."

"Chris?' she calls out a minute later, "Are these towels your idea of a joke? I've seen bigger face cloths."

"You hold them in front of you. It's the tradition."

"Bloody stupid tradition," mutters Sam.

"Come on, we need to scrub ourselves before we can soak in the hot tub."

Sidling back into the main room, she keeps turning to face

Chris, although this isn't made easy by him moving around her.

"Sit yourself down on one of these. Here's your soap and shampoo."

"Thanks, put them down there."

"I can't believe you're so shy."

She notes he keeps his gaze fixed firmly on the wall behind her. Probably hoping to put her at her ease.

"Well, sorry, but I'm not used to standing in the middle of bathroom the size of a football field, armed with nothing but a sodding hand towel!"

Sam realises she'll have to ditch the towel so she can scrub herself as instructed, but she may as well be in the middle of a naked-at-school dream for all the notice he takes of her when she drops it and hunkers down next to him on one of the Playschool-sized stools.

"And now we rinse." Chris takes a small wooden bucket, filling it with water from a big cedar trough in front of them and upends it over her before rinsing himself.

"Grab your towel."

"Yeah, I might want to dry my hands." Sam turns to pick it up from behind her and is horrified to see that what she's taken for more wooden panelling is in fact a floor to ceiling mirror. Chris grins at her reflection.

"Come on," he says, walking in front of her to a sliding door. She grabs the opportunity, expertly twists her towel, and flicks him on the bum.

"Ow-w-w, what was that for?" Chris spins back to face her and she doesn't have time to get her towel back in place. She looks him straight in the eye and says, "For sneaky peeking."

"Should I have been more blatant?" His gaze drops and she can feel herself tightening under his scrutiny. She yanks her towel back up in front of herself as quickly as she can. Chris turns away and slides open a door that leads out into the private courtyard.

"This is gorgeous," says Sam, when she takes in the hot tub partially obscured by tropical plants.

"Get in. I'll join you in a second." He opens a panel in the wall and starts fiddling with buttons. While he's concentrating on this, she drops her hand towel, climbs into the huge cedar tub and sinks up to her neck in the water thankful to be concealed at last. At least she is until Chris hits the underwater light switch. Never mind boobs and pubes, it's so bright he'll be able to see she's had her appendix out.

"Do we have to have those on?"

"Hang on, I haven't finished yet." He hits another button that has millions of bubbles erupting out of pipes at the bottom of the pool. Sam jumps. The bubbles rid her of any remnants of sand and turn the water a luminous, milky white colour. "No wonder you wanted this place when he left."

"It has its advantages." Chris climbs in and pulls Sam over and settles her against his chest. He sluices water across her shoulders letting it trickle down between her breasts. She relaxes back against him to discover he's not relaxed; not at all.

Later that evening, she walks up the path leading to the flat. She can't believe she's even here. She'd thought everything was going well, but after the hot tub she'd followed Chris's lead and dressed. They hadn't even showered. She reeks of chlorine; and frustration.

The flat is in darkness so not only is she home, she's home alone. Scrabbling around in her handbag for her keys, she's unable to locate them. Holding her bag up toward the glow from the street light, she finally finds them hidden at the bottom. Then follows the usual rigmarole of jerking the key around in the lock, before being able to make it turn. Closing the door and snibbing the lock, Sam's shocked by a blood curdling scream from somewhere in the house.

Her keys fall from nerveless fingers, her handbag slides to the ground and her heart jumps up into her throat.

"What the hell?" Sam stands, hand on chest, and gets her bearings in the darkened house.

Her heart hammering, Sam slowly and quietly picks up Brenda's baseball bat from its spot next to the front door. She listens intently for any sounds of movement, but has trouble hearing anything over the blood pounding in her ears. The lounge appears deserted apart from grainy images flickering on the telly.

Taking an extra deep breath, she leaps into the lounge with a banshee scream, the bat raised high above her head. She's ready to brain someone if necessary.

She's met with louder screams from Jennie and Brenda who are crammed together on the couch, knees up to chests, blanket up to chins, eyes wide.

"Bleedin' hell, you scared the bejeezus out of us!" yells Brenda at Sam, although her eyes don't leave the screen. Jennie's eyes also refuse to stray from the action on the telly.

"What the hell are you watching?" She looks at the screen in time to see a wooden stake jammed into someone's chest, causing her jump. The staking is accompanied by more screams from the couch.

Brenda drags her eyes away from the screen. "What the hell are you doing home anyway? We thought you'd be getting your brains screwed out."

"You and me both!" Sam puts the baseball bat on the coffee table. Sure Chris had said he'd call, but she'd heard that line before. She is feeling dejected and rejected, although this doesn't stop her lusting at thoughts of Chris naked. Brenda having drained the hot water tank, again, her lust is soon washed away with the chlorine.

Sam's warming up after her shower when the phone rings, causing yet another outbreak of screaming from the lounge. It's Mrs Farquhar wanting her to pop around the following day to get briefed on another outfit for Sapphire for a Canine Capers customer shindig.

Promptly at six thirty the following evening, Sam pushes the brass button next to the highly polished black front door. She's on her own with no one else wanting to join her, no matter how tempting it is to eyeball how the other half live. Without the impediment of a solidly engineered German sewing machine, it's only taken her ten minutes of brisk walking to make it from the flat to the mansion. The bell chimes her arrival throughout the house and it isn't long before Mrs Farquhar and Sapphire are at the door.

"Come in, come in," says Mrs Farquhar, sweeping to one side. Sapphire doesn't move and she has to manoeuvre her way around the obstinate dog before she can take her sneakers off. They're a recent purchase from the local Presbyterian Church op shop and cost just fifty cents. They're a little on the rough side but Sam refuses to risk any more of her good shoes being full of Sapphire's slobber when she leaves. Mrs Farquhar's eyebrows elevate as Sam puts them neatly next to the front door.

As they make their way upstairs, Sapphire stays put.

"I was thinking something with sequins like this." Mrs Farquhar delves into the wardrobe and pulling out a particularly putrid jumpsuit. It's the colour of a bad head cold.

"Ah, it's ah, um …" stammers Sam.

"You don't like it?" Mrs Farquhar's nostrils flare, warning Sam to be careful how she answers this question.

"No, it's, ah, lovely. When do you need the new outfit by?"

"The party's next Saturday afternoon."

"Wow, so soon." Sam calculates how long the hand sewing of sequins will take.

"I don't know why you don't give up the office work … with some careful planning you could set yourself up with a tidy little business."

Sam's calculations stop in their tracks. "A business? I don't think I'm ready for that. I don't have the skills. I wouldn't even know where to begin."

"Goodness me, if you put as much effort into a business as you just have into why you can't, you'd be halfway there.

We're not talking a multi-national, global conglomerate here, just a simple little start-up."

"But where would I even begin?"

"It's easy, I could help. I've been on the board of the family's saddlery for years and my nieces, who I trained, manage the day-to-day running of the place nicely. You don't need a business degree. A good head on your shoulders is sufficient. You don't strike me as stupid."

"Oh, no, I'm definitely not that!" Sam'd managed a credible 140 points on an IQ test in high school – she wasn't sure who was more surprised, her or her teacher. Not that her recent behaviour had been that of a near genius.

The design of the outfit agreed, Mrs Farquhar takes her to an office. The room is dark and masculine, and so at odds with the rest of the house that it's obvious to Sam the late departed Mr F must have been allowed free rein in having this room exactly to his tastes.

The areas of wall not shelved with boring-looking books carry an impressive array of diplomas. There's a Telex machine, a photocopier the size of a Mini and a couple of phones on a large and imposing oak desk. The top is dark green leather and carries enough ink blots and scratches for Sam to realise it's not a rich man's prop.

Mrs Farquhar sits, pulls a pad and a pen from the top drawer and drops them on the desk before sliding the drawer closed. Because of the size of the desk, it's as though the woman has halved in size. Removing the top from the fountain pen, she clips it on the end and sits with the nib balanced over the clean sheet of lined paper. As she looks up at Sam, a mask has been removed. The little old lady who's bonkers about her dog has been replaced by a woman who looks like she could hold her own on Wall Street.

Whoa, will the real Mrs Farquhar please stand up!

Together, they work on a business plan and when they're both happy with it, Sam is surprised to see it's after nine. Getting up to leave she takes a closer look at some of the degrees on the wall and is not surprised to see they're all Mrs Farquhar's.

Sam arranges to come back the following night so they can continue to work while she starts the hand sewing required for Sapphire's latest ensemble.

Sapphire is still guarding the op shop sneakers at the front door when Sam goes to leave. The dog looks like she's stoned which shouldn't be a surprise given how many people will have worn the sneakers. Inside the sneakers she can see the tell-tale glisten of dog drool but with a ten-minute walk ahead of her she has to put them on regardless.

The return trip is completed in less than eight minutes as she resorts to running given the lateness of the hour. Sam had been expecting to have to vehemently turn down the offer of a ride home from Mrs Farquhar but the offer hadn't been forthcoming.

By the time Friday night rolls around, she has been over at Mrs Farquhar's place every evening, alternately stitching and empire building. Unfortunately more empire building than stitching, so she's still putting the finishing touches to Sapphire's outfit, having to miss going out with the others.

Making the outfit look truly incredible is all part of their business plan, the Canine Caper's party being the perfect place to showcase Sam's skills to the other 'mothers'. With enough orders she can give up work and concentrate on Doggs' Toggs – as she and Mrs Farquhar have decided to call it – full-time. To speed up production, Mrs Farquhar is letting her hold onto the sewing machine. She suspects Mrs Farquhar never wants to see it again.

The phone rings. Sam ignores it given she's in the middle of a fiddly bit.

Eventually it stops, starting again seconds later. After the third time, she realises she'll have to answer.

"Hello," says Sam, tersely.

"Sam? It's Chris."

"Oh, hi," her voice softens.

"I saw your flatmates at Donovan's and they said you were home."

"Yeah, I've got a special christening outfit to finish for Sapphire."

"Do you fancy getting away this weekend?" says Chris, after he manages to stop laughing.

"What did you have in mind?" Sam has to ask, because after the hot tub she doesn't have a clue where she stands.

"A few of us are heading up to the lake in the morning and then back on Sunday afternoon."

"I guess," says Sam, cagily.

"Just friends, no pressure."

The only pressure Sam is likely to feel is resisting the urge to jump him at the slightest provocation.

"Brilliant. We'll pick you up in the morning. Eight-thirty too early?"

"No, that'll be fine."

"Great, see you then," says Chris, before hanging up.

Eight-thirty! Why did I agree to that?

It's already gone nine and she still has a good couple of hours to complete Sapphire's outfit. It's midnight before she finishes the outfit and starts packing for the weekend. Just choosing underwear takes half an hour. She still hasn't found a pair as lucky as those she'd had to leave with surfer boy.

16

That night the boys cook steak on the barbeque while Sonja and Sam prepare a salad and garlic bread. They spray their arms, legs and around their plates with insect repellent to ensure the only protein they eat is the steak. Sam is glad the caravan has mozzie screens fitted; even smothered in repellent she's started to feel anaemic.

Dinner over, the boys build a fire in a stone circle down on the beach, although more in hopes the smoke will keep the mozzies away than any need of warmth. Mark hooks up a hose in case of stray sparks.

The fire is burning brightly by the time the girls finish the washing up. Sonja falls on Mark with as much gusto as the resident blood suckers.

"That's what we must have looked like that night at Brighton Beach when the old guy gave us a hard time," says Sam.

"Except Mark doesn't have a terrier humping his leg."

"Only a Dalmatian," giggles Sam in Chris's ear.

Sonja and Mark mumble goodnight and disappear in the direction of the van. It starts rocking minutes later.

Chris suggests going for a dip at the same time as stripping off. It's late and dark with no one around and so rather than be left on the beach, she strips too before scuttling after him.

She's glad of a cloud that slips in front of the full moon, making it dark enough for her to feel comfortable being buck naked in a public place. Chris stops when he's thigh deep and she runs straight into him sending both of them sprawling in the water.

Chris surfaces smiling and pushes his hair back out of his eyes. He strikes out for the floating platform they'd seen kids jumping off earlier in the day and Sam follows, keeping pace. The cloud moves on, leaving everything glowing in the moonlight.

Making it to the raft first, Chris holds onto the side with his back against it and his arms spread wide, crucifix style. She treads water in front of him keeping herself out of his reach.

"Come closer."

"It's okay. I'm all right here."

"I think you should be closer." Chris's legs snake out and hook her around the waist, drawing her toward him. He's obviously not finding the water cold. She puts her arm over his shoulder to steady herself on the side of the raft and keep some distance between them but all this does is bring her breasts in contact with his chest.

"Are you cold?"

"No." Sam's gaze follows his to her breasts just below the surface and gleaming in the moonlight. "Oh. Maybe a little."

"This'll help." Chris lets go of the raft with one hand and pulls her hard against his body. "Better?"

"Tell me about it." Sam looks into his eyes before dropping her gaze to his lips. Unable to resist she moves in and drops a small kiss on the side of his mouth. He returns the favour then slowly moves his mouth to cover hers and after flicking his tongue over her lips, he explores her mouth when her lips part on a sigh. If she thought his kisses were electric before, they were nothing compared to this, given her whole body is in on the act.

Her nerve endings are screaming where Chris caresses her; the water swirling around adding to the sensation. Chris lets go of the raft and they sink beneath the surface only coming up for air.

"Hold on," says Chris, and guides Sam's hand to the ropes hanging off the side. She's dangling by one arm when Chris takes her other hand and places that, too. Their positions reversed, Sam's tempted to grab him around the waist with her legs to repeat his action of earlier but before she can do so his head drops below the surface and she can feel his mouth pulling on one of her nipples. He surfaces and slides up her body taking her into another long kiss which has her starting to take her arms down.

"No, don't move." He takes a big gulp of air before slipping below the surface. He slides down her body then his hands expose that most sensitive part of her, caressing and tugging. The stream of bubbles he finishes with cause her to lose it. She's still trembling when he surfaces.

"Come on." Chris climbs up the ladder on the side of the raft.

"I don't think my legs will work."

"Give me your hands."

Sam does and he pulls her up. He needs to hold her as her legs won't do the job. They sink down and Chris lays her on her back before starting to explore her body with his hands and mouth. The sensations on her front are all soft and smooth, while underneath there's the scratchy Astroturf covering the raft. This combination soon has Sam back at the brink.

Chris stops touching her so she can level out and when her breathing is more settled he scoops her up, onto his lap and with what seems like practiced ease enters her, nearly sending her over the edge again. He's incredibly hard and large.

He's thrusting into her when Sam pants "Wait, wait, cramp, my hip." Shifting herself around, she's able to straddle him, her legs dangling over the edge of the raft and into the water. She can feel the full length of him and each time he lifts his hips and pulls her forwards he fills her so completely she gasps in pleasure. They're both close to climax when Chris stills. "God, these mozzies are killing me."

"*What!*" says Sam, through gritted teeth.

"Big breath," he says, and locking his legs behind her back, topples them backwards over the edge of the raft. She just has time to get a lungful of air and hold her face against his chest before they're under the water still firmly locked together.

Chris grabs one of the trailing ropes and steadies himself on the side of the raft while Sam catches hold of him and her breath.

"Lock your legs." Chris grabs one, then the other of Sam's ankles and tucks them up behind his back. He trails his hand along one of her legs to its source causing her to give an involuntary buck and nearly lose her hold on him. Locking her ankles more securely, she draws him in even further, then experiments with how much she can move. Not as much as on the raft, but enough. She finds she can float out until he almost leaves her body and then using her leg muscles drag herself back in for a long slow thrust.

Chris brushes his hand over one of her breasts slowly decreasing the circles.

"Oh, god, I ..." Sam gasps.

"Relax," he says, gently.

Any response from Sam is lost as her body starts to contract and the air slips from her lungs in a sigh.

"Relax." Chris trails his hand down her body to where they join and with a little more coaxing, she shatters, the ripples racing up and down her body mirrored by the water around her.

She's floating in his arms when she comes back to her senses. Later, when they're up to it they swim back to shore, struggle into their clothes with wet skin and arrive at the caravan pleased to see it's stationary. As quietly as they can they make up the bed by dropping the table down and rearranging the cushions. Leaning over, Sam switches off the lamp on the end of the bench, before frowning. Flicks it on and off a few times, she says "Why doesn't it get darker when I turn the lamp off?"

"There's a security light right outside, that's as dark as it gets."

"Damn, I have trouble sleeping when it's this light."

She's just finished when Mark starts snoring loudly enough to have the glasses on the bench rattling. "Bloody hell, no wonder Sonja goes at it so hard," says Sam, sitting up. "I could have coped with the light but here's no way I can sleep through that.

"I'm sure I can think of something to keep us occupied." Chris runs his hand up her back to her shoulder, pulling her down and covering her body with his before dropping his head to a hardening nipple.

17

*S*team fills the kitchen as Sam pours the pot of macaroni into the colander sitting in the sink. The moist air has her hair either curling in wild tendrils or plastered to her skin. Shaking the colander to get rid of any water still lurking in the pasta's little cavities, she looks up to see Jennie trudge past the kitchen window.

Putting the colander down, she walks into the lounge. "You're late home for a Monday."

"Yeah, I had a whole stack of typing for a big meeting in the morning," says Jennie, flatly, before dropping her handbag on the coffee table and falling into the couch. "This heat is a killer."

"I managed to get away early so dinner'll be ready soon. Just need to make a cheese sauce for the macaroni and we're set." Sam pops back into the kitchen and opens the fridge. "Ah, bloody hell, we're out of milk."

"I can go and get some if you like." Jennie starts to climb out of the couch.

"Nah, don't worry, I'll go, you've just got home." She gently pushes Jennie back down before rummaging in the junk bowl on the coffee table, counting out the spare change into her hand, and then shoving it in her pocket. "Won't be long," she yells over her shoulder as she skips down the front steps.

Jingling the change in her pocket, she wanders up the hill to the corner store, mesmerised by the pavement disappearing under her feet with each step. The humidity, together with the waves of heat coming up from the startlingly white concrete, makes it feel like she's wading through warm water. Speed is impossible, with her progress measured by how many steps to a section break between the meticulously poured slabs. Step on a crack and you'll marry a rat, is set on repeat and given she's already had enough of those in her life, she takes the occasional short or long step.

The next crack disappears from view when a Mercedes mounts the footpath and screeches to a halt right in front of her.

"Arrrgh!" Sam staggers back, her heart speeding in her chest. Looking at the tyre scuff across the toe of her left sneaker, she releases her death grip on the change in her pocket and steps back to put some distance between herself and the car.

The handbrake cranks on and the window winds down. She can see Sapphire sitting in the passenger seat. The dog looks as green as Sam feels.

Mrs Farquhar leans over Sapphire. "Sam, I'm so relieved I ran into you!"

Bloody Norah, ran into me is right.

Sam's hand strays to her throat where her pulse is slowly beating a retreat from heart attack territory. Leaning heavily on the car, she bends over to look inside. She'd crouch down but doubts her rubbery legs would hold. "What's the problem?" stutters Sam. No point pulling Mrs Farquhar up on her driving. It's a lost cause.

"I've had the most marvellous idea. I'm going to host a fifth birthday party for Sapphire."

"A birthday party?" says Sam, stupidly. The near-death experience has slowed her responses, although finally, up pops an image of a cake made out of blade steak and 'iced' with pâté.

"Yes. Think what a fabulous outfit you could make for Sapphire. She'll be the talk of the town. Oh, and of course, it'll be a wonderful showcase for your skills too. But we need to get moving on the design. The party's only three weeks away."

"I suppose I could come around later tonight," says Sam, reluctantly.

"And what's wrong with right now?" Mrs Farquhar gives the motor a gentle rev.

"I'm in the middle of making dinner." Seeing Mrs Farquhar's reaction, she adds, "I've popped out to get milk."

"Well, will you be long? I'm anxious we start my angel's outfit directly." Mrs Farquhar absently rubs her fingers back and forth on Sapphire's head. The dog's eyes glaze over and her mouth goes goofy.

After a few rapid calculations, she says, "I promise I'll be around there in an hour and a quarter." Although to fit everything in, she's going to need to step it up a gear.

"Make it an hour," commands Mrs Farquhar. The window closes and the Mercedes backs off the footpath and straight into the path of an oncoming car.

Mrs Farquhar is oblivious to the squeal of tyres when the startled driver of the other car brakes hard to avoid her. She graunches the Merc into first gear and drives off down the hill with the engine desperately trying to claw its way out of the bonnet.

Second gear for god's sake. Second gear!

Sam's teeth are clenched tight, her eyes squeezed shut and her head angled to stop the horrendous sound in its full-throttle assault on her eardrums.

"Bloody hell, an hour!" says Sam, when the screaming Mercedes turns the corner at the bottom of the hill. A slow jog up to the shop has the sweat running seconds after she does. She'll need a hose down when she gets home, albeit a quick one.

Leaning against her headboard with a sketch book propped on the easel formed by her knees, Sam works on Sapphire's party outfit. She'd sketched up the basic design at Mrs Farquhar's on Monday night, but it'd taken a couple more days to nut out the accessories.

"Sam, there's a fraightfully naice bloke on the phone about an outfit for a mutt," says Brenda, her head craned around the door of Sam's room.

"Whay, thank you seooo much." Sam does her best plum-in-her-mouth accent in return. Brenda's is better.

"You'll need to shout, he's a deaf old bastard," yells Brenda, at full volume, given she's returned to the lounge.

I bloody hope he's deaf. Sam, puts aside the sketch pad and swings her legs off the bed. "A man?" she questions Brenda en route to the phone in the hallway.

"Yep, old dude. Must be gay."

The girls are used to a succession of old ladies calling about outfits for their pooches but this is the first guy who's ever called.

"Hello?" The only response from the other end is raspy breathing.

"Hello!" says Sam, slightly louder. There's rustling, but still no actual response.

"Told you," says Brenda, from the lounge. "Deaf as a post."

"HELLO!" yells Sam into the phone.

"Julia de Graaf speaking, John-John's mother," rumbles back at her so loudly that she instinctively yanks the receiver away from her ear.

"YES!" yells Sam in return. With a name like Julia she's obviously not a man but sure sounds like one.

"You won't be aware but there's going to be a fancy dress party next month to celebrate Sapphire Farquhar's fifth birthday," announces Mrs de Graaf, as though imparting a state secret. Given the volume, it isn't a secret any longer.

"That's right, I've already started on Sapphire's outfit and have other orders coming in thick and fast!" She speaks loudly, her mouth close to the receiver, her ear well clear.

"This won't do! John-John would never forgive me if he was the only one not in costume," is shouted down the phone louder than ever, before a softer "I'm not too late, am I?"

"No, you're not too late!" shouts Sam, her voice full of sympathy, her eyes rolling in disbelief.

Sam and Jennie drop around the same evening. Sam's amazed to see the place is even bigger than Mrs Farquhar's. John-John probably has his own bloody wing. For all Sam knows, John-John could even be human.

It's a two storey stone house with a tall iron security fence with spikes atop. She hopes this is to keep the bad guys out and not John-John's mummy in. They crunch their way up a side path and around the right hand side of the mansion as instructed through the squawk box at the tradesgirls' entrance. The place isn't as tidy back here, with leaves piled high in corners. The large concrete area in front of the garage and leading up to the back door is liberally dotted with small piles of dog poo. The owners obviously don't give a rat's arse about the impression they give to the working classes.

Jennie's nose wrinkles in disgust. "Golly, it reeks."

"It's bloody gross," gags Sam.

"Blooming heck, watch your feet." Jennie narrowly misses one of the canine landmines.

"Aw, hell, too late!" Sam eyes the flattened splat beneath her foot. Limping over to the lawn, she gives the sole of her shoe a vigorous wipe on the surprisingly long grass before zigzagging her way back to Jennie. The wire mat beside the back door appears to be a demilitarised zone.

"God, I hope I got all of it. I wouldn't want to track it through the house." Angling her foot up first one way and then the other, Sam checks the bottom of her shoe. Her nose is so full of the smell of dog poo that sniffing it wouldn't help; if she breathes in too deeply there's a good chance she'll barf. Even with shallow breathing, a couple of dry heaves pop out.

"It looks okay, no brown showing," says Jennie, nasally

after inspecting it for her. "Block your nose like me, it'll stop you wanting to be sick."

Sam pinches her nose with one hand and knocks with the other on the mullioned glass back door and they wait. Nothing. She knocks again, louder but the only response is sore knuckles.

"There's no way she's going to hear us, I had to yell just to make myself heard on the phone," says Sam. "We don't stand a chance knocking with a place this big."

They walk around to the front with its imposing porch complete with Greco Roman columns that run the full width of the house. The front door is bordello red and shiny enough the girls can check their hair is tidy. The whole area must be serviced by the same door-polishing bloke.

Sam pushes the gleaming brass door bell and they wait. They can hear the extra loud *BING BONG* echoing throughout the interior; in the end it's answered by a woman with dark grey hair set in a perm so unforgiving that all that's missing is a chinstrap. Her face is crumpled and her nose squashed in to a point that Sam can see right up inside the woman's nostrils. The eyes dissecting them are the colour of unpolished stainless steel and about as warm. Her head is cocked to the side in the attitude of someone favouring an ear.

Sam's adrenaline kicks in and it's all she can do not to bolt.

"I was expecting you at the back," booms the woman in a deep baritone that firmly identifies her as the lady of the house.

Any money must have been on her side muses Sam; there's no way she could have married into it without a shotgun being involved – although the woman appears more than capable of using one. She's chunky and dressed with military severity in a tweed pinafore dress in an ugly shade of mushroom. Supporting all of this is a pair of legs that are the same width from knee to heel, like drainage pipes. Her shoes are so tight they appear painted on, like a chain-store dolly.

"We knocked a few times but I don't think you heard us!

We're so sorry!" says Sam, with as much apology as she can, given she's yelling at the woman. She hopes she's not laying it on so thick as to be unbelievable.

"Which one of you is Samantha?" Mrs de Graaf scrutinises them, as though they're on the parade ground.

Sam waves her hand to identify herself as this seems a quicker option than speaking.

"And who is this?" The woman examines Jennie as she would road kill.

"Ah, this is my friend, Jennie. I didn't want to walk here on my own."

"Walk? Walk! Oh, right, a little joke." Her laughter sounds like a concrete mixer working on a full load. "Come in." She inches the front open. "You can put your shoes there." She points to a cane basket next to the front door.

"Our shoes?" says Jennie, quietly to Sam.

Sam toe taps the carpet that lies beyond the marble they're standing on. Drifts of snow white carpet lie passively in all directions.

"Whoa." Jennie ditches her shoes and then checks carefully for sock lint.

"John-John, come here, darling," trills Mrs de Graaf in a falsetto akin to eating tin foil; Sam's astounded the woman's larynx is even capable.

They hear yapping from the back of the house that makes its way in their direction them confirming for Sam that John-John is not human. He flies around a corner and into the entrance hall. Once he clears the white carpet and hits the marble, he demonstrates cornering skills more commonly seen in competition-level speed skating. He comes to a barrelling halt in front of them, and eyes them expectantly.

This has to be the ugliest pug Sam has ever seen. His forehead is a road map of deep, furry wrinkles giving him a permanently pissed-off air. His underbite is an orthodontist's wet dream.

"There's Mummy's little darling."

"He's beautiful!" shouts Sam, with what she hopes is an appropriate tone.

"He's lovely, can I hold him?" Jennie speaks at a volume designed not to be heard.

Mrs de Graaf's reaction, however, suggests her hearing loss is selective. Jennie edges behind Sam.

Unaware he's under discussion, darling sits and proceeds to demonstrate the ability to lick, in quick succession, his nostrils then his balls.

"Agile, isn't he!" Sam fights to keep the laughter out of her voice.

"He's gorgeous, that's what he is," booms Mrs de Graaf, picking him up and peppering small kisses all over his nose. There's a muttered, "Gross," from behind Sam

No sooner has John-John been put back down than he starts jumping on the spot causing the slobber running down his chin to arc off in all directions. Sam and Jennie step back in tandem, out of the mucus radius.

Mrs de Graaf calms the dog enough that Sam can take his measurements. He's stocky and as round as he is long, but quick, given the number of nips he manages to get in. Sam will have to include the cost of a rabies shot on this one.

"Have you given any thought to what you'd like his outfit to be?" says Sam, in a professional bellow.

Mrs de Graaf's blank look is answer enough.

"How about I design something for him?" roars Sam, in hopes of avoiding this woman having anything to with the design, given her own dress sense. When Mrs de Graaf seems doubtful, she yells, "A few of the other mothers *have* left the designs up to me."

Sam is horrified at some of the outfits the other mothers want and is still thinking on how to dress a King Charles spaniel as King Charles II, complete with sceptre, orb and crown. Conversely, the Maltese Terrier who's going as Marilyn Monroe only requires a couple of glasses of Champagne to be in-character. The British Bulldog going as Winston Churchill, bears an uncanny resemblance to the great man, and will be set with a black Homburg, a cigar and a bottle of whisky.

"If you could design something then," says a relieved Mrs de Graaf. "Do I take it that will be extra?"

While Sam's still considering this, Jennie yells, "Yes!"

18

eturning from a trip to the fabric store, Sam sweeps aside the usual assortment of crap on the oval, mahogany dining table and spreads out her purchases. It doesn't take her long to decide what she'll use for John-John's costume and, because of the relatively small size of the dog, the outfit is almost complete by that afternoon when Jennie gets in from work.

Because of the number of outfits she's making, Sam's taken the week off temping in order to get through the bulk of them. She's making more from doggie fancy dress costumes than she ever could from typing; exactly as predicted by Mrs Farquhar.

"How'd you go?" says Jennie, keen to see what she has come up with.

"Brilliant, have a look at this for John-John." Sam holds up a small all-in-one, made from pale blue spandex and astrakhan fabric, which is about as poodle as you can get without resorting to taxidermy. The outfit replicates Sapphire's lion clip perfectly and Sam has even fashioned a fake tail with a pom-pom at the end. This was easier than attempting to make John-John's little piggy, swirly tail resemble Sapphire's straight-as-a-rod appendage.

"That's awesome. The spandex feels exactly like Sapphire's

135

skin where she's shaved. Are you putting ribbons at the top of the ears?" says Jennie, enthusiastically.

"Oh, right, I forgot all about them."

"I hope John-John's mummy doesn't mind you cross-dressing her darling."

With the outfit finished to her satisfaction, Sam rings Mrs de Graaf and arranges to deliver the outfit the next evening.

"Please come with me, Jennie?" says Sam in a wheedling tone after she's hung up. "*Pleeeeease.* She scares the hell out of me."

"But that's Friday night."

"We'll be quick. I have to be home by seven 'cause I'm going out with Chris."

"Well, can't we deliver it on Saturday morning?"

"I don't think I'll be home by then." Sam's sure the jingle of excitement must be evident in every word.

Dead on 5.30 p.m. the next evening, the girls are buzzed through the gate at Mrs de Graaf's. Sam's pleased Jennie's going out later with mates from work because she worries about her sitting home alone if Brenda does one of her usual no-shows.

They've knocked on the back door until their knuckles are nearly bleeding, when they spy John-John through the glass door.

"Go get mummy, darling." Sam uses her best talking-to-a-minor voice. She's pleased the concrete has been hosed free of doggie bombs so she doesn't have to block her nose this time.

The response is a lot of yapping, bouncing and spraying of body fluids.

"Come on, sweetie. Let mummy know we're here," she sing-songs.

"I can't believe it – you're talking to him like she does. It's a *dog.*"

"Hey, at least he can hear us. And anyway it's worked hasn't it?" She points at the pug trotting away from them.

They're about to give up and brave the front door when John-John waddles back into view with what looks like a human femur held firmly in his jutting-out bottom teeth. Obviously proud of himself, he makes a a production out of dropping it on the floor. His bum hits the lino soon after.

Sam looks at the huge bone. "Crap, do ya think he's eaten her?"

"Get real. He doesn't have the power to take her down," Jennie proceeds to pull faces at the dog through the glass. There's no response and Jennie is spurred on to even more gruesome expressions, much to Sam's delight and Mrs de Graaf's horror when she walks into the kitchen and spots Jennie at it.

"Samantha, is your friend all right?" she says, loudly through the safety of the glass.

"Yeah, she's fine, she was … ah … playing with John-John," gasps out Sam, before repeating it at double volume so Mrs de Graaf can hear her.

Jennie's mute, her face scarlet.

Mrs de Graaf opens the door scarcely wide enough for the girls to squeak through. They make it into the kitchen, where she inspects Jennie closely before giving her the okay. "Come through to the conservatory and you can show me John-John's ensemble."

The girls perch themselves on the edge of a cane settee and Sam pulls the outfit from her bag and holds it up for scrutiny.

"Hmm. I don't know?" says Mrs de Graaf, doubtfully, leaning over to take the costume from Sam. "I don't know if Cynthia will be pleased."

While Mrs de Graaf turns the outfit first one way and then the other, Sam and Jennie gently poach in the heat of the conservatory, the temperature being ideally suited to the various tropical palms and orchids surrounding them. It doesn't appear to bother Mrs de Graaf, even though she's dressed in her standard tweed.

Sam rubs the back of her hand over her top lip then sneakily puts it down between the cushions of the flowery settee and slides it back and forth to dry it. Pulling it out, there's a small dog biscuit stuck to the end of one finger. She flicks this away without being spotted, although John-John's head does pop up briefly.

"Maybe if we put it on John-John so you could see what it looks like," yells Sam, encouragingly. She clicks her fingers to get John-John's attention away from the large bone he's dragging around the black-and-white-tiled floor in a bovine-inspired game of chess. At the lack of response from Mrs de Graaf, who's still busy turning the outfit back and forth, Sam has a good dig down the side of the settee and comes up with a couple more dog biscuits, one of which she flicks in John-John's direction. It hits the back of his head and he drops the bone and turns toward her, growling.

Oh great.

Sam holds out the other small biscuit and is relieved to hear the growling stop. He trots over and drops his butt to the seagrass matting, drool already pooling on his bottom lip. She holds the biscuit out with a grimace; fully expecting to get snotted on at the very least, but John-John is all manners when he gently takes the biscuit from her. While he crunches contentedly, Sam quickly puts a hand on either side of his chunky abdomen and prompts Mrs de Graaf to hand over the outfit.

At the lack of response, Jennie leans over and slides the jumpsuit stealthily from Mrs de Graaf's fingers. The woman's gazing at a spot well past Sam's left shoulder, apparently deep in thought as to the pros and cons of John-John's get-up.

She and Jennie successfully wrangle the mutt into his costume, then Sam bellows at Mrs de Graaf, "What do you think?" Then trying to keep the second-hand car salesman impersonation to a minimum, she adds, "Doesn't he look fabulous?"

"He looks great," shouts Jennie, obviously hoping to close the deal.

Mrs de Graaf unglues her gaze from its spot on the far wall to look at John-John. "I don't know," she says, her voice still full of uncertainty. "He does look good, but let me think about it. I'll speak to Mildred and Sarah-Jane and see what they say."

Sam's not sure if Mildred and Sarah-Jane are friends, relations or dogs but hopes she doesn't have to make another outfit.

"I'll call tomorrow and let you know." Mrs de Graaf shows them out. They say goodbye but she doesn't notice.

"Blooming heck, you'd think the outfit had fake boobs," says Sam, when they're safely out the gate.

Sam's kept busy over the next week making fancy dress outfits for most of the small yappy dogs of Toorak. It's getting to the point where no dog worth its diamante-studded collar is going to be seen sporting anything other than a Doggs' Toggs original. Jennie has even designed a proper logo. She lets Mrs Farquhar know about this at one of their regular strategy meetings, insisting Jennie is an integral part of the fledgling company. Thus it is that both she and Jennie are invited to Sapphire's party. Jennie immediately starts freaking out about what she's going to wear.

"It's only a bloody party for a dog. You don't need to go to any trouble, I'm not going to," says Sam, laughing.

"But don't you want to look as though you belong?" wails Jennie. "You can guarantee they'll all be dressed to match their dogs, like they usually are."

"Hell, you're right." Sam realises she'll have to make two more outfits. Ten times the size and twice as furry.

Attempting to apply her mascara without risking minor eye surgery, Sam squints in the bathroom mirror. Chris is taking her to a flash Italian restaurant for dinner tonight and she wants to look her best but with the light bulb being so far above her, she has to angle her head back to a point her eyeballs can hardly swivel enough to see the mirror.

In the end there's more mascara on her eyelids than her lashes and she has to wipe everything off in preparation for starting over. She gives up on the bathroom and retreats to her bedroom, moving the lamp from her bedside table and stretching the cord out so it can sit on the edge of her dressing table. The angle of light is weird but at least she can see her eyelashes now.

She's adding the final touches to her make-up when the phone rings. After three or four rings the calls of, "Can someone else get that?" from both Brenda and Jennie's bedrooms leave Sam in no doubt that if she doesn't get it, then it won't be answered and by now it's getting to the stage that if she doesn't move quickly she'll miss it. Tossing the glowing lamp onto her bed, rather than waste time crawling under the cord, she races through to the phone. Her arm is outstretched to make the pick-up.

"Hello!" says Sam, when the rest of her body catches up.

"Sam? It's Chris."

"Hey, there, I'm nearly ready." Sam's voice softens.

"Yeah, about that. I'm sorry, but I have to fly up to Japan."

"Why are you sorry about that? That's cool. When are you going?"

"They've managed to get me on a flight tonight."

"Tonight!" She sinks to the seat of the telephone table.

"I know it's short notice but we'll have to cancel dinner. I'm truly sorry."

"No, that's all right, we can go another time. When will you be back?" She tries hard to sound more enthusiastic than she's feeling.

"Not sure, hopefully by next weekend, but I'll phone you as soon as I get home."

"Have a good trip." Sam knows her voice has gone into business mode but this is better than blurting out something she might regret ... isn't it?

"Okay. Will do, 'bye," says Chris, abruptly in response.

She listens to the dial tone for a while before hanging up. *Damn.* She'd wanted to tell him that she'd miss him, that she'd be thinking about him, that she'd do something special for him when he got home, but she'd gagged on the words.

Her hand hovers over the phone; she lifts the receiver and dials.

But what if he thinks I'm too clingy, too serious, too soon? Is it too soon to say that sort of stuff?

After hanging up again, she wavers between phoning him back and returning to her bedroom. Eventually she grabs the handset.

She's started to dial again when a burning smell makes its way up her nose and into the "oh hell" centre of her brain.

Bloody hell, the lamp!

She slams the phone down and runs to her bedroom. The shade is well alight and given it's sitting in the middle of her bed, it's seconds away from taking out her whole room.

Sam grabs the base of the lamp and lifts it clear of the patchwork quilt; while blackened, thankfully it isn't alight. "Oh my god oh my god oh my god." This mantra spews forth while she holds the flaming lamp up and away from her like an indoor version of the Statue of Liberty; she'd biff it out the window but worries about it setting fire to the lace curtains. Realising she's still attached to the power point by the cord, she yanks the plug out of the wall hoping to stop any possible sparks.

The plastic-lined shade is burning merrily away with flaming globs dropping onto the carpet at regular intervals. She stamps these out as soon as they hit its godawful random, black and orange pattern. Even if she left them to burn out on their own, they wouldn't be noticeable. By the time the flames die down, her room is full of black, acrid smoke and she's trembling while she waits for her body to use up all the adrenaline it's produced.

Shakily closing her bedroom door to contain the smoke, she puts the lamp on the floor and ties the lace curtains in knots to get them out of the way. Swinging her pillow around helps force the smoke out of the wide-open window, she keeps this up until it's down to a slight haze.

She examines the patchwork quilt for damage. It's not too bad apart from a couple of bits she'll have to replace. She can already see the correct-shaped hole cut in an old pair of shorts and the bottom chopped off one of her nighties. Hopefully the landlord won't notice her patch job.

Removing her never-worn-before black patent heels, now with scorch marks on the sole, Sam puts them back in the box; her brand new dress is next. She slips the hanger through the neckline then smooths the dress into place. The dark purple of the fabric glints in the evening sunlight when she hangs it outside the window to rid it of its smoky smell. After dragging on her dressing gown, she attacks her perfectly applied makeup, swiping a baby-oiled cotton pad first across one eye and then the other. She smears her lipstick.

Her reflection looks blurry, thanks to some of the oil making its way into her eyes. But that's okay because she feels blurry, too. After some judicious scrubbing, there isn't a scrap of makeup left. Her eyes and lips are back to their normal size and her whole face is as greasy as a chip.

The phone rings again. She hopes to hell it's not Chris telling her his flight's been cancelled. Again there are calls of "Can someone else get that!" from both Brenda and Jennie. With the lamp out of the way, she walks leisurely through to answer the phone.

"Hello."

"Hi, it's Chris."

"Oh, hi."

"I just wanted to say I'll miss you while I'm away," says Chris, without preamble.

"Me, too. But about you." She'd like to say more but it's enough for now.

"Bye."

"Bye." Sam gently replaces the receiver.

Back in her bedroom, she stands unmoving in the middle

of the room. A smile works its way up from her stomach and explodes onto her face; the spell is broken. Opening the top drawer of her dressing table, she rummages around until she locates the pale pink satin bag. Loosening the drawstring, Sam shakes the silver chain with its small button out onto her hand along with a flurry of dried lavender. She's about to put the necklace over her head when her hands still.

Examining herself in the mirror, she's surprised to see there's no outward sign of the gymnastics her stomach is performing. Her gaze wavers from her reflection down to the button before she drops it back into the small satin bag, re-ties the cord and once again buries it deep amongst her underwear.

"Hey, can I borrow your white denim jacket," says Jennie, coming into Sam's room.

"Help yourself." She waves casually at the wardrobe.

"Have you been burning incense again?" Jennie sniffs repeatedly.

Sam's not keen on admitting to her stupidity. "Ah, not exactly."

"What on earth happened?" Jennie has spotted the burnt-out lamp tucked in the corner by the wardrobe.

"Just a small accident, all under control now."

Satisfied the lamp isn't going to flare up again, Jennie starts riffling through the clothes in Sam's wardrobe. "I thought you were going out with Chris."

"I was, but he has to fly up to Japan on business. Tonight!"

"Tonight? Gosh, that's unexpected. You want to come out with me? It won't be a huge night, it's drinks at Penny from work's place."

"Thanks, but I can't be arsed getting all done up again now," says Sam, as a way of excusing herself. This sounds better than saying she doesn't trust herself to not drink too much when Chris isn't around.

Sam jumps out of bed the following morning with an unusually clear head for a Sunday. She's sipping a coffee and flicking through a magazine when Jennie drifts through the lounge.

"How was last night?" Sam asks out of habit, her eyes straying briefly from the latest *Cleo* male centrefold lying in her lap. *Cute.*

"It was fun, you should have come," says Jennie, from the kitchen over the roar of the kettle.

"I had a nice night in." Sam holds the *Cleo* up at arms' length so she can take in the centrefold properly.

"Did you come up with any good ideas for our costumes?" Jennie sits in the chair across from Sam and puts down her coffee.

"Yeah." Sam drops the centrefold face down into her lap and spins her sketch pad around on the coffee table so Jennie can see. "What do you think of these?"

Jennie looks closely at the sketch. "What are we going to use for whiskers?"

"I thought we could glue on a few bristles from the yard broom."

"Glue!" yelps Jennie.

"Draw them on with eyebrow pencil?"

"I thought we decided we wouldn't wear anything revealing?"

19

olding a ruler across her right cheek, Sam carefully draws in a neat line with a sharpened eyebrow pencil. Taking the ruler away she's annoyed to see her final whisker is crooked, like a cat that's chewing on a particularly tough mouse. It'd been much easier doing Jen's whiskers. Even then they'd had a close call with the phone ringing while she was just starting a whisker and unable to stop. By the time she'd finished, the ringing had stopped too.

Her whiskers will have to do, because straightening them would involve removing all her foundation and starting again from scratch. And one twitch and she'd still end up looking like she was chomping on rodent.

Resigned to an evening of crookedness, she replaces the cap on the pencil and checks out the rest of her costume. Not bad; shame Chris is overseas. He'd love it.

Sam's practicing licking the back of her hand and cleaning behind the ears perched on top of her head, when Jennie comes in.

"Sam, can you help me with this?" Jennie tugs on the tail of her cat suit. "It keeps bending the wrong way." With a minor adjustment and the addition of another small safety pin, Jennie's tail is perfect.

Turning her face first to one side then the other, for

145

Jennie's appraisal, Sam realises her whiskers aren't as bad as she'd thought. Once everything is tweaked to perfection, they don coats and call for a taxi. Even though it's not far, they're not keen on traipsing the streets dressed as they are.

Instead of being whisked straight up to the front door as she has expected, their taxi joins a queue of cars up the driveway. It's mostly taxis but there are also a couple of chauffeur-driven European stunners.

They walk up the front steps behind an older couple both with silver hair and both in ankle-length dress coats. Tailing them is a small Jack Russell; he's au naturel without a costume.

"I can't wait to see what they're wearing," Jennie whispers to Sam.

"Bloody hell, if they're like most of the others, they'll match the dog!" says Sam, looking at them under the lights in the foyer. *I hope they're in good physical shape.*

She finds out soon enough when the four of them all take their coats off at the same time. Sam can't decide who's more stunned, though she doubts the couple in front of her feel like throwing up in the middle of the foyer.

"I didn't think it was fancy dress for everyone," says the woman, who's wearing an off-the-shoulder electric blue, satin sheath dress that must have cost a fortune.

Sam and Jennie are so shocked at seeing the others aren't in fancy dress,they hand their raincoats over when the older couple relinquish their beautiful, and more than likely Italian, designer coats. Cheap and chic alike disappear with the coat-check girl through a doorway off the foyer.

"Yes, I thought the fancy dress was only for the dogs," says her companion, looking down at the terrier sitting next to his tuxedoed leg. "Although I must say, they are rather fetching outfits." His smile is as wide as his eyes.

"Come on, Alfred, let's find Cynthia." The woman drags dog and husband away.

"Righto, Milly. I'll catch you girls later for a dance."

"There's no way I'm going in there dressed like this," says Jennie. "Where on earth did that girl take our coats?"

They examine the spot in the wall where they think she disappeared, but there's no door.

Sam examines the wall. "God, I could have sworn she walked through there."

They're pushing at the wall experimentally when several elderly gents make their way through the front door. The posse of costumed dogs in their wake and a faint aroma of cigars and dog poo is testament to them all having been out for a comfort stop. The girls try to get out of the way but they're swept purposefully into Mrs Farquhar's lounge on a wave of Grecian 2000 and Old Spice, and just as promptly abandoned.

Conversations stutter to a standstill around the room and the quartet playing in one corner grinds to a halt, their flautist finding it impossible to blow and gasp simultaneously. After what seems an eternity, tête-à-têtes start up again, with the girls painfully aware they're the subject of all of them. The music eventually follows, although it's nowhere near as smooth.

"I wish this shag pile was deeper," laments Sam. "We'd have somewhere to hide."

Jennie takes in the looks they're receiving from the society matrons, many of whom she's met when on measuring sorties with Sam. "Anyone would think we'd dressed like this to lure their husbands away from them," she says, before shuddering.

They're sidling their way slowly back to the front door when a herd of small zebra gallops across the savannah of cream carpet, chased by a couple of giraffe and a hippo.

"Sam, they look so much better when they're on the dogs. It's like David Attenborough does Toorak. Only smaller."

The girls momentarily forget their own costumes as they look at the small animals milling around them.

"Yeah, when I saw those animal prints, I just knew. I was lucky Mrs McGowan let me dress her lot the same way otherwise it wouldn't have worked as well." She points at a smoked glass coffee table where the herd of zebra are hiding next to King Charles II. He's still sporting his crown, but she suspects he's already buried the orb and sceptre.

They're nearly knocked off their feet by a small but surprisingly solid elephant flying past at speed. He doesn't get far before accidentally standing on his 'trunk', pitching into a couple of out-of-control forward rolls and taking out one of the waitresses. Her plate of hors d'oeuvres shoots up before raining down to be ripped apart by a ravenous 'lion'. The girls step back out of the kill zone.

"My god, was that Sapphire?" Jennie spins around when she spots the familiar blue zip past.

"No, it was John-John."

"The fabric is spot on, it's exactly the right shade of blue."

"Hey, it's not blue."

"It's Gentian Silver," they say in unison and burst out laughing before again heading toward the front door. They're so focused on their escape they don't see Mrs Farquhar until she pops up in front of them. The orange lipstick is even brighter than usual. It's almost audible.

"What on earth are you girls playing at?" say Mrs Farquhar's lips, the real Sapphire beside her.

"We're so sorry – we thought it was fancy dress for everyone. We were trying to leave when we were forced in here by that group of men." Sam indicates the offenders. "We're trying to leave."

"For goodness sake, the damage has been done now, you may as well stay." Mrs Farquhar's voice is full of resignation, although Sam notices a small sign of amusement flare in the woman's normally cold eyes. This is soon extinguished when a mental bucket of ice is chucked over it and the public persona donned once again. "I'm sure I can feel a migraine coming on." Sapphire follows on her heels, wings flapping, halo wobbling madly.

The girls wander around taking in the dogs' outfits and receiving startled responses to their own, before passing the group of elderly men who are the reason they're stuck here.

They receive cat calls from several of the old chaps as they pass.

"Here, kitty, kitty, kitty,"

"Nice tail."

"Meow." The last more frog croak than cat.

As the phlegmy laughter dies down, Jennie retorts, "Yeah, yeah, don't laugh too hard, you might backwash your colostomy bags."

Proving their hearing is up to snuff, the old chaps guffaw delightedly at this comment, following up with grossly productive coughing.

Sam battles revulsion and surprise, with surprise winning out. "Jennie! Have you been taking lessons from Brenda?"

Jennie's hand flies to her mouth when it dawns on her that she said that last comment loud enough to be heard.

They're standing in the foyer thinking about doing a runner without their coats when part of one wall opens out to reveal the coat-check girl. "Thank goodness," says Jennie, "can we have our coats, please?"

With a nod the girl disappears through the wall.

Sam looks at the concealed doorway. "So we weren't going mad. Don't suppose she'll have much trouble remembering which coats are ours. Shame."

"It's not late, shall we walk home? It's not far and we may as well save on a taxi?"

"Yeah, why not, although with our luck we'll end up at the SPCA."

They're walking through the double gates set in the high stone wall that borders the front of the property when they see headlights swinging into the driveway.

"God, the fewer of my customers who see me in this clobber the better." Sam shoots behind the nearest manicured shrub, followed closely by Jennie. They're crouching down next to the small bush when a taxi drives slowly past.

An immaculately groomed blonde sits next to a man who looks a lot like Chris. If she hadn't been crouched down, Sam wouldn't even have spotted him. The girl turns and looks straight at them; her mouth forms a perfect O when she spots their ears and whiskers. It widens into a broad smile seconds later. They can hear her giggly laughter as the car crunches on down the driveway.

"Chris!" says Sam, "with another woman."

"Are you sure? I'm not sure I'd call her a woman either, she looked young to me."

"Old enough!" Sam takes off across the front garden, nipping from bush to bush, Cat Woman-style. She's close enough to the front steps when the couple emerges from the car to see that it is Chris.

"I can't believe he's here with another woman," she hisses to Jennie who's caught up. "I didn't even know he was back," chokes Sam, past a huge lump in her throat. "What's he even doing here? I'll bet he thought I wouldn't be invited." Her legs give way and she sinks to the ground. Maybe if she wasn't dressed as a cat she might confront him, but her pride has taken enough of a battering for one evening.

"Oh, Sam." Jennie hunkers down and wraps her arms around Sam's trembling shoulders. "At least it's not that serious."

"Yeah, yeah. Not serious," sniffs Sam, into Jennie's shoulder.

Jennie softly rubs her hand round and around on Sam's back. "Come on, let's go home." Jennie helps Sam to her feet.

At the end of the drive they step aside to let a taxi with more guests pass them and when it reappears after the drop-off, they flag it down. Sam's in no fit state to walk home.

At home, Jennie helps her out of the taxi and leads her up the path to the bottom of the steps. After confirming she's all right, Jennie nips up, opens the front door and turns on the light in the hallway. With some coaxing, Sam is led up the stairs and into the house. The door swings shut behind them with the help of Jennie's foot.

Sam stops in the lounge, unsure what to do with herself.

"I'll make us a cup of tea," says Jennie, already on her way to the kitchen.

As Sam hears the kettle kick into life it's as though a switch is flicked in her head and she wanders into her bedroom. She doesn't bother with the light, preferring to let the dark press in on her. Her handbag drops from her fingers and she sinks to her bed.

What the hell is it about me that I keep attracting losers? It's like I'm a jerk magnet. I'm going to end up a lonely old woman like Mrs Farquhar.

This spiral of thoughts is interrupted by urgent knocking at the front door. Sam hears Jennie walk through and call out, "Who is it?" without opening the door. Jennie is safety conscious.

"It's Chris. I need to speak to Sam."

"I don't think that's a good idea."

"It wasn't what it looked like," says Chris through the letterbox slot in the door, a remnant of more refined times.

"It never is," yells Sam, who's now joined Jennie in the hallway.

"Sam, will you please open the door? You have to let me explain."

"No, bugger off."

"It is not what you think."

"Oh, go away, Chris. You've done enough damage already," says Jennie.

"This is between Sam and me," comes back through the letterbox.

"Not when I'm the one who has to pick up the pieces," says Jennie, indignantly, crouching down beside Sam, who's now in a heap on the floor.

"Fine, I'm leaving, but this is not over."

"Yes, it is," says Jennie.

"Yes, it is," echoes Sam, in a small voice that acknowledges the truth of this.

20

Glaring at the ceiling Sam confirms her count on the number of fly spots on the light fitting. She's sure she's in the same position she was when she went to bed and her eyes feel as if they've been open all night. They're gritty and they hurt but at least the tears have stopped, although only as a result of dehydration.

Her chest aches and it feels like there's a big ragged hole where her heart used to be. It does feel like someone's ripped it out; something she'd always thought was simply a corny phrase. The pain she'd felt when she was two-timed by Darren was nothing compared with how she's feeling now. This time it's so bad it almost doesn't hurt at all.

How could I have missed all the signs?

It's obvious she's as thick as a brick when it comes to guys; better she concentrates on the stuff she has control over.

"Bloody hell, what happened to you?" says Brenda to her later that morning. "You look like you've got a couple of shiners." She blows on her mug of coffee to cool it.

"Chris, that's what happened to her," says Jennie, coming in with two more coffees and handing one of them to Sam.

"He slugged her? That doesn't sound like him."

"No, they broke up."

"It's last night's make-up," says Sam. "No point taking it off." Her voice is screaming, "what's the use?" but the others don't take it up.

"How was last night?" says Brenda, obviously trying to steer the conversation away from Chris, but causing Jennie to frown at her.

"The fancy dress was only for the dogs," says Jennie.

The mouthful of coffee Brenda had been about to swallow shoots out of her out of her mouth and back into the mug. This is followed by a snort of laughter. As the giggles subside, she wipes her face on the bottom of the large Kangaroos T-shirt she's wearing as a nightie. "Hell, you're joking?"

"That and I caught Chris cheating on me."

"You're joking?" Brenda's no longer laughing.

"Yeah, there's nothing like being two-timed when you're dressed as a sodding cat." Sam's face burns with humiliation.

They're drinking their coffees in a reflective mood when the phone rings.

"If that's Chris, I am not home," says Sam, emphatically.

"I'd better not take it, I'm likely to give him a piece of my mind," says Jennie.

"Hell, I've got no problem ripping him a new one." Brenda stalks through to pick up the phone. "Hello!"

Sam and Jennie, wait for the outburst that's sure to follow but are disappointed when Brenda says, "Yeah, I'll get her for you. Sam."

"It's not him, is it?"

"Nah, it's another one of those batty old birds." Brenda doesn't bother dropping her voice.

"Hello, Sam speaking."

"Hello there, it's Mrs Courtney speaking, I'm the batty old bird you met in the foyer at the party last night," she says, in a wry tone.

"Ah. Right," says Sam, cringing.

"Yes, well. I was most impressed with the outfits you made and because my little Monty turns six in a few weeks, I'd like to commission you to make an outfit for him to wear at the party we're throwing to celebrate."

"Really? I wasn't sure I'd get any more work after dressing a lot of the dogs the same way."

"But that's what I liked. I'm having a *Star Wars* party for Monty."

By the end of the day Sam has orders for over forty outfits.

Another *Star Wars* outfit is materialising out of the sewing machine in front of Sam, when Jennie walks in the door with a heavily bandaged hand. "I swear the next time Honey-Bun the killer Corgi bites me I am going to bite him right back." Jennie's trying to sound tough but Sam knows she wouldn't hurt a fly. Even if the fly had it coming.

Sam finishes the seam she's working on before giving Jennie her full attention. "Bloody hell, how hard did he bite you?" says Sam, when she sees the large crepe bandage.

"It's not as bad as it looks. I think Mrs Moreton fancies herself as Florence Nightingale." Jennie starts to unwind the dressing and when she'd finished, a pile of bandage rests at her feet and a small bite mark showing on her hand. "See," she says, holding it up. "A decent plaster is all that's needed."

"I should have warned you about him. I whacked him around the chops first time he tried it and he's been fine ever since."

"I'll bet that went down a treat with mummy." Jennie flexes her hand experimentally, and then checks for fresh blood.

"She wasn't around. Hey, I appreciate your help with this. If I didn't have you out there measuring their chubby little butts I'd never make it."

"Have tape measure, will travel," says Jennie, jauntily.

"Yeah, you will. We're going to make enough out of this lot to finish saving for both our airfares to England."

"Gosh. Really? Both of them?"

"It's the least I can do, with the way you're helping me out.

And ..." Sam's words die in her throat. They'd feel far too real if she said them aloud.

"Are you doing okay?"

"I guess. Each day I don't hear from him it gets a little easier." Sam's words are strained; her hands grip the sides of the sewing machine like it's an anchor.

"That's a good thing, then, isn't it?" says Jennie, her tone unsure.

"I suppose. Part of me hoped he'd try a little harder. I'm obviously not worth the effort." Sam's voice is tinged with bitterness.

"Don't say that."

"Come on! He hasn't exactly been breaking down the door." Sam rips the tissue that's appeared in her hands into confetti. She doesn't even remember taking it out of her pocket. "But I don't ever want to see him again after what he's done."

She hasn't heard from him since the night of Sapphire's party apart from a couple of phone calls later on the Sunday afternoon that Brenda answered. Even if it was over, she'd hoped he'd try a lot, lot harder.

Sitting with her legs slung over the side of the lounge chair and fanning herself with an Aussie *Woman's Weekly*, Sam is waiting for the shower. Jennie's first, then Brenda, so the odds are that Sam's shower will be cold, whether she wants it that way or not. Chances are she will. It's only 10 a.m. and already the temperature is in the low thirties, even with all the doors and windows open.

Sensing movement on the edge of her vision, she turns her head to investigate. "Crap!" If she can see him clearly through the wide open front door, then chances are he can see her too. She hopes the dark interior works in her favour and will allow her to escape. She struggles out of the lounge seat, dives into her bedroom and immediately drops to the floor next to her bed. A cloud of dust envelopes her, her coughs muffled by her armpit.

"Chris?" queries Brenda, who's lying on the couch watching Sam's antics through the open door of her bedroom

"Shh." Sam's finger seals her lips.

"What?" whispers Brenda.

There's a sharp knock on the front door.

"Who?" mouths Brenda.

"Salami Boy," says Sam, in a hoarse whisper followed by another bout of muffled coughing.

Sheesh, when did she last vacuum?

Brenda grins, and arches off the couch with cat-like grace. She doesn't bother covering the cut-off men's pyjama bottoms and mini cropped t-shirt that constitute her sleeping apparel before going to answer the door. The ensemble shows her Barbie-perfect body to advantage.

Sam wriggles her way across the floor to keep an eye on Brenda, but she's careful to stay out of sight of the front door itself.

Brenda leans languidly against the wall and looks down at Salami Boy.

"Great, I've got the right place." He obviously recognises Brenda from the night in the club when Sam had picked him up. Brenda is fairly hard to forget. "Is Sam here?"

"Nope, she isn't. Aren't you hot in that jacket?" Brenda flaps her crop top.

"Bloody hell, don't chat to him," mutters Sam, to herself, "get rid of him." Her heartbeat is hammering loudly in her ears.

"Baby, I'm always hot," says Salami Boy, causing Sam to make quiet gagging sounds. She can't believe it when she sees his hand snake toward Brenda's exposed stomach. He trails his finger across the top of the elastic of her pyjama pants, finishing with a small tug. The bottoms ping back into place. Brenda stands straight and steps back into the hall. Salami Boy takes this as an invitation and steps off the top step and into the hallway.

Sam sucks in her breath and muffles the coughing as she shimmies away from the bed and ever so slowly pushes the door to. She jams her eye hard against the small gap left allowing her to see a sliver of the action in the front hall. What the hell is Brenda playing at?

"And who the hell invited you in?"

"Well, you didn't exactly say no."

"Trust me, if I was interested, you'd know."

Salami Boy thrusts his pelvis in a manner designed to increase the value of his jewels. "But, baby, I'm hung."

"Yeah, and what's the use of a big dick when it's attached to an even bigger prick?" Brenda pushes in the middle of Salami Boy's chest sending him back onto the top step.

Realising he's not going to succeed with Brenda, he says, "Can I have the phone number again then? Sam must have written it down wrong."

"She doesn't live here anymore." Brenda folds her arms tightly, her look mutinous.

"But that's the jacket she was wearing the night we hooked up."

"This piece of crap?" Brenda grabs the jacket off its hook in the hallway, "She gave it to me. Like I'd wear it!"

"Like you'd be able to get the buttons done up?" he says, laughing. He grabs at her breasts to emphasise his point.

Brenda smacks his hands away with the jacket. "You wanker!" He's given a few suggestions by Brenda that Sam doesn't think are physically possible, although she'd love to see him give them a try.

After Brenda finishes, he calmly says "Yeah, yeah, whatever. So do you know where I can find her?"

Sam's nearly out cold from holding her breath when she hears Brenda give him the address of the hostel in South Melbourne.

Hearing the front gate slam shut, she jumps up.

"What a complete and utter turd," mutters Brenda, picking up the phone.

Sam stumbles into the hallway. "What the hell did you give him that address for? They'll just send him back here."

"Stow it." Brenda's fingers are suspended above the dial while she waits for it to rotate back to its home position. She whistles tunelessly waiting for the call to be answered. "Ace, the very person," she says into the receiver. "Thought I'd warn you that the creep that Sam screwed is on his way round there looking for her. Any chance you can put on a welcome?"

She snorts at the reply before hanging up.

"What are you up to?" says Sam, taking in Brenda's evil expression.

"A little bit of revenge."

"What have you got in mind?"

"Maria and Janey! They're going to drink him under the table on that rocket fuel their uncle makes and when he's out cold they're going to strip him and handcuff him to something solid."

"Do you think he'll drink with them?"

"Sam, they're both gorgeous!"

"Oh, right." Sam's head bobs up and down in time to the pennies dropping. "It'll be nice to see the crap being flung in the other direction for a change."

Brenda stands deep in thought for a couple of seconds before hanging Sam's jacket back on the coat rack. "Dammit, this is too good to miss. Get dressed, we're going out."

21

*S*am feels sticky in her thrown-together outfit, partly due to no shower but mostly due to sweating like an overweight old bloke at thoughts of what they're about to do. Because of Jennie's propensity to panic, only Brenda and Sam are in the car. They've driven over to the hostel using a circuitous route to avoid running into Salami Boy and arrive in time to see him driving away with Maria and Janey in a bile coloured Corolla. His black BMW sits out in front of the hostel.

Even though he's not looking in her direction, Sam sinks lower in her seat. "Do you think this is a good idea?"

"Hell, yes." Brenda rubs her hands together before putting them back on the wheel and accelerating toward the corner the others have just turned. There's not much traffic and Brenda has no trouble keeping a safe distance behind. The Corolla stops outside a large wooden building in St Kilda, and Brenda barks with laughter.

Sam can see nothing about the building to warrant this sort of reaction. "What's so funny?"

"It's where they're taking him. He has no idea."

"About what?" She looks closely at the building. It's a large, two storey, turn of the century structure, with no signs or markings to give a clue as to what might be inside.

"They've just gone in the back entrance to one of the most notorious gay bars in Melbourne. Maria works there."

After turning off the engine and yanking on the handbrake, Brenda opens her door. "Wait here, I'll be back in a second."

Before Sam can formulate a question, the door slams and Brenda runs to the building the others disappeared into. Brenda uses the same door as they had, causing Sam to suck in her breath. "What the hell."

Brenda's hasn't been gone five minutes when she shoots back through the doorway and over to the car. She settles in her seat and looks at her watch. "They said to give them half an hour."

"Half an hour? They're never going to get him drunk in that time."

"Are you kidding? The stuff they're pouring down his throat is closer to paint stripper than alcohol. Half an hour'll be plenty."

According to Brenda's digital watch, twenty-eight minutes have passed when they see Janey beckoning to them from a second storey window.

Brenda throws open her door. "Come on, it's show time." She realises Sam hasn't moved, leans down and looks in through the door. "You coming?"

"I can't go in there with him." Sam's voice trembles in unison with the rest of her body. "I don't want to go anywhere near him."

"What if he doesn't know it's you?" At Sam's blank look, she adds "We can wear disguises."

It doesn't take long for Brenda to convince her she'll be unrecognisable, especially when Sam clocks the clobber pulled out of the boot. Although thoughts of wearing a black balaclava and dark grey overalls in 35°C have her sweat glands increasing production in anticipation. Finally kitted out, not even Sam's own mother would know her.

Creeping her way up the stairs after Brenda, Sam wipes more sweat out of her eyes. A burst of female laughter from off to their right somewhere, indicates the direction they'll be taking.

They 'Pink Panther' their way down a narrow hallway, stopping outside a four-panel mahogany door at the end. Brenda turns the door handle in minuscule increments, with time slowing to match, then inches the door open enough to jam her head into the room. As she swings the door wide and tiptoes right into it, Sam freezes. Only when Brenda turns and beckons her to come in too, does Sam start moving forward again. She's creeping for the door and is about to ask what's going on, but Brenda puts a finger to her lips, visible through the mouth cut-out of her balaclava.

She makes it into the room in time to hear Janey say, "Come on, baby, let's turn things up a bit," before cranking the volume knob on a boom box as far as it will go. It wails loudly in response, drowning out any creaking floorboards or heavy breathing.

Looking properly into the room, Sam's glad of the wall of sound that stops her gasp being audible to Salami Boy. Not that he would have heard her; he's out of it. He's hog tied to a brass bed that looks to be original to the building, is starkers and seems happy to see everyone despite a skinful of paint stripper.

Standing at the back of the room next to Maria, Sam can feel sweat tickling her back; droplets running its length before hiding deep between her cheeks. She probably doesn't even need a disguise – she's safe behind the wall of bright lights pointing at their captive.

The music staggering its way around the room stops Sam from hearing what Maria says to Janey, her partner in crime, but whatever it is has Maria laughing when she leaves the room. Leaning her head toward the open door, she can hear Maria is still laughing all the way down the stairs. It cuts out when a door slams below.

"What's the plan?" says Sam, right into Janey's ear.

Rather than shout an answer over Salami Boy, who is now

bellowing along to the music, Janey holds up a Polaroid camera and raises and lowers her eyebrows menacingly.

As the song ends, Salami Boy continues bellowing but now it's for the girls' company, rather than lyrics. Janey hands the camera to Brenda and picks up a bottle of "no more paint" and a glass, and sashays over to the bed.

A couple more shots have him singing and gyrating on the bed again, causing his erection to bounce in time to the music. This has Sam giggling nervously and Brenda howling with laughter behind the muffle of her hand.

Even with this racket going on, Sam can hear feet thundering up the stairs, accompanied by shrill, girlish laughter. It doesn't sound like Maria, whose voice is deep and sultry. She pops her head out of the door and immediately has to jump to one side to avoid being trampled by a small gaggle of gay men. Seeing Salami Boy spread out in all his glory, the gaggle's laughter turns to shrieks of joy. Maria, who's followed them in, is holding a large bowl of whipped cream with a spatula standing firm in the middle.

Janey looks at the three brightly-dressed men peeking through the bars at the end of the bed with the eagerness of five-year-olds, checking out an exhibit at a petting zoo. "Once I told them what was going on, there was no way they weren't going to be part of the action." She walks over and hands the bowl to them along with some instructions.

Sam doesn't hear what's said, but doesn't need to. The look of delight on the faces of the three men says it all. After an initial scuffle that is only missing handbags, one of the men, who Sam has now identified as Brian, holds the bowl high above his head and squeals in triumph. Walking away from the bed, he takes the spatula and licks some cream off the end. "Ooh, yuck."

"What?" says Janey, a frown marring her beautiful face.

"No vanilla essence."

"Oh, for goodness sake, it's a prop, not a bloody condiment," says the gay man called Gary.

Brian sighs dramatically. "I suppose so." Making his way around the side of the bed, he pauses before slapping a spatula's worth of whipped cream smack bang on top of Salami Boy's dancing dong. The captive's mouth curls into a leer before his eyes open languidly and he looks up at Janey who's now at the head of the bed. Confusion clouds his face when he sees her hands are empty. His gaze swings to the other side of the bed where Maria now stands, also empty-handed. He looks farther down the bed and spots Brian lasciviously cleaning the spatula with his tongue. All hell breaks loose.

Salami Boy fights hard to free himself, arching up off the bed and screaming obscenities. "Dang, those are good knots," says Brenda, to Sam.

After a particularly hard wrench, Salami Boy passes out. He's not looking so perky now, in any department.

"Smile," says Brenda, ready to take a photo. Her voice is gruff to disguise it. She has stayed at the end of the room.

"Ooh, hang on, I don't think this is my good side." Gary flips his head the other way and sucks his cheeks in for a gamin effect.

"Oh, for god's sake, you don't have a good side," snipes Pip, the third of the gay trio, from his spot on the other side of Salami Boy's genitals.

Brian adds another liberal dollop of cream to Salami Boy's crotch; the captive's eyes snap wide open and he's blinded by the flash going off.

"What the hell?" he roars.

"Smile," they all chorus.

"What the hell are you fags up to?"

"Hmmm, well, we've changed our tune, haven't we?" lisps Gary, camping it up.

"Yes, you've been insatiable. My bum's killing me," adds Pip.

"No way," screams Salami boy, thrashing around wildly.

Realising he's not getting anywhere with the happy trio, he turns his venom on Janey and Maria. Sam's never heard such vicious words aimed at women. Salami Boy promises pain and lots of it.

A look of cold loathing settles on Maria's face and when Salami Boy's rant degenerates into muttered oaths and threats, she says. "Gary, Brian, a nipple each for the next shot."

"Ooh, teeth or fingers?'" says Gary, a look of anticipation on his face.

"I think fingers might be safer," says Maria, looking at Salami Boy, who's once again thrashing as much as his restraints will allow.

Brenda is about to take the next photo when Gary puts up his non-nipple-tweaking hand. "Make-up, I need make-up." His voice is overly dramatic and very Hollywood.

Sam's sure Salami Boy's going to break free any second; he's straining hard against the ropes. It's not until her back bangs into the window frame that she realises she's even moved.

Pip grabs the bowl and using the spatula smears cream across both his and a surprised Gary's chin, although it's not long before Gary starts to giggle too. Not to be left out, Brian juts his chin out for some 'make-up' of his own.

'Oh, that's great,' rumbles Brenda.

The flash going off coincides with Gary's tongue snaking out to collect some of the cream off his chin. "Ooh, I think Brian's right, you should have added a dash of vanilla. It tastes so flat."

"For goodness sake, this isn't a bloody cooking show," says Janey.

Salami Boy renews his thrashing and is rewarded with a smack from the spatula. Cream splatters in all directions and his now limp member pokes its head through the mound of cream.

"Doesn't it look so cute nestled there?" says Pip, lifting the flaccid appendage with the spatula and flicking it from side to side. This has the effect of it losing some of its limpness much to the horror of Salami boy and the delight of Pip, who increases the speed of the spatula.

"You like boys, do you?' says Janey, archly, unable to hide a smirk.

Salami Boy's expression quickens from angry to something a hell of a lot scarier. "I'm going to get you for this, you bitch!" He turns his face to include Maria in his threats. "You have to sleep some time. I know where you both live."

"Now, now. Play nicely," says Pip.

Salami Boy's gaze narrows as he glares at Pip "And you can sod off and all, ya turd burglar."

This insult earns him an extra-hard smack with the spatula. Pip then holds it over Salami Boy's scrotum waiting for the opportunity to give it another whack.

"Yes, play nicely, or these lovely pictures will find their way onto the notice board at your rugby club!" says Brenda gruffly, flapping a handful of Polaroids in Salami Boy's direction before slipping them into the pocket of her overalls.

Leaving Salami Boy to the tender ministrations of the others, Brenda and Sam scarper. It's not until they're a block away that Sam feels safe enough to remove her balaclava. She uses it to wipe the sweat off her face. "God, I hope that's the last I'll see of him."

"Yeah, I bloody hope so, 'cause after that there's no way you can go to the pigs ..." Brenda trails off.

22

Sam's bed is strewn with fabrics of every colour and texture but when she tries focusing on them they swirl together like paisley. Sighing raggedly, she starts stuffing the material into a large carry bag.

She's finishing up when Brenda bellows from the front steps. "Sam, ya taxi's here."

"Be. Right. Out!"

Hurrying out of the front door with the bulging bag slung over one shoulder, Sam's brought up short by Brenda who's hogging the top step, painting her toenails. Inching her way past, Sam's lip curls unbidden when she spots the gangrenous shade of green.

"Don't let the little bugger bite you," mumbles Brenda. She's scrunched over in an attempt to look as closely as possible at her toenails.

"If he does, he'll be getting it right back." Sam snaps her teeth together and Brenda's laughter follows her down the path. Shutting the gate, she turns but instead of a beaten up Ford she's faced with a late-model, silver Mercedes. Next to it stands a guy in a suit that shrieks "tax audit".

He looks to be in his thirties, over six foot and doesn't look to have a spare ounce on him, but he's not muscle-bound either. Sam thinks he's cute but it's as though he's made a conscious effort to blend. The bean-counter suit is middle of the road; not too flash, not too cheap. The white shirt could headline a bleach commercial; the dark grey tie that bisects it is perfectly matched to the suit. His black, round-toed shoes have been polished to a see-up-skirts level while his hair hangs product-free from a straight, side parting.

He opens the back door with a fluid swing, revealing the car's dark interior.

She baulks. "Mrs Courtenay said she'd send a taxi. Who are you?"

"I'm her taxi service."

"You're joking."

"Does it look like it?" he says, with a face that could sell you a full house even if all he had was a pair of threes. "If you'd like me to be more authentic I can close the door, get in and beep the horn impatiently."

"No, we're cool, but no politics or sport."

"As you wish." He gestures to the inside of the car.

She takes the hint and throws her bag of fabrics across the leather-clad back seat, causing him to grimace. She follows the bag in and the door is clicked shut after her before the driver walks around and gets behind the wheel.

Sam's heart thumps double time when all the doors lock and she's forced back in her seat when he floors it. After all the white glove treatment of the car up until this point, it throws Sam – literally – when he takes the corner at the bottom of the hill without touching the brakes. Obviously, he's still a typical bloke underneath all that buttoned-down conservatism.

The journey passes in silence although when they turn into the property, she can't help a "whoa" of appreciation and a small sigh of relief. You just never knew, did you? Stranger danger and all that.

There's an impeccably trimmed hedge spanning the front of the property, although she notices it's backed-up by a utilitarian hurricane wire fence, so close in places as to be part of the foliage. The car drums its way up a dark-grey, general issue gravel driveway that's considerably noisier than the more grandiose white gravel that's ubiquitous at these places. You'd never be able to drive in here on the sly.

Sam watches the borders on both sides of the driveway slide by, her eye occasionally straying to one of the large specimen trees dotted about the cricket-ground-striped lawn that spreads out behind the hedge. She spots at least three young gardeners seemingly hard at work.

The car breaks through the foliage and into a large open area in front of the house. Actually, there's no greenery of any kind near it and it stands clean and proud on the plot as though any weeding has been completed using Agent Orange.

The Mercedes creeps to a halt at the front door.

"Shouldn't you be dropping me around the back?" says Sam, in an I-don't-want-to-get-blamed-for-your-screw-up tone.

"I was asked to drop you at the front."

Once out of the car, she looks up at the large, wooden house with its wide verandas cuddling both the ground and first floors. Every door and window is flung wide open, making the place more like a pavilion than a house. Any woodwork visible between the openings sports warm cream paint, with trims of dark burgundy. The overall effect is crisp, but welcoming.

Mrs Courtenay waits regally at the top of the steps, affording Sam her first proper look at the woman since Sapphire's birthday party. Mrs Courtenay stands tall and strong in an outfit that screams quality. The white top has three-quarter sleeves and there's a blue and white striped jumper draped casually over her shoulders. Below that sit dark blue, wide-leg pants. Sam comes to a halt at Mrs Courtenay's footwear.

Sneakers! I want to be just like her when I'm in my seventies.

"Hello, Samantha." Mrs Courtenay holds her hands out to Sam who's still making her way up the wide wooden steps. Sam reaches the top with her hand already extended for the anticipated shake. Instead, it's given a reassuring squeeze by a pair of warm, smooth hands, the product of regular manicures.

"Please, call me Sam. Only my mum calls me Samantha … and that's usually when she thinks I'm up to something." She steps up onto the veranda.

"Right, Sam it is. Please come in."

The house couldn't be more different from the others Sam's visited. The solid oak panelling lining the foyer has been polished to a golden shine, so that rather than being dark, it glows with inner warmth. Sam's eyes roam skyward and, sure enough, there hangs the de rigueur chandelier, although rather than the size of a cooker with enough crystal to keep time on a million analogue watches, it's a modest affair with a few crystal droplets hanging from each of the five lights.

It's the staircase that gobsmacks Sam. Rather than being an ostentatious monstrosity of marble, wrought iron and gold leaf, it appears serviceable and designed to simply get you from one floor to the next. Intricately carved spindles support a balustrade that looks perfect for sliding down if the dings and scratches that mar its surface are anything to go by. A Turkish-inspired carpet runs up the middle of the wide, round-edged treads; dark, brass rods bolted to the inside of each step keep it tightly in place.

Even though she can see the parquet floor herringbones its way into the rooms leading off both sides of the foyer, Sam starts removing her shoes.

"Don't worry about those, dear."

"Are you sure?"

"Absolutely. Come, let's sit in the front room." Mrs Courtenay glides into a room off to their right. "Make yourself comfortable and I'll ring for tea." Picking up a small bell from the round side table beside her chair, she gives it a little shake. She puts it back down, and the gentle tinkle stops with an abrupt *clunk*.

Sam drops slack-jawed onto a large, comfortable sofa covered in faded damask. Her gaze roves around the light-filled room, through the open windows and doors and out into the garden. A soft breeze and perfume from the many vases of flowers dotted around the room make it feel garden-like inside too.

"Right, that's all settled. Shall we get underway?"

"Sure." Sam pulls her attention away from the room and retrieves the fabrics from her bag, before laying them out on the polished, mahogany coffee table in front of her.

"I like this one." Mrs Courtenay holds up a sample of steel grey silk and rubs it between her thumb and forefinger. "Too good for Monty, though. He'd ruin it in five seconds flat."

"What about this?" Sam hands over a square of black leatherette. "It's, ah, very robust."

"Yes. I think you're right." Mrs Courtenay tugs the plasticky fabric first one way and then the other. "Definitely Monty-proof."

Sam is retrieving her sketch pad and pencils from her large handbag when the taxi driver arrives with afternoon tea on a tray almost equal in size to the coffee table. She doubts she'd be strong enough to lift it even when it wasn't chocker with tea paraphernalia and tiny homemade cakes.

"Thank you, Stephen, that's lovely." Mrs Courtenay makes room by sweeping the fabrics to one side.

Stephen places the tray on the table. The precision with which he does this is testament to the strength that lies beneath his mild exterior. Sam knows that if she'd tried the same manoeuvre, someone would have ended up wearing something.

"Milk?"

In answer to Sam's nod, Mrs Courtenay pours some from a small silver jug into an ornate rose-patterned cup, sitting on a matching saucer. Sam automatically says, "When," to convey the desired level has been achieved. Mrs Courtenay adds a similar amount of milk to another rose-patterned cup. "We'll wait a few minutes for it to brew. Rock cake?"

Sam shakes her head to avoid eating something that looks like it'll produce a bundle of crumbs. It will be traumatic enough as it is, managing the fragile cup and saucer. While they wait for the tea leaves to release their flavour, Mrs Courtenay makes small talk about the forthcoming party.

"Right, I'm sure that's ready now." Mrs Courtenay picks up the silver pot and pours tea into both their cups.

Sam's relieved to see the tea isn't crowding the lip of her cup. Using both hands, she picks up the cup and saucer, before moving them slowly over to her lap. She lowers them just as carefully onto her knee, keeping hold of the saucer with her left hand then picking up the eminently smashable cup with her right.

Taking a tentative sip of the brew, she's surprised at its rich, smoky flavour.

Mrs Courtenay sees Sam's surprised expression. "It's Lapsang Souchong."

"It's delicious." Sam takes another, larger mouthful.

Between sips of tea, they discuss possible outfits for Monty, settling on Darth Vader for the small terrier. Putting her cup and saucer to one side, Sam sketches furiously before holding the pad up for Mrs Courtenay to see. After a few adjustments, they're both happy with the final design.

"Right, I think that's everything. I'll ring for Stephen to take you home."

"Mrs Courtenay, there's one more thing."

"What's that, dear?"

"I need to take Monty's measurements."

"Oh dear, I hadn't thought about that." Her tone borders on anxious.

"Look, if he's having a nap I can come back."

Mrs Courtenay regards her strangely before calling the dog. She leaves Sam to walk out on to the front steps all the while calling the dog's name and even resorting to loud whistling. She's back inside the sitting room when Sam hears barking that gets louder and louder, attaining a crescendo when Monty charges into the room and straight through Mrs Courtenay's legs. Spotting Sam, the little Jack Russell changes course without slowing, screeching in a four-paw skid to a stop in front of her. He shakes violently, starting with his head and working in a tsunami action down to his tail. The brown splotches on his back blur and water flies in all directions.

"I'm so sorry, Sam, the little devil's been in the pool again."

Sam wipes some mud off her face. "Followed by a spot of gardening?"

Both she and Mrs Courtenay start to laugh at the same time. With each chuckle, the Chris-shaped knot in Sam's stomach loosens a little more. God, it feels good. They've subsided to the occasional snigger by the time Stephen comes in to collect the tray. On seeing the chaos, he says, in a deep, authoritative voice, "Monty, over here, now!" pointing to the spot beside his feet for emphasis. A few seconds later the dog is standing next to him, although it appears anything but chastised, judging by the delighted wagging of its tail.

"Stephen, be a dear and clean him up so Sam can take his measurements without getting any dirtier."

"Not a problem." He looks down at the little dog sitting next to his highly polished shoes and points at the back of the house.

The dog's butt stays firmly on the ground and Sam could swear it's smiling. Stephen glares down at it, the dog's smile slips, the tail stops wagging and it adopts a woebegone expression.

"It won't work, Monty," says Stephen, to the dog. "I know you too well."

Realising the jig is up, Monty jumps to his feet and jauntily trots off to the back of the house, leaving a trail of little muddy footprints in his wake.

23

*B*renda's still painting her toenails when Sam arrives home.

"How many coats have you got on? You'll be lucky if your shoes fit."

"Nah, I hated the other colour and started over. Weren't you wearing something different when you went out?"

"Yeah, I was." Sam starts to explain.

She doesn't get far into the story before Brenda holds up her hand. "Stop, I don't give a rat's arse. So … what's … the … mutt's … outfit …going … to … be?" Brenda's query comes out in time to the brush strokes as she paints one of her big toenails a bright, baboon-arse red.

"Darth Vader, complete with mask and light sabre."

"Classic, you could record deep breathing on a tape recorder and mount it on his back," says Brenda, cackling.

"Ripper idea! I'll see if Mrs Courtenay wants to spring for a Dictaphone, Monty's too small to lug a tape recorder around all night."

Brenda looks up at her with a flabbergasted expression, the polish dripping forgotten from the brush. "I wasn't serious."

177

"How'd it go with Mrs McGowan?" says Sam, when Jennie walks in the door later that afternoon.

"Well, she wouldn't let me any further than the kitchen and kept her eyes on me the whole time like she was expecting me to try for the cutlery."

"Bloody hell. How much did you get?"

"Half a dozen knives and a couple of spoons." Jennie's tone and eyebrows are a perfect Groucho Marx.

"Laaaaammmme," sings Sam.

"A hundred dollars." Jennie hands over a wad of fives that smell strongly of mothballs. The girls have set up a Doggs' Toggs account and bank all the money so they won't be tempted to spend it. Not that they could, with Mrs Farquhar having double knotted the purse strings.

"I managed to get a *Star Wars* book too," says Jennie, handing it to Sam.

"Fantastic. I'm thinking Storm Troopers for Mrs McGowan's lot."

"Princess Leia for Sapphire is a must."

"I wouldn't be brave enough to suggest anything else. I can get a pair of those doughnut things you use for putting your hair up in a bun and stick them on either side of her head."

They're flipping through the book assigning characters to the various dogs when the phone rings. "You'd better get that." Sam hasn't answered the phone since the night of Sapphire's birthday party and leaves it ringing when at home on her own.

"Hello," says Jennie.

Sam waits with breath held, absurdly hoping it's Chris.

"No, she's out, can I take a message." Jennie looks at her but taking in the optimism on Sam's face, she shakes her head.

Sam's hand pauses mid-knock. Does she want anything to do with this guy; he's more than borderline weirdo. He's seriously creeped her out on the few occasions she's had to pass him in the hallway and who the hell dresses like someone from Star Trek just to hang out their washing? That's not normal in anyone's book.

Damn, she wishes she knew someone else who could record Darth's trademark breathing for her. The girls had all tried and even though Brenda had come close, it still sounded like a woman having an asthma attack. Because the rest of the costume had turned out so well, she didn't want to let it down with a lame-arse soundtrack.

Focusing on the picture of Vader stuck crookedly below the large number 2 on the door, she takes a deep breath and knocks Darth on the head four times. Hearing no signs of life, Darth gets another beating, harder this time. Sam puts her ear to the door and is rewarded with the loud creaking of a staircase.

The door opens a sliver and she can see one of the weirdo's eyes examining her. His gaze snags on her chest and she has to fight the urge to fold her arms.

Who the hell's he expecting?

The door opens a little further to reveal two eyes, the rest of the face and a body type only achieved after years of non-activity.

"Yes?"

"I'm Sam from over the hall. I know this is going to sound strange, but I'm hoping you can record something for me."

"Record? Me?"

"Uh huh. I need a recording that sounds like Darth Vader and, well, because of this," Sam taps the picture on the door, "I was hoping you might be able to help."

She can't believe the transformation that takes place. He stands taller and sucks his gut in so hard it puckers the front of his T-shirt. Even his face changes.

"You've come to the right place." His voice is pure James Earl Jones and on seeing Sam's reaction, he laughs deeply, still in character.

She holds out the hand-held recorder to him. "If you could just do the breathing, that'd be perfect."

"I can do better than that." He hits the record button and launches into a perfect imitation of Darth Vader.

A tape's-worth of Vader later, he hands the recorder back to a stunned Sam. "That okay?"

"Yeah. More than I could have hoped for," says Sam, coming out of the trance she'd slipped into while listening to him record Darth's exact breathing, interspersed with every famous quote from the movie.

Task over, the guy's face droops to normal and his body deflates, with the exception of the hard-on, straining against the zipper of his jeans. He closes the door on Sam leaving her to dwell on what he'll get up to now. She doubts he'll even need a poster of Princess Leia to achieve the money shot.

The sewing machine *tink-tink-tinks* its way through the outfit Sam is working on, soon to feature in the weird and wonderful world of Canine *Star Wars*. "How are you going with Monty's outfit?" Jennie looks at the corner behind her with its ever-increasing pile of C-3PO, Chewbacca, Obi Wan Kenobi and R2-D2 outfits.

"Bloody brilliant. Mrs Courtenay bought me a Dictaphone. Listen to this." Sam holds it up and presses the play button.

There's a whole lot of Darth Vader heavy breathing then, "The force is strong in this one". It keeps repeating phrases until the tape runs out.

"Who'd you get to record it?"

"That weird guy from upstairs. He's creepy though – kept touching his 'light sabre' while he was recording it."

"Eeeuw. I'll be glad when we've got enough plastic to complete the outfits for Mrs McGowan's lot. I've never eaten so much ice cream in my life." Jennie is finishing up yet another bowl in their bid to empty enough tubs to make articulated white armour for six small storm troopers. "Heck, is that the time, I'd better get ready." Jennie takes her empty bowl back into the kitchen and rinses it.

"Where are you off to?"

"Just out with mates from work. You should come too. Have a break from the sewing."

"Another time, maybe." Taking a deep breath, Sam shakes the stiffness out of her shoulders and mentally prepares herself to start on the Storm Trooper outfits.

Only these six outfits to go, you can do it.

It doesn't take much chopping up of ice cream containers for her to realise she'll need to empty another couple of tubs to have enough plastic for Fifi McGowan's outfit.

Chubby little mutt.

Jennie comes up behind her when she's up to her waist in the chest freezer.

"You sure you won't come? It won't be late a late one and the guys from work are super friendly," says Jennie, down into the frozen void.

"Nah, thanks. I'm not in the mood." Sam's reply echoes back from amongst the blocks of rock-hard peas and lumps of freezer-burned meat. Trust the blasted ice cream to be right at the bottom of the damn thing.

"If you're sure. Catch ya later."

Sam's transferring ice cream from the second tub into a bucket when Brenda walks into the kitchen.

She pauses briefly in her scooping. "Hi, there."

"What the hell are you doing?"

"Needed more plastic for Storm Trooper outfits and couldn't face eating any more ice cream, even if it is double chocolate chip."

"Hell, yeah, I think we've done enough already." Brenda gives her bum a good double squeeze.

"What the hell, it doesn't matter anyway."

"You should go for old blokes like me, they're so desperate they don't care what shape you're in."

"No, thanks." Sam puts the empty ice cream tub in the sink with the first one and turns the hot water tap full bore on them.

"Let me know if you change your mind. Hook up with the right bloke and you sure as hell wouldn't need to worry about making all this clobber for scabby dogs. You could just ask for the airfares." Brenda fingers a heavy gold chain around her wrist.

"Thanks, but I think I prefer my way." Sam turns off the tap and scrubs furiously at the plastic containers with the dish brush.

"Have it your way, but just so you know, this here's a return trip to Paris." Brenda deliberately jangles her bracelet all the way to her bedroom.

"This here's a return trip to Paris", mimics Sam, brutally stabbing holes through pieces of plastic with a nail so she can sew them together by hand. They're too thick to go through the sewing machine.

Her hands fall still in the middle of the task. Maybe Brenda's right. The chunky gold bracelet isn't the first gift Sam's seen her flashing about. And when it's all over, she sells the goodies, meaning Brenda's bank balance is probably a hell of a lot healthier than Jennie's, Sam's and the Doggs' Toggs' accounts combined. But Sam doesn't think she could be mercenary enough to get past the shuddering heebies at the thought of old-guy sex.

Sam folds the last *Star Wars* outfit neatly and puts it on top of the pile of costumes stacked in the wicker basket sitting in the middle of the dining room table. Thank god Jennie's helping deliver this lot, although it will still take them a few trips and the best part of the day.

"You ready?" says Sam, through the partially closed door of Jennie's room.

"Hang on a second, don't come in," yells Jennie. "Just give me five minutes."

A few moments later Jennie backs out of her room and into the lounge. She spins around and deposits a pile of paper and ribbon on the coffee table in front of Sam. "Ta da!" says Jennie, her arms wide. "Official Doggs' Toggs' wrapping paper and tags."

Sam lifts one of the little bone-shaped tags. These feature the Doggs' Toggs' logo and have the words "This outfit belongs to ...." handwritten in beautiful copperplate. Putting the tag down, she picks up a sheet of the sandy-coloured tissue and looks closely at the all-over pattern of little dark-brown doggie footprints.

"Jennie, these are incredible! Thank you so much." Sam stands and hugs her friend hard. Both for the gift and all the other support Jennie is giving her.

"You're welcome." A pink flush of embarrassment works its way up Jennie's face like a Tequila Sunrise. "Let's get wrapping this lot." She bustles away.

Not letting Jennie simply brush away her thanks, Sam adds, "I do appreciate it though."

It takes close to two hours to personalise the labels and wrap all the little outfits to Jennie and Sam's exacting standards, but they do look brilliant. She knows the wrapping won't last two minutes in the hands of an eighty-year-old determined to see their dog's new outfit, but it's a nice touch and adds to the professionalism of the Doggs' Toggs' brand.

But they're now running late and Sam can imagine these same octogenarians hopping from foot to foot, anxious to see the outfits packed and ready on the dining table next to her.

"Hey, Brenda, can we borrow the car?" yells Sam, over the music blaring from the new stereo in Brenda's room; more than likely a gift from one of the hopping octos' husbands. "We need to deliver the outfits and it'll take bloody ages on foot."

"Even better, I'll drive." Brenda comes out of her room. "I want to check out some of these hovels."

"You won't be allowed in."

"That's cool, I'm happy to look from the outside."

"If you're sure?" Sam doubts Brenda's attention span is up to waiting more than five minutes in the car.

24

The last delivery of the day is at Mrs McGowan's. "I can't wait to see her face when she clocks the storm trooper outfits," says Sam. "Next on the left, and then it's number 14. Park outside."

"Turning," says Brenda. "Ten, twelve, here we go."

"Okay, park here." Sam points at the kerb. As the car keeps rolling she adds, "The kerb, here!" pointing repeatedly for emphasis.

Brenda turns and grins. "Ain't gonna happen."

Sam cringes mentally. "Well, at least promise you'll behave." The lack of commitment in Brenda's smirk doesn't bode well.

The massive overhanging jacaranda trees make it dark after the road and it takes a few seconds for their eyes to adjust to the gloom. This is the first time Sam and Jennie have come in through this entrance; it's a different experience from the small side gate and the footpath that snakes its way through the outer edges of the garden to the back of the house.

The car creeps down the driveway, soon filling with the smell of damp vegetation from the shadowed areas on either side. The trees crowding overhead amplify the sound of tyres on gravel. Leaves rustle in the breeze but obviously don't dare drop given none mar the raked perfection of the drive. Eventually the car pulls into a huge open area in front of the house, leaving the living tunnel behind them, dark and foreboding.

"Sheesh, I can't believe the size of this place," says Brenda. "Whoa, it's even got a turret. Who does she think she is? Rapunzel?"

Sam has to agree, the place is ridiculous for a couple in their seventies to rattle around inside, even with six French Bulldogs. The overall design is less spacious and gracious than it is ostentatious and voracious. Still, it's old enough that Sam can't blame Mrs McGowan for the design. The white stonework is blinding in the early afternoon sun; it's like this every time she visits, as though repainted weekly. The mansion is guarded by huge columns that stand sentry at regular intervals on all sides. One thing's for sure, the McGowan's will never come up short for the electricity bill.

"Drive around there." Sam points to the left of the massive house in front of them. "We need to at least park out back." She's bending over, putting the six storm trooper outfits into a carry bag, and doesn't notice until too late that Brenda has pulled up at right next to the front steps. "Hell's teeth, you can't park here."

Brenda's cranking on the handbrake when Mrs McGowan rushes down the front steps. Her wig bounces with each drop to the next step. Sam knows it's a hairpiece because, even though beautifully made, it contains more hair than a woman in her seventies would have on her *entire* body even if you included her chin. It's also dark auburn. Sam suspects the only grey in the whole thing is on the manufacturer's label sewn into the netting holding that abundant mane together.

"You can't park that rusting heap there." Mrs McGowan's eyebrows are raised in astonishment. Actually, this is how they always are, it's how they're drawn on. Mrs McGowan is enduringly amazed.

"Why not?" says Brenda, indignantly.

"Move it. Now!" Mrs McGowan points repeatedly to side of the house.

"Okay, okay, keep your knickers on."

"Sam, who is this person?" Mrs McGowan crosses the cardigan of her twinset firmly over her bosom.

Sam leans in front of Brenda. "Ah, Mrs McGowan, this is Brenda, our flatmate. It's her car."

Never again is Brenda coming on a delivery run.

"I could have sodding answered you know, I'm sitting right here," growls Brenda straight into Sam's ear.

"Well, you can't park there, we might have company. You'll have to move it around the back," orders Mrs McGowan.

"Jeez, okay."

Satisfied the riff-raff is moving, Mrs McGowan turns with a reel of tartan skirt and heads back up the stairs. The auburn curls once again spring into life.

"Brenda!" warns Sam. "Don't even think about it."

"It's all right. I'll behave," says Brenda, sweetly, before moving the car around to the back at the slowest speed she's managed all day. She pulls to a sedate stop in the middle of a turning circle in front of the enormous triple car garage.

"Happy now?" she says, her snark level set at ten.

"*Please* promise you'll behave while you wait for us," pleads Sam, before getting out the car. The lack of response doesn't instil confidence.

"Do you trust her?" says Jennie, quietly to Sam as they wait at the backdoor of the Tara-styled house.

"No, but there's not much we can do about it right now."

It takes forty-five minutes to fit all the little dogs with their articulated armour and Sam worries Brenda will have ditched them. She's relieved to see the Toyota still sitting in the same spot when they're let out the back door.

"Bloody hell" says Sam, when they arrive next to the car. "Where is she?"

"She could be anywhere. Does Mrs McGowan have a son?"

The rumble of a male voice and giggling from over the hedge that frames one side of the parking area answers their questions.

"Never mind a son. Heaven help any males back there over fifty." Sam eyes a path cutting through the chunky hedge. They put their stuff in the car and go in search of Brenda.

They find her resplendent in her underwear on a sun lounger next to the pool, as good as naked, her bra see-through after a dip. She's chatting away to a man in the lounger next to her. His face is turned away from them, but the lean muscular legs and deep tan look to be those of a gardener getting in a sneaky smoke-o. Unaware they're behind his chair he puts a pen down on the table next to him and slides a piece of paper into the pocket of his shorts.

"Brenda?" says Sam, politely, unsure who her companion is.

"Hi, guys. Come and meet Martin McGowan," says Brenda, playing the gracious hostess.

They move forward so they can see his face and are shocked that it mismatches his legs by about thirty-five years.

"Hi," say both Sam and Jennie, weakly.

"Hello, girls," says Martin, absently. His glassy stare firmly locked onto Brenda's breasts.

"Sam? Are you through here?" Mrs McGowan's voice warbles through the hedge.

"Bloody hell." Martin springs to his feet with remarkable speed for his years. He doesn't get far once upright, starting off in several panicky directions before returning to his original spot and then freezing.

"Now we know how he gets the muscle tone," whispers Jennie to Sam.

"Move it." Sam picks up the small pile of clothes from beside the lounger and shoves them at Brenda. "If she finds you like this she'll go frigging ape." Any sense of decorum Sam had at being in front of Martin has fled with Mrs McGowan being a far more formidable foe than her husband.

"Sam, there you are." The rest of the sentence dies on Mrs

McGowan's lips when she spies Brenda struggling out of the sun lounger still only dressed in her undies.

With his wife's attention momentarily caught, Martin attempts escape again.

"Martin! Don't even think about it."

"No, dear."

"Out, now!" screeches Mrs McGowan at the girls, pointing in the direction of the car.

"Jeez, anyone would think I pissed in the sodding pool."

"Stow it, Brenda." Sam hustles her to the car while Jennie trails behind picking up dropped articles of clothing. Sam opens the driver's door and shoves Brenda in and is startled when she rockets straight back out again.

"Now what?" Sam manages to force through her clenched teeth.

"The vinyl's hot, I'll burn my arse."

"For God's sake, get dressed." While Brenda is putting her clothes back on, Mrs McGowan is giving Martin a right dressing-down on the other side of the hedge. The accusations leave the girls in no doubt that today's conduct is a common occurrence.

Settled in the car, the look on Brenda's face has Sam warning, "Brenda, don't," for all the good it does. Brenda pops the clutch, causing gravel to fly hard against the garage doors and Jennie and Sam to sink low in their seats. Sam hopes Mrs McGowan is too distracted to notice. Brenda hits the horn when they're in the middle of the tunnel of trees and doesn't let up until they drive through the front gates. She then waves wildly out the window before completing a burn-out on the road outside.

Never again is Sam going to let Brenda within a bull's roar of any of her clients. That's if she can even count Mrs McGowan as a client. Hopefully the woman won't put a stop on the cheque she's just handed over.

25

With underwear, make-up and hair sorted for Monty's party, Sam pushes the hangers to one side in her wardrobe and spelunks her way into the far recesses, pulls out her interview dress and drags it on. The outfit's a bit funereal but at least she'll be a lot less conspicuous than she was dressed as a bloody cat.

She pulls the black patent heels out of their box, the scorch marks from the lamp fire still visible on the soles from the night she'd – almost – gone out to dinner with Chris. Before she'd found out about *the other woman*.

Sam slips a foot into the first shoe, and then elevates herself into her new standing height before slipping on the other. Satisfied she's looking as good as she can, she goes to check on Jennie. Putting her head around Jennie's bedroom door, Sam finds her friend struggling to zip up her navy dress.

"Sam, can you help me with this?" Jennie's arms windmill – first one way and then the other – trying in vain to grab the zipper that's halfway up her back.

"At least I'm not pinning on a blasted tail this time." Sam zips up the dress before neatly tucking in the pull tab at the top. "Where's Brenda?"

"I'm pretty sure she's out with the same guy she went out with on Monday night."

191

"A *second* date! The guy must be loaded. Where'd she meet him?"

"Don't know, she wouldn't say. She was super cagey."

"Maybe she's embarrassed that he's too young?"

It takes a second for Jennie to process this, but her laughter soon joins that of Sam's.

"God, I hope tonight is more fun than the last party," says Sam, when their taxi joins a queue of cars up to the front of the house.

"I was surprised when you said yes to the invitation."

"It didn't want to, but Mrs Farquhar said it's good for business."

Sam's leaning between the front seats to pay their driver when she recognises the woman getting out of the Bentley in front of them. Pulling back quickly, she drops the money she'd been about to hand him and ducks behind his seat. She looks over at Jennie who's hiding behind the passenger seat, obviously having spotted Mrs McGowan too.

"Do you think she saw us?" whispers Sam.

"If she'd seen us, I think we'd know by now," Jennie whispers back.

"I'd rather not start the evening with an ear bashing about Brenda."

"Wonder where Mr McGowan is?" Jennie risks a peek.

"Probably faked a heart attack or rabies," says Sam, snorting.

By the time Sam gathers up the money off the floor, she's relieved to see Mrs McGowan and her vanguard of small storm troopers disappearing through the front door.

"Coast's clear," she says to Jennie, who's still hiding.

The girls make their way up the front steps, across the front veranda and into the foyer. They shrug off their jackets, toss them at the coat-check man and head in the opposite direction to Mrs McGowan, straight into the middle of what looks like a scene from *Star Wars*.

"For gawd's sake," is out of Sam's mouth before she can stop herself.

This elicits a response of, "Language, young lady," from an Obi Wan Kenobi next to her.

"You've got to be joking," wails Jennie.

Mrs Courtenay comes up to greet them. "Girls, you didn't come in costume."

"Sorry, Princess Leia. After the last debacle, we're rather gun-shy on the costume front," says Sam.

"Never mind, we've got some spares that you're more than welcome to wear."

Mrs Courtenay takes them upstairs to the bedroom Sam had changed in before. Several different *Star Wars*-inspired outfits lie on the bed in readiness. "I didn't twig until too late, that of course Princess Leia is just about the only woman in the whole movie unless you count Luke's Auntie. And who on earth is going to want to dress like her?"

"I don't even remember her," says Sam.

"Exactly, the woman had no dress sense whatsoever." Mrs Courtenay hands a voluminous, long, white dress and necklace to Sam and a tan and cream dress to Jennie.

The girls put the outfits on and recognize that while they're both Princess Leia, they're her from different times in the movie. Jennie is the Princess in her caught-in-the-trash-compactor-on-the-death-star phase, while Sam is lucky enough to be dressed like Princess Leia at the awards ceremony finale. Sam is happy her costume requires she simply put her hair up on top rather than in buns on either side of her head. Jennie, because of her chin-length hair, has no option other than don a hair band with a couple of horsehair bun fillers stuck to it.

"Where's Monty?" says Sam, when they're making their way back downstairs.

"Most likely lying prostrate under the buffet by now."

"That's a shame, I wanted to see him in his outfit," says Jennie.

They reach the bottom of the stairs and Mrs Courtenay

turns to them. "Well, I must away and play the gracious hostess. There's a buffet in the morning room and there'll be dancing starting soon in the ballroom." These instructions are accompanied by graceful indications of direction.

"We'll be fine," says Sam. "Thanks again for the costumes."

"Yes, thank you," chimes in Jennie to their retreating hostess.

"Come, let's eat." Sam spins on her heel and marches into what must be the morning room.

"Whoa," says Jennie. "Hope you're hungry."

The girls gawp at the tables that run down each side of the room. They're bowing slightly in the middle under the weight of food spread out along their lengths.

As they wander through the maze of downstairs rooms, they feel they're part of a cheer squad – nearly every woman at the party is dressed as Princess Leia. A few brave souls wear Imperial Guards outfits that are a lot skimpier than those in the movie and far more revealing than should be worn by any woman in her seventies. No matter how much tennis she plays.

Praise is heaped on Sam for her costumes, especially Mrs McGowan's small squad of Imperial Storm Troopers in their adapted ice cream tubs and for Monty as Darth Vader, although they've yet to spot the small terrier.

"Sam, I am disappointed in you," says Mrs Farquhar, coming up to stand next to Sam.

"What's wrong? I thought you were happy with Sapphire's costume?" Sam looks down at the poodlely Princess Leia sitting next to Mrs Farquhar.

Mrs Farquhar looks pointedly at Sam and Jennie's outfits. "Yes, but it's hardly original is it?"

"Sapphire is definitely the only dog here dressed as Princess Leia, I made sure of that," says Sam, defensively.

"Do try harder next time to ensure Sapphire's outfit is one of a kind," says Mrs Farquhar, annoyance dripping from every syllable. She straightens the buns on either side of her head before walking off with a haughty, "Come Sapphire."

"Bloody hell, just when I think she's starting to thaw, she sideswipes me like that." Sam shakes her head in amazement.

"Maybe you should make the costumes for the mothers, too," suggests Jennie.

Sam's eyes widen, her eyebrows raise. They both break into the opening bars of Pink Floyd's 'Money' dead on time, before cracking up with laughter.

Once the giggles have subsided, they take a glass of pink punch from a large bowl. They clink their glasses together and drink to being filthy rich.

"Whoa!" Jennie breathes out through her mouth.

Sam, likewise, is panting like John-John after a big walk, in hopes of cooling the alcoholic burn. "Bloody hell, you could take nail polish off with this stuff."

They nod in agreement and put the still reasonably full glasses down on the nearest flat, unpainted, surface.

"No way I'm gonna risk getting hammered in the middle of this lot."

Jennie looks at a group of old Leias who are glugging back punch like it's the last night on the death star. "Although they're all coping okay."

"Come on, let's get some food before all the good stuff is gone," says Sam.

"Bloody hell."

This language is so out of character that Sam's head swings toward Jennie in surprise. "You have got to stop hanging out with Brenda so much."

At a lack of reaction, she follows Jennie's gaze and spots the reason for the Brenda-like outburst. She'd know that immaculately coifed blonde hair anywhere. It's been featuring in her dreams for weeks.

Sam's rooted in place as she stares wide-eyed at the bitch she's lost Chris to. She's sure the pure venom must be showing on her face and so is surprised when Blondie sees her and smiles broadly. Placing her index finger briefly in her mouth, Blondie draws a score line in the air in front of her.

Sam feels the heat rush to her face. "That cow!" She jerks

around to face Jennie. "I should wipe that smile off her face right now."

"Sam! You can't. We should leave," says Jennie, no longer channelling Brenda.

"Oh, my god!"

"What?"

"If she's here, then that means Chris must be, too!" Sam bolts for the nearest set of French doors, worried she's about to throw up, pass out or both.

She's leaning over the railing that enfolds the veranda gasping and staring out into the darkness, when Jennie catches up.

"Are you all right?"

"No," says Sam, trying to settle her breathing. "I feel all spinny."

"Here, sit down." Jennie steers her backwards and onto a wicker couch. "Breathe nice and slow." Jennie rubs Sam's back and this small act is enough to start the tears.

So much for kidding herself she was over him.

As a Wookie and an Imperial Guard walk out onto the veranda, Sam twists away from them to hide her tears.

"C'mon, let's find somewhere a bit quieter." Jennie gets to her feet and pulls Sam upright.

They walk away from the couple and find a patio area around the back of the house that's free of anyone else. It's beautifully lit with fairy lights strung over the gazebo and through the trees and underwater lights have the pool sparkling like a precious gem. The back of the house is alive with reflected ripples, but dead otherwise.

"What do you want to do?" says Jennie, once they're comfortable on a couple of loungers beside the pool.

"I'd like to go home, but I can't go back into the house to change looking like this." Sam's hands flutter up to frame her face.

"You stay put. I'll go find Mrs Courtenay and let her know we're leaving because you're not feeling well."

"But what about our stuff?"

"I can grab everything from upstairs and tell her we'll drop the outfits back tomorrow.

26

With Jennie gone, Sam slumps down and is wiping her eyes with the bottom of her dress, when she's startled by the sound of heavy breathing.

Monty crawls out from under the lounger and holds a paw out to her, just as the tape moves onto, "The force is strong in this one."

"Hey, there, Monty. How are you little guy?" Sam scratches him underneath the headpiece. The look on his face proves answer enough. "Here, let's give you a rest from all this." She removes the headpiece then undoes the clips down the back of his outfit. The last one has only just snapped free when Monty launches himself at the pool. He's makes it right out into the middle with a single joyous leap.

Sam is splashed a little and the water feels so good that she kicks off her shoes, gets up and wanders down to the curved steps at the end of the pool. Lifting the costume up around her knees, she steps down onto the wide top step. Monty dog-paddles over to join her, the splashing caused by his wagging tail helping her to cool down even more. "What am I going to do, eh, Monty?"

Sam absently walks back across the curved step. Monty follows, tight on her heels and up to his undercarriage in water. She swings around and starts the return journey.

Monty doesn't. She overbalances and does a headlong tumble into the pool.

Monty propels himself in tight circles around her, yapping delightedly, his tail wagging so hard that Sam thinks he'd be moving even if his little legs weren't powering away under the water. She tries standing but the bottom is beyond her reach. "You little rat bag, you tripped me on purpose," says Sam, spluttering. She's treading water when a shadow passes over her. Spinning around, she looks up. Damn, she's just been caught in the pool by Darth Vader.

"What on earth are you doing?" Darth's voice is metallic and hollow thanks to the voice modulator in the mask. He sounds the real deal.

"It was an accident, Monty tripped me." She continues to tread water but the weight of the costume is making it difficult to stay afloat and Monty isn't helping by trying to stand on her shoulders.

"Don't you think you should get out?"

"I'm *trying* to!" Sam kicks futilely at the costume that's wrapped itself tightly around her legs.

Darth holds his light sabre out to her. "Here, grab hold of this."

Grabbing onto it, Darth to pulls Sam slowly to the side of the pool, while Monty makes his way out and around to join her rescuer.

"Give me your hands," says Darth.

Sam grips his hands with all her strength and is nearly clear of the water when Monty gets caught up in her rescuer's legs and they all end up in the pool. Managing to claw her way to the surface, it's to find Darth has lost his mask and she's face-to-face with Chris. Any air left in her lungs whooshes out and she starts to sink again.

Chris grabs her and pulls her to the surface. Her lungs fill gratefully.

"Bloody hell, this cape is lethal." Chris ditches it, before swimming over to the steps with Sam and Monty in tow.

By the time they scramble out of the pool, Sam's breathing is laboured.

Chris leans over Sam who's lying face down. His hand rests lightly on her shoulder. "Are you okay?"

"I'm fine." She shrugs her shoulder to dislodge him.

"Doesn't sound like it to me."

"Shouldn't you be getting back to your *date*?"

"What *date*?"

Dragging herself up on her elbows so she can glare at him, Sam doesn't try keeping the bitterness out of her voice. "Oh, come on, I saw her myself." Her words echo stridently off the surrounding concrete surfaces.

"No, you didn't. You saw my little stepsister, Pita."

"Yeah, your stepsister, sure she is," says Sam, sinking back down to the paving.

"Hey, if you don't believe me, you can ask my grandmother, Milly." Chris struggles to his feet then bends down to drag her upright, something made difficult by the weight of her sodden costume.

"Milly?"

"Milly Courtenay?"

"Oh." The cogs in Sam's brain work overtime as she digests this snippet. "But that means ..." Sam's voice stutters to a halt. "But ..."

Arms crossed tightly over his chest, Chris raises his eyebrows.

Sam looks down at the sopping wet dress, moulded to her body and alarmingly see-through in places. "But I can't go in there like this. Jennie'll be back with my clothes soon."

"You might be waiting a while. I asked Mark to stall her."

"Well, I'm not going inside looking like this."

"Fine. I'll go get Milly so we can bloody sort this out once and for all." Chris drags his cape out of the pool, wrings it thoroughly and throws it over Sam's shoulders. "Don't you dare move."

"As if," says Sam indignantly, crossing the cape in front of her and marching over to plonk herself back down on one of the sun loungers.

She doesn't have long to stew before Chris is back, but rather than Milly, he's accompanied by Blondie. She feels even more bedraggled next to the immaculate Princess who is looking down at her, with a smugly superior smile.

"Go on, tell Sam who you are," prompts Chris.

"I'm a *close* family friend," simpers Blondie, her hand resting on Chris's chest in a proprietorial manner.

Chris removes her hand. "No. You're Pita, my little step-sister and a right-royal pain in the arse."

"We're not related though, are we? Well, not yet."

"But hang on," Sam struggles to her feet and looks at Pita. "What was all the scoring stuff about earlier?" At the blank look on the girl's face, Sam repeats the action putting her finger in her mouth, then scoring in mid-air.

"Oh, that," says Pita, innocently, "just having a little fun."

Sam is swamped with relief and annoyance in equal parts. Seeing Monty walk behind Pita, and then stand there and look up at her as if to say, "Go on, I dare you," Sam gives in to temptation. For a little girl, the princess makes a big splash.

"Not looking so clever now, are you?" says Sam, when Pita surfaces.

Chris is fighting not to smile. "I can't believe you did that."

"She had it coming." Sam glares at the girl clambering out of the pool and running soggily to the house.

"Yeah, she did, but we'd better scarper, because I can guarantee she's going straight inside to dob you in."

He takes Sam's hand and leads her away from the pool and into the dark. They stumble around the back of a potting shed and through undergrowth, until they're close to the side of the house, but still hidden.

Taking advantage of the dark, Sam blurts out, "I'm so, so sorry. I jumped to conclusions, I know that now. Please say you'll forgive me."

"You wait here and I'll go get your stuff." Chris ignores her apology but when he rubs his hands up and down her arms in response to her shivering, it gives Sam some hope. "Whereabouts are your clothes?"

"We left them in the back bedroom, to the right at the top of the stairs. My dress is the black one with the white collar." She leans closer to him. "I am so, so sorry. You have to believe me."

"Hmm," is his less than satisfying response. He leaves her side and races Kung Fu-style over to the house and monkeys his way up a trellis. Sam can hear him swearing and cursing the roses regularly before he disappears over a rail and into the house.

Sam waits, and waits, and waits.

What in god's name's keeping him?

The wet clothing chafes, she's getting colder by the second and she's not keen on standing in the undergrowth with bare feet. Who knew what creepy crawlies were lurking close by? Seeing movement on the upper veranda, she's relieved to see it's Chris, dressed in jeans and a T-shirt, climbing back down the trellis. He has a plastic bag firmly gripped in his teeth.

"Come on," he says, as he leads her back in the direction of the potting shed.

"I could just get changed here. No one will see me."

"Best if you go into the potting shed, you never know who's lurking in the bushes."

"There's no one else out here," says Sam, and immediately has this disproved by rustling foliage nearby. A gardener pops out from behind a bush. "Arrrgh." She attaches herself to Chris like a lamprey.

Chris unclasps Sam's death grip from his T-shirt. "Hey, Jack. You're working late."

"You know how it is," says the gardener, before disappearing back into the undergrowth.

Before she can voice any thoughts on gardeners still working at ten at night, Chris is leading her back the way they'd come earlier.

He opens the door of the potting shed for her and Sam's breath releases when he switches on a dim light. She'd been worried about heading into the dark in what would be creepy crawly Nirvana. Handing Chris his cape, Sam slips in another apology before closing the door. She wastes no time changing and is soon back out with her soaking wet Princess Leia outfit crammed into the plastic bag along with her wet underwear.

"I need to grab my shoes. They're by the sun lounger." She twiddles her muddy toes for emphasis.

"You left them with Monty?" says Chris, horror evident in both his tone and on his face.

"He wouldn't?"

"Is the Pope a Catholic?"

They make it back to the sun lounger and Sam is dismayed to see only one shoe sitting next to it.

"Monty!" barks Chris, out into the dark.

"Monty," sings Sam in a less dogmatic tone. Peering out into the darkness, she spots a flash of white farther down the property. "Look, there," she says, pointing.

They take off at a run, arriving just in time to see Monty finish filling a hole that must have been quite the excavation, considering the state of him.

"Mark the spot," says Chris, already heading for the potting shed. He's back moments later with a shovel.

While Chris digs, Monty shows his disproval by howling loud and long. "Shut up, Monty!" says Chris, for all the good it does.

Chris unearths the shoe and gingerly hands it to Sam. It'll never be the same. While she can clean the mud off and out of the shoe, the bite marks on the heel will never wash away. "Bugger."

"Beyond repair?" says Chris, loudly to make himself heard over the howling.

In answer, she drops both shoes next to Monty. The "I'm being murdered" wailing stops instantly and Monty gets stuck into digging a two-shoe sized hole.

Chris looks down at the little cream and brown excavator. "Come on, let's go."

"Yeah, okay," says Sam, unsure where it is they're going.

27

*W*hile Chris goes inside to find Jennie and Mark, Sam perches back on the sun lounger. Even without the benefit of a mirror, she's conscious she must look a mess. Swivelling her eyes to the side, she can see her hair is hanging in rats' tails. She's also certain her mascara is slowly working its way down to her jawline.

Having successfully buried both her shoes, Monty is back in the pool, swimming in ever-widening circles and leaving blooms of muddy water behind him.

"What happened to your costume?" says Jennie, sitting down next to Sam. "And you!"

"I ran into Chris, *in* the pool." Sam looks over to where he and Chewbacca are chatting on the other side of the patio, both of them occasionally turning and looking at her and Jennie.

"Did he push you in?" Jennie's voice has gone squeaky.

"No! It was Monty. He tripped me, and then clobbered Chris while he was dragging me out of the pool. Then the little devil buried one of my shoes."

They watch the happily yapping dog as he half-heartedly attacks the floating chlorine dispenser, deems it not worth the trouble and continues on, sporadically biting at the water.

"Mark told me all about Pita," says Jennie, gesturing to the mountain of hair standing next to Chris. "She's an orphan and Milly's her godmother. Apparently she's had a crush on Chris since puberty."

"She a spoilt little bitch, that's what she is. And what the hell sort of name is Pita? She sounds like Lebanese bread."

"It's not pita, it's P-I-T-A." At the look of confusion on Sam's face, she adds "Stands for Pain In The Arse. The boys came up with it," says Jennie, nodding at them.

"Hmph, they got that right."

"Does this mean you and Chris are back together?"

Sam shrugs her shoulders in confusion. "I don't know. I've said I'm sorry over and over but I get the feeling I'm not forgiven." Sam wrings more water out the ends of her hair.

"I said 'sorry' to Chris, too."

Sam swings to face her. "What for?"

"Well, I assumed he was cheating on you, too. I fobbed him off heaps of times when he phoned."

"He phoned heaps?" Sam's heart unfurls in her chest.

"He rang at least once a day for the first week," says Jennie, guiltily. "I'm so sorry … I thought you wanted a clean break, so I didn't say anything."

"Oh, Jen, that's all right." Sam hugs her friend. "You weren't to know."

Seeing Chris and Mark heading in their direction, Sam says "Is it okay with you if I head off with Chris now? I can't stay here without shoes or underwear."

Jennie eyes widen. "Monty buried your undies too!"

"No! I've still got them, but they're soaking wet." Sam lifts the plastic bag from the ground next to her. "You can stay on here if you want."

"I can't stay here on my own."

Mark overhears this when he and Chris come up next to the girls. "I can keep you company if you like," he says to Jennie. "It'll make a change to dance with a chick whose eyes aren't level with my naval."

"I suppose." Jennie's voice is tinged with uncertainty, as she looks at him.

"Come on, let's leave these two alone." Mark pulls Jennie to her feet and urges her inside. His big, hairy Chewbacca paw easily spans her back.

Sticking to the bushes, as they'd done earlier, Sam and Chris keep out of sight of the house on their way to his car. At the gravel driveway, Chris scoops her up to save her feet.

"Was Milly angry that I pushed Pita into the pool?"

"Not exactly, she knows what a little brat Pita can be."

"Was she all right about you leaving?" says Sam, while Chris manoeuvres his car out of its parking space.

"She was when I told her it was with you."

"Really?"

"Tickled pink. The party was Milly's way of getting us back together."

"I thought the party was for Monty sixth birthday."

"Hah! Monty's nine, if he's a day. And his birthday is sometime around August." Chris then concentrates on not reversing into a car worth more than his house.

"She lied about the dog's age?" says Sam, in amazement.

"I think that pales when you consider she's throwing the dog a fully catered party for two hundred people to get us back together."

"I hadn't thought about it like that." The corner of Sam's bottom lip soon finds its way into her mouth, to be chewed on while she looks unseeing out the side window.

"So?" Chris stops between the double gates before steering the car out into the street, "Left or right?"

Sam turns her head and focuses on the road in front of them. Left is the direction of her place and right, the direction of his.

"I think that's your call." Sam fully expects him to turn left.

Chris sighs heavily and quietly mutters "I must need my head examined," before turning right. She puffs her held breath out on a sigh.

The journey passes in relative silence with any gaps filled

by the car stereo. Going through what will happen when they get to Chris's place, has Sam's heart rate kicking up a notch. She's maybe pushing it, imagining a darkened room and bright light shining in her eyes, although that's what it will feel like.

Sam looks at Chris's back while he opens the front door. The dripping plastic bag containing the Princes Leia costume and her undies has created a small puddle by the time he swings open the door and stands aside so she can enter.

She lifts the bag. "I'd better leave this outside."

"Not if you want it to be there in the morning."

"I am sorry, you know." Sam hopes her apology will finally be accepted.

Her hope nosedives when Chris simply says, "Give it here," and holds his hands out for the dripping bag. Their hands touch, he jerks his away, then up-ends the bag, squeezes out a good amount of water and walks swiftly inside.

She closes and locks the front door before following Chris's watery trail through to the bathroom.

Sam's nose wrinkles at the reek of chlorine filling the room. "I'd better rinse the outfit and hang it up, otherwise it'll be ruined in the morning." Kneeling next to the bath, she drags the costume out of the plastic bag and is jamming the plug in when Chris sighs heavily behind her.

"Sam! It can wait!" says Chris, gruffly. Leaning over, he takes her wrists and pulls her to her feet. She steps toward him, but he moves away before leading the way to the lounge.

Sam's feet drag their way along the hallway.

If he doesn't want to accept my apology, then what am I wasting my time for? I may as well go home.

Chris comes to a stop in front of the couch. "Gumboot or Earl Grey?"

"Sorry?" Sam's having trouble keeping up.

"What sort of tea do you want?"

"I was thinking of something a bit stronger." Because of the events of the evening, she sure as hell doesn't have enough

Dutch or any other nationality's courage in her system for this little chat.

"Oh, no, I want you present for this discussion."

Sam's saliva evaporates and her heart goes into free-fall. He leaves her to stew while he goes to the kitchen to make the tea.

Discussion?

She's wishing he'd turned left at the junction.

By the time Chris returns with two mugs of tea, Sam's hands are clammy and her heart is beating irregularly from its new location in her stomach. Her stomach is knotted so tightly, it's a wonder it can beat at all.

"So," says Chris, looking at Sam, "you want to start?"

Sam, who has the mug halfway to her mouth, freezes. She's unsure what she's meant to do, apart from apologise, again. She's said sorry so many times, the word doesn't even sound like English anymore. "Hey, I can only say I'm sorry so many times. If you don't want to hear it, then I'm wasting my time here."

Sam slams the mug down on the coffee table and only feels a little guilty when she sees some of the liquid slosh over the side. "What more do you want from me!" she shouts.

"Maybe you'd like to explain why you thought I was guilty of screwing around?" Chris shouts back.

"I, ah—"

"Why you wouldn't give me a chance to explain!"

"Ah, I, ah—"

"Or why you even thought I'd cheat on you in the first place!" shouts Chris, before adding more quietly, "Have I ever given you even the slightest reason to think I'd do that?"

Sam squirms under his scrutiny. Suddenly the darkened room and bright light is looking like the better option. At least then, she wouldn't be able to see the hurt and disappointment in his eyes.

"Why didn't you trust me? We're not all arseholes you know."

"I know you're not! But I can't just turn distrust off."

"Yeah, okay, I can see that. But if you're not sure in future, can you at least talk to me about what's going on inside that head of yours?" He knocks gently on her forehead for emphasis.

"I guess." A tear escapes its duct and makes a run for it down her cheek.

"Hell, I'd rather you got mad at me than find me guilty without a trial." Chris pulls her into his arms.

28

Sam's eyes pop as she spots who's strutting confidently up the front path. "Hell, hell, hell!" Being drunk under the table by a couple of chicks and having his willy spatula-slapped by a gaggle of gays hasn't put him off tracking her down. Her legs buckle and she hits her bedroom floor with a knee-jarring thump.

Luckily the others aren't home meaning they won't have to deal with him. The front door is shut

Shame she can't say the same about her bedroom window. With any luck the fluttering lace curtains won't catch his eye.

A loud hammering on the front door is followed by a pause, then more hammering. Then quiet, thank goodness. She's about to get up when she hears movement under the window.

Hell's teeth, he's tall enough that he'll be able to see in.

She's just made it safely under her bed when she hears the curtains being wrenched aside.

"I know you're in there. Alone. Open the door, sweetie."

She breathes as quietly as she can; difficult given she's hyperventilating.

How on earth does he know she's alone? How does he know which room is hers?

"I've been watching you."

Sam's breathing screeches to a halt before starting up again double-speed when she hears scuffling and thumping against the side of the house right by her head. This is followed by a heavy grunt, crash and stream of vitriol. Big, but thank god, not super-athletic.

"I'm not giving up! I'm gonna screw you again, whether you like it or not!" is screamed venomously through her window.

Lying frozen amid the debris under her bed, Sam soon finds the lack of oxygen has her panting in air raggedly, making her feel dizzy and more than a little nauseous. The trembling starts out gently enough, but gains in strength until she's shaking like a cold, wet dog. Her ears feel like they've doubled in size, so hard are they listening for any movement outside.

Eventually she hears, "Bitch," from outside, followed by heavy footsteps and finally the front gate slamming.

She stays where she is, listening hard for any further movement outside the window. Unsure if he's bright enough to fake an exit, Sam's not leaving her dusty sanctuary just yet. She lies there until the shaking has stopped and her breathing has returned to normal. She burps softly, until the nausea abates. The house and garden are unusually silent, as though they too are listening for Salami Boy's return. Even the cicadas have stopped their racket.

The phone smashes this eerie silence and her head whips up and straight into one of the metal bars of the bed base. Never mind stars, she can see planets and entire bloody galaxies. It takes a few shakes before her head's clear enough to allow her to scramble from under the bed and through to grab the phone before it stops ringing.

"Hey, there," says Chris.

"Hey, back." She sinks to the floor on legs still a little on the rubbery side; her ears attuned for approaching footsteps.

"... catching up tonight?"

"Sorry, what was that?"

"I said, are you still keen on catching up tonight?"

"That'd be nice," says Sam absently, while rubbing the back of her head where she can feel a Pluto-shaped bump forming.

"You don't sound sure? Are you all right?"

"What? Oh, yeah, I'm fine." Sam tries to concentrate on the conversation.

"I was thinking we could grab a meal at that steak house in Lonsdale Street."

"That'd be good," says Sam, with forced enthusiasm – she hasn't managed to burp away all the nausea. "Can you pick me up at the back gate?"

"Yeah, sure?"

She can tell by his tone that he thinks this is odd but thankfully, he doesn't ask why. This is one of those things she'd rather explain face to face.

Chris escorts her in the back door after dinner. "Sam, I don't like the idea of you staying here while that crazy is lurking about. Let me have a quiet word with him."

She doesn't want Chris anywhere near Salami Boy. "No!"

"That'd be bright," says Brenda, walking out of her bedroom. "He is one seriously screwed-up bloke. Trying to reason with him would be like poking a snake with a stick and not expecting it to fang ya."

Chris arches one eyebrow. "I can be very persuasive."

"Sure, two blokes punching the crap out of each other. That always works," says Brenda, sarcastically. "There are better ways of dealing with the likes of that prick."

"What did you have in mind?" says Sam, hopeful at the thought of getting Salami Boy out of her hair once and for all.

"Oh, I'd stitch him up good and proper. He wouldn't be bugging you again, that's for sure."

"Hang on a second. I think I should be the one to sort this out!" says Chris.

"No. Please, I don't want you anywhere near him." Sam rests her hand on his puffed up chest and rubs it in circles. She feels his body relax, and so does she.

"Hmm, okay, but if it doesn't work, then I'm going to have a little *chat* with him," says Chris, causing her to tense up again.

Brenda's plan had better work.

"In the meantime, I don't think it's a good idea for you to stay here," says Chris.

"I agree," says Jennie, joining them. "He sounds like a nutter." So seamlessly does she join the conversation, Sam's in no doubt that Jennie's heard everything from her room.

"Guys, I think this is my decision." Sam grabs Chris by the hand and leads him to the back door. After a lengthy kiss goodnight next to his car, she convinces him it's safe for her to go back inside.

Walking into the lounge, she's met by Jennie and Brenda standing shoulder to shoulder and eyeballing her.

"What?" says Sam, defensively.

"I found this stuffed under the door." Brenda hands her an envelope with 'SAM' scrawled across the front.

By the time she's finished reading the note, she feels like throwing up. The paper drops from her fingers, to be picked up by Brenda, who scans the note.

"He is one sick little arsehole." Brenda folds the note and puts it back in the envelope, ignoring Jennie's outstretched hand.

"Did you know he's *still* parked out front?" says Jennie.

"He *is?*" Sam's hand flies to her chest as her breathing pattern suffers a couple of dropped stitches. The thought of him lying in wait has her teeth chattering. She drops onto the sofa and her arms snake over her chest in a comforting hug.

By the time she finishes telling them about her encounter earlier in the day, Jennie's wide-eyed and her mouth is all goldfish. "But Sam, you have to call the police," she says, her voice rigid with fear.

"Hah, after the whipped-cream-kidnapping-thingy, that's a dumb idea," says Brenda. "Go and pack, I'll bring the car around back."

Sam lifts her gaze from its close study of her knees. "What?"

"You're getting the hell out of here. I've seen first-hand the damage crazy bastards like him can inflict," says Brenda, emphatically, before muttering. "You're staying somewhere else. Especially with what I've got planned."

Sam is vaguely aware of Jennie on the phone to Chris telling him they'll be over shortly. She comes back to reality when Jennie drops an overnight bag on the coffee table in front of her.

Sam's still trembling when she follows Chris into his place on legs that are more liquid than solid. Jennie is right behind, lugging the sewing machine and a bag of material. Brenda's already inside, "checking out the place". Chris drops her bag in the hallway, closes the front door after them, and Sam feels some of her tension dissipate.

Hearing splashing and laughter, they all look at the central courtyard.

"Hell, that didn't take long." Chris looks at Brenda, now buck naked, in the hot tub. "Join her if you like."

Jennie and Sam shake their heads and roll their eyes in unison before following Chris into the lounge and leaving Brenda to it. The three of them are finishing their coffees when Brenda comes in, clothed but still slightly damp. A large dark blue towel is wrapped turban-style around her head.

"So, Brenda, what exactly have you got planned for crazy boy," says Chris, causing Sam to tense up again.

"Hah, you mean Salami Boy!" says Brenda, snorting.

Jennie and Sam stare at each other in horror, hoping Chris won't notice this slip.

"Salami Boy?" says Chris.

There's a moment's silence before Jennie says, "We call him that because, ah, his breath smells of garlic."

Sam mouths "thank you" to Jennie for her quick thinking.

"So, Brenda?" prompts Chris.

Brenda's eyes go all squinty. "I'm still working out the details. I'll let you know when everything's ready."

Sam's sure she can hear the faint whir of cogs rotating at twice their recommended speed.

"I still think I should—" says Chris, only to have the three girls shout "No!" at him in unison.

Standing by the front door with Chris, his arm casually draped over her shoulder, they wave Brenda and Jennie off. Sam's surprised at how natural this feels and she's only been here an hour.

Chris pushes the front door closed, swings around and drags her into his arms and kisses her soundly. "I have you alone at last," he says, in his best Dick Dastardly voice, before throwing her for a loop when he adds, "Damn, I just realised she took my towel."

Chris picks up Sam's bag and takes it through to his bedroom and drops it on the end of the bed. He opens the wardrobe to reveal he's already cleared some space for her; he pulls open an empty drawer in the dresser.

She does feel safer here, although this isn't how she'd ever planned on moving in with a guy. For one thing, it's not permanent, anything but. Even so, sharing a toothbrush mug with a guy is the biggest commitment she's made in her life, so far. There was never anything official between her and Darren and, looking back, that was a good thing.

"Yell if you need more space."

Sam's surprised that, even on such short notice, he's made room for her in his life. "Ah, thanks. I can live out of my bag, it's not like I'll be here long."

29

*H*er first night staying at Chris's place on a semi-permanent basis and Sam lies neat in the bed, her arms resting on the covers, parallel to her body. Having let her go first, Chris is now in the bathroom brushing his teeth. It's the first time she's ended up in his bed without already being naked and she feels scruffy in the oversized T-shirt that doubles as her jammies.

Hearing gargling, she breathes into her hand and sniffs.

Damn, too close to call.

She folds the bedclothes neatly to one side, gets up and straightens a stray wrinkle, before wandering back into the bathroom. Chris is replacing the cap on the mouthwash but when she holds out her hand, he gives it to her.

She pours herself a capful of the bright green liquid and tips it into her mouth, squelching the involuntary reaction to swallow. While swishing it around she watches Chris clean out the pale grey ceramic toothbrush mug.

Sam awkwardly spits out her mouthful of green fizz, before breathing in deeply. Her nostrils tingle in response. A final swirl of water ensures the sink is spotless again.

She indicates the mug on the vanity. "Your mother brought you up well."

"My parents died in the same plane crash as Pita's." Chris straightens the hand towel. "Milly and Fred raised us."

"I'm so sorry." Sam's instinct is to hug him but she's not sure how this would go down. People were funny about sympathy. Sometimes it was all that was needed to push them over the edge. Sam isn't sure she wants to see Chris like that.

"No biggie. I don't remember a time before living with my grandparents, so it's hard for me to get down about it. They were amazing when we were growing up. Still are." Chris leads the way back to the bedroom.

"I don't know Fred, but Milly is lovely."

"Yeah, she's great. Fred is too, but in a different way." Chris gets into bed on Sam's side. "He used to let us do things like play cricket in the ballroom when it was wet outside. Milly used to pretend to be annoyed ... it was all part of the excitement for us kids."

"Sounds like you were lucky, in some ways." She walks around the bed and gets in on the wrong side.

"What time should I set the alarm for," says Chris, the small beside clock in his hand.

"I'm working on Doggs' Toggs stuff tomorrow, so I can get up whenever."

"Wish I could say the same. I've got an early meeting."

Sam wakes alone the following morning. She hadn't heard Chris leave for work which is a surprise as she's a reasonably light sleeper. Focusing on the bedside clock, she's alarmed to see it's 9.30 a.m.

"Bloody hell!"

She'll have to haul arse to get through all the sewing on her list for today. Damned birthday parties were becoming all the rage and, while she likes the extra work, the deadlines are a little crazy.

Standing beside the bed she sniffs her armpits. Good enough. She'll shower later in the day and that way she'll look nice for Chris when he gets home. Thank god they didn't have sex last night. "Ha, never thought I'd say that."

Dragging on the nearest clothes to hand, she's ready to face the day in minutes. Looking at herself in the full-length mirror on the back of the wardrobe door, she hopes Chris doesn't come home unexpectedly. His sweatpants ride low on her hips and the only thing holding them up is the waistband being rolled over several times. One of Sam's oldest crop-tops finishes off the outfit.

What a slob.

Sam laughs aloud.

In the kitchen, she finds a medley of breakfast things laid out for her along with a note from Chris. The selection is staggering and far wider than she's used to. Vegemite on toast and a mug of tea is the winning combination. While the water is boiling and the bread toasting, Sam puts everything else away. There's a little trial-and-error involved and she's sure Chris will have trouble finding one or two items she couldn't decide on, but she knows he likes things tidy. By the time she's finished wiping and tidying, the kitchen is up to a Handy Andy advert quality.

With breakfast prepared, she goes in search of her sewing room. Chris had said he'd set it up in the far bedroom and, sure enough, at the end of the hallway, she finds a bedroom with her sewing machine at the ready on a small student desk. There's an Anglepoise lamp perfectly angled and poised to illuminate her work, but not blind her.

Once she's concentrating on her sewing, she blocks everything else out and so she's surprised when she hears the back door opening what feels like only a couple of hours later. When she looks at her wrist to confirm the time, it's bare except for a freckle and hair that have never proved accurate.

"Hi, there," calls out Chris.

Looking down at the bunched-up track pants and her washed-thin top, Sam responds weakly. "Hi." She's digging crumbs out of her moderate cleavage when Chris walks in.

"Whoa, what the hell happened?" says Chris, although he quickly follows up with, "I mean, did you have a good day?"

"I did." Sam pulls her hand out of her tank top. When she realises she's just put the crumb into her mouth, she feels her face and chest bloom crimson.

"What else have you got in there?" says Chris, his eyebrows raised.

"You weren't meant to see me like this. I didn't realise the time. I thought you wouldn't be home for ages. I was going to have a shower."

Chris grabs Sam's hand, pulls her to her feet and leads her to the bathroom. "I'll scrub you down."

Once Sam is squeaky clean and properly dressed, Chris gets dinner underway. This involves a lot of tinkering with the barbeque in the courtyard. She offers to help but after being turned down the second time, she leaves him to it. While he works on getting the charcoal to the right heat to cook their steaks, she nips inside and prepares drinks.

"We can go out later, if you like." Chris holds his hand above the glowing charcoal to check the temperature. Pulling it back sharply, he announces, "Good to go." He stabs the stainless steel barbeque fork into a half-a-cow steak sitting in a pool of blood in a smoked glass Arcopal roasting dish on the picnic table. Holding the steak above the dish for a second so it can finish bleeding to death, he then swings it over to the barbeque and gently lays it on the grill. The process is repeated with a much smaller steak for Sam.

He looks intently at the steaks for five minutes before poking them experimentally. "There's some potato salad and coleslaw in the fridge," he says without taking his eyes off the steaks.

Glad to have something to do, she puts her drink down and goes back inside to grab salads, plates and cutlery.

Chris flips the larger of the two slabs of meat. "How do you like your steak?"

"Ah, cooked?"

"No. Still mooing, well done, incinerated?"

Sam's slightly nauseated by the pool of blood congealing in the bottom of the roasting dish. "Well done, thanks."

Sam's tummy has never felt so full. The steak was good and she hadn't been able to stop herself eating the whole thing. It'll take a couple of hours lying flat on her back to give her stomach enzymes a fighting chance against the chunk of meat she's managed to gnaw her way through.

Chris rubs his distended stomach. "Would you mind if we didn't go out?"

Sam undoes the top button of her jeans with a groan of pleasure. "Not a problem."

Sam wakes on Saturday morning to find she's on her own again. She's wondering where Chris is when her eyes focus on a note sitting on his pillow.

Have to go out for a bit.

Back soon.

xxx.

Sam's heart warms at the kisses at the bottom of the note. "Hope he's not too long," she says to the room.

She's nodding off again when she feels a warm body creeping into bed beside her. Smiling into the pillow, she opens one eye, but has trouble focussing on the face that is too close to hers. "Good morning, gorgeous," says Sam, before her eyes close again. A tongue slurps its way across her chin and she pulls away, gagging. "Good lord, your breath stinks." She rolls away from him, desperately seeking fresh air.

"Monty! Out of there now," says Chris, coming into the room.

"What on earth has he been eating?" says Sam, not moving her head until Monty is safely on the ground.

"He was wolfing down a plate of fresh liver when I arrived."

"Gross. No wonder his breath reeks." She sits up to look at Monty. "Can't you brush his teeth?"

The expression on Chris's face is all the answer she needs.

"What about giving him a peppermint?"

"They make him fart and believe me, that's a hell of a lot worse." Chris grimaces at the memory. "Common, get up, after breakfast we're taking him to the P-A-R-K."

The K has just cleared Chris's lips when Monty howls, bounces on the spot for a bit, then runs to the door and looks back at them. Tongue hanging out, face expectant.

"I think he can S-P-E-L-L."

After spending all day at the park, running the legs off Monty, they drop him home late afternoon. Fred and Milly are still out but Stephen is back and takes the tired little dog off their hands. Because Sam and Chris have also done a lot of running around with Monty, they opt for another night in.

It's midday before they surface on the Sunday. Sam's body is nicely achy from all the time spent playing with balls, plus the time spent playing with Monty at the park. They're tackling the housework after a late breakfast when the phone rings. "Can you get that?" shouts Chris over the roar of the vacuum.

"Yeah," Sam shouts back, before putting the furniture polish and duster down and walking out to the hall to pick up the phone.

"We're all set for Wednesday night," says Brenda.

"What's going to happen?"

"Just make sure you're here by eight o'clock," says Brenda, without giving anything else away. "Oh, and wear black."

"Wear black?" says Sam, into the dead phone.

30

*S*am walks down the lane at the rear of the flat, keeping to the deep shadows formed by the tall wooden fence that backs all the properties. Even though she's checked that Salami Boy is parked out front, part of her still expects a hand to clamp over her mouth at any second. Easing open the gate, ensuring any squeaking from the hinges is kept at mouse-level, she sneaks up the back path. "Jen, are you there?" she stage whispers through the back door of the flat.

"You're not meant to be here until Wednesday," says Brenda, loudly, out the kitchen window right next to her. Sam spins around, loses her balance and bangs into the door frame hard enough to know she'll soon be sporting a bruise. Brenda's sniggering suggests the scare has been done on purpose.

Bitch.

Scuttling through the lounge, Sam says "hi" to Jennie, who's sitting on the couch with a magazine, and walks straight into her bedroom without slowing down. To make her time in front of any windows as brief as possible, Sam keeps walking until she's right inside her wardrobe. "Has he sussed yet there's a back gate?" she says, to Jennie, from its safety.

Jennie follows Sam into her room. "Nope. Brenda's hardly been around and if I go out at night I use the back gate and leave the telly on with the volume cranked up. That way if he gets out of the car to take a leak in the garden, he more than likely thinks I'm still home."

"Oh, my god! He doesn't?"

"He does! It's not doing the landlord's roses any good."

"Stefano was bitching about them when he last collected the rent," says Brenda, who lurches in to join them, a half-empty tumbler of red wine hanging dangerously from one hand.

"Brenda, just how are you planning to sort him out?" says Sam, from behind the safety of a rain coat.

"Easy, I just let Stefano know who's been screwing up his roses. His boys will sort the prick out." Brenda wavers on her feet.

"Now that's gonna be entertaining," says Sam.

By the time she's packed more clothes to take over to Chris's, Jennie is in the shower and Brenda is sitting sideways on one of the lounge chairs doing serious damage to another tumbler of red wine.

"How's it been living with the stud muffin?" slurs Brenda, her eyes fighting to focus on Sam.

"I never thought it'd be so easy living with a guy. He even cooks!" Sam is unable to keep her eyes off the wine sloshing from side to side in Brenda's glass.

Brenda swings her feet randomly with the contents of the glass getting closer to the rim with each swing. It was only a matter of time before red wine ruined something. "You should keep him."

"But I can't let Jennie down. We've only been away five months and she's planned everything. And Mum and Dad would freak if I told them I was going to settle down in Australia. And—"

"And. And. And. Jeez, it must be exhausting keeping all those people happy. What do *you* want?"

"What do *I* want?"

"Yeah. What. Do. *You*. Want? Hell, I'm the one who's been drinking."

"Uh," stutters Sam.

"Just because you do stuff to keep other people happy doesn't mean they will be, and it sure as hell doesn't mean you will be. It's your life."

"But, what if it doesn't work out?"

"What if it does?"

"What if he wants to control me?"

"What if he doesn't?" Brenda drains her glass, arches her way out of her chair and heads into the kitchen, forcing out a couple of belches on her way.

"Turn into that street there." Sam points to the no-exit road up the hill from the flat. With Sam standing behind the car using her hands to indicate the narrowing space, Chris squeaks into a spot not much bigger than his car. She shivers, even though the night is warm, rubbing her hands up and down her arms while she waits for Chris to get out and lock the car. She's looking at the main road when Salami Boy's car slides past and disappears down the hill. Violent trembling starts in her chest before skittering all over her body.

As Chris starts walking to the main road, she firmly hooks her arm through his and veers him toward the back lane. "We can't go around the front, he's out there already."

Chris stops in his tracks. "I still think it'd be easier if I just had a word with the guy."

"I'd hate you to get hurt because of me. I think we're better sticking to Brenda's plan."

"Hmm, I'd worry more about something dreamed up by that crazy tart."

With more urging, Sam gets him moving again and they walk in silence down the back lane and in through the open gate. She opens the back door and nearly pees her pants when Brenda and Jennie materialise just inside. "Hell!" says Sam, "You scared me."

Jennie and Brenda are dressed from head to toe in black

the same as Chris and Sam. No balaclavas this time though. Brenda carries a humungous bowl of popcorn in one arm while Jennie is holding onto a bottle of wine and some plastic cups.

They're all crowded into the small hallway, the back door is shut, and Brenda taps her nails on the neighbour's door. The large number 2 and Darth Vader picture are just visible in the gloom. Sam's glad Chris is with her tonight, as old Vader from upstairs seriously creeps her out. So fast is the door opened that Sam knows he's been waiting on the other side. Probably for ages. The sad bastard. They pass him single file and make their way up the darkened stairs. Sam hopes Salami Boy isn't already in the front garden because the loud creaking emanating from the wooden staircase could keep Hammer Horror in sound effects for the foreseeable future.

Brenda, who's leading the way, stops at the top of the stairs causing the others to bang into each other. Sam hears a hoarse "Straight ahead" from Darth Vader, who's bringing up the rear and they move off again. Sam's relieved to see they'll be watching tonight's show from the lounge rather than a bedroom.

The lounge is bad enough. Even with the lights out she can see that one wall is wallpapered with posters of what looks like every sci-fi alien to ever appear on celluloid. There are a lot of raised eyebrows amongst the group, although Vader himself seems proud of the set up. The furniture in the room consists of a large stereo, an even larger television, a small, beaten-up coffee table and a couple of bean bags the colour of overcooked oats.

Even safely behind the hard-angled venetian blinds, Sam feels exposed when she looks down at Salami Boy's car and jumps when she hears a loud crunching right behind her. Spinning, she realises the noise has come from Vader, who's dumped himself into one of the bean bags. The half-light makes it difficult to see where his body finishes and the bean bag begins. It's like looking down on a big bowl of porridge. He picks up a *Star Trek* branded glass of Coke from the tripod coffee table next to him and takes several large gulps before putting it back down. He clicks a remote and the TV flares into life, revealing what looks like a episode of *Star Trek*. The room is bathed in a harsh blue light and Sam worries their silhouettes will be visible.

"Do you have to have that on? It's pretty bloody hard to stay hidden when we're lit up like a soddin' Christmas tree." The look Brenda impales him with has him shakily switching off the TV, although it takes a couple of stabs for him to hit the right button on the remote.

"Better yet, go to your room." Brenda points to the back of the flat and Sam's amazed when Vader struggles up out of the bean bag like a cast sheep, never once letting his gaze waver from Brenda's. He picks up the nearly empty glass of coke and shuffles off to his room. Sam can feel Chris shaking with suppressed laughter beside her.

"Weirdo," mutters Brenda.

"That was a bit mean," says Jennie. "It is his home."

"Give it a rest. He's the sort who'd be happy to pay for someone to smack him repeatedly on the arse with a tennis racquet. You can be sure he loved it." Brenda walks over and grabs the wood-grain Formica-topped coffee table with one hand then plonks it down so hard next to their viewing area that Sam worries the little angled black plastic legs will give out. Brenda dumps her bowl of popcorn in the middle. "Help yourselves," she says, tipping her head at the bowl.

Jennie puts the bottle of red wine down next to it, splits the plastic cups into a neat row and sets about opening the bottle of wine with the corkscrew she's pulled from a pocket. They're all standing with a glass of wine and munching on popcorn when the action outside gets underway.

Sam's gaze fixes on a dark green transit van that's crawled to a stop further up the hill from Salami Boy. "Do you reckon that's to do with us?" says Sam, quietly to Chris.

"I think so. The lights were turned off at the top of the hill and it coasted down the rest of the way. Brenda?" says Chris, turning to her.

"That's the boys." Brenda looks at the illuminated numbers on her watch. "Bang on time, too."

"And now we wait," mumbles Jennie, her mouth chocker with popcorn.

They've finished the wine, the popcorn's as good as gone and they're feeling twitchy before they see Salami Boy's car door finally swing slowly open. He hoists himself out and into the light streaming from the sodium street lamp next to the car. Seeing him again, this close, has Sam shivering strongly enough that Chris pulls her into his arms, and watches events with his chin resting on top of her head.

Sam can't begin to imagine what Chris is thinking? He has to realise I was off my face to go anywhere near the creep below.

Salami Boy softly closes his car door, walks confidently around the back and up to the front gate. He opens it and leaves it swinging wide behind him. He takes a couple of steps up the front path and does a right angle turn straight into the rose garden without slowing down.

"Cheeky bastard." Brenda drains her wine then throws the plastic cup into the far corner of the room.

Jennie's too busy absently shovelling the dregs of the popcorn into her mouth to comment. Some tooth-shatteringly loud crunches come from her direction.

Salami Boy weaves his way through the artfully planted rose bushes until he's in the centre of the garden and mostly hidden from the street. He halts, and then turns around several times before stopping to face away from the house; he bends down to look at the ground.

"What the hell's he doing," says Chris, right into Sam's ear. "This is the sort of rigmarole Monty goes through before he takes a dump."

"He wouldn't! Would he?"

In answer to this question, Salami Boy fiddles with his belt. His jeans drop in a heap around his ankles. His jocks follow and Jennie spits out a horrified, "Whoa, moon's out."

"This is tooooo good." Brenda snaps open the venetian

blinds causing the others to jump back. She then drags a torch, from where it's stuffed down the back of her trousers and flashes it through the venetians toward the van. She then adjusts the blinds back to their former angle.

From their vantage point they watch the van's back doors inch open and six large guys all get out just as slowly.

"Do you think they're going to kill him?" Sam jams her fists against her mouth, scrunching down and knocking Chris's chin off its perch.

"I doubt anything too bad is going to happen. The boys are more likely to belong to Rotary than the mafia," says Chris.

"Yeah, Rotary," snorts Brenda.

Sam watches them lumber down the hill and in through the gate. They're much larger than anyone belonging to her dad's Rotary Club. They're square, and seemingly as wide and deep as they are tall. They don't walk; they rock from corner to corner. Their dark suits steal light from around them. "They don't look like Rotary members to me."

"Maybe not Rotary," says Chris.

Sam looks at the scene below. "Shame we won't be able to hear them," she whispers. This is immediately followed by her hissing, "No, don't!" when she sees Brenda slowing lifting the bottom of the venetian blind. Sam holds her breath and swivels her gaze from Salami Boy to the window and back, until the window is safely pushed to its full open position without detection. They all kneel down next to the gap where it's possible to hear what's going on below.

The six blokes line up, shoulder to shoulder, along the front path causing Salami Boy to splutter, "Oh, hell." The irony is lost on him

He's still squatting when they surround him.

"Jeez, talk about the number two equivalent of coitus interruptus." Brenda's voice is loud in the quiet of the room and Salami Boy's gaze swings from the men surrounding him up to the window causing the group at the window to all fall backwards into the safety of the lounge.

"Do you think he saw us?" whispers Jennie, nervously.

"I don't see how he could." Brenda kneels back next to the window and peers down into the garden. "Nah, we're good," she whispers, over her shoulder.

"Our boss don't like you doing this sorta crap in his garden," says one of the besuited cubes.

This has Brenda snickering quietly and saying "Ha. Crap! Get it?"

"Wow, they sound like gangsters to me," says Sam. "Brenda, who are these guys?"

"Relax – they're just playing a part. If you think they sound dangerous now, you should see them in Hamlet."

"Hamlet? Shakespeare or cigars?" says Chris.

"Shhh, stow it," says Brenda.

Back down in the garden another cube rumbles "Yeah. He. Don't. Like. It." Bullet pointing his sentence by punching his right hand into the palm of his left.

"Did Sam put you up to this?" says Salami Boy.

Sam swallows deeply to get her heart from her mouth and back down into her chest. Her ears strain. Waiting for a cube to respond.

"We don't know nuffin' about a bloke called Sam," says a cube.

"Screw me, what've ya been eating," says another cube, waving his hand in front of his face. "You smell rotten."

"Yeah," agrees the largest cube. "Best you pick your stuff up and piss off."

"Do they mean what I think they mean?" whispers Chris.

"What?" Salami Boy straightens and pulls up his underpants. He grasps the top of his jeans to pull them up into place.

"Not so fast, mate," says the widest cube. "I think you've forgotten something." He points at the small pile of excrement between Salami Boy's feet.

"I'm not touching it," says Salami Boy, defiantly.

The largest cube taps Salami Boy on the shoulder with a garden stake. "Pick it up." He then hefts the stake above his head. "Now!"

"Where the hell did he get that from?" Not getting a response, Sam turns to discover she's the only one still looking out the window. Chris is lying on the ground and laughing so hard he's having to breathe through his mouth to keep the noise down. Brenda's fist is stuffed in her mouth to stifle the laughter and there are tears rolling down her face. Jennie simply looks nauseated.

Sam won't feel free to laugh, or throw up, until this is over. Looking out of the window, Salami Boy is bending over scooping up the pile of poo and stuffing it into the front pockets of his jeans. He tries to step out of them, but all of the cubes shake their heads. Salami Boy can't bring himself to pull the jeans all the way up. His expression reflects what it must feel like to have pockets full of warm poo.

The cubes rock to the sides leaving the way clear for him to exit the garden. He does so with no finesse; his jeans, grasped at mid-thigh, make his gait awkward. He walks doubled over to the driver's door of his car. Still holding his jeans up with one hand, he tries to open the door with the other, but his hand slips.

As soon as he sees the Rose Protection Team rock out of the front gate, he lets go of his jeans, grabs at the door with both hands and wrenches it open. He backs himself into the driver's seat and kicks his feet free of denim. There's no skill involved in how he starts the car, with the engine still screaming when he reaches the bottom of the hill.

His dirty jeans lie abandoned in the middle of the road.

The Transit Van rolls down the hill to meet up with the team and they climb in; the van settling a little lower on its springs as each of them disappears inside.

The last cube pauses with one foot on the back step, looks up at their window and completes a jaunty salute before climbing inside.

31

*R*ather than move home immediately after the demonstration of gardening by the phases of the moon, Sam stays on at Chris's place until the weekend. She walks into the bathroom and opens the glass door of the shower. Bending down, she collects her razor, shampoo, conditioner, finishing rinse, shower gel and loofa, shoving these into a plastic bag. She turns to look at the numerous bottles and jars that litter the top of the vanity. Apart from occasionally corralling the bottles back to one corner, Chris hasn't said anything about the takeover.

She sweeps everything into the bag, wincing slightly when she hears a couple of glass bottles make the trip. Looking tentatively, she's relieved to see everything's intact.

Wandering through to the bedroom, she crams the bulging plastic bag into the end pocket of her carryall bag. There seems to be a lot more stuff than there was when she moved here just over a week ago. With her clothes packed, three-quarters of the wardrobe is empty; Chris's clothes are still jammed down one end.

"Got everything?" Chris surveys his near-empty wardrobe. "I'm not going to know what to do with all the space."

"Yep, all set. If you grab the bags on the bed and I'll get the other two. I'm sure I will have forgotten something."

"Well, it's not like you're not coming back. I don't know why you don't leave some stuff here anyway."

Sam pauses briefly in her bag collecting.

"Welcome back," Jennie greets Sam when she carries some of her bags through the back door. "Do you need a hand?"

"No, thanks. Chris is bringing the rest in now."

Chris staggers into the lounge laden down with the sewing machine and a few more bags of Sam's belongings. "Where shall I put this lot?"

"Sewing machine on the table and if you could throw the rest in my room, that'd be great."

Chris is dropping the bags in her room when they hear impatient beeping from the back alleyway.

"I'd better go move my car," says Chris, already on his way with Sam following.

"Gonna miss you," he says, settling into his seat.

She leans down next to the car. "Me, too." Chris puts his head out the window to give her a brief kiss, although not brief enough for the driver of the blocked car.

"Better go. I'll call you later."

"How was it staying at his place?" says Jennie, when Sam wanders back inside.

"It was nice. How's it been around here?"

"Quiet. Haven't seen hide nor hair of Salami Boy. Haven't seen much of Brenda either."

"Where's she been?"

"Out with some guy every night. Getting home at all hours. If at all."

"I hope this one's younger than the last bloke was. Even someone in their sixties would be an improvement."

"Don't know. She's staying tight-lipped." Jennie's unable to quash a shudder. "Thank goodness."

Walking into her bedroom, Sam feels like a trespasser. Still, the bags piled on the bed are all hers. Apart from a couple of pairs of underpants, she's been careful not to leave anything behind at Chris's.

After removing her toiletries bag, she upends her carryall into the middle of the bed and sorts through everything. A depressing number of items make it into the washing pile. Damn, she should at least have taken Chris up on the offer to use his washing machine. No loss of independence there.

She drops a solitary pair of clean undies into the empty top drawer of her dresser, spotting the small satin pouch stuck in the back corner, forgotten. She hasn't thought of the button in weeks, and doesn't feel tempted to wear it now.

"Mrs *Chris* Drayton?" says Sam aloud to the room. It doesn't feel right. She likes being called Sam.

Why do I have to give that up because of marriage? God, to think I was so ready to give up everything for that arsehole Darren. Sam shudders at how close a call she'd had there.

While she loves going out with Chris, and maybe even loves him, she'll never hand over her life to a guy again; ever. She drops the unopened pouch back into the drawer.

"Jennie, I have to go and do a load of washing. You need anything done?" says Sam, going into Jennie's bedroom.

"No. I'm good," says Jennie, who's lying on her bed reading. "I did all mine yesterday."

"Do you want to come for the walk?" Sam isn't looking forward to a solo trip to the laundromat but on seeing the drop on Jennie's features and her furtive peek at the book propped open on her chest, she answers herself, with "Hah! What was I thinking! Of course you don't. Catch you later."

With a backpack of laundry slung over her shoulders, she heads out the back gate and up the alleyway. It's longer than through the front gate but it'll take her a while to believe Salami Boy has given up stalking her. Even knowing he hasn't been around, the feeling that someone is watching her is still palpable.

Rather than stare vacantly at the washing machine, she reads through an hysterically old Aussie *Women's Weekly*.

It's 1978 for goodness sake! Thank goodness things have moved on.

The idea of standing at the front door in a nice 'frock', with full make-up and holding a drink ready to greet hubby home from a hard day at the office has Sam snorting. Darren would have loved that. Chris would prefer a different outfit, thinks Sam, grinning.

"Good afternoon, Sam," says Mrs Farquhar, causing Sam's head to pop up from the napkin folding how-to she's concentrating on.

"Hi, there. Hey, Sapphire?" Sam scratches the small blue dog behind the ears.

While Mrs Farquhar empties a dryer-load of Sapphire's clothes, Sam continues to scratch away at the dog's thinning coat.

"Well, I must be off. I'll see you Thursday evening," says Mrs Farquhar, referring to one of their Doggs' Toggs' catch-up meetings. Sunnies on, she looks both ways then scuttles across the pavement to the Merc. After opening the door to let Sapphire in and popping the basket of washing in the footwell, she makes her way quickly around to her side before driving off at speed.

Her Mata-Hari-does-washing getaway is ruined when she slams on the brakes and reverses wildly. After beckoning frantically for Sam to come out, she lowers the electric window far enough for a bag of fabric to be shoved through and into Sam's waiting hands.

"I think Sapphire will look gorgeous in this, I'll leave it up to you to design something unique." This instruction has only just squeezed its way majestically through the gap before the window is closed and the Merc shoots off again.

Sam looks inside the bag and her initial reaction to the purple alligator embossed vinyl is to gag. "Something unique?"

With the washing transferred to the dryer, she mulls over possible creations using the hideous purple plastic. By the time her laundry is dried, folded and packed, she has the beginnings of an outfit in mind.

Even dried, the clean washing feels heavier than the load she'd stuffed into a machine earlier; possibly because she's close to falling sleep, rather than the actual weight of the washing. Hoisting the backpack over her shoulders, the straps cut in and she feels herself lose a couple of inches in height. A deep breath is required before she can swing open the glass door of the Laundromat and head for home.

Her pace starts out leisurely enough, but the feeling that someone is watching her naturally ramps it up. She trips over an uneven spot in the footpath and foregoes looking over her shoulder every twenty seconds, although this doesn't stop her listening intently for footfalls gaining on her. She's unable to stop her pace increasing to a slow jog, even though the shoulder straps dig deeper with each hasty tread.

Thundering down the hill to the front gate her breathing is so laboured a rubbish truck could sneak up on her. Unlatching the gate, she takes a quick look back the way she's come. The footpaths on both sides are empty, with no one in sight. It's not until she's closing the gate that she sees bushes moving in the front garden of a house across the road.

Dumping her backpack of laundry on the front step, she unlocks the front door with some difficulty. Her hands are shaky from a combination of the unaccustomed jogging and the fear that Salami Boy might still be in her life. After throwing the laundry on her bed she goes into the kitchen where Jennie is rattling around to a background sizzle from the frying pan.

"Brilliant, wiener schnitzel," says Sam. "Hey, are you sure Salami Boy hasn't been around? I think I was followed just then."

"No!" Jennie drops the edge of the piece of schnitzel she'd been checking for colour, slopping some oil over the edge of the frying pan in the process. "Are you sure?"

"It was just a feeling, but then I saw the bushes moving at that white place opposite. It might have been a cat. Or something." Sam's tone doesn't convince herself, let alone Jennie.

"Look after this while I go and check." Jennie hands the tongs to her and nips out the back door. Sam sees her walking past the kitchen window, presumably on her way around the side of the house to check out the place across the road without being seen.

By the time Jennie returns, Sam has plated up meals for the two of them, plus one for Brenda who's not home.

"My imagination?" Sam hands the loaded plate to Jennie.

"I had a good look over that way and then a cat fight erupted, so that might have been it."

"God, I hope so."

After dinner, Sam powers through the washing up. It's eight-thirty when she wanders through the lounge to the bathroom to brush her teeth. She's already in what passes for pyjamas.

Jennie looks away from the TV. "Isn't it a little early for bed?"

"Normally, yeah. But I'm knackered. I haven't exactly had a lot of sleep lately."

So much for an early night thinks Sam, hours later when she's memorised by the pattern on her ceiling caused by the street lights shining through the gaps at the top of her curtains. She leans over and grabs her alarm clock. The red digital readout shows it's a smidgeon after midnight.

With a sigh, she throws the covers back and makes her way quietly out to the lounge, not bothering to switch any lights on. After checking Jennie's door is shut, she turns on the TV, setting the volume so low she can hardly hear it. She's hoping this, combined with the snow pattern on the screen, will mesmerise her into nodding off. Tough if she ends up spending the night on the couch.

An hour later and Sam's still looking at the blizzard on screen when Brenda staggers in.

"Can't sleep?" slurs Brenda, stating the obvious.

"No. It's weird being in bed on my own."

"You were only at his place a week or so – you can't be that used to it."

"You'd be surprised. I am."

<hr>

It's Thursday evening and Sam sits at her dressing table waiting for her curling irons to get hot enough to brand heifers. She shouldn't be going out with Chris tonight – her sleeping pattern has just returned to normal. Maybe she should spend the night with him rather than get home late. She sleeps better when she stays at his place but that might be because hot sex works better than hot milk.

With Brenda raiding her wardrobe, Sam absently stares into the mirror at the backwards view of her room. Brenda's decided Sam's got enough clothes that she can spare an outfit for her to wear that night on a special date. Sam isn't too concerned; she knows she'll get whatever is chosen returned. Eventually.

Movement reflected in the mirror causes her to focus. "I wonder what they want."

"What who wants?" says Brenda, from her spot halfway inside the wardrobe. She's working her way through the outfits in the furthest recesses, where Sam keeps her better clobber.

"The cops." Sam swings around to watch them walk up the path and knock on the front door.

"I'm not here, you don't know me, I've moved." Brenda is now right inside in the wardrobe. Her hand snakes out through Sam's clothes and pulls the door closed.

"Oh, all right. Mum's the word." Sam gets up to answer the door.

Walking slowly to the door with a smile pasted on her face, she thinks of possible Brenda alibis.

She's moved to Africa, joined the Peace Corp, become a nun. Brenda who?

Unfortunately her smile isn't reciprocated by the male and female officers standing at the open front door. Brenda must be in deep do-do.

"Is Samantha Bennett here?" says the male officer. His tone is official.

It takes a second for Sam's brain working on all those missing Brenda scenarios to click as to what they've just asked. Her stomach drops.

"Is it Mum? Dad? My brother? What's happened?" fires Sam, at the officers. "It's bad news isn't it? Please tell me. Please, please tell me." She wrings her hands together tightly, her eyes darting from one officer to the other. Her heart is hammering in time to the thoughts of car accidents, house fires and heart attacks marching relentlessly through her head.

The officers are momentarily stuck for words. "No, miss. We're not here to discuss your family."

Sam's sudden relief has her bursting into tears. "Thank god," says Sam, before wiping her arm across her eyes "Oh, thank god. Oh, thank god." Then she remembers the Rose Protection League. Her heart speeds up again.

"We'd like to talk to you about the disappearance of John-John de Graaf."

"John-John?" Sam's having difficulty following the conversation. "He's missing? But I was only over there the other day to measure him for a new autumn coat." Despite a circuitous route to Mrs de Graaf's, Sam hadn't been unable to shake the feeling that she was followed. But no matter how quickly she'd looked over her shoulder, she hadn't been able to spot anyone. In the end she'd put it down to paranoia.

32

*S*am's home alone, putting the finishing touches to John-John's autumn coat, when the phone rings. Sticking the needle part-way through the fabric, she piles it carefully on the table. She's kept going with the outfit because she figures John-John has to turn up soon or later, and she'd rather Mrs de Graaf pay for the fabric than have to cover the cost of it herself if she doesn't deliver the finished garment.

"Hello?" says Sam.

"Samantha! I need to see you now," booms out of the earpiece, firmly identifying the caller as Mrs de Graaf. "John-John's back!"

She holds the receiver a safe distance from her ear and wonders why Mrs de Graaf would want her anywhere near John-John if the woman thinks she's the one who dognapped him. "Is he okay?"

"No, he's not!" comes back at such volume that she moves the receiver even farther away than usual. "He needs a new coat. Urgently!"

Damn it.

Sam's loath to go over and do more work for the woman after she's obviously dobbed her in to the cops. If she wasn't such a good customer, Sam would tell her to shove it. But she locks up tight and walks slowly to Mrs de Graaf's place.

She doesn't bother going around the back. If it's as urgent as the woman made out on the phone, there's no way she's going to waste half an hour hammering at the back door. Mrs de Graaf doesn't snarl at her about this obvious breach of protocol. The woman is not her usual self. John-John can't be in a good way.

Mrs de Graaf leads the way from the foyer to a large, over-full sitting room where she sits on a French reproduction sofa and strokes the lump of blanket next to her. Sam can hear soft whimpers from somewhere under the pink heather-and-tan checked wool. "They shaved him. Completely."

"Shaved him?"

But he was as good as bald already.

"Yes. Just look at him." Mrs de Graaf lifts the covers off a violently shivering John-John.

"That's *awful*." Sam's genuinely appalled. While not being the dog's biggest fan, she doesn't hate him, either. Whoever did this sure as hell doesn't like animals. And they'd done a crap shaving job, with the little dog's body covered in scabby nicks. "Quick, cover him up again, keep him warm."

"Can you make a warm outfit for him to wear? I don't know what else to do for him," says Mrs de Graaf helplessly, the fluttering hands out of place on this Sherman tank of a woman.

"Do you have a hot water bottle?"

"Yes, I do! Would you look after him while I sort that out?" Mrs de Graaf struggles to her feet.

"Of course I will," says Sam, to the empty room. Sitting down next to John-John, She rubs away at the top of his head. The whimpering has died down by the time Mrs de Graaf returns with a hot water bottle and hands it to Sam. It's the temperature of molten lead, so Sam tucks it under several layers of woollen blanket to avoid parboiling the pug.

She leaves Mrs de Graaf, promising to return later with a jumpsuit that will be perfect at keeping John-John warm until his hair grows back. Even if it was the old bag who fingered her, Sam doesn't feel John-John should suffer.

. . .

Sam pulls an orange stretch towelling jumpsuit from her handbag and holds it up for Mrs de Graaf to see. "It's a little rough in the finishing, but it should do the trick."

"That doesn't matter, just so long as he's warm," says Mrs de Graaf, shivering in sympathy.

Pulling the blanket to one side, Sam gently eases one of John-John's front legs into the first leg of the all-in-one jumpsuit. Usually, this resulted in him trying to bite her, but he hardly stirs. Given how floppy the poor little dog is, it's like trying to get a couple of pounds of sausages into a pair of pantyhose. Finally she's able to dome the stretchy outfit closed along the back. John-John has been the soul of patience and despite his shivering and whimpering hasn't reacted to the new suit at all. Sunken and dull, his eyes stare up at Sam. She can feel him relax; he then dips his head and licks her hand when she rubs his chest.

She turns to see Mrs de Graaf looking down at her in wonder. "I told those policemen you had nothing to do with this, but they wouldn't believe me." She goes back to murmuring sweet nothings to the sad little dog. This mantra of endearments continues, until Sam feels herself glazing over. Shaking her head, she pulls herself out of the trance she's slipped into.

"Mrs de Graaf. I think you should take John-John to the vet."

"No, he'll be fine. He hates the vet. He just needs his mummy."

"But it's been half an hour and he's still shivering. He can't be cold now. I think it might be shock."

"Shock?" Mrs de Graaf's face is creased in confusion.

Wow, the woman surely isn't firing on all cylinders?

"Yes, shock. It can't have been nice for him." Sam rubs a dark ear poking out from the blanket.

"Do you think I should?"

"I think you need to get him to the vet pronto. Shock can

prove, ah, dangerous," says Sam, narrowly avoiding the word "fatal".

Leaning against the only wall in the lounge that isn't peppered with windows or doors, Sam stitches away by hand at her latest project. She's completed as much as she can on the sewing machine but this outfit is like no other she's ever made. "God, what is that smell?" She sniffs the air all around her but can't button it down.

Jennie watches her wrestling with the mountain of white satin. "What on earth are you making? Don't tell me one of them is getting married."

"Ah, no. It's a burial shroud."

"John-John?"

"Yep. Poor little bugger didn't even make it through the night." Sam's surprised at how much this has upset her.

After an initial look of surprise, Jennie says "That's awful! I know he was always biting me, but I wouldn't wish that on him."

Sam isn't surprised at this response. Jennie is so soft hearted she's been known to ferry spiders outside rather than see them squished. "He did seem to be partial to your ankles," says Sam, sniffing again.

"It was like I'd painted them with gravy." Jennie leans down to push the corner of her latest plaster back into place. "Surely you won't need all that fabric. He wasn't that chubby."

"Ah, it's not only a shroud." Shoving the satin to one side, Sam reveals what she's sitting on.

Jennie steps gingerly back from the small glossy white coffin. "He's not in there is he?"

"I didn't think to check when it was carried in here. I bloody hope not." She jumps up and tips the coffin lid off with the toe of her boot.

"Is that an oven bag?" says Jennie.

"Bloody hell, that's what the smell is. Gin!"

"Do you think she embalmed him herself?"

"I think losing him has her close to losing her marbles, so if she has, it wouldn't surprise me."

"Yeah, if you're capable of kissing a dog on the mouth when he's just finished licking his ah, crotch, you're capable of anything." Jennie shudders before adding practically "Is there enough room in the freezer?"

"Yeah. But we'll need to leave all this other crap in the coffin." The girls look down at the dog treats, fluffy toy and framed print of Mrs de Graaf, crammed in with John-John's bagged up body.

With the dog safely on ice, Sam gets back to work on his final outfit.

Poor wee thing. what a way to go. Whoever shaved him like that is a complete and utter arsehole.

Sam wonders how much Mrs de Graaf had to pay to get her pet back.

Sam looks across the checked tablecloth at Chris, his face reflecting the flicker of candlelight. Her right hand is held securely by his across the table. Gino, a waiter at their favourite Italian restaurant, has already taken the order and left them on their own.

"I still can't believe John-John died. Mrs de Graaf is beside herself with grief. Who'd do such a thing?" says Sam.

'Did you know six or seven owners have had dogs taken?" Chris rubs his thumb over the back of her hand, sending waves of pleasure up her arm and off to more covered areas.

"What about the police?" says Sam, in a distracted manner. "What are they doing? Apart from hassling me!"

"There's not much they can do. The owners don't say anything until the ransom's been paid and the mutt returned." Chris runs his finger up Sam's wrist, watching for a reaction.

She picks up her glass of water and takes a large mouthful.

"But Mrs de Graaf called the cops before John-John was returned."

"From what I hear, that's the worst shaving job to date." Chris places a foot between her feet and nudges them apart. His smile broadens in response to her intake of breath.

"Poor little guy. Apparently it was the shock that killed him, along with far too many tranquillizers." She moves her chair back slightly so she's out of Chris's reach and can concentrate on the conversation.

"Chicken," says Chris, with a knowing look.

Refusing to bite, she says "What I don't get is why the cops are looking at me. It wasn't Mrs de Graaf … she said she'd told them I had nothing to do with it. The cops wouldn't say who pointed them in my direction."

<hr>

Sam and Jennie sit at the dining table, devoid of dog outfits in various stages of construction. It's beautifully set, complete with candles and a white tablecloth that Sam recognises as one of her sheets. Brenda is banging around in the kitchen as though she is "knocking something together," as promised.

"Isn't this nice?" says Jennie. "It's the first time we've all managed to be home together for dinner. I still can't believe Brenda has cooked."

Sam shakes her head in wonder. "I didn't even know she could."

"Should we be afraid?"

"Bloody hell, this weighs a ton." Brenda staggers up to the dining table with a huge roast on an even bigger platter. It's surrounded by veggies that are more crucified than cruciferous.

"My god, that looks scrumptious, I don't remember us buying a roast that big." says Jennie, as the platter is slammed down in the middle of the table.

"The glaze looks incredible," says Sam.

Jennie's face bleaches out. "Is that a collar?"

"Brenda, where did you get this meat from?" Sam stands and stumbles away from the table.

"In the freezer … wedged between the ice cream and a couple of birds."

"Ah, would those be chickens?" Jennie also stands, although she gets no farther.

Rushing into the kitchen, Sam lifts the lid on the freezer, terrified of what she's going to find. Spotting John-John still at eternal rest amongst the peas she gasps out a heartfelt "Thank god!" This is soon echoed by Jennie, still frozen next to the dining table.

"Gotcha," crows Brenda.

Sam walks back into the lounge. "You bitch – I thought you'd cooked the frigging dog."

"Serves ya bloody right, it scared the hell out of me. Little beady eyes looking up at me, his tongue sticking out like that. It was obscene."

"I don't remember his tongue sticking out," says Jennie.

"Me, neither," says Sam, "I didn't bother unwrapping him just then."

"Jeez, I hope it goes back in when you defrost him," says Brenda.

"Defrost him?" says Sam.

"Well, you can't leave him frozen. He'll skid around inside the casket like an ice cube in a kitchen sink. And what if the crazy old cow wants an open casket? Freezer burn ain't pretty."

"Crap," utter Jennie and Sam in unison

"You'd better get the little sucker out if you want him soft in time for the funeral," says Brenda, gleefully.

Jennie prods the roast with the tip of her knife. "What exactly is this?"

"Pork," says Brenda, with conviction, before adding, "I think."

Sam checks her appearance in the mirror and satisfied with the outfit, closes her wardrobe doors and stuffs a few bits and pieces of make-up into her handbag. Chris is taking her shopping so she can buy something suitable to wear to John-John's funeral. Catching movement out of the corner of her eye, she watches him walk up the front path. The sight of him is enough to have her heart speeding up.

"Hi, there," says Sam, opening the front door.

"Hi, back," he says, before kissing her soundly. "Hey, before we head off I'll quickly use the loo, had a couple of coffees with breakfast."

"Okay." She's standing by the front door ready to go when she hears Chris calling from the bathroom.

"Sam, you want to come in here for a second?"

Chris is looking down at the bath. "Please tell me that's not a dead pug in the bottom of your bath."

"John-John. We're thawing him out."

"Ah, I didn't recognize him without the studded collar."

"Bloody hell." She nips through to the kitchen, holding it up triumphantly on her return. "Can I get you to put it back on? I'm starting to get grossed out now."

"Only now?" Chris takes the collar and bends down to put it back on. "What's this?" he says, straightening and holding out his hand.

"Ah, that'd be gravy."

33

*S*am tucks the tails of her new white shirt into the skirt of her new black suit and zips herself up. Shrugging into the jacket, she looks at herself in the mirror with a critical eye. She thinks the outfit is better suited to going for a job in a bank than a funeral, but Chris had assured her it was perfect.

She walks out into the lounge for a second opinion. "Do I look all right?"

Brenda, who's the only other person home at ten on a Monday morning, is lying on the couch and, worryingly, reading a book. "Yes, if you're going to a funeral."

"Phew, I thought it looked too interviewy." Sam tips up the book so she can read the title. "*Heart Care for the Elderly*. What the hell are you reading that for?"

Brenda grins broadly. "Don't want anyone popping their clogs on me."

"More than I needed to know." She lets the book drop back down.

"I still don't understand why The Tank doesn't just say a few words and toss John-John in a skip," says Brenda, waving at Sam's black suit.

"Can you honestly see Stephanie de Graaf down a back alley, dressed from head to foot in black and calmly standing there while her dearest John-John is flipped into the nearest dumpster?"

"Now, even I'd turn up for that!"

"Speaking of turning up, how come you're not at work?" Brenda looks settled in for the day on the couch. "How do you even manage to hold that job?"

"It's my charm. That, and I've got enough on my boss that he wouldn't dare flick me."

"Hmm. Well, gotta go, here's Chris." Sam watches him walk through the open front door "And, wow, doesn't he look hot in a suit?"

Brenda drags herself upright. "This I gotta see."

"Hey, there." Chris walks into the lounge, eliciting a wolf whistle from Brenda. He ignores it and kisses Sam on the mouth.

Brenda makes a spinning motion with her finger. "Hey, stud, give us a twirl."

"Careful, that's my stud you're talking to." Sam grabs Chris by the arm and is dragging him out the front door when Brenda speaks.

"How long do you think the ceremony will last?"

"An hour maybe," says Chris, over his shoulder.

"Why are you interested all of a sudden?" Sam stops so abruptly that Chris tugs on her arm.

"If you must know, I'd like the house to myself for a while."

"And?" says Sam.

"I've got, ah, a friend coming over."

"Brenda, are you blushing?" says Sam, in amazement. "How long do you need?"

"Not long."

"You've got two hours, tops," interrupts Chris, playing referee and calling full time on the girls' verbal ping-pong match.

"I wonder who's coming around," says Sam.

Chris walks around to his side of the car. "I really don't care. She's a complete flake."

"Yeah, but underneath it all she's okay. And she cooks a

mean pug."

"I can't believe you said that!" says Chris, sternly, before giving into laughter.

"Hey, we're going to his funeral aren't we?"

"But I'm going because my grandmother said she'd like me there. I wonder why you're going." Chris looks at her as she settles herself in the car.

"Are you kidding? After what the poor wee guy's been through over the past couple of days, I want to make sure they get him in the ground in one piece. I'm going to miss him, and I guess I'll miss her, too."

"Now that's the girl I know and love."

Love mouths Sam to herself, her hand straying to her chest where her heart has started to beat erratically; unfortunately in a "stand clear we need to use the defibrillator kind of way". "Well, you know me." She laughs weakly, and then sits quietly the rest of the way to Mrs de Graaf's.

They have a hike after parking because both sides of the street are chocker with flash European cars. Walking along the footpath to the house, she spots a couple of dark BMWs that have the nerves up her back skittering. She'll never be able to look at another one without thinking of Salami Boy.

They're about to walk in the driveway when Martin McGowan's Bentley drives slowly out and swings into the road, never gaining any real speed.

"Do you think he ever gets out of second, and more importantly why isn't he staying for the service?"

"I don't think he and John-John saw eye to eye, so he's probably dropped the wife off and done a runner."

"Wow, it's quite a turn out," says Sam, when they wander through the gap in a tall red brick wall to the left of the house. The service is to be held poolside.

John-John's little coffin sits on a black-swathed trestle table set up at right angles to the pool. An 'aisle' leads away from this, bordered on both sides by rows of folding chairs, adorned with black bows. Tall vases of lilies stand sentinel at the end of each mathematically-aligned row.

Flocking around this set up, the biddies are, to a woman, dressed from head to toe in funereal black. Flapping about, like blackbirds on a worm-filled lawn after a downpour.

Circling them is an assortment of small dogs in unsuitable funeral attire. Sapphire is even wearing her purple vinyl condom outfit. Given it's a muggy day, Sam hopes it's not possible for a girl poodle to get jock rot. Still, the dog's lucky it's socially acceptable for her to scratch in public.

Mrs McGowan's pack of French Bulldogs is racing around and through the legs of the trestle table, threatening to send John-John's coffin into the drink. Sam is alarmed to see water pooling by one corner of the small coffin. "Looks like he started thawing eventually," she says, under her breath to Chris. "Hopefully no one will notice with the mess the McGowan mob is making."

"Shouldn't we try to calm them down?"

"And risk Mrs McGowan biting my head off for stifling their creativity?"

Seconds later, one of the little dogs barrels into the trestle at the pool end, turning the plank on top into a ramp. The small casket slides majestically down the wooden slope and into the pool. "No!" Sam's hand covers her horrified expression.

The small craft lists to one side before sinking into the deep end of the pool.

"We have to get it out. We can't leave him in there!"

"Hey, I'm not going to ruin a perfectly good suit fishing a dead dog out of a pool and I'm sure as hell not stripping off in front of this lot." Chris looks at the group of old ladies. "One of them's likely to kark it."

They're still deciding what to do when the lid pops off the coffin and John-John floats to the surface where he bobs about like a grotesque, white satin pool toy.

"Quick, we have to fish him out before Mrs de Graaf comes out and sees him. It'd destroy her." She indicates a leaf skimmer propped up against the pool house, but before Chris can move, the McGowan pack are in the pool and nosing

John-John around with all the skill of an international water polo team.

"Oh, my god!" Sam can see Stephanie de Graaf walking across the paved area in front of the garages. She's wearing what must be her funeral tweed and a demeanour reminiscent of the Queen Mother. "Quick, someone delay her," says Sam, to the women in general. "She can't see this."

"Oh, I'll do it," says Mrs McGowan, finally taking responsibility for her dogs and tottering off to intercept the chief mourner.

Sam, again points to the leaf skimmer. "Hurry, Chris, now."

He's dragging John-John's body to the edge of the pool with the giant sieve when Stephen strolls up with Mrs Courtney. He grasps the situation in seconds, rips off his shirt and trousers, causing one old lady to sink gracefully onto a sun lounger, and dives into the pool. After a few duck dives, he manages to retrieve the coffin plus the items Mrs de Graaf has put in it for John-John's trip to Canine Heaven. Chris and Sam get everything set up again, while Stephen dresses.

"Margaret, will you please get out of the way! I have to say a proper goodbye to my baby," booms Julia de Graaf, managing to push her way past Mrs McGowan.

"Whoa, that was close." Sam's standing shoulder to shoulder with Chris while Stephen hides behind them. She's in a reflective mood by the time the ceremony starts and is surprised to find herself sneakily wiping away a few tears.

She thinks no one has noticed until Chris hands her a pristine white handkerchief.

She's still in a sombre frame of mind when they pull up outside the flat, having given Brenda the two hours they'd promised. "Hey, isn't that Mr McGowan's Bentley?" She points to the dark green monster parked in front of a house a couple of doors down. "He must be visiting one of our neighbours."

"C'mon, let's get you slipped into something more comfortable and go back to my place for the afternoon," says Chris, who's managed to wangle the whole day off work, supposedly on compassionate leave. He hurries Sam along the path and up the front steps.

"And would that be so you can slip into something more comfortable later?" She arches one eyebrow, before unlocking the front door

"You read my mind," says Chris, although anything else dies on his lips. He and Sam stop short when they spot Brenda and Martin McGowan, naked, on the couch and going for it.

Sam isn't sure what to say. "Glad the couch is vinyl," wins out.

"I wouldn't have called that a plus."

"Makes it easier to take outside, scrub it with disinfectant and hose it down."

Chris nods at the writhing couple. "And speaking of needing to be hosed down."

"Brenda!" Sam shouts "will you please stop?"

"With you in a minute," Brenda pants, seemingly undeterred at having an audience. Martin is similarly inclined. Realizing they have company, he gasps, "Hello" over his shoulder and carries on.

The sight of his white bum pumping up and down is more than Sam can stomach. She covers her eyes and turns away. "This is likely to put me off sex for life."

"Can't have that!" Chris drags her out of the front door. "You can wear something of mine."

"That was 'special' although not in a good way," says Sam, getting in the car. "I'm going to need therapy to rid myself of that particular image."

"I'm sure I can replace it with something more pleasing." There's a definite glint in his eye.

"The hot tub's switched on?"

"Absolutely."

"Good, because I'm feeling very, very, dirty," says Sam, looking at Chris through her lashes.

Chris looks at her before breaking into a huge grin. "What a coincidence."

She's still shaking her head and having the occasional involuntary shudder, when they arrive at Chris's place. "I can't believe she'd shag an old guy just to get her hands on his cash."

"He's worth a lot and it looks like he can still get it up."

"Arrrgh. Don't even talk about it."

Chris leads her into the house. "Relax. I'm going to replace it with something much nicer." He closes the door behind them and takes Sam through into his bedroom.

"So?" says Sam, smiling.

"Patience." Chris rummages in a drawer, "Here we are." He holds up a black scarf. "I think the best way to get rid of those images is to replace them with feelings."

"How's that supposed to work?"

"Trust me." Chris carefully ties the scarf behind her head, covering her eyes.

"I can't see a damn thing."

"Good."

"Chris?"

Chuckling when he realises she's not going to shut up, he kisses her, taking her by surprise, blindfolded as she is. She's lost for words when Chris finally stops.

"Well?" he says, to her.

"It's good. I know I always close my eyes when we kiss, but this is different."

"Want to go on?"

"Yes," she breathes out raggedly.

Chris moves away slightly and waits. Sam is jumpy with anticipation, knowing he's about to do something but has no idea what it will be. She jumps when he peels off her jacket, before slowly unbuttoning her crisp white shirt. His hands brush her skin in the process and she can't help a quick intake of breath.

She can feel the air on her breasts where the shirt gapes. Chris pushes it back over her shoulders and collects it behind her, his tongue trailing the side of her neck. Sam breathes deeper in an attempt to brush her breasts against him. He runs a finger across the front of her bra, the friction caused by the lace sending small tremors through her body.

Chris skims his hands across her shoulders, sliding the straps of her bra down and over her arms. Moving behind her, he undoes the two tiny hooks that were all that was holding it in place.

He runs his tongue up the back of her neck while he reaches around and tugs at both nipples. Sam's gasp catches in her throat and she arches against his hands. She moans when he removes his hands to unzip her straight black skirt. In seconds this is sitting on the ground and Chris reaches around in front of her again, running both his hands down her body and over the front of her lace knickers, adding more tremors to those already making her shake.

He lifts her clear of her skirt and she sways against him unsure her legs will hold. He straightens her up and steps back from her, she can hear clothing rustling and when he joins her again she can feel his bare chest, the crisp hair tickling her back. His hands skim down her body, then his thumbs hook the side of her knickers and slide them down to her ankles, where he leaves them. She frowns that he's left them there and goes to step out of them, but he holds her legs in place and nips a buttock.

"Stay still," he admonishes and stands, rubbing himself against her on the way back up. He steps away again and she hears more clothing being removed. "Don't move," he whispers in her ear and walks away.

Time moves slowly for her and she's starting to feel silly standing there with her knickers around her ankles when she hears him returning. He stands in front of her for a few seconds, doing nothing, and the anticipation is killing her. His hands close over her breasts and she groans when she realises they're slick with oil. They glide over her, slipping their way down her stomach and his thumbs push themselves into her, parting her and making everything they touch slick and hot. He moves his hands around and kneads her buttocks and pulls her up against him. He's naked, oiled all over and ready for her. Sam's legs start to buckle.

"Put your hands around my neck." His voice has turned croaky.

Even without a blindfold Sam would be doing his bidding blindly, passion having overtaken; all her senses are screaming. Chris reaches around behind her again and grasping her by the thighs lifts her until she can feel him nudging for entrance. With a slight swivel of her hips he slides all the way in causing a gasp to catch at the back of her throat.

"Hold on," says Chris. Sam's expecting to ride him like this but he has other ideas and starts walking with them as they are. Each step pushing him even deeper.

"What are you doing?"

"Shhh."

Sam is still too caught up in the moment to work out where he's carrying her but realises they're outside when she feels the sun on her back.

"I hope we haven't just walked out the front door?"

Chris's response is a snort of laughter that she feels deep inside.

Sam's legs are wrapped firmly around his waist and so she feels safe when he starts to tip her back but is surprised when her back comes into contact with fabric.

"Relax," urges Chris. "Let yourself drop back."

Sam does and realises she's lying across the hammock, which Chris starts to swing with one hand, while his other rubs back and forth across her clit. The hammock gains momentum and he runs his hands up the front of her body and over her breasts. Sam's senses are on fire, it's as though he's touching her everywhere and still the thrusting keeps on.

"Think how good it would be if your legs were over my shoulders," he suggests, without actually telling her to do it. Thinking about it for a second, she feels incredibly wanton when she takes up his suggestion. More than she would if she had simply been told to do this. His thrusts go deeper and she feels he's touching the very core of her.

The heat of the sun shines on her naked skin, invading her body, filling every bit of her. Holding her hips, Chris pulls almost all the way out of her before burying himself in her, he keeps this up until she's whimpering and the warmth has spread beyond her body. It crashes in, concentrating itself between her legs, before exploding. Sam cries out, the orgasm washing over her in waves. She's pulsing the length of Chris, fulfilled when at last he follows her over the edge, coming hard and collapsing on top of her, sending the hammock swinging wildly.

Chris pulls her back against him in the hot tub and massages her shoulders. "You know you could enjoy that every day of the week if you moved in."

"But I can't leave Jennie on her own." Sam's body goes still under his hands. "We're travelling together, we've made plans. She needs me."

"She's not your dependent, she's an adult. Would she stay by your side if it was the other way around?"

"Of course she would!" says Sam, her tone bolstered with forced conviction.

"It's crazy to put your life on hold because you're second guessing her."

"But what would Mum and Dad say?" She throws out another argument.

"Hey, if you don't want to move in, you only have to say," says Chris, his voice cracking at the end.

Sam doesn't need to turn to know he's feeling hurt by her rejection. She feels trapped into a response. "I don't know if I'm ready."

"Okay, if that's your decision." Chris pushes her gently away from him until she's kneeling in the middle of the hot tub. "But you know where I am if you change your mind."

She keeps her back to Chris rather than risk eye contact. "You think this is easy for me?"

"Yeah, I do. You're taking the easy way out. Again."

"Again?" says Sam, unable to stop herself from spinning to face him.

"Wasn't that why you left New Zealand? It was easier than facing Darren and telling him what a complete prick he was. You haven't stopped running since you left Auckland. Have you?"

"I'm outta here." Sam throws herself over the side of the hot tub in her haste to get away. "Stay where you are. I'll call myself a taxi."

"That's right, Sam, run away. Again."

"Bastard," she mutters to herself before stalking to the bedroom to get dressed. Chris is still in the hot tub when the taxi arrives although she hears him call out, "You know where I'll be when you're ready to stop running."

"Well, I hope ... I hope you shrivel like a prune," she screams back at him. It even sounds stupid to her ears, but she's incapable of a more grown-up response.

Sam's relieved to see Martin McGowan's Bentley missing from the front of the house when the taxi drops her off, although she must have just missed him as Brenda is still lying on the couch wearing nothing but a smile.

"I hope you're going to scrub that sofa," says Sam, stomping through to her room.

"Didn't last time," is the airy response from Brenda.

"You mean we've been sitting in the remains of your old-man sex?"

"Nah, I always make him wear a rubber – he might not be shooting blanks. How was the funeral?"

"The coffin ended up in the blasted pool. Sort of put the ceremony on fast forward."

"How the bloody hell did that happen?"

She gives a blow-by-blow of the ceremony as Brenda dresses. By the time Brenda is fully clothed, and Sam has finished, Brenda's in tears, she's laughing so hard. She stops chuckling when she clicks that Sam isn't sharing her amusement.

"I didn't think you were that keen on the mutt?"

"It was just sad seeing Mrs de Graaf so distraught. It brings it home that these dogs are sometimes the only family they've got."

"Surely they've got rellies waiting for them to kick the bucket?"

"If they do, then they bloody aren't going to turn up until after the funeral. I'd never abandon Mum and Dad like that."

"So, spit. What's got you all depressed?"

Damn.

She'd been hoping to steer the conversation away from herself. She outlines the scene with Chris, but rather than the expected sympathy, Brenda gives her an ear-bashing about her not being able to keep everyone happy.

Sam slams her bedroom door on Brenda's lecture; although this doesn't stop it continuing without pause. She drops her handbag and peels off her clothes. They smell of chlorine.

Is Chris right? Am I running?

"Stow it Brenda, I don't want to talk about it," Sam yells through the door.

She feels as if she's running the gauntlet when she goes

back through the lounge to the bathroom. Brenda's still going strong, although she has trouble hearing with her fingers jammed in her ears while "la, la, la-ing" at the top of her voice in an effort to drown out the lecture.

Once she's under the shower, mercifully she can no longer hear the non-stop lecture, or maybe it's stopped. She stands and lets the water beat on her head, cascading down her face. Wasn't love supposed to be easier than this?

The water sluicing down her body causes a faint scent of chlorine to waft up. Breathing it in, Sam's thoughts are back in the hot tub. The water on her back as caressing as Chris's hands had been. She sighs deeply, drawing water into her lungs in the process. She's down on her hands and knees in the bath and feeling faint before the coughing stops. She stays there letting the water pummel her; it's still pounding away when the hot water runs out. Still she doesn't move.

Eventually, she makes her way back to her bedroom and Sam's relieved to see that Brenda has disappeared. Fighting shivers, she shuts the door to her bedroom and crawls into bed, a towel still wrapped about her head. She rolls over and faces the wall to further blot out the world and is still shivering and focusing on the wallpaper when Jennie comes in hours later.

Jennie sits on the edge of her bed. "What happened?"

"I think it's over," says Sam, her voice catching.

"But why? I thought everything was going great with you guys." Jennie rubs Sam's back in a comforting circle.

"So did I, but he started to get all serious. He asked me to move in."

"But would that have been such a bad thing?"

Sam rolls over to face her friend. "But what about us travelling together?"

"It's great travelling with you, but love is rare. You never know when it'll be taken from you."

Looking at Jennie staring into space, Sam is reminded of what her friend has lost; with events beyond her control. No matter how much Jennie had loved Steve, he'd still left her in the end.

"But if it's meant to be, how come I feel so cornered?"

"It can be scary, but so can letting go. Just promise me, you'll think about it?" Jennie pulls the covers up to Sam's chin and pats her shoulder through the blankets. "You need to think carefully before you throw it away."

After the door closes behind Jennie, Sam lies looking at the wallpaper. Every now and then a tremor works its way through her body. She's not sure if these are from being cold or being scared of the thought of commitment.

So much for love making you feel all warm and cosy.

35

Sam spits out a piece of wool bouclé fluff. Even having zigzagged all the raw edges, everything in her corner of the lounge is covered in pink snowflakes, including her. Chewing away at the side of her bottom lip, adding to its rawness, Sam wishes she could stop everything unravelling.

Jennie walks into the lounge and catches her biting hard on her lip. Jennie's dressed for a night out. Her small black evening bag dangles from one shoulder. "Have you phoned him yet?"

Sam lifts her foot from the pedal. "No! Why the hell should I phone him? He's the one who should be phoning me."

"And if he doesn't?"

Sam sucks her bottom lip into her mouth, along with some fluff. Her gaze drops back to the pink fabric to break eye contact. Risking a peek, she's relieved to see Jennie's looking toward the front door in response to beeping at the gate.

"Well, my mates from work are here," says Jennie, yelling, "Phone him!" as she pulls the front door closed behind her.

"Why the bloody hell should I? It's his stupid idea to get serious, not mine. I'm too bloody young to settle down!" No sooner has this been screamed at the empty room than Sam's mouth drops open, her eyes widen and a snort of nervous laughter escapes.

Shaking her head in disbelief, she turns her attention back to the sewing. Well, most of her attention. While unpicking yet another crooked seam, she also works on a tangle of random thoughts.

What happened to being excited about being engaged to Darren? Has hasn't changed that much, hs she? What is it that's got her freaking out about making a commitment now?

No answers crop up and she goes back to her sewing with better results. Poor Sapphire had been shivering when they'd seen her at the Laundromat. If the dog had been able to, Sam thinks it would have crawled inside one of the tumble dryers. The problem with all the satin, lace and feather outfits that currently make up Sapphire's wardrobe is that none of them are up to keeping the dog warm, now that autumn is creeping closer.

Knocking on Mrs Farquhar's door, Sam hopes the woman will be okay with her dropping in unannounced. This is the first time she's made an outfit without it specifically being commissioned.

"Hello, Sam. I wasn't expecting you this evening," says Mrs Farquhar. Sapphire stands next to her, trembling.

"No, I know this is unusual but it's been a bit colder recently and I thought Sapphire might enjoy something a little warmer to wear," says Sam, in explanation.

"That's so kind of you. Please come in."

Sam ditches her shoes and follows Mrs Farquhar through to the lounge where she takes the new outfit from her bag and hands it over for inspection.

Mrs Farquhar holds it up and twists it front and back, inspecting it from every angle. She fingers the fabric, a smile making itself comfortable on her face. "It's beautifully made, as always. The design is fabulous and I love the fake fur trim on the hood."

Mrs Farquhar rests the outfit on her lap. "Seeing this gives me an idea."

"A silk version?" Sam tries to second guess the direction of their conversation.

"No. I was thinking more about a Ready-to-Wear Collection."

"A collection for Sapphire?"

"Fabulous, we should call it the Sapphire Collection."

A range! Lordy, talk about cash to spare.

"I can come back with my pad and pencils and start on some sketches of outfits that will work with what she already has."

"No, you misunderstand. The range wouldn't be for Sapphire, just named after her. I'm talking mass production."

Images of herself physically chained to a sewing machine flit through Sam's head. "Mass production! I don't think I'm capable of that."

"No, no. You wouldn't be sewing them yourself. You'd just be designing them. I've got a couple of ladies who'd be perfect for that sort of thing."

"Really?"

"Yes, they've retired from the saddlery because the horse blankets simply became too much for them. They're excellent seamstresses and I know they're finding retirement leaves them with too much time on their hands."

She doesn't feel as though she has any choice but to go along. "Right you are."

"Excellent, I'll phone Theresa and Nancy and see when they can come over. In the meantime, I want you to give some thought to a basic range. Ten or so styles should do."

"Ten or so," says Sam, weakly as she's leaving.

Mrs Farquhar's hand holds the edge of the door. "More if you like."

"More?" says Sam, to the now closed door.

Sam sits in the middle of a flock of wool bouclé, with pastels from every hue of the rainbow. The new autumn outfit has been such a hit with both Mrs Farquhar and Sapphire that she's been commissioned to make six more. The only colour she couldn't bring herself to buy was baby blue, worried it would look as if Sapphire was sporting a toupee.

In tandem with this, she's been working on designs for the new Sapphire Collection and has met the two women Mrs Farquhar recommended. She'd simply given them a sketch along with some fabric and basic instructions and they'd assembled a sample beautifully. Thinking about it, the main difference between coats for horses and coats for dogs is the size.

One plus about this frantic activity is that it's stopped her dwelling on Chris. Damn him for being so bloody stubborn. She'd be stuffed if she was going to be the one to buckle under and phone him.

Brenda eyes the material churning through the sewing machine. "Good lord, what on earth are you making?"

"Autumn suits for Sapphire."

Brenda picks up one of the crested, gold buttons from a small bowl. "Jeez, she'll look like Jackie O."

She takes in the chic navy pant suit Brenda is modelling as though on the catwalk, albeit without the crazy cross-over walking. "You're looking a bit Jackie O yourself. Where are you off to?" The ensemble's not Brenda's usual look at all, and makes her look a little too *Stepford Wives* for Sam's liking.

Brenda runs her hands down the side of her jacket, smoothing it into submission. "Martin and I are off to the races at Ballarat."

"You're seeing him again!"

"Why wouldn't I? He treats me well. We're a lot alike." At Sam's reaction, she continues "It's true! He wasn't always rich. He clawed his way up. I like that about him."

Sam is so gobsmacked at Brenda being able to manage this statement without it being liberally splattered with "effings" and "craps", that she's quiet for a second.

Maybe Martin McGowan is good for Brenda?

"And, anyway," says Brenda, reverting to type, "he throws buckets of cash at me. Says I make him feel young."

"He's feeling young, that's for sure. What does Mrs McGowan think?"

"She's screwing the gardener to get back at him."

"You're joking!" Sam snorts, having trouble with this combo. "Is it working?"

"Yep! He's pissed off all right. Says the garden's looking scruffy."

"But what about Mrs McGowan?"

"He reckons the gardener had the blade set too low last time he *mowed* her, if you get my drift."

Unfortunately, she does.

Sam looks at the phone, willing it to ring. Its silence is needling when Brenda comes to stand next to her. She also looks at the silent device.

"I take it he still hasn't phoned."

"Hmm. I don't understand. Why won't he phone? What the hell's the difference to him if we're living together or not? I don't get why we couldn't just go on like we were?"

"When you've worked that out, maybe you should call him."

Brenda wanders off to her bedroom before Sam can ask her what the hell she means. She presses her index finger to the corner of her right eye to quell the twitching and after one final glare at the silent phone, returns to her sewing.

She makes a good show of working away at another of Sapphire's Jackie O suits but is unable to concentrate, her mind churning. After a muttered, "Damn it all to sodding hell," she stomps back to the phone, pounces on it and dials Chris's office. She's thrown when it's answered by someone other than Barbara, the usual receptionist. This one's name is Rachel. Her forced perkiness and squeaky voice put her at around twelve, even if she is so obviously trying to inject some professionalism into it.

"Ah, hello, could I speak to Chris Drayton, please?" Sam winds the curly phone cord so tightly around her hand she almost straightens it.

"He's out of the office at present, can I tell him who called?"

"No, that's okay, I'll phone back," Sam's too chicken to leave a message with a pre-pubescent stranger, although she can't help but ask, "Do you know when he'll be back?"

"He didn't say. Are you sure I can't take a message? It's probably the best idea." The young receptionist subtly puts the pressure on.

"Ah, okay. Will you tell him ... Samantha Bennett phoned?" Sam immediately regrets it. She's still pissed off that she's been the one to fold.

"I'll make sure he gets the message." The receptionist's tone is less perky now she knows who's calling.

Or am I being paranoid?

She's in for the rest of the day but doesn't get a call back. Part of her is relieved. He wants a level of commitment she's not certain she's ready for. At least not yet.

Unsure if he's been given the message by the snotty receptionist, she tries him at home the next evening.

Why in god's name doesn't he have an answerphone?

The following morning she leaves another message at his office. She's politely assured the previous message has been passed on but after several more attempts over the following days, the receptionist eventually says, "I've told him you've called," without even bothering to ask who it is.

36

*C*hris stands at the workbench in his garage surrounded by a pile of cardboard boxes. For a self-professed minimalist, he's got a lot of stuff to pack. He takes down a wrench from the board at the back of his workbench and after oiling it, wraps it in an old pair of grots, the arse of which is long gone. All that's left to show the tool had ever hung on the board is its painted outline.

A click in his ears announces the end of the first side of the cassette he's listening to.

Bloody clever of the Japanese to invent a mobile tape deck.

Without unclipping the Walkman from his belt, Chris hits the eject button, flips the cassette over and reinserts it ready to play the B side. He's been listening to music pretty much non-stop since picking it up on his last trip to Tokyo. He pushes the play button and listens to static before the music kicks in. The bobbing of his head soon follows.

He continues oiling and wrapping tools until the board is a shadow of its former self. He's hacking an old T-shirt in half ready for the final tool, a set of feeler gauges, when a hand lands on his shoulder causing him to drop the scissors. They sail point down toward his feet, inadequately protected in a pair of flip-flops. His feet shoot out to both sides and clear of the scissors by the time they attack the concrete.

273

He swings around to find Mark right behind him. A downside to having the music cranked up. He hits the stop button and pulls the headphones back so they sit around his neck, the foam ear pads snug on either side of his Adam's apple.

"That's a relief. I thought you'd gone deaf."

"Jeez, mate, you scared the crap out of me."

"Sorry, I got sick of yelling your name." Mark tugs at the electronics hanging on Chris's body. "I only sussed you were out here by the bloody awful singing."

"I wasn't singing."

"Mate, you sounded like a cat that'd just had its nuts removed with a butter knife."

Chris untangles the Walkman and piles it at one end of the workbench. "I'm glad you're here, I could do with some help with this lot." He swings his hand wide to encompass the garage.

Mark eyes a collection of used paint cans, their contents visible by the long since dried-out drips fringing their rusted sides. "I hope this crap is all going to the dump."

"Yeah, chuck that lot in the drum." He jerks his head in the direction a dark red 44-gallon drum standing just inside the double roll-up door.

Turning back to the bench, he wraps the feeler gauges and stows them in a cardboard box with some other tools. He seals the box with brown packing tape that shrieks in annoyance every time he uses it. Once closed, he stacks the box with an assortment of other cartons. The boxes he's packed today are easy to spot in that they're not covered in cobwebs and a fine layer of dust and engine oil. He'll have to re-tape some of the older boxes as the parcel tape has split into clear plastic and a residue of sticky brown goo.

Mark swings paint cans across the garage and into the drum. "Is Pita okay with you hanging onto all this stuff?"

"So long as she's got somewhere to park her car, she's cool."

"Where are you going to park yours?"

"Out in the carport. More important I keep the Ghia inside." Chris pats the bonnet of his beloved 1959 Karmann Ghia.

"You *still* waiting for that part from Germany?"

"Yeah, it's taking bloody ages to find one that's gonna fit without paying an arm and a leg. It'll be coming up to a year since I even took her out on the road." He flips the cover back down over the gleaming gunmetal paintwork. It slithers down the polished sides, then pools on the ground, hiding the blocks supporting the vehicle. The car's whitewall tires are stacked in a corner, waiting for the day they once again savour the tarmac. "How's the Foul Can going now?"

"Hah bloody hah! Smooth as a baby's arse since I fixed the front ball joints," says Mark, defending his beloved Falcon. "Have you told Sam you're going away?"

"No point. Haven't heard from her." Chris still can't believe how bloody stubborn she is. He would have expected her to cave by now. It isn't like he's asking for a lifetime commitment, just something less casual than their relationship had been. It's that or she's found someone else.

Mark's response to this revelation is to chuck another rusting paint can in the direction of the drum. He's getting good; this one doesn't even bounce off the rim but drops cleanly in. Unfortunately the noise isn't lessened by his accuracy, with the loud clang filling the aluminium garage to bursting point. The cobwebs on the inside of the windows pulse like the woofer speakers of Chris's stereo.

"I'll bet Pita wishes you weren't going away," says Mark, archly.

"Hah. Every time I walk through reception she visually frisks me. I can feel her eyes all over my arse when I walk down the hall to my office."

Mark responds by tossing the final two paint cans together at the drum. He misses with both of them and their lids fly off like Frisbees and out down the drive. Luckily any paint left in the tins has long since dried to a plastic-like consistency.

"Careful mate."

"You still think buggering off overseas is a good idea?"

"It's a no-brainer, considering." Chris pulls ruined tape off an old cardboard box. "If I want to get ahead, it's not going to be in Aussie. And anyway it's only a month's leave of absence."

37

Staring at the phone until it blurs, Sam dives on it and calls Chris at home. She's given him a week to call her back.

"Pita speaking," says a now-familiar voice after a couple of rings.

She's stunned when she twigs that Pita the snot-nosed step-sister and Rachel, the receptionist at Chris's office, are one and the same. The girl hadn't said much the night they'd met at Monty's birthday party and her *telephone* voice is different. "Hello? Is anyone there?"

"Hi, is Chris there?" says Sam, on auto pilot.

Damn, I should have just hung up.

"He is, but I'd hate to wake him … the two of us didn't get much sleep last night. Is this Samantha?" says Pita, sweetly. There's a smile pasted all over the smug little bitch's voice.

"I don't believe you!" Sam's not making that mistake again. "Can I speak to Chris?"

"No, you can't."

"Dammit, if you don't put him on, I'm coming over there. Now!"

"It was worth a try." Pita drops the phone heavily enough that Sam automatically yanks the receiver away from her ear.

She's still waiting ten minutes later but doesn't want to

hang up now she's managed to get through. A couple more minutes and Pita is back on the line. "Oh, I've just remembered, he's working overseas."

Sam's anger threatens to choke her. "When's he back?"

"He's not coming back. Don't you get it?"

"Get what?"

"You lose. I'm joining him over there and we're announcing our engagement." Pita's voice is brimming with spite when she continues. "He's mine. Always was and always will be."

She listens to the disconnect beep for a minute before numbly replacing the receiver.

———

Gloria Gaynor's, 'I will survive' warbles out of the cassette player on her bedside table while she lies limply on her bed staring at a spot on the ceiling. She's startled when Brenda storms into her room.

"I thought you were over with him? How can you be moping when you dumped him? I can't take this anymore." Hitting the eject button, Brenda brings Gloria to a garbled halt; leaving her *afraid*, but not yet *petrified*. She throws the cassette on the ground and stomps repeatedly on it until all that's left is a small pile of shattered plastic and a spaghetti of tape.

Dragging herself up onto one elbow, she glares at Brenda. "I can't believe you did that."

"Hey, it was the cassette or you. What the bloody hell's happened now?"

"He's gone."

"Gone?"

"Working overseas. Japan, I guess."

"Who told you that?" says Brenda.

"Pita."

"And you believed the little bitch?"

• • •

Walking back to her room after hanging up, Sam berates herself.

This is all my fault! I should have done what Jennie said and phoned him straightaway.

She's lying on her bed, thumping her head into the pillow and muttering, "stupid, stupid, stupid", when Jennie walks in.

"Brenda told me what happened. Is it true?"

"Yeah. I just checked with Mrs Courtenay. She was vague on their engagement, but confirmed he's overseas."

"What are you going to do?"

"Not sure."

"Something you *could* think about is England. Steve and I planned to go there so I've already checked everything out. What if we head over for their summer?"

"Oh, you and Steve. Oh, Jennie, I'm so sorry. I've been so wrapped up with what's happening to me, I didn't even think."

"How many times do I have to say I'm ... oh," Jennie rolls her eyes and shakes her head. "A new country is just what you need."

Hearing the back door open, Sam looks up from the final Jackie O suit she's working on, to see Jennie coming in from work. "Hey, there," says Sam, flatly.

"Hey, back. How are you?" Jennie's face shows her concern.

"I'm okay." Sam knows she looks a sight, with dark circles under her eyes and skin covered in breakouts from eating rubbish.

Jennie pulls some red plastic wallets from the depths of her handbag and places them carefully on the dining table.

"What are they?"

"Our tickets to England."

"You've bought them!" Sam squeaks. "But I thought you were only checking flights?" Sam's hands fly up to frame a face that's rigid with shock.

"They were half price, Sam! Otherwise I couldn't have

stumped up for them. We'll be flying Air New Zealand and everything." Jennie seems to think this fact alone is enough to travel to the other side of the world.

"I can't believe you bought them without even speaking to me! What if, what if, Chris—"

"Sam, there isn't a '*what if*'. You said so yourself."

"But, but. When, when are the flights?"

"June the twentieth."

"That's only three weeks away! You'll have to change the flights." Sam's still grasping for a reprieve.

"They're non-transferable, that's why they were so cheap."

"But what if ..." The rest clings to Sam's larynx, when she spots Jennie's pitying look.

"They were the last two seats at the cheap rate. I couldn't pass them up."

"God, I wish you had!" yells Sam, causing Jennie to quietly pick up the bright red wallets, put them back in her handbag and walk to her room. The door closing softly behind her signals an end to their discussion.

Sam's still glaring at the peach bouclé, half swallowed up by the sewing machine, when Brenda waltzes in.

"Fu ... ah, I mean, heck, what's wrong with you? You've got a face like a smacked arse ... er, bum."

"Shut, the hell up."

"Well, excuse me. It's Chris again. Isn't it? As if I need to ask."

"No actually, it's not."

"Makes a fu ... ah, flipping change."

"No, it's Jennie. She's bought our tickets to London," says Sam.

"London! When?" Brenda stills while she waits for Sam's response.

"Twentieth of June." Sam readies herself for the explosion.

She's surprised when the only response from Brenda is, "You can leave before then if you like," accompanied by her moving again, but only to rub her hands together.

"But you'll be covering the rent on your own."

"Martin said he'd be happy to pay. That way we can have the place to ourselves."

Sam is amazed that once again Brenda has landed on her feet.

Why on earth can't luck be more evenly distributed?

She takes the bouclé out of the machine, snaps the threads roughly by hand and tosses it to one side.

"You don't *have* to." Brenda's gaze roves around the lounge assessing it. "Just so long as you're cool with Martin being around most evenings."

Leaving Brenda mentally re-arranging the furniture to suit its new love-nest status, Sam walks to her room. She's shutting the door when Brenda announces that she intends turning Sam's room into a walk-in wardrobe.

Hearing this, she sits at *Brenda's* dressing table, in *Brenda's* wardrobe and stares in the mirror. Hah, correction. *Brenda's* mirror. Maybe Jennie is right, and it is time for them to get out of Melbourne. She focuses on the mirror and her reflection. With her acne, hollow eyes and greasy hair, she's glad she doesn't run the risk of Chris seeing her. She's still staring at herself when the evening light fails along with her reflection. A knock at the door brings her back to reality, her thoughts solidifying in that second. "Come in." Sam's expecting Brenda to appear with a tape measure, but it's Jennie.

"I'm so sorry, Sam. I thought I was doing the right thing. I'll cover the cost of your ticket. But, I'm still going to England. Steve would want me to. I want to."

"No, you're right. Sorry I yelled at you."

"I'm sorry I sprung it on you like that. I did phone from the travel agent's, but there was no answer."

Sam swivels to look up at Jennie. "So apart from leaving on the twentieth, what else am I up for?"

"Does this mean what I think it means?"

Sam gets to her feet. "I guess it does." If she focuses on the future maybe it'll help bury the pain of her recent past.

Hugging each other, the girls chant, *sotto voce,* "We're going to London. We're going to London." As the excitement builds, so does the volume until they're yelling it out and jumping around in an impromptu dance, although Sam's aware of sadness picking at the scab of this new-found joy.

Jennie stops suddenly and Sam almost tumbles. "But what's Brenda going to say about us moving out?"

"Hah, she's thrilled. She's going to turn my room into a walk-in wardrobe."

"But what about the rent? She won't like having to cover that on her own."

"She won't have to – Martin McGowan's going to pick up the tab." She can't help but laugh at Jennie's grimace which deepens when Sam breaks the news about Martin McGowan soon being a common sight. "I'd rather sleep in the park than be treated to seeing that man's bum again," says Sam, laughing.

The girls sink to the floor and start planning their trip to London in detail.

"I'll pay you back for the airfares, Jen."

"You will?"

"Yeah, I said the dogs would be paying for our flights and that hasn't changed. Half price? Bloody bargain!"

Leaning against the bed they survey the contents of Sam's wardrobe, the doors of which are flung wide open. "You'll have to get rid of some clothes," says Jennie.

"Hey, after all Brenda's done for me, I'm happy to leave them in the wardrobe."

Crunching her way reluctantly up Mrs Farquhar's driveway, Sam's fairly sure the woman will go ballistic.

Seeing herself in the gleaming black door she rearranges her features in an attempt to look less guilty. Satisfied with her expression, she rings the doorbell hoping it'll remain unanswered.

"Samantha. I've been expecting you." Mrs Farquhar's gaze

latches onto the large brown parcel jammed under Sam's arm. "Is that what I think it is?"

Sam needn't have bothered preparing her expression. The woman's only got eyes for the new package of autumn outfits. "Yes, it is."

Mrs Farquhar swings the door wide and Sam enters and follows her into the small sitting room. Sapphire turns up not long after Sam is comfortably seated.

While Mrs Farquhar's attention is focused on opening the parcel, Sam takes the opportunity to break the news. "There's something I need to talk to you about." Sam's aware she's stuttering slightly.

"That doesn't sound good." Mrs Farquhar looks up after snipping the string holding the package together.

Absently stroking Sapphire's ears, she blurts out the news about leaving for London. Being nervous does strange things to her mouth.

"You're going where?" Mrs Farquhar's eyebrows are now just under her hairline.

"London." Sam rubs Sapphire's ear that she'd accidentally tugged when recoiling from Mrs Farquhar's tone.

"When are you going? The launch of the Sapphire Collection is only two weeks away." Hearing her name, Sapphire's head pops up and she looks at her mistress as if to say "Yes?" As there's no response, her head drops back onto Sam's knee.

"We're flying out on the twentieth, so I'll be here for the launch. I've nearly completed the designs and Theresa and Nancy have made up most of the samples. We're on track for the launch."

"But what happens to the business when you leave? You've already got a big pre-order from Simon at Canine Capers. Did you know he has salons in Sydney and Adelaide too?"

"No, I didn't. I guess, after that order is filled, I'll have to close up. Unless?"

"Unless what?" says Mrs Farquhar, sharply.

"Unless you would manage the business for me. You're so

much better at all that than I am." The words rush out of her and she's unable to slow them down. "All I'm doing is coming up with the designs and Theresa and Nancy seem more than capable of the manufacture."

"I suppose." Sam can see by the faraway look in Mrs Farquhar's eyes that she's going through a mental checklist.

"Honestly, if I could stay I would, but ..."

Hearing her trail off, Mrs Farquhar stops putting ticks against her mental agenda and looks properly at her. Sam's fully expecting the third degree but all that follows is, "But what about Sapphire's personal wardrobe?"

"I can airmail outfits back for her. They don't weigh much and I've got all her measurements."

"I suppose that could work," says Mrs Farquhar, slowly, before rushing on with, "and that way her outfits would be different from anything anyone else was wearing."

Dread unpacks its bags in Sam's stomach. "That's right."

"Oh, I can just see her now in a purple velvet outfit with an Ermine collar, very regal."

"Yes ..." Dread now makes itself comfortable in the pit of Sam's tummy.

By the time she leaves, they've covered all the logistics of Mrs Farquhar running the business in Aussie. Sam offers the woman a percentage of the profits in return but it's firmly dismissed. Money doesn't appear to be an issue and Sam has the feeling Mrs Farquhar is enjoying being of use again.

She spends the rest of the day phoning clients and in the process receives half a dozen more orders that will see her flat out for the next week. All extra spending money for her and Jen, although she'll need Jennie's help to get everything finished. The final call she makes is the hardest.

"Hello."

"Hi, Mrs Courtenay."

"Sam. We haven't seen much of you lately."

"Yes, sorry about that, I've been, ah, busy."

"Well, you know you're always welcome here even though you and Chris, well, yes …" she peters out.

"Right. Well, anyway, the reason for the call is to let you know I'm leaving for London in a few weeks."

"Oh, Sam, I am sad to hear that. We will miss you."

Sam is now used to this response, although it had come as a surprise that so many of her clients had seemed genuinely upset she was leaving. Hard to believe given how truculent some of them are. Even more incredible was how many of them had dog-loving relatives living in London. Sam's address book is chocker.

"Promise you'll make an outfit for Monty before you go."

"Monty? I thought you only dressed him up for parties."

"Usually, yes. But he will insist on going into the pool to the point Stephen emptied it to stop him running through the house dripping wet. Then he discovered the fish pond which makes him even dirtier. So we've refilled the pool. Anyway, the upshot is his rheumatism is giving him grief and I think if he had a warm coat to wear, it would help."

"Right, I think I can come up with something no-frills and bullet proof enough to suit him." Sam smiles when she thinks about the only real dog amongst all her clients. She'll miss him.

"Oh, Sam, look at you," says Mrs Courtenay, when Sam walks into the living room at the Courtenay house.

"What's wrong?" Sam's hand subconsciously strays to her face. She's certain she's managed to conceal the worst of the spots.

"Oh, Sam, I'm so sorry it turned out how it did," says Mrs Courtenay, but on seeing her stiffen, quickly changes the topic. "So what have you got for that scallywag, Monty?"

"This!" Sam reveals the little coat she'd finished just that morning.

"Oh, it's perfect."

"Yes I found an old oilskin in an op shop, and then lined it with quilted polyester because I thought it would dry better than anything else. Even so it might not survive a dunk in the pool. That's why I made this." She pulls a second outfit from her bag.

"Oh, it's brilliant, he'll love that."

"When I saw the old wetsuit, I couldn't resist."

"Let's get the little rascal in here and try it on." Mrs Courtenay calls out to Stephen to find Monty. He walks in a while later holding a still damp Monty in a big fluffy grey towel.

"Looks like you finished that outfit just in time," says Mrs Courtenay, taking Monty off Stephen. "Let's get this on you, you little devil." She puts the outfit onto the patiently waiting Monty and has just zipped up the back when Alfred Courtenay walks in.

"I say, that's brilliant. Hello, Sam."

"Hi." Sam looks briefly at Alfred Courtenay, before her gaze drops away. His eyes remind her so much of Chris.

"How have you been?"

Seeing her struggle for an answer, Mrs Courtenay interrupts and says, "Yes, well, how about we try out this wetsuit?"

This doesn't prove to be complicated, as all Mrs Courtenay does is put Monty on the floor and let him go. Stephen opens the back door and the pool works like a magnet. By the time the humans have made it as far as the patio Monty is throwing himself off the end of the diving board.

3 8

Finally! Sam hadn't believed they'd be able to pull it off, but so far so good. She looks out at a sea of Ladies Who Lunch through a chink in the soft cream curtains leading to the, ah, dogwalk. Nearly show time.

Hearing someone behind her, she turns. "Mrs Courtenay, I can't thank you enough for letting us use the ballroom for the launch."

"It's nothing. I know most of the audience anyway. It makes a nice change from the usual affairs we host." Mrs Courtenay has only just slipped through the side of the curtains to take a seat before she's back. "Break a leg."

With the show due to start, Sam does a final check on her models, courtesy of the local obedience school. This had been Jennie's idea and Sam agreed it was a much safer option than taking up the many offers made by her current clientele. Because of the unruly nature of most of them, expecting them to walk sedately down a catwalk would be pushing it. The launch would end up in chaos.

She wishes her friend was here but with no holiday owing and a boss put out she's leaving, Jennie hadn't wanted to risk missing out on her final pay cheque.

With bladders empty and buckles and domes secure, Sam gives the nod to Stephen who hits the play button on the

287

cassette player that's hooked up to the large speakers standing on either side of the stage. Music from Vivaldi's *Four Seasons* fills the room and the chatter of voices on the other side of the curtain, subsides in anticipation.

Mrs Farquhar pops up next to her with a sheaf of papers in her hand. "Right, I'm ready."

"Ready? For what?" Sam's aware her frown of confusion is so strong, she more than likely has a uni-brow.

"To narrate the collection of course."

She's still pondering on what this means when Mrs Farquhar slides through the curtains and out onto the stage. Her appearance is met with a smattering of gloved applause that sounds like a flock of sparrows flying just overhead.

Sam's still glued to the spot when Mrs Farquhar's head appears back through the curtains. A hand appears below this, holding a single sheet of paper. "Here's the running order."

Scanning the list, Sam can see the first outfit is one of the simpler ones. The range then progresses through to the star of the show, a Burberry-inspired trench coat complete with belt, fold-up collar and checked lining.

She looks at the dogs milling around and spots number one on the list. She's just finished a last-minute check when she hears Mrs Farquhar announcing the range. This is followed by a squeal of feedback and cries of pain from every hearing-aid wearer in the room. Peeking through the curtains, Sam sees several devices being held aloft, well away from ears.

"Stephen?" She looks across at him and without a word he walks through the curtains, to a round of applause. He adjusts the microphone to give it some distance from Mrs Farquhar's bright orange lipstick. Any sound effects in the room are now courtesy of Vivaldi. Mrs Farquhar apologises and presses on.

She coughs loudly after a brief silence and Sam realises this is her cue. Stepping to the centre behind the closed curtains, Sam is conscious her hands are trembling due to stage fright. She doesn't have more than a second to imagine the audience naked before Stephen opens the curtains and she automatically moves forward, dragging a now-nervous boxer wearing a knitted vest.

She still feels this makes the dog look like he's missing his shorts but Mrs Farquhar had assured her it was *darling*. Seeing Mr Courtenay slap his hand over his mouth and leave the room with shaking shoulders, she knows he's in agreement with Sam. However, the ladies in the audience like it and she only hears positive comments when she drags the boxer, now sitting, to the end of the lino-covered runway. Just as well they hadn't gone for the carpet option or the boxer would be de-sexed by now.

The rest of the show goes smoothly with the audience response building as each new outfit is revealed. The star of the show, the Burberry trench, gets a standing ovation, although Sam feels this is overkill.

Mixing and mingling after the show, makes her realise she's going to miss some of these old dears. They may be cantankerous and demanding but they do love their pets and they've never treated her badly exactly, although they could be bloody rude at times. They simply prefer maintaining the class divide.

Hearing her name boomed out, she turns to see Mrs de Graaf forging her way through the crowd. She pulls up next to Sam, then bends over and picks up the small, black pug travelling in her wake.

"Samantha, I'd like to introduce you to Baxter." As the woman hands her the puppy, Sam realises she's just been afforded a huge honour.

"He's gorgeous." The little pug is one of the cutest things she's ever seen and the puppy seems taken with her too, nestling up under her chin and licking at her neck, causing her to giggle.

"Promise you'll make something for him before you leave?" Mrs de Graaf's eyes are suspiciously moist.

"Absolutely. I know exactly what I'll make for him." Sam is already imagining a small royal blue coat, with a red triangle on the back and a large white 'B' for Baxter centred in that.

What a super little dog.

Sam smiles, handing Baxter back to his besotted mistress.

"Sam there's someone here I'd like you to meet," says Mrs Farquhar, coming up with a woman at her elbow. "This is Madga Roberts, she's a buyer at David Jones. They're interested in talking to us about stocking a few things from the range to support a campaign they're planning, where the models will be photographed with dogs."

"I don't think I've seen that done before."

"Exactly why we're doing it." Magda's smile heads toward her eyes, but stops mid-cheek.

"Yes, well, leave the details to me," says Mrs Farquhar, "I'll sort it out with Brian Mackley. He's a *good* friend of mine."

The response from Magda is immediate. Sam has no idea who this Brian bloke is but Magda does, and the superior look in the woman's eyes has been replaced with something closer to sycophantic. As Mrs Farquhar turns away from her, the woman gets the message and quietly moves off.

"Jumped up little madam," says Mrs Farquhar, bristling.

"Way to go," says Sam, before she can stop herself. "So who's Brian Mackley?"

"Her boss, although not her immediate one. I suspect Brian is far enough up the pecking order that young Magda hasn't even been allowed to speak to him."

"Mrs Farquhar, you'll do an incredible job of running Doggs' Toggs."

"I'm enjoying it too." She backs this statement by smiling broadly.

By the time the hire company return to collect the stage, runway and chairs, the Sapphire Collection is an official hit with enough bulk orders to keep Theresa and Nancy sewing full time for the next couple of months.

Mrs Farquhar is leaving with a bone-weary Sapphire in tow when she passes Sam, who's sitting on the front veranda changing her heels for sneakers. "Can I give you a ride, Sam?"

"No! That is, no thank you. I'm looking forward to a walk to clear my head after being inside all day."

"All right then. I'll see you tomorrow, shall I? We can go over the production schedule and shipping arrangements."

Sam's conscious she should start packing soon. "Do you need me there for that?"

"Yes, I think it's important you have some understanding of the business. There could be further opportunities in England."

39

Swinging open the double doors to the Piano Bar, Jennie and Brenda don't get much farther. They're faced with a seemingly impenetrable wall of grey suiting.

"Man, it's like a morgue in here." Brenda takes a deep breath before elbowing a gap between two patrons.

"What do you mean? The place is packed." Jennie fights her way through the crowd to stay in the small gap behind Brenda, the human battering ram, who is now shoving and pushing her way toward the bar. Jennie hopes she'll be able to find her mates from work in this mob.

"It's all these suits … it's like a funeral, although no priests tonight." Brenda scans the room before adding, "Just some phoney Arabs. Complete with tea-towel headgear."

Due to Brenda's pigheadedness, they reach the bar and seeing she isn't looking for her wallet, Jennie buys the first round. They inch their way over to the grand piano sitting like a mahogany island in the sea of people.

"What can I play for you girls tonight?" says the dapper-looking chap who's thumping out requests although he's presently in a jazz holding pattern.

"How about the theme music from Laurence of Arabia?" Jennie indicates at the pseudo Arabs as she slides a dollar bill into the brandy balloon sitting on the ledge above the keys.

"Coming right up," he says, launching straight into it.

It takes a few moments but tea-towel-draped heads pop up. Jennie's gaze meets that of the tallest Arab, his bright blue eyes checking her out. She smiles when she recognises him.

"Nice choice on the music," says Mark, into her ear a moment later.

Jennie turns to face him. "It seemed appropriate." This is the first time she's seen Mark in the flesh, she only knows what he looks like without a Chewbacca costume from having seen Sam's photos of her trip up to the lake. Of course, Mark had a rabid Sonja hanging off various body parts in all those shots. "Glad to see you got the Chewbacca outfit off okay." On seeing the blank look on his face she adds. "Your zip stuck. Remember?"

"Oh, yeah, I forgot. I ended up taking to it with a steak knife so I could have a slash."

Brenda laughs so hard at this comment that rum and coke shoots out of her nose. Grabbing the end of Mark's tea towel, she blows her nose then pats it back into place on his shoulder.

"Gross," is the response from both Jennie and Mark.

"For god's sake, lighten up. It's only rum and coke, no boogers."

Mark delicately picks up the corner of the tea towel and flicks it back over his shoulder. "That makes it so much better."

"There's Martin, I'll catch up with you later." Brenda flounces off in the direction of her older lover. Jennie doubts it's a coincidence he's here.

"Where's Sam?"

"At home. Doesn't go out much these days after she and Chris ..."

"Ah, yeah, right." Mark looks fixedly at a point over Jennie's head.

"Yeah, she's at home and I'm stuck with booger girl." Jennie looks around the bar in hopes of spotting some of her friends.

Now she's been abandoned by Brenda, if they don't turn up, she's on her own.

Noticing Jennie's continual scanning of the room, Mark says, "Are you meeting someone?"

"Not officially, but some girls from work are meant to be here. But I don't see them."

"If you like, you can come to the party with us. There'll be heaps of dancing."

Jennie looks pointedly at Mark's outfit. "But I'm not dressed properly."

"No worries, we can call in at my place and get a sheet and some rope."

"What am I going as? A corpse!"

"Good idea, but no … I thought we could jury-rig a dress using the sheet, then use the rope to hold a tea towel on your head."

Looking at the sheet Mark has given her, Jennie says "I don't think this is going to work."

"Why not?" Mark looks up from the bottom drawer in the kitchen where he's rummaging about for string. He's already sporting a booger-free tea towel on his head.

Jennie demonstrates her fitted sheet. "Maybe if I were going as a starfish."

"Ah. Right, I'll get you another one."

He does, and before you can say, "baba ganoush", Jennie's looking like someone dressed in a sheet.

"Hmm, not exactly authentic, is it?" Jennie tugs at her sheet in an effort to make it more Arabian than Sheridan. "I wish Sam was here. You could give her a sack and a pair of nail clippers and she'd come up with something amazing."

Jennie's anxiety doesn't diminish when their taxi pulls up outside the party. There are flaming torches lining both sides of the driveway and what looks like a Bedouin tent pitched on the front lawn. Jennie looks for camels but figures they must be around the back.

Pushing palm leaves aside, Mark ushers her into the lounge. "Your friends go all out." Jennie doesn't know how they've done it, but the whole room looks like the inside of a tent. She's conscious the thread count of her costume is about 350 more than any other female's in the place. She feels overdressed next to all the *I Dream of Jeannie* costumes most of the girls are wearing. Still she doesn't know that's she'd feel as safe around Mark in anything that diaphanous, although he's obviously not interested in her that way, given how he's checking out the genies over her shoulder.

An hour of non-stop dancing and she's ready to ditch the sheet and reveal her street clothes. After begging for a breather, she and Mark make their way through to another room where a Middle Eastern feast has been laid out on long tables. Jennie walks the length of the buffet. "This is amazing. I can't believe the trouble the hosts have gone to." She doesn't recognise a lot of the food and is tentative about adding anything to her plate other than the dishes she knows.

"I'll give you more warning about the next one so you can get an outfit sorted."

She stops tugging at her sheet. "I doubt I'll be here for the next one. Sam and I already have our tickets to London. We leave on the twentieth of this month."

"That's only a couple of weeks off. Where are you staying when you get there?"

"We've booked a B&B for the first week, and then I'm not sure." Jennie follows Mark out to a candle-lit patio.

"You should look up my auntie. She rattles around in a huge old place in Chiswick and I know she's always thankful for some extra income. It'd be much nicer than any bed and breakfast."

"Chiswick. I think that's close to where our place is!"

"That's settled. I'll give Eadie a call and see if you can stay with her. I know she'd like the company."

They're back dancing when Jennie looks up at Mark to see his eyes have glazed over. Completing a dance spin to see what's caught his fancy, Jennie spots her immediately. A stunning redhead in a genie outfit that, when compared with the one worn by Barbara Eden on the telly, is positively tiny. Jennie bursts out laughing. This girl is going to chew him up and spit him out.

"Go on, go ask her to dance."

"What?" It takes a second for the words to filter through Mark's veil of lust.

"Go ask her to dance. Poor girl is standing there all on her own." Jennie can't believe she's just called the stunning creature a "poor girl", but Mark does seem to be in need of some encouragement to leave her side.

"But?"

"But what, you and I are just mates and I'm ready to bail anyway. I'm going to call a taxi and leave you to it."

40

The morning after the fashion parade and Sam's going through Doggs' Toggs' paperwork with Mrs Farquhar. She finds it hard to believe how much she's enjoying it. She thought it'd be a bore but Mrs Farquhar's mind is like a steel trap, and her grasp of marketing inspiring.

Mrs Farquhar scrolls down a frighteningly long list with her Parker pen, stopping occasionally to write notes next to a name. "When you get to London, you must set up meetings with everyone on here." She taps the page with the pen to emphasise her point.

"Should I concentrate on the private clients first, or the businesses?"

"Definitely the private clients." Sam's about to ask why, when Mrs Farquhar continues. "You get them on board and you'll be amazed at the doors that will open."

"I should still follow up with Harrods though, shouldn't I? For the ready-to-wear stuff."

"Yes, that's a good lead and they're expecting your call. Who knows, you might even get an exclusive deal with them."

She runs her eye down the list after Mrs Farquhar hands it to her. "Are the numbers next to the names to show who'll buy the most?"

"No dear, those are in order of gossipy show-offedness.

There's nothing like a society matron who's full of herself blabbing about her dog's new outfit to advertise your product."

Sam smiles at this comment, coming as it does, from one of Melbourne's biggest show-offs. It gives her confidence though. Sounds like the society matrons from London's posher suburbs are exactly like their Melbourne counterparts. Just different accents and more titles, if the list is anything to go by. There are a lot of The Hon, Lady, and other abbreviations that mean nothing to her.

"The main thing to remember with the Ladies of London is … Show. No. Fear!"

She straightens the list she's instinctively crumpled. "Fear?"

"Yes, dear. A lot of these women are bullies, used to getting their own way. If you buckle in the slightest, they'll stomp all over you. Still, you've stood up well so far." The smile Mrs Farquhar aims at her, has Sam's mouth dropping open. "Well done, by the way."

"Thank you. I think." Sam's aware she's passed some unwritten test.

Mrs Farquhar looks at her closely before saying "You remind me a lot of myself when I was your age."

Sam can't help but mentally compare herself to the beautifully dressed battleaxe in front of her. For one thing, she'd never wear that colour lipstick. "Really?" Much to her embarrassment, her incredulity is palpable in that one word.

"Oh, I wasn't always like this, but sometimes life isn't fair. It changes you." Mrs Farquhar stares at the ceiling in the corner as though searching for the right words.

Leaning forward, Sam settles in to hear the full story, but is disappointed when the woman mentally and physically shakes herself and carries on with the business of running Doggs' Toggs as though this aberration has never taken place.

On leaving, Sam's brain is fit to explode. She's a little overawed with how much she's got to do when she gets to London. It will be weeks before she can fit in a visit to the crown jewels and that won't sit well with Jennie who has their sightseeing planned out like a military assault. London won't have seen anything like it since the arrival of the Vikings in AD842, although there'll be less bloodshed.

Sam works on more scheduling when she gets home, scribbling names and addresses into the appropriate slots of her jam-packed diary. After rubbing out the third entry, thankfully in pencil, she writes everyone's details on bits of paper and shuffles them around on the cat-vomit-hiding carpet. It takes a while, but eventually she's happy everything is where it should be. It will be a juggling act seeing Ladies in the right order and, if possible, by location too. As it is, she'll be rattling around London like a blue-arsed fly.

Of course, the current schedule is based on all these women agreeing to see her as and when suits her proposed itinerary. After writing all the entries into her diary in pencil, she scoops up the bits of paper and is about to bin them when she has second thoughts. She forms a small envelope out of a larger piece of paper and slides it into the back of the diary.

Her diary sorted, she moves, reluctantly, on to working her way through her closet. She'll have to leave a surprising number of outfits behind, especially with Mrs Farquhar telling her the contact at Harrods has insisted she take samples of the complete ready-to-wear range over with her. Safer to pack them, than risk them getting lost in the mail.

Sliding items along the rail, Sam selects things around a mix-and-match of black and a couple of accent colours. If the garment doesn't slot in with this plan, then it's staying behind. She lays things on her bed, grouping them by type. She considers the various combinations, before grabbing a couple of tops and a skirt and hanging them back in the wardrobe. She's still busy sliding hangers when Brenda comes up behind her.

"Whatcha doing?"

"Just working out what I'll have to leave behind." Sam throws a red top in the direction of the bed.

Brenda dodges another skirt heading the same way. "You're leaving stuff behind?"

"Yeah, but if you don't want it, I can give it to the Sally Army." Sam stares hard into the wardrobe, eventually crossing her arms in a business-like manner and "hmming" in consideration. Finally decided, she pulls a green jacket from the wardrobe and throws it onto the frighteningly large pile on her bed. She then shoves anything still hanging up roughly to one side before pushing hard on the front item until she jams everything into the hard-to-reach end of her wardrobe and well out of the way.

"Hang on a second. Are you saying what I think you're saying?"

At Sam's nod of confirmation, Brenda's fully into the wardrobe, forcing her way to the end and pushing all the hangers back along the rail and into the light. She flicks her way through the hangers with comments ranging from, "Are you sure?" through to, "Sally Army." The Sally Army items are tossed in a pile on the floor under the window. By the time Brenda's finished there are still a good number of items hanging in the wardrobe.

"Are you sure?"

"I can't take everything with me. And anyway, I'd like you to have the stuff to say thanks for all your help. You know with Salami Boy and the flat and everything."

"You're welcome." Brenda's eyes are suspiciously moist when she shoves the selected items into the back of the wardrobe out of Sam's way.

"Are you crying?" Sam can't help the surprise in her voice. She didn't think Brenda was capable of tears.

"Of course I'm bloody not." Brenda rushes to leave the room. "Thanks again for the clothes," she says, over her shoulder.

41

*W*aiting on the footpath outside the flat, Jennie wonders at the wisdom of what she's doing. She stands directly under the street light where she feels safer. Normally she'd wait inside but there's no way she wants Sam to see who she's catching up with.

Scanning the road to the left and right looking for the headlights that will announce her ride, Jennie angles her wrist toward the street light. She's on time. She always is.

She twists her hands together then plays with the buckle on the shoulder strap of her handbag. Several cars pass without slowing, although this doesn't stop her from stepping forward as each of them nears. In due course a car with headlights duller than any she's seen before, slows, and pulls up next to her. The car is like something out of a museum. No wonder the headlights are so faint, they're old. Really old.

Jennie examines the car slowly from front to back. Surely he wouldn't drive anything like this. The paintwork is black, only interrupted by strips of chrome running the length of the body just under the windows. A Cro-Magnon visor sits above the windscreen. Unable to see the driver, she stalls, unwilling to march up and get into a strange car. Her back stiffens when the driver's door swings open.

It's not until he faces her, that she recognises Mark. "Are you coming?"

"Ah, yes." Jennie moves forward, still unable to comprehend Mark driving this museum piece. She grasps the shiny silver handle of the door and tries to open it. Thinking it must be stiff due to age, she tries again. Nothing. She hears a muffled "Sorry" from inside the car and Mark reaches over and unlocks the door by pulling up on the skinny, black plastic knob set in the door, next to the window.

Even unlocked, the door is difficult to open. It must weigh a ton and the graunching sounds when she swings it wide have her worrying it'll drop off the hinges any second. She exhales when she's safely seated in the car with the door shut.

"She's a beauty, isn't she?" Mark runs his hand over the top of the steering wheel. "1960 Ford XK Falcon."

Jennie doesn't hear much after 1960. "She's a Classic then," she says, hoping "Classic" goes down better than "Ancient".

"Sure is." Mark plays around with the gear shift on the steering column until he finds first.

Jennie searches in vain for a seat belt. "I'll bet this impresses your dates."

"I don't use this one on dates, just when I'm meeting up with mates." Jennie lets out the breath she hadn't been conscious of holding.

They move off so slowly that it's not until she sees a tree sliding past that she realises they're on their way. "Very smooth." She's unable to keep the surprise out of her voice.

"Of course she is." Mark sounds slightly defensive. "Did you tell Sam where you were going?"

"I wanted to, but in the end I told her I was out with friends from work." The lie sits in her gut, like a bad pie. She's told more lies in the last three months than in all the years up until that point. She knows it's been to save Sam from hurt, but this doesn't make it any easier.

Fiddling with knobs in the middle of the dash, Mark announces, "The radio's original."

Jennie has no trouble believing this when music pours

from the speakers, tinny and thin. It fills the space between them, just.

They head toward Toorak Road, with Jennie recognising landmarks familiar from the many trips to the Laundromat. Mark pulls over not far up the road from the scene of so much washing. "I think you'll like this place."

He's out of his side of the car, locked the door and around to her door while she's still struggling to open it. He manhandles it open for her and she notices that even his eyes widen as the door drops when opened to its widest point. She'd always thought it was an etiquette thing that men opened doors for women, when it would seem it was more to do with brute strength.

While Mark closes and locks the door, Jennie looks at the bar they're about to enter. It's tiny and dark but, looking at the family group she can make out through the front window, seems to be a neighbourhood local, unlike most of the bars she's visited in Melbourne.

He holds the door open for her and she enters tentatively, not knowing what to expect from the depths of the place. The bar is lit throughout with soft, yellow light making the whole space glow. Solid wooden rafters slice the ceiling from side to side, while shelves line the length of each wall. In the bigger shelf spaces there are framed reproductions. On the smaller shelves there are Toby jugs and other bric-a-brac. Very English and maybe a little contrived, but nice for all that.

Mark leads the way to a minuscule, round, wooden table at the back where there are fewer people and pulls out a leather upholstered chair for her. She's pleased when he doesn't push it in after she sits. She hates that. She always ends up feeling too crowded by the table. Mark takes off his leather jacket and throws it in the general direction of his chair before turning to her and asking what she'd like to drink.

While Mark is at the bar, Jennie shrugs out of her bomber jacket and swings around to drape it over the back of her chair. She straightens her top and is smoothing the nap on her velvet flares when Mark ambles back. Seeing he's unable to put down the drinks, she moves the small lamp, squatting in the middle of the table, to one side to make room.

She's about sip her wine, when Mark proposes a toast. "To travelling." He holds his glass of beer out to her.

She takes her glass away from her mouth and clinks it against his and repeats, "To travelling." After a small sip, she puts down her glass. "This is a nice place." Jennie looks around, peering at the patrons mostly sitting at the other end of the bar. There's the family group by the window, some older couples and a few more people around her and Mark's age. Obviously all locals, judging by the interaction between the tables.

"I've been coming here since I was a little guy." He nods at one of the older couples in response to a small wave. "Thought you'd like it."

"Have you spoken to your auntie yet?"

"Yeah, I managed to catch her last night."

"And?" Jennie's not sure what she wants his answer to be. "Yes" would mean an easy transition to living in London but would mean they were stuck at his auntie's place whether they liked it or not as they couldn't simply up and move if it didn't suit. Well, not without hurting the auntie's feelings. "No" would mean having to start looking for permanent accommodation as soon as they got to London, while they stayed in the B&B.

"She's thrilled. I've told her when you're arriving so she'll make sure she's home." He gulps a mouthful of beer before putting his glass back down. "Here's the address." He pulls a crumpled piece of paper from his trouser pocket and slides it across the table to her. "Best if you don't tell Sam who you got the contact from."

"Right," says Jennie, the chardonnay not mixing well with the dodgy pastry of guilt lying in the bottom of her stomach. "I suppose that's best." Carefully folding the still warm paper, she slips it into a side pocket in her purse. "I'll say Eadie is a workmate's auntie." Jennie worries about how good she's become at telling fibs.

"Stacey and I stayed with her a few years back." His voice fades when he adds, "We loved it. Being over there with her feels like a dream now."

"Sorry. I heard what happened."

"People avoid mentioning her so much, it's almost like she never existed."

"I know what you mean." At the look of "yeah, sure you do" on his face, she adds, "My fiancé, Steve, died last year from cancer."

This changes his expression to one of understanding. "There've been times I wanted to talk about it, but couldn't get anyone to engage. They were also so busy sparing my bloody feelings," says Mark, with disgust.

"The crystal effect, I call it. People treat you as though you're about to shatter when the fact you've survived up until that point says otherwise."

"The crystal effect? Hmm, that works."

They sit in companionable silence for a few minutes before Mark starts talking again.

"Chiswick is great, and Eadie's place is close to everything. You can walk to the Thames and the shops. The tube station is within spitting distance and there's even a pub right around the corner. Only drawback is the church," says Mark.

"Why would a church be a problem?" Her forehead is wrinkled in confusion.

"It's right next door and the bloody bells start at eight o-bloody-clock every Sunday morning," he says, disgustedly. "Killer on a hangover."

"Seems a small price to pay." Jennie is unable to stop chuckling at the look on his face as he thinks back to bell-ridden hangovers of past. "Speaking of price, what is the rent?"

"Bugger all, just enough to cover the electricity and gas. Cheaper than anywhere else you could stay in London."

"Are you sure about that? We wouldn't want to take advantage of her."

"Honestly, she'd be happy for you to pay nothing. She's mostly after company."

They're onto their second drink when Jennie notices that all the paintings around the bar are by the same artist. "Hah, I just twigged that all the paintings are Gainsborough's." She swings her head to glance at the paintings in her line of sight. "Well, reproductions."

"Gainsborough's is the name of the bar."

"Ah, that makes sense then. *Mr & Mrs Hallet, Blue Boy, A Pug.*" She rattles off the names of some of the paintings.

"You know the names of them?" says Mark, astonished.

"Yeah, I was doing a fine arts degree before ..." She fades, hoping Mark doesn't notice and ask her to elaborate.

"Do you do any art stuff now?"

"Don't have the space for it," says Jennie, as an excuse rather than let on that she hasn't picked up a paintbrush since Steve got sick. Watching him fight for his life had bled any creativity out of her soul. If she'd attempted any painting, the canvas would have ended up solid black.

"You'll have to see if Eadie will let you use her studio. It's at the top of the house and full to bursting with all sorts of arty stuff. Her arthritis means she can't hold a brush."

"That's so sad." Jennie is unable to imagine what it must be like to not be able to paint, when you wanted to.

She's about to have another sip of her wine but realises the glass is empty. Funny she hadn't even noticed. Seeing this, Mark offers to get in another round, but checking the time, she says she'd better not.

He also checks his watch. "I didn't realise it was that late. I've got to get up at some godawful hour tomorrow to catch a flight.

She drags her jacket off the back of the chair. "Where are you off to?"

Mark gets to his feet and shrugs on his jacket. "I'm flying out of town on business."

topping halfway up Mrs Farquhar's drive, Sam gently lowers the sewing machine tot he ground. She swings her arm wildly to get the blood flowing again. She'd arranged to use Brenda's car for the drop off, but both Brenda and her car had been AWOL all morning. She'd called for a taxi, but was told there'd be a twenty-five-minute delay due to some event in town.

This left her with no option other than to lug the machine around here herself. Better to suffer permanent back damage than go through a dressing down for being late.

Sam shakes her hand free of the final pins and needles, walks around the sewing machine and picks it up again, with her other hand.

Facing the familiar gleaming black door, Sam waits for it to be answered. She rings the bell again and waits. This is unusual. Even if Mrs Farquhar hasn't heard her, Sapphire should have. There's only a few days left before she and Jennie leave Melbourne and time is running out to get everything sorted with the business.

Surely she doesn't have to lug the bloody sewing machine all the way home again?

She's turning to leave when the door opens. Mrs Farquhar is a mess. Tears have furrowed their way down through her liberal coating of face powder and the orange of her lips is diluted. As she focuses on Sam, the sobbing starts in earnest.

"What's wrong?"

"It's Sapphire, she's been dog-og-napped. She was taken this morning."

"No! That's awful. Have you called the police?"

"Goodness me, no. Not after what happened to John-John."

She follows Mrs Farquhar inside, puts the sewing machine down and closes the door. Unsure of the reaction, Sam wraps her arms around the distraught woman. It's like hugging a half-empty packet of potato crips. All crinkly, with no substance. Initially, there's about as much response too, although the woman eventually relents and returns the embrace with surprising strength. Their hug over, Sam ushers Mrs Farquhar into the lounge and steers her into a seat. "Do you need a cup of tea?"

"That'd be lovely."

Leaving Mrs Farquhar filling a hanky with ladylike tears, Sam goes in search of the kitchen. After a couple of wrong turns she locates it and sets about making a cuppa. Thank goodness even the rich set their kitchens up following the same basic rules, although she notes Mrs Farquhar doesn't use an old peanut butter jar for *her* sugar. Sam even manages to rustle up some biscuits.

"Here you go." She puts the tray on the glass coffee table in the front room, but there's no reaction from Mrs Farquhar who's muffled behind her sodden, lace-edged hanky. Sam turns the pot three times before pouring a cup of tea.

"Do you have any idea who took her?"

"No-o. All I've got is this note," Mrs Farquhar hands her a limp piece of paper. The tear-soaked demand is hardly legible but the note paper and handwriting have Sam's heart firmly in her throat. "That rat bastard."

"What's that, dear," says Mrs Farquhar, looking up from the ball of damp cotton she's cradling in her hands.

Sam points to a small pile of blue fur on the table next to Mrs Farquhar's chair. "Is that what I think?"

"Yes, it came with the note."

"No, that's terrible, it's not like she's got a lot to spare."

"I worry she'll catch cold."

Let's hope she still can, thinks Sam, surreptitiously stuffing the note in her pocket.

Mrs Farquhar is still looking at her cup of tea as though not sure what to do with it when Sam leaves. She had thought the dognapping was over and it had simply been a coincidence that she'd been implicated.

If only I could remember where the creep lives.

Storming into the flat, she slams the door shut behind her. Her leg muscles are burning from stomping all the way home from Mrs Farquhar's. It hasn't helped reduce the tension zinging around her body. "Arrrgh, that effing, effing, effing bastard!" Sam stamps her feet for emphasis.

Jennie walks into the lounge from the kitchen, a tea towel hangs limply from her hands. "Who is?"

"Salami Boy!"

"That bastard. I thought we'd seen the last of him," says Brenda, joining them.

"So did I, but I think he's the reason the cops were asking me about John-John. I've just discovered he's the arsehole who's been nicking all the dogs. He's dognapped Sapphire."

Jennie's brow is creased with confusion. "What makes you think that?"

In answer Sam marches into her room and digs in the top drawer of her dresser before returning to the lounge. After flattening the piece of paper against her thigh, she holds it up next to the ransom note she's pulled from her pocket.

"Spot the difference?" She shakes first one note and then the other. Both are on the same blue paper and both in the same untidy scrawl.

"Tenacious, isn't he?" says Brenda.

Jennie twists the tea towel until it resembles a thick rope. "Sam, you've got to show those to the police."

"I can't do that," says Sam, noting Brenda's shoulders relax.

"I'll call the boys. They'll sort the bastard out."

Brenda's already walking in the direction of the phone when she's stopped by Sam's forceful, "No!"

"Why not? It's what guys are for."

"Because I've had enough of having guys sort stuff out for me. Don't you get sick of always having to *phone the boys*? I thought you had more guts than that."

"Sam, you need to go to the police."

"No!" shout both Sam and Brenda, causing Jennie to take a step backwards.

"Whatcha got planned then, Wonder Woman?" says Brenda.

"Not sure yet, but he's not going to pull this crap. Ever again." Sam crushes both notes until her knuckles whiten.

Back in her room, she drops the crumpled notes on her dressing table. Bloody shame she doesn't know where he lives. She'd been too busy hiding her face from the world to notice her surroundings when he'd driven her home.

After ruminating on the problem for a while, she yells through the partially closed door of her room. "Brenda, can I borrow the car Friday night?"

'Yeah, sure," comes the unadorned reply. Sam's relieved she doesn't have to explain her plan in order to borrow the car. She suspects the reason she hasn't been subjected to the third degree is the gift of clothing still hanging in her wardrobe.

Her relief is short lived when Jennie's head appears around the door. "What are you going to do?" Jennie's face is a picture of parental concern. "Promise me you won't do anything silly."

"Haven't got anything planned. Yet. But I thought if I park outside the RSL club, I might be able to follow him and see where he lives."

"I'll come with you."

"No, Jen. I need to do this on my own." On seeing the look of rejection on her friend's face, she adds, "I can move faster that way, keep out of sight. You understand."

"Sure I do." Jennie's tone states the opposite. Without another word, she slips backwards out of Sam's bedroom.

Sam doesn't like leaving things like this but neither does she want to drag Jennie into anything. At least not until her plan is better fleshed out.

Friday night Jennie's expression is still dark when Sam walks into the lounge and grabs Brenda's car keys out of the bowl on the coffee table. Sam's dressed top to bottom in black, with her blonde hair stuffed under a cap. She appreciates the irony of this when she unlocks the driver's door of Brenda's bright red Celica. It's hardly stake-out material.

Driving into the club car park, she looks for a suitable spot. She needs a clear view of the entrance but not so close that Salami Boy might spot her. She also needs to be able to drive off quickly. After circling the car park a few times she backs into what she hopes is the perfect space. The parking lot is soon heaving and after the second car pulls up in front of her and gives her the evils, she climbs over into the back seat and scrunches all the way down.

Hours later, and Sam's pleased she hadn't had that second coffee after dinner. Although she suspects the full feeling in her bladder has more to do with nerves than pee.

She's about to give up and go home when she spots Salami Boy leaving the club. She'd obviously missed him arriving which didn't say a whole lot for her surveillance skills. The girl at his side would be face down on the asphalt if it wasn't for the firm hold Salami Boy has on her. The girl is plastered to his side, her feet skipping along the footpath like a marionette on uneven strings.

Climbing into the front, Sam catches her reflection in the visor vanity mirror. Unable to endure her own scrutiny, she flips it up settling herself into the driver's seat.

Unfortunately, by the time she's got the engine started, Salami Boy and his latest conquest have disappeared into the darkness of the car park. There's nothing for it but to pull out into the street and hope she's pointing in the right direction when he leaves.

She isn't and only a dangerous U-turn in front of a speeding taxi has her safely following him. Her driving is erratic after the near miss and it takes a couple of blocks for her to settle down and her driving to smooth out.

As recommended in all the cop shows on telly, she keeps a few cars between herself and her quarry, but after being forced to run a couple of red lights, risks it and gets a little closer, until she's sitting right behind him. She hopes he doesn't recognise the car.

He swings wildly to the curb, forcing her to pass him and pull over a little farther along. In her rear-view mirror she sees him running around the front of his car and wrenching open the passenger door. He bodily drags his date from the car and drops her unceremoniously on her hands and knees on the nearest front lawn where she proceeds to rid herself of the alcohol in her system.

"Poor bitch! She is so going to hate herself when she wakes up tomorrow."

After five minutes, the girl is still throwing up, although she's slowing up. Salami Boy storms back to his car and leans into the passenger door, which is still open. He doesn't walk back, and instead throws the girl's handbag in her general direction. The contents spill when it hits the ground next to her. He slams the passenger door closed and walks back around to his side of the car.

"He wouldn't?" says Sam. "He would," as the black BMW accelerates past her.

She's torn between going to help the girl and pursuing Salami Boy. In the end she decides she can do both. The girl is tucked in next to some shrubs and the road they're on is reasonably quiet, so she should be safe for a little while.

43

*S*am's concentrating so hard on catching up with the creep that it takes a second for her to realise he's stopped for a red light. Slamming on her brakes, she comes to a squealing stop a gnat's whisker from his back bumper. Seeing him adjusting his rear-view mirror, she puts the car into reverse, ready for a quick getaway. This prompts the car behind her to start beeping frantically.

She slips the car into neutral hoping to silence the beeping from behind her and is relieved when this happens. Unfortunately, Salami Boy seems to think it's her who's been beeping. Her eyes widen when she sees his door opening. He hauls himself out of the car and stares hard at her before walking in her direction.

She locks the door and winds up the window but before he can get level with her door, she hears angry shouting from behind. "It's a green light, ya moron. Move it!"

Peeking out from under the brim of her cap, she looks up to see Salami Boy glaring at the occupants of the car behind her. He mustn't like the look of them, because he jogs back to his car, jumps in and floors it, heading straight down the road.

She debates turning left for a couple of seconds, before she moves off. She takes her hands off the wheel one at a time and wipes them down her jeans.

Fear controlling her accelerator foot, she drops back. Realising he's no longer in front of her, she panics. "Relax. He can't have gone that far," she pep-talks herself. Continuing slowly, she looks carefully down every side road.

"Gotcha," she crows when she spots the familiar tail lights disappearing down a street off to her right. She turns and follows at a safe distance but when she sees his indicator go on, she pulls over and kills the lights and engine.

"That has to be his place."

While he waits for a car heading in the other direction, Sam gets out of the Celica and locks it. As he turns into his driveway, Sam is off at a run, keeping to the shadows where possible and is almost outside his house when she hears movement. She slips into the nearest bushes, breathing through her mouth to keep as quiet as possible.

She watches from her hiding place as he clears the letterbox. She's close enough to hear his muttered, "Bloody waste of alcohol," as he stomps back up the driveway.

Hearing a door slam somewhere above her, she slithers out from under the trees and over to where she can see the BMW parked in the driveway for the night. She waits, conscious the ground beneath her is damp. The air is full of the scent of leaf mould.

The lights in the front room turn off and getting onto all fours, she gropes around until she finds the perfect stick.

Sneaking up next to the car, she takes the cap off the valve on the front, right tyre. Jamming her stick into it results in a hissing so loud she thinks she might have to check her undies when she gets home. Reducing the amount of force, she's rewarded with quieter hissing. After decreasing the tyre pressure, she puts the valve cap back in place and moves to the next tyre.

Rather than flatten the tyres, reducing the pressure in them ensures the car will handle like crap and all the tyres will end up buggered.

She skips back to her car, smiling broadly.

· · ·

Pulling up next to where the girl had been abandoned, Sam thinks she must have crawled off but when she squints at the shadows under a small tree, she sees movement.

"You are one lucky chick," says Sam, to the mound of clothes on the ground in front of her. "C'mon, let's get you home. She picks up the girl's handbag and collects the scattered belongings, before zipping it shut.

It takes all her strength to drag the girl upright, with progress stalling when the girl has to throw up a couple more times. Once the girl is safely in the car, her head leaning over the side window, Sam chucks the handbag into the footwell.

Because of the girl's slurred speech, it takes a while to understand the address. After checking the map a couple of times, they reach their destination.

The following morning, the other two grill Sam. All three are quiet after she explains how she helped Salami Boy's date get home.

"Shame you didn't throw up," says Brenda.

"Now you know where he lives, you'll have to phone the police?" says Jennie.

"No way, I think it's about time we put the little bastard in his place," says Sam.

Jennie's face is full of confusion. "But we're flying out tomorrow morning."

"Exactly. It's tonight or never," says Sam.

Seeing Salami Boy walk out to his car that evening has Sam sucking in a ragged lungful of air. "What's he doing, what's he doing?" She's scooted right down in her seat. Jennie's in a similar position. Sam still feels Brenda has parked too close.

"Relax would ya, he's driving off now. We're on." Brenda checks the rear-view mirror and tightens the scrunchy that's holding her hair off her face.

Sam's having second thoughts. If it wasn't for Sapphire she'd be tempted to forget about the whole thing. "Hell, I don't know if I'm ready for this."

"Me neither," says Jennie.

"We can't chicken out now." Brenda opens her door and gets out, propelling Sam and Jennie into action.

"Right! The sooner we get in, the sooner we get out." Sam squares her shoulders and then walks briskly up the drive toward the front of the house.

Jennie and Brenda are still walking up the front steps when she smashes one of the small glass panels flanking the front door. They all wait nervously to see if this results in lights coming on anywhere.

"I thought you said you knew where he kept the key?" Jennie's voice is squeaky with nerves.

"Oh, silly me." Sam smiles before lifting the corner of the coir door mat where the key nestles in an accumulation of grime and scurrying earwigs. After gingerly retrieving the key, she drops the mat back into place.

The door opens easily and they step over the threshold.

"Common, check around and see if you can find Sapphire. We'll start down here and then head upstairs." Now that she's committed to breaking and entering, nothing is going to hold her back.

The ground floor doesn't reveal any shaved poodles, so they make their way upstairs. Sam knows he lived on his own when she was here, but there's no guarantee this is still the case. They're in full-on sneak mode.

The staircase is a combination of wrought iron and solid wooden slabs. It creaks alarmingly when it takes the full weight of the three of them. They freeze to see if anyone's going to jump out, but all is quiet – until they continue creaking their way up to the next level.

"Sapphire," calls Sam, softly padding along the upstairs hallway. She's not keen on simply trying doors. She doesn't want to risk finding the master suite with all its awful memories. She's relieved when she hears whimpering from a room at the end.

Opening the door, she's hit by a wave of hot air reminiscent of what she and Jennie encountered when leaving the Melbourne airport terminal.

God, is he trying to cook the poor dogs?

Sapphire seems okay apart from panting hard. Hopefully this is because the room's like an oven. There's a bucket in the corner, with some water in it, but not much. "Looks like we found you just in time," she says to the three miserably bald dogs crowding around her knees.

Apart from Sapphire, there's what she thinks is a Scottish terrier, although it's hard to tell with only its head remaining furry. The other is a de-bearded collie. The floor is covered in urine-sodden newspaper, with little brown piles scattered liberally about. The smell has her eyes watering and she understands why the dogs are so keen to escape.

Sam realises she can't only rescue Sapphire. She has no idea who the other two dogs belong to, but doesn't think it will be difficult to find out. She's sorting out make-shift leashes when she hears a door slamming below. The ropes dangle forgotten from her hand.

Opening the door a crack, she looks out into the hallway. Jennie and Brenda are standing still in the middle of it. Jennie's eyes are wide and she looks to be frozen to the spot. Brenda seems unconcerned by this new development but when the stairs start to creak complainingly, the two of them immediately disappear through doors on opposite sides of the hallway.

Sam's relieved that Salami Boy can't have spotted the smashed window.

Hopefully he won't see it on the way out either.

Sam holds her breath as she closes the doggie prison door.

The collie, sensing its freedom isn't coming, kicks up a stink. "Shut up you mangy mutt!" is yelled from down the hallway. She throws the rope back in the corner before squeezing into one end of the wardrobe. She pulls the door almost closed. Salami Boy storms into the room yelling at the dogs to, "Shut the hell up". The barking doesn't stop. There's a thump then a lot of yelping and finally silence.

Sam has to bite her lips to stop herself from saying anything. She's so angry she's shaking. She's only able to see a slice of room from her hiding spot but it's enough see Sapphire staring intently at the wardrobe. Go away, go away, go away thumps through her head. Obviously not loudly enough, because the dog doesn't budge.

"Jeez, no you can't go in there." He slams shut the door to the wardrobe and Sam's heart tries in vain to claw its way out of her throat. It slows when she hears the door to the prison slam shut. She empties her lungs of air and breaths in again. Big mistake! Obviously he hasn't always been so vigilant about keeping the door shut. The overpowering smell lets Sam know she's sharing the wardrobe with a few more little brown parcels. She doesn't care if she runs into the creep. She has to get out of here or she's going to chuck.

She pushes against the door. Nothing. She shoves against the door. Still nothing. Panic rushes through her system. She's about to lose it when the door opens to reveal Brenda.

"Come on, stop mucking about in there, we don't have all night." She's sounding nasal because her nose is pinched closed with her thumb and forefinger. "Jeez, it reeks in here."

"Tell me about it," says Sam, followed by a small dry heave. Retrieving the ropes, she ties up the three dogs. The collie gets an extra pat to calm it down after being belted. They make their way out of the room and along the hallway. The dogs nearly send her sprawling a couple of times in their eagerness to get out of the place. "Where's Jennie?"

"Not sure," says Brenda.

"Jennie. Jennie. Jennie!" Sam says up and down the hallway, getting progressively louder. Eventually a door opens and a dusty Jennie emerges.

"What the hell?" Pulling her sleeve down to form a glove, Brenda peels a used condom off Jennie's back before holding it up to show Sam. At the subtle shaking of Sam's head, Brenda just as delicately drops it where Jennie won't see.

"I realised I was in his room. The only place to hide was under the bed."

"Come on, let's get the hell out of here in case he comes back again," says Sam.

They're all safely down in the lounge when the front door is thrown open by Salami Boy. "Damn it!" he says, taking a golf club from an umbrella stand next to the door. "I thought I could smell cheap perfume underneath all the dog poo." He stands in front of Sam, legs wide, hips thrust out, causing his cream trousers to pull tight.

The guy should consider being circumcised if he's going to go without undies when wearing pants that snug.

Italian loafers as big as *ciabatta*, anchor him to the ground. A T-shirt, also too small, stops short of covering the parcel of Italian meat he's obviously so proud of. His man-breasts strain against the stretch of the white cotton.

Sam's halfway through freaking out and ready to bolt, when Brenda saunters up next to her.

"C'mon baby, don't be like that, let's have some fun," says Brenda to Salami boy.

He hoists the golf club threateningly, his face glistening with a fine sheen of sweat. Even though he looks to be freshly showered and dressed, there's something distinctly grubby about him.

Brenda takes hold of the bottom of her T-shirt. "Don't you want to play with me?"

"Brenda, you *wouldn't?*" says Jennie.

"But I want to." Brenda whips up the front of her T-shirt. Once clear of the hem, her breasts bounce free. No bra for Brenda.

He stares at Brenda's breasts jiggling in front of him. His mouth is slack, the golf club held forgotten above his head.

His attention captured, Sam puts every bit of the pain and heartache he's caused her into the kick she aims squarely at his nuts. Connecting, the golf club clatters to the ground and he doubles over, retching.

Brenda takes the opportunity to bring up her knee, connecting hard with his face. Something breaks with a sickening crack and he concertinas onto the floor, rolling into a protective ball.

"And he's soooo stupid," says Brenda, pulling her T-shirt back down into place.

Dragging the dogs along with her, Sam walks over to a small table that's threatening to buckle under the combined weight of a huge pile of phone books and a dirty beige phone. Pulling a small card from her jeans pocket and checking it, she dials. She makes her voice gruff and sports an atrocious American accent. The call is short.

"Let's get the hell out of here," says Brenda, already on her way out of the front door.

Jennie avoids eye contact with Salami Boy when she steps around him, but Sam can't resist looking down. He's rolling around clutching his crotch, his nose is streaming blood and snot and as tempting as it is to put the boot in again, she decides not to push her luck. While she's thinking on this, the Collie takes the opportunity to empty its bladder on Salami Boy's back.

"Good boy." Sam pats the Collie's head before leading it and the other two dogs to freedom.

She meets up with Brenda and Jennie at the bottom of the front stairs.

"Angels, Charlie will be proud of us!" says Brenda, causing Jennie and Sam to immediately strike two thirds of the opening credits pose. It doesn't take long for Brenda to complete the set up.

As they pull away, a police car races past, lights flashing.

"Wow, they were fast." Actually, much faster than Sam would have liked. She looks out of the side window and spots the male cop who'd searched the flat only weeks earlier. "Damn it. Brenda you'd better floor it."

Brenda does as instructed and Sam is pushed back into a pile along with the three dogs.

Once the acceleration slows and she's able to peel herself off the back seat, Sam chucks her dog-poo-encrusted sneakers out of the window. The trip to Mrs Farquhar's passes in silence apart from Brenda's tuneless whistling, the car radio having gone on the fritz. The dogs settle down in the back with Sam where they snuggle up for comfort. They're still shaking, so she covers them and her, with the car blanket, so the back seat is positively steaming when they hit the gravel drive at Mrs Farquhar's.

Sapphire's head pops out from under the blanket and she starts to whine when she recognises her surroundings. Sam undoes the rope threaded through her collar and Sapphire's out of the car as soon as the door opens. Sam takes the other two dogs along too, just in case Mrs Farquhar knows who they belong to. She'd also rather they weren't at the flat in case the cops decide on a snap inspection.

She rings the doorbell and waits impatiently; Sapphire is jumping on the spot on one side of her while the other two dogs wait patiently on the other. The outside light comes on and the door swings open to reveal Mrs Farquhar, dressed from head to foot in black and devoid of make-up. "Yes," she says, dully.

Sam doesn't say anything. She doesn't have to, with Sapphire becoming vocal when she sees her mum.

"Sapphire darling," says a reanimated Mrs Farquhar. "But how?"

"It's a long story, but I recognised the paper the ransom note was written on and we checked it out. Best the police don't know we were involved." She waves her hand in the direction of Brenda's car.

"And why not? I think you deserve recognition."

"Because we broke the law, plus a few bones, getting her back. The culprit paid for it big time."

"Paid? How much?"

"He won't be reproducing any time soon."

"Good," says Mrs Farquhar. "No less than he deserves. But whose dogs are these?"

Sam looks down at them. "I was hoping you'd know. They were with Sapphire."

"Leave them with me and I'll sort it out. Oh, Sam, I don't know how to thank you."

"You don't have to. You're not the only one who loves Sapphire."

44

*L*eaving Mrs Farquhar's, Sam's surprised when she realises how much she will miss Sapphire and her mum. They've become a large part of her life. With moist eyes, Sam runs back to the car as fast as her stockinged feet will allow.

As soon as her bum hits the back seat, she yells, "Move it!"

Brenda doesn't need to be told twice and redistributes a good quantity of gravel as she fishtails the Celica down the driveway. After sliding across the seat on the first turn, Sam jams herself in sideways for the next few corners. Brenda screeches to a halt in the dead-end road up from the flat and the girls sprint down the deserted back lane and into the house. They're in the middle of the darkened lounge when there's an urgent knocking at the front door.

Sam has never been so relieved in all her life when Martin wanders out of Brenda's bedroom in a dressing down. "Right girls, I suggest you all get into bed immediately. Leave this to me."

They scatter when he walks ever so slowly through to answer the front door.

Once in her room, Sam rips off her outer layer, stuffing everything into the bottom of her wardrobe. She drags a nightie on over her bra and pants, rips the covers back and is "deep asleep" in seconds. While her eyes might be jammed shut, her ears are working overtime, trying to hear the conversation taking place at the front door. Damn, she shouldn't have closed her door properly.

She stops feigning sleep when there's a gentle knock on her door, followed by Martin calling her name. This results in her heart hammering away at double time, something she hopes doesn't show. After pulling on her dressing gown and belting it tightly, she messes her hair and stumbles into the lounge, squinting hard against the light.

"What the hell?" Sam's voice is laced with confusion. She hopes the lacing isn't too tight. Pausing a minute for effect, she acknowledges the officer's presence, then starts raving, "Oh, my god, it's my parents isn't it? Please tell me. I can't stand it. Please tell me what's happened." She wrings her hands together, her face a study of earnest pleading.

She's knows she's going through the same rigmarole as last time this policeman turned up, but her brain is mush and it's all she can think of. He steps back, and she thinks she might have overdone it a bit.

"Relax, this is nothing to do with your family." His "for feck's sake" hangs heavily in the air.

She plasters on a confused and innocent mask. "But what then?"

"Officer, perhaps you'd be good enough to explain why you're here?" Martin's tone, while calming, has a nice ring of authority to it. The officer stands a little straighter in response.

God, he's good.

Sam looks at Martin with new-found respect.

"There was an incident earlier this evening and Ms Bennett's name came up."

Sam stands mute, her mouth dropping open as though in shock. Actually there is a lot of shock involved.

The bastard's still trying to implicate me!

"How so?" says Martin.

"A person who is helping us with our enquiries regarding

the recent dognapping has just made some rather serious accusations against Ms Bennett." He turns back to her "Are you able to confirm your whereabouts for the past two hours?"

Now it's her turn to step backwards. This just became serious. Before she can formulate a reply, Martin speaks.

"Officer, I can confirm Ms Bennett's whereabouts during that time." His voice has a sharp edge to it, any calmness now taking a back seat.

"You can?" says the officer.

Sam just thinks it.

"Yes, she's been here all evening. As have I. The officer who's been watching the front of the house would have seen my Bentley parked outside since approximately 7:30 p.m."

"There's someone watching the house!" Sam tries to remember how they'd left the house earlier and is relieved to recall they went out the back way. Sam's sure she heard a muttered, "Sodding pigs" from the direction of Brenda's bedroom. She hopes the officer didn't hear it too. His expression suggests not.

"Officer, I think it's time for you to leave now. It's obvious Ms Bennett has an alibi for whatever it is this person is accusing her of."

After gulping a couple of times, the officer regains his voice. "We will need to speak to her again on this matter though." He flips open the small notebook he's retrieved from his trouser pocket. "Would one o'clock tomorrow afternoon be convenient?"

"N-n-no, not really," stutters Sam.

"But you'll be here," says the officer, emphatically, before turning and leaving.

By the time Martin returns to the lounge after shutting the front door on the policeman, Brenda and Jennie have joined her. Jennie is wide-eyed with shock, and Brenda looks pissed off. "I can't believe the place is being staked out by the pigs!" Her hand covers her mouth when she realises she's sworn in front of Martin.

"That's all right, dear," he pats her hand. "In this case, you're entitled to swear."

"This doesn't mean I have to stay here? Does it?" Sam's face carries every ounce of the horror she's feeling. "Oh, screw it, it wasn't meant to turn out like this." She drops into one of the lounge chairs and curls herself into a tight ball. "I thought tonight would be the end of it for sure. Screw him."

"Are you serious?" Brenda's expression is one of incredulity. "Screw missing your flights because of this."

"She's right, you know," says Martin. "I doubt the local constabulary will bring Interpol in on a dognapping case. They'd never live it down. No, they've got their man and you've got an alibi."

Sam uncurls from her armadillo pose. "Good point! And we'll be well away before the cops realise we've gone."

"I can deal with any fall out. You'd be surprised who I play golf with. But now it's time for bed." Martin salutes the girls, wishes them "bon voyage" and disappears into Brenda's bedroom.

Sam's hand strays to her chest. "God, I'll be lucky to sleep after that."

"I'm going to make a cup of tea." Jennie wanders into the kitchen and the kettle roars to life soon after.

"No tea for me, sleep is the last thing on my mind." Brenda's wide grin leaves Sam in no doubt as to what's on the agenda.

"Oh, I'm going to miss you." Sam hugs Brenda who is rigid for a second before relaxing into the embrace. "There's no one like you."

She feels Brenda's hands wrap themselves around her back. "Ditto back. Maybe I'll come over to England and look you up."

"You've got our address. We'd love to see you."

Jennie hands her a cup of tea, and Sam can't help but hold the mug close, drawing warmth from it. It's been one hell of a night. They settle themselves into the two lounge chairs but soon move into Jennie's room and turn on the radio. The sounds coming from Brenda's bedroom announce Martin is close to climax or a coronary. For the sake of her alibi, Sam hopes it's the former.

"I'm so relieved we got away with it tonight." Jennie's voice is shaking, the tea not yet having worked its magic.

"I can't believe how good I feel to have done it." A few months back and Sam knows her voice would have been full of surprise that she'd managed to pull it off at all. She blows noisily on her tea before taking a sip.

"You feel good about it!"

"Yeah, I do." She takes a gulp of the brew. "Really good. I haven't had to rely on some guy for help and I've stood up for myself."

Silence invades the room as they both swallow this development and their tea.

"Crap, I've just remembered the cop car out front." Sam's mouth forms a grimace. "At least I think it's still out front."

"Of course!" Jennie's already wringing her hands together in worry when Sam stands.

"Hang on, before we freak out, let's check they're still there." She walks through the darkened house and unlocks the back door leaving Jennie in a lather of worry. Thank god her dressing gown is black as this will make her harder to spot for any copper on stake-out duty. Sam nips out and around the side of the house then, keeping under the trees, runs up to the front fence. Standing on the bottom rail she hoists herself up so she can peek over the top.

Hmm.

There's a car parked in the road opposite, but Sam's not sure there's anyone inside.

Her arms are tired by the time a car makes its way up the hill. Its headlights momentarily illuminate the inside of the car and sure enough there are two guys sitting in the front of the parked car. The flat seems to be their main focus.

"Screw them!" She drops off the fence and makes her way back inside. A minute later and she's on the phone to the cab company.

She pops back into Jennie's room. "Sorted. The taxi's going to pick us up at the back gate."

"The police are still out there then?"

"Sure are." Sam relieves Jennie of the cups. "'Night, Jen, sleep well."

"Don't forget to set your alarm."

"Hah, there's no way I'm getting up at 4.30 tomorrow morning without it."

45

After dragging their suitcases out to the back gate, Sam does a final quick walk-through to check she's left nothing behind. She stops next to the hall table and looks down at the note next to the phone asking for anyone answering a call from Chris to take a message. It's faded and hard to make out, but she carefully folds it and puts it in her pocket, next to the small satin covered button.

As the taxi approaches down the alley dead on 5 a.m., Sam stands in the middle of it and waves her hands. With any luck they'll be in the air before the cops work out they've gone.

"We're as good as out of this town," says Jennie, doing up her seatbelt.

Sam looks back up the alley, her view blurred with a few sneaky tears. "I guess we are."

Even though they know they're far enough down the hill from the cops, when the taxi exits the alley, they both slink well down in their seats and the trip to the airport is carried out in silence. Neither of them wants to discuss their getaway in front of the driver.

After parting with a good wad of cash for the taxi, the girls stand looking at the international terminal. "And so the adventure begins again," says Sam.

They join the queue to check in their bags. There are only

a couple of people ahead of them, so they don't have much of a wait before slinging their bags onto the scales.

"And where are the other members of your party?" says the uniformed, wise arse behind the counter they're directed to.

"What party?" says Sam, confused.

"Well, I assume there are more of you given the amount of luggage." He looks bored already even though his day must only just have started.

"Just us," says Jennie, the sole of her platform firmly wedged under the plate of the scales.

"You've got seventy-two, no make that seventy kilos between the two of you. You should only have forty. If you don't want to pay excess baggage, you'll have to take something out."

"I thought we were allowed more if we were emigrating?" says Sam.

"You're emigrating?"

"Well, we're not coming back so I guess you'd call that emigrating ... see." Sam waves her one-way ticket at him.

"That still only allows you thirty kilos each."

They reclaim their paperwork and drag the suitcases off the scales and back between the queues to a spot out of sight of the check-in counters.

"What the bloody hell are we going to do?" says Jennie.

"We can wear some extra stuff and I'll flick all my hair products. It'll be cheaper to buy new stuff when we get to England. What shoes are you wearing?"

"Shoes?"

"Are they your heaviest?"

"No!" Jennie dives gleefully into her bag, dragging out a pair of five-inch wooden platform clogs that if burned could keep a Mongolian hill tribe warm for the winter. "That should save a couple of kilos."

Sam, who's similarly engaged, says, "And you know how cold it can get on those planes," pulling out a bulky woollen jumper and a coat.

"Thank god they don't weigh the carry-on bags." Sam hefts her bag over her shoulder and almost falls off her platforms.

They drag their bags back to the check-in queue and can't believe their lousy luck when they're directed back to the same miserable git. Jennie gets her shoe ready as Sam throws the bags up onto the scales. They settle on forty kilos so Jennie eases the upward pressure and they read a more believable fifty-nine kilos.

"We made it," says Sam, with relief.

"And put on twenty pounds and grew a couple of inches while you were at it," is the sarcastic response.

Given there's not much else he can say, he allocates them seats and heaves their bags off the scales and onto the conveyor belt behind him. Sam nudges Jennie, who shifts her foot allowing the scales to drop back to zero.

"Hell, that was close," says Sam, walking in the direction of customs, all while shedding layers.

"Yeah, you're not wrong, although we're gonna have to find a trolley, my shoulder is killing me." Jennie lowers her carry-on bag to the floor.

They find a trolley that wouldn't be out of place in a supermarket given its tendency to crab sideways, no matter how much effort they both put into keeping it in a straight line. They struggle with the trolley for all of thirty feet before coming to the first check through to customs. "I'm sorry, you'll have to leave that there," says the customs man, pointing at their trolley.

"Really?" says Jennie, bleakly. "But I've got a bad back."

"I'm not surprised," he says, looking down, "you should wear more sensible shoes."

The flight is a long twenty-eight hours with stopovers at Perth and Bombay. Perth is so short it's not worth getting off the plane. At Bombay the girls would rather have stayed put, but it's compulsory to disembark. This involves a pat down from a sari-clad security officer before entering one of the dirtiest terminals they've ever been in. Every surface is coated in a combination of dust and aviation fuel residue.

Almost as long as the flight, is the walk from their gate to the bag collection point at Heathrow. Wearing most of their excess luggage doesn't make it any easier and by the time they get their hands on a trolley, they're ready to collapse.

"God, it's going to take an hour's soak in a hot bath to get the airlines logo off my arse," says Sam.

Customs and immigration are straightforward and it's not long before they're looking at the underground map on the back of their A-Z and working out how to get to Eadie's place in Chiswick.

Nervously, they watch the stations ticking away against the underground map and get off as quickly as possible when the train pulls into Chiswick Park.

Sam looks up at the three-storey house where the black cab has dropped them. "Wow, it's a nice place. We struck it lucky here."

The bay windows on either side of the glass front door make the house look as though it's lifting itself clear of the garden, in an effort to keep clean. Unlike the rest of the house, the garden is untidy and rampant with weeds.

"I guess she can't garden with arthritis," says Jennie.

"If the rent's as cheap as your workmate says, then maybe we can do some weeding for her." Sam looks over the low front wall before her gaze travels up, taking in the rest of the house. The windows on the second and third floors are mullioned; crisscrossing the lace curtains hanging behind them.

Seeing a curtain twitch at the bay window to their right, Sam drags her suitcases up the tiled path, before heading back to help Jennie manhandle the beast up to the front door.

"Well, knock on the door then," says Jennie.

"No, you knock. You know them."

"I don't know them."

"For goodness sake, I need to get in and lie down." Sam's hand is raised to knock on one of the glass panels, when she notices a small button to the left of the door. She pushes it, but not much happens. She pushes until the end of her finger turns white and is rewarded with a no-nonsense *rinnggg* inside the house.

Examining the bell-shaped indent on her finger, Sam waits for the door to open. When it's eventually answered, the girls look down at their new landlady. She's bird-like, with her legs visible at the bottom of the flowery dress being no thicker than Sam's forearm. Looking at the full head of snow-white hair that tops this fragile body, Sam's reminded of a dandelion. It's refreshing to see the hair hasn't been dyed.

Sam introduces herself and, through force of habit, puts out her hand. The tiny hand she engulfs is soft, and beautifully manicured, but she can almost feel the pain emanating from the swollen joints. Sam clasps the hand as gently as she can but Eadie still flinches slightly, although she tries to hide it.

"And this is Jennie." Sam keeps hold of Eadie's hand, thereby avoiding Jennie having to shake it too.

Jennie waves a small greeting. "Hi."

"I've so been looking forward to meeting you." Eadie's hands drop uselessly in front of her. "Come in, girls. Can I help you with anything?"

They decline. They all know there isn't any way she can help but she obviously finds it impossible not to offer.

"Why don't you go and sit back down while we bring our bags in," says Jennie. "We can re-lock the front door and join you then, if you like."

"That'd be lovely, but best you don't lock the door. It's a bit stiff and if it's locked I have to use the back door." This is said in a matter of fact manner, with no thought of seeking sympathy. Sam sees that while Eadie's body might be under attack, her spirit has yet to go down fighting.

The bags stowed to one side of the hallway, Sam has a

chance to take in her surroundings. She supposes this is how 'old money' decorates, as everything is refined, tasteful and understated. Feeling eyes on her, she looks up and spots a large black and white cat sitting at the top of the staircase. It stares at her as if to say, "Go on, I dare you".

"Wow, what a monster," she says, to Jennie, nodding at the cat.

"Shoot, he's bigger than some of your clients back in Melbourne."

Conscious their hostess is waiting for them, they enter what proves to be a light and stylish sitting room. Eadie has settled into a large armchair, part of a chesterfield suite. It's upholstered in a quiet floral that has her looking like she's sitting in the middle of a garden. Small tables on either side of her chair carry an assortment of knick-knacks designed to ensure that once seated, she can stay put in comfort for long periods of time.

"Please sit down girls, you must be exhausted." She gestures toward the sofa with a crippled hand.

They sink gratefully into its soft hold. Sam can feel her body liquefy into the cushions and keep going through to the floor. So complete is her exhaustion, she feels boneless.

Eadie's chattering away to Jennie, who's managing to hold it together enough to respond, when Sam's ears prick up at the mention of a glass of sherry. She checks her watch on the sly before realizing it's still set to Aussie time. In that case, it's exactly the right time for a small glass of something.

Eadie leans awkwardly in her chair and grabs at the decanter of pale, golden sherry set on the table to her right. She miscalculates the distance and the cut crystal container wobbles alarmingly before again finding its centre of gravity. "Perhaps one of you could do the honours." Her tone leaves the girls in no doubt the woman finds her condition exasperating.

They all settle again with their glasses, she holds her glass aloft with a trembling hand and toasts, "Here's mud in your eye."

This is so out of keeping with the genteel air of the small woman that both Sam and Jennie burst out laughing, before they too, toast to mud in their eyes.

By the third glass of sherry, Sam is seeing double and her words are slurring. Not because she's drunk, but because she's utterly exhausted.

"Oh, dear, I've just realised you girls must be pooped and here I am chattering away. Would you like to have a little lie-down?"

"That'd be lovely," say both Sam and Jennie, almost in unison. They look questioningly at Eadie, hoping for some clue as to where the longed for lie-down will take place. Sam's so knackered, she'd happily kip on the plush cream carpet with its cut-pile patterning.

"Jennie, you're up on the top floor, just follow the stairs as far as they go and the door is off to the right. Samantha, you're on the next floor up, the door to the left on the landing."

Closing the door on her, they look at their bags, then the stairs, then their bags again.

"Stuff it, I'm going to collect mine after I've had a sleep," says Sam.

Jennie agrees.

Dragging themselves up the stairs proves trial enough, with each step achieved individually. Finally they reach the landing and Sam is faced with the door to her room. "Spot ya later."

She turns the brass handle of the panelled, white door and swings it open. It does so soundlessly on what must be well-oiled hinges. Sam stops when the room beyond is pitch black. It's the middle of the morning, how can it be so dark? She looks beside the door for a light switch but the wall is smooth and free of any protuberances. As her eyes adjust, she can make out the bulk of a large, four-poster bed, centred against the far wall.

Entering the room, she sinks into carpet that feels even more luxuriant than that in the rest of the house. Closing the door behind her, she waits until her vision adjusts before inching her way over to the bed and swaying next to it. She peels off all her travel-tired clothes and as each item is removed, she holds it at arm's length and drops it, hopefully into a reasonably neat pile.

A wonderful feeling of anticipation warms her when she folds the covers back and climbs in. Sure enough the mattress proves to be even more inviting than the sofa downstairs. Coupled with a down pillow and crisp, clean sheets, it's bedded bliss.

Consciousness waning, she rolls over. Straight into a warm body, sending adrenaline cascading throughout. She goes from barely conscious to very, very alert and moving in a sickeningly short time.

Sam's legs pump frantically before her brain is fully engaged, desperately kicking at the covers to free themselves along with the rest of her body. As soon as the bedspread is bunched around her ankles, she throws herself backwards over the side of the tall bed.

She's suspended in mid-air for a few seconds, like someone out of Scooby Doo, before she drops like a stone to the carpet. She lands hard, even bouncing a couple of times and suspects there'll be a few cheeky dents left as a result. Her arse is going to sport matching bruises.

A light flares on the other side of the bed and Sam gropes blindly for her recently ditched clothing, holding up whatever she can lay her hands on in a futile attempt to hide her nakedness.

Damn, I'm sure Eadie said the room to the left on the landing.

Her eyes adjust and she peeps over the top of the mattress, the beginnings of an apology already half-formed. Any words die when she realises she's looking over at Chris. He's alone.

"You took your time," he says, sleepily.

Sam crouches transfixed, unsure what she's meant to do now. Her forehead is creased in confusion. "Where's Pita, your fiancée?"

"Fiancée? In her bloody dreams she is!" Chris pats the bed in invitation.

Elation starts low in Sam's stomach, but soon bubbles up and onto her face as a broad smile. Her exhaustion drops away with the clothes.

Sam springs to her feet and launches herself at Chris, easily making it across the broad expanse of bed in one joyous leap.

Chris grunts in pain when she lands on him in a tangle of knees and elbows.

"Oh, I'm so sorry."

"You always did know how to make an entrance," squeaks Chris.

He doesn't get any more words out, with Sam kissing him like her life depends on it before having to stop for air. "I've missed you so much." Tears streak down her face in a mixture of relief and happiness.

Chris kisses her back, before wiping her tears away. "I really hope you love me as much as I love you." His expression is as tentative as Sam's.

While she might not be able to say the words out loud, she has no trouble showing him her love. Where they go to from here, only time will tell, but her heart tells her being with him is the right thing.

I hope you had as much fun reading as I had writing. If you did, I'd be thrilled if you could give it some **STAR LOVE** before you leave.

Read on to discover others in this series. For a heap of fun with your friends, check out the **BOOK CLUB QUESTIONS AND EXTRAS** at the very back. There may be cocktails involved.

Happy reading

Andrene

ABOUT THE AUTHOR

Andrene is a multi-genre author who writes edgy chick lit under her own name, and paranormal cozy mysteries, as Andie Low.

She also writes short and steamy curvy girl romance under the pen name Hope Malone. If you'd like to stalk her, you can sign up to her newsletter on her website.

THE LOW DOWN comes out once a month and includes new releases, special offers and comps.

www.andrenelowauthor.com

Written in British English, the series is a lot like the late seventies, in that it's full of bad language, bad behavior and Farrah Fawcett hair. There's also a lot to laugh about.

COOGAN'S BREAK
CURVY ROMANCE SERIES

HOPE MALONE

Welcome to Coogan's Break where the girls are curvy, and the guys hotter than hell. If you're short on time, but long for romance, this series of short and steamy romances might just be what you've been looking for.

Meet Frankie Bonny, a jinxed witch with Bruce Lee moves. With the 'help' of Dex, her snarky Jack Russell, she's out to solve murders, mysteries, and more. Add in Zane, Frankie's mystical, but equally gorgeous, neighbor, and things are about to get interesting.

BOOK CLUB QUESTIONS

- What was your favourite part of the book?
- What was your least favourite?
- Did you race to the end, or was it more of a slow seventies-style burn?
- Which scene has stuck with you?
- What did you think of the writing style? Are there any standout sentences?
- Do you think the author captured the animal's personalities authentically?
- Do you think the author captured the seventies authentically?
- Would you want to read another book by this author?
- What surprised you most about the book?
- What's the worst way you've ever been dumped?
- Have you ever had revenge on someone who's treated you badly? If so, how?
- What's the best revenge you've ever heard of? (My boss's current wife sending the marital bed to the girlfriend's office is up there for me. Not sure if it still had the sheets and duvet in-situ, although that would have made it funnier.)

- Do you think Samantha was responsible for a lot of the problems that befell her?

346

BOOK CLUB EXTRAS

Just as you can pair a fine wine with fabulous cuisine, we believe in the perfect drink to accompany a spirited book club discussion. Read on for a few seventies-inspired drinks and recipes to get you started.

GRASSHOPPER

- 1 ounce green crème de menthe
- 1 ounce white crème de cacao
- 2 ounces heavy cream

DIRECTIONS

- Combine all ingredients in a cocktail shaker filled with ice
- Shake well
- Strain into a martini glass

DISCO DANCER

- 2 ounces freshly squeezed orange juice
- 1 ounce Galliano
- 1 ounce vodka
- Dash orange bitters
- Ice and Cold club soda

DIRECTIONS

- Combine orange juice, Galliano, vodka, and bitters in a cocktail shaker with ice and shake.
- Strain into a chilled cocktail glass, top with a splash of club soda, and serve.

TEQUILA SUNRISE

- 2 oz tequila Lots of ice
- 3/4 cup orange juice
- 1/4 cup pineapple juice
- 2 oz grenadine syrup
- 1 maraschino cherry for garnish

DIRECTIONS

- Pour the tequila in tall glass, then top with ice.
- Pour the orange juice over the top without mixing. Then pineapple juice.
- Finally carefully pour in the grenadine, which will sink to the bottom.
- Top with a cherry, orange slice or pineapple slice as desired and serve immediately.

Remember, it's best to drink responsibly even if the first rule of your book club is 'What happens at Book Club, stays at

Book Club'. As the perfect host, why not serve some suitably kitsch 70s snacks? Here's a recipe to get you started.

CHEDDAR FONDUE

- 1 large garlic clove
- 12 ounces / 330g Emmental Cheese
- 12 ounces / 330g Medium Cheddar
- 1 cup dry white wine
- 1 tbsps corn flour
- 1 tbsp lemon juice
- Salt and Pepper
- Some nice fresh crusty bread

DIRECTIONS

- Cut the garlic in two and rub the inside of the pan with the cut edge of the garlic. Add the wine and heat slowly until warm.
- Cut the cheese into smaller pieces. Then add the cheese to the pan, bit by bit until it is all melted. Stir regularly to mix with the wine.
- Then add some salt and pepper to taste, the corn flour and the tablespoon of lemon juice. Make sure the heat is adjusted so that the cheese is slowly bubbling.

Emmental is a very mild, neutral cheese so good substitutes would be Gruyere, French Comte, or Jarlsberg. You may also try slightly aged Provolone, Havarti, or mild Cheddar. But you can basically use any cheese if you aren't very picky. So other options include regular Cheddar, Gouda, Parmigiano-Reggiano, or Brie.

Finally, if you do go ahead with your seventies-style book club, I'd love it if you could send me some photos.